Kali Napier worked in Bangladesh as an anthropologist on gender programs before working as an Aboriginal family history researcher for the Queensland government and as a Native Title anthropologist in the mid-west of Western Australia, the setting for *The Secrets at Ocean's Edge*. The novel was longlisted for the Bath Novel Award, as was her first manuscript – also a finalist in the Hachette Australia Manuscript Development Program. Kali is currently an MPhil candidate in creative writing at the University of Queensland. She now lives in Queensland with her two children.

For all the latest news from Kali Napier please visit:

Facebook: KaliNapierAuthor
@KaliNapier

KALI NAPIER

PIATKUS

First published in Australia and New Zealand in 2018 by
Hachette Australia, an imprint of Hachette Australia Pty Limited
First published in Great Britain in 2018 by Piatkus

1 3 5 7 9 10 8 6 4 2

A CIP catalogue record for this book
is available from the British Library.

ISBN 978-0-349-42184-1

Printed and bound by CPI Group (UK) Ltd, Croydon, CR0 4YY

Papers used by Piatkus are from well-managed forests
and other responsible sources.

Piatkus
An imprint of
Little, Brown Book Group
Carmelite House
50 Victoria Embankment
London EC4Y 0DZ

An Hachette UK Company
www.hachette.co.uk

www.littlebrown.co.uk

To Ruby and Rory

so that you may always know where you come from

Author's note: At the time this novel was set, the present-day town of Dongara, in Western Australia, was spelt 'Dongarra' and this is the spelling used throughout.

CHAPTER ONE

LILY

The wheat rippled in the late winter's breeze like dusty, crushed velvet flung out across the field. Ernie was still out there, late. The weather would come good for the young green wheat ears to ripen in time for a November harvest.

Too late.

Lily flexed her wrist in small circles against her side. Why couldn't he have waited for just one more harvest? The wheat buyers might have offered a better price than last year's. Though she had thought these things, she held her tongue. Ernie had taken the risk, thrown in years of hard work to abandon it all, when other blokes around here held out, in faith.

The dark spot of Ernie's head and shoulders flitted in the top field, moving towards her. She dropped her wrist with a sigh. Flinched, at the slam of the door, followed by a flurry of footsteps along the verandah.

'Girlie,' she said, as her daughter bounded towards her. Lily took stock of her appearance: barefoot, the cuffs of her cardigan dirtied brown, her knickers showing beneath her pullover dress. 'Don't run. Walk,' hardening her tone.

Girlie slowed for three paces before breaking into a skip again. 'It's not fair. Jenny says—'

Lily held up her palm, the burn scar on the back of her hand a flesh-coloured moon. 'Without whining, please. Now, start again.'

Girlie sucked in her cheeks. 'Jenny's telling lies, Mummy. She says she isn't coming with us all the way to Dongarra.'

Lily tugged at the end of a ribbon that had slipped out of its bow at the end of Girlie's dark pigtail, re-tied it, smoothing her daughter's untidy curls behind her ears.

'She's going back to the mission.' Jenny's movements were of little consequence to their own with all it entailed, packing and selling off furniture.

'But who'll cook our tea and show me how to . . .' Girlie bit down on her bottom lip.

Lily rested an arm around her daughter, letting her head drop against her shoulder as they walked together slowly towards the house. Girlie had grown tall this winter.

'You're old enough to help me with the cooking,' she said. It had been a year since the cook had been let go, and now Jenny. Little by little losing the life Ernie had promised her. Lily tipped her chin up towards the house. 'Tell Jenny to boil up some water for a bath.'

Girlie tripped against the raised edge of the garden path. 'Walk,' Lily called. But Girlie kept running until she disappeared inside the shadow of the house.

Lily stopped to look at the house, to really look at it, imprint it on her memory. The large water tank bleeding rust down the side, tucked in behind the gum that shaded the sitting room, providing the only relief in the sweltering heat each summer. A deep verandah that wrapped around three sides of the house. The frame of the flywire door, wire missing, that creaked on its hinges as the dry wind blew down the hill across the wheat. The house was as bleached and dust-coated as the fields beyond, a washed-out ochre palette.

Lily glanced over to the dray, held up on the low bough of the gum tree. After thirteen years of marriage, these were the sum effects. Four tea chests stuffed with her mother's linens and remnants of a Royal Doulton dinner setting, two iron bedsteads, the easy chair with its worn grey tapestry, the pine kitchen table, iron pots and kettles, yards of canvas, and the upright piano. Her Singer sewing machine gone. The argument they'd had over that still twisted in her stomach.

She couldn't leave behind all that weighed on her spirit, as burdened as the dray. But this move would make it harder for her to be found.

Lily took a deep breath and walked through the front door.

She checked each room, surveying the wooden floors of the bedrooms, picking up Girlie's cardigan and a book left face down. There was little else to pack, other than the bedding they would sleep on tonight and a few odds and ends. In the sitting room was an open tea chest, half-filled with their essentials for their new life in Dongarra: a shirt for Ernie, a clean dress for Girlie. Besides her crepe wedding gown, which she kept good for socials, Lily had two dresses; all the others had been patched and mended until there was no more fabric left in their seams.

She shoved Girlie's book down the side of the chest, tapping her fingernails on the metal of the old Arnott's tin. Inside, beneath the twists of embroidery threads, lay her savings of nearly eighty pounds, and the photograph that kept her moving forward. She flicked a glance over her shoulder, then unfolded Pa's greatcoat to take with them on the dray.

With her knife, she went out to the vegetable plot in the back yard, to tear at the tangled vine, grasped shrivelled pumpkins, half-grown and gnawed at by rats, and discarded them among the bolting cabbages. She spat on the greenish stain crossing her palm, wiping it dry on her apron as she gazed to the far reaches of the yard, across the geraniums and Michaelmas daisies to the scrubby patch of grass.

She hadn't finished. The yard had all been sand when they'd arrived here at Cowanup Downs six years ago – the farm a two-day journey north from Perth by train and dray, and untended by civilisation apart from the newly constructed weatherboard house. The town itself had only been gazetted ten years before, in 1916. She'd brought a geranium cutting with her. Once she'd organised the domestic servant to ready the house fit for habitation and instructed the cook on Ernie's favourite meals, she turned the first sod of the flower garden directly off the left-side verandah so the heady rose scent of the geraniums would one day waft through the children's bedroom windows. Since then, the garden had wrapped around the back of the house. A wicker chair had once nestled in the shady corner between the steps and the verandah rail, a cool spot where she'd sipped tea and gazed across the flowers to the vegetable plot. Every aspect designed for colour, throwing into relief the drabness of the house and surrounding fields. The ladies in the Country Women's Association had once said it was the prettiest garden in all of Perenjori.

She crushed a geranium leaf, releasing the scent before dropping it to the ground. The sheer waste of it – the countless hours digging, tilling, planting and pruning – to walk away . . .

The iron garden gate squealed, a clang of metal.

'Ern?' She wandered round the corner of the house. He was tying the rabbit traps to the side of the dray, his singlet flung over his bare shoulder like a rag. Dried blood crusted his knuckles and dirt etched the lines in his face as he grimaced.

'There's no room for the wire netting,' he said without looking up. 'I'll have to leave it.'

'Did you stow the guns?' Ernie's rifles each had their own wooden box; he'd been an amateur marksman before the Great War.

He gestured towards the bench seat at the front of the dray. 'The .22's under the seat. Sold the others to Dillon.' He turned his head away from her, knotting and reknotting a rope on the dray. The muscles in his neck worked as he swallowed hard.

It was like words were stuck there, but he wouldn't say them. Not to her anyway. She imagined he might have talked about abandoning the farm with the other blokes at the pub in Perenjori or further away where he'd started to drink in the past year. The only words he'd given her had been assurances. *This year will be better than last. The subsidies will see us right.*

'You're filthy, Ern. Wash before coming inside.'

He dropped the rope. She felt his hotness, the grease on his skin as he closed the space between them, and reached for her waist. 'Come on, darl,' he said, squeezing her shoulder with his other hand, smelling of iron dirt and blood.

She shrugged free from his grasp. He groped the air for her but she skittered towards the tank and turned the tap. Water spurted, flowing to the ground. 'May as well use the whole lot. We don't need it anymore.' The muddy water splashed her shins and snaked over the hardened earth.

She wrung the hem of her skirt as she walked away. At the foot of the verandah steps she paused to look back. He stood beneath the tap, water sheeting from his shoulders, each droplet flashing with the rays of the setting sun so it looked as though he were a firework, a sparkler.

He closed off the tap and rubbed his chest and shoulders dry with his singlet. 'You're a tease, Lil. Can't a man get a kiss from his wife after working all day?'

She came to him, took his singlet and wiped down his back. 'Looks like it would have been a good harvest this year.'

He snatched his singlet back and tucked it into the waist of his clinging trousers. 'Not now. Don't have a go at me, will you?'

'I wasn't, Ernie. I didn't mean that,' she said, feeling a flush in her cheeks. 'It's just a shame, that's all.'

She despised herself. Couldn't say what she really felt.

He glanced at her and nodded, then headed inside. Rust-wet blotches soiled the steps she'd scrubbed only an hour ago, determined that nobody could say she hadn't kept a neat house.

CHAPTER TWO

GIRLIE

Girlie pulled back the sheet and lay down on the sacking, her stomach rumbling. It sort of fizzed the way it did when she was going to the fete. But she felt sad too. The sheet was cold and her coverlet was gone, packed away. She spread over herself the old towel that would be her blanket tonight. It reached from her toes to just below her chest, so she tucked the corners over her feet and wrapped her legs and bottom – as if she were a present – and then lay back down, hugging her arms.

Her mother's footsteps, shuffly, came down the hallway. She opened the door and poked her head through the gap. 'Big day tomorrow. We're starting out early.'

Girlie tried to say, 'Goodnight, Mummy,' but the words came out with a sob that had been waiting for her to open her mouth.

Her mother pushed the door open wider and shone the kerosene lamp into the room. Her face was still in shadow. It made it hard to tell if she was cross with Girlie for acting like an infant. Placing down the lamp, her mother sat on the edge of the sacking.

'I've watched you grow up on this farm.' She sounded tired, and as though she were about to cry.

Girlie breathed out in relief. She was a big girl; she'd turned ten last month. 'I can't imagine being anywhere else. Will I still be me in Dongarra?'

Her mother stroked her forehead. 'Who else would you be?'

'Katie says people are different in other places.' Her school friend had been down to Perth once, which was where all the important people lived. Like the Emerald City in the book Miss Glaston had read to the class last year.

'They might be, but that doesn't mean *you* have to be different,' her mother said.

Girlie wrinkled her nose. How could she control how she felt? 'But I won't know anybody there. I'm scared I won't make another friend like Katie.' Or Jenny. Nobody in Dongarra knew everything about her like Jenny did.

Her mother started to sing. She always did that when Girlie asked questions she didn't want to answer.

'Did you used to wrap me in a rabbit skin?' Girlie asked when the lullaby ended. She'd see her father go off with his gun into the wheat fields and come back with sometimes three or four rabbits that he'd shot.

'You'll never get up in the morning at this rate,' her mother said for an answer, picking up the kerosene lamp and walking over to the doorway. Girlie lifted her head to see her better, but when her mother spoke again she sounded cross. 'Go to sleep.'

Then she closed the door and the line of light underneath dimmed.

People were different in different places. The thought struck her sideways. It wasn't just what Katie had said. Their old cook, Ah Lee, had told her that in the cattle stations up north where he'd worked as a young man, they'd called him a Chinaman. But the people around Perenjori called him a half-caste Aborigine.

Girlie strained to catch the sounds of the house. Her father mumbling, the slam of the front door as he went out for a smoke on the verandah. She sat up, the towel twisting around her legs. The glass of the window was foggy and she pressed a fingertip against it and drew circles, one inside another. The sides of her face hurt from gritting her teeth at the cold air stealing up through the floorboards.

Outside, a squelch.

Her finger paused on the glass. She could hear nothing but the blood in her ears as she concentrated on the sound. There it was again. Someone was in the side garden. It had rained this evening, and the paths had quickly become muddy again.

The front door closed and her father trod softly down the hall to the main bedroom.

Girlie's breaths came out raggedy. It wasn't her father out there. Though she was scared, it wasn't of the dark – it was of Jenny leaving without saying goodbye. Careful not to stand on the squeaky boards, she found her cardigan, her fingers shakily threading the buttons. She tiptoed over to the door, and turned the handle as slowly as she could. The house was quiet except for the wind sighing against the shutters.

'Girlie?' Her father's voice came muffled from the front bedroom.

'Just going to the privy,' she answered, keeping her voice even. He grunted, and she put on her shoes.

Outside, the wind blew her hair, strapping her face. She pushed the strands behind her ears as her eyes adjusted. It was a light kind of darkness. A clipped moon swung low in the sky, shining on the wall of the wash house. The door was open. Girlie looked inside towards the alcove at the back. Even in the dark she could see the emptiness of Jenny's bed.

An urge pressed below her stomach. She really did need to use the privy. She finished her business, springing from the seat before a redback could find its way into her nightclothes. She hesitated at the privy door. Outside, the night was blacker, and shadows moved across the wall.

She stared at the wash house door, her chest hollowed out, the changes from their move already happening. Where would Jenny go? Girlie couldn't remember a time in her life when Jenny hadn't been there – taking her down to the creek, lacing grass stems through her hair, teaching her to whistle like a peewit.

Girlie stepped out into the night, towards the dark end of the yard. A hand grasped her wrist. She let out a squeal, pulling away, twisting from the phantom holding her tight.

'Sh!'

'Jenny,' Girlie said, then lowered her voice. 'I thought you'd gone.'

'Come with me.' Jenny tugged her further away from the house. She scuffed her shoe and stumbled, but Jenny didn't stop, zig-zagging along the path as sure-footed as if she had a candle to light the way.

'Where are we going?' Girlie's heart stuttered as Jenny slowed. Scratchy stalks caught at her skirts. They were in the strip of land at the end of the garden; her mother had never finished making it pretty with flowers. It was scrubby, sandy land. Here, Girlie used to throw boondies, little bombs of baked sand that shattered when they hit the ground. But that was during the day, when she could see it was just long grass and not dead fingers poking at her legs.

Jenny stopped. A shadow rose up in front of them, bleeding into the blackness. Girlie froze, her whole skin prickling with electricity.

It was a man, with skin so black he was more night than the night. He stepped forward, opening his mouth of stark white teeth. One was missing in the top row. Girlie fell backwards onto her bottom, staring up at the man looming above her.

Jenny helped her to her feet, holding her close. 'This one's my husband, Jimbo.'

Husband? The word was like a thump in the chest. 'I didn't know you were married.'

Jenny touched the man on his arm, familiar, the same way she touched Girlie. 'Not married the white way. Tribal way.'

Girlie looked at Jimbo. *Tribal.* That word stirred a part of her that she knew her mother wouldn't approve of. The part that made her want to wade in puddles when it rained.

'You didn't see Jimbo here, all right?' Jenny said.

Girlie nodded. But she didn't know why it was a secret; they were leaving anyway and Jenny was going back to the mission in the morning. Was that why Jenny was being sent away – because her mother had found out something secret about her?

'I promise,' she said. She couldn't help looking at him. Jenny's husband. There'd been other Aboriginal men around the town; they came in from the stations in drays and on the back of farm trucks. They'd jump off and go to wherever such men went, with the town's eyes watching them from across the road. Not to where her father and her friends' fathers would meet: the pub, the hall.

Girlie hadn't seen one up close, not like this. The scars on his chest were shiny like slugs. And instead of being frightened, she wanted to know more. He was a secret. She liked secrets, she collected them. Like when Katie found Miss Glaston crying behind the school tank, ripping a letter into confetti. Or when she and her mother ate a tray of chocolates with Christmas still a week away and she wasn't to tell her father.

Jenny was speaking in her own language now, mumbling then almost-singing. That was something else her mother wouldn't like. Jenny's native ways weren't allowed in the house. Girlie had heard her mother tell Jenny she was lucky she was so concerned with civilising her. Her mother told Jenny off for doing exactly what Girlie liked doing. Puddles. Making up stories about Mr Emu and his wife. And walking as far as the blackboys on the ridge.

Jenny stopped her sing-song, seemed to be listening. Girlie focused on the sounds below the wind, the whoosh of grass and the faintest chirrup of a cricket. Jimbo grabbed Jenny's shoulders, rubbing his face against hers. Girlie realised they were kissing and crying. She turned away, embarrassed. But Jenny stepped backwards, clutched Girlie's hand.

As Jenny led her back to the house, Girlie cast a glance over her shoulder. Jimbo had disappeared into the night.

'He's gone, Jenny.'

'Yes, he's gone,' Jenny said, walking fast.

'But he's your husband. Why are you going back to the mission?'

Jenny paused. 'It's not like that for us, Girlie. He works jackeroo for the McConnells. He's gotta stay with them. I've gotta go back to the mission if I ain't working.'

They heard a mournful humming now, floating away into the night. Jenny didn't go after it. She stood and listened, and when Girlie looked at her, the moon lit up streaky tears running down her cheeks.

Girlie had so much more to learn. Changes in life she didn't understand. She'd thought she'd known all of Jenny's secrets. But not the secret of Jimbo. How could adults keep secrets this big?

CHAPTER THREE

LILY

They travelled for three days. Through Morawa the first day, then to Mingenew where they left Jenny at the railway siding. Girlie had clung to Jenny's waist, until Lily prised her away and then had to endure her snivelling day and night.

Now they crossed a sand plain, where giant gums grew sideways, bent by the wind hurtling off the sea. A black motor car rumbled past them, setting off the horse. Brownie nickered and weaved until Ernie stopped and got down from the dray. He handed Lily the reins and she nudged Girlie's head from her lap, covered with Pa's greatcoat.

'Are we there?' Girlie squinted her eyes as she looked across to the sand hills fringing the blue sky. She wiped her nose with her cardigan cuff.

Lily passed her the handkerchief she'd tucked inside the wrist of her sleeve. 'Nearly.' Nearly was a sigh, a refrain, a place she'd rather settle than to reach Dongarra and have her hopes dashed. Folk had built houses down at the foreshore, Ernie had said. *They line the road along the beach.*

Ernie whistled as he walked, holding Brownie's bridle, kicking stones to the side of the gravelled road. He seemed without a care, but then he had already been ahead, organised their new home, met a few locals at the beach. She could almost believe in his conviction that a guesthouse and shop at the beach settlement, despite their isolation from the main town, would be a success. To say otherwise would undermine their marriage. She maintained her part by following him into his next venture, patching and mending and making do, so he couldn't see the strain he put on her.

The sun had started to dip behind a pink-coloured cloudbank when he squeezed her shoulder. 'Look.' Following the direction his finger pointed, she saw a smoking chimney behind a clump of trees.

'Dongarra?'

He nodded.

The huge fig trees cast shadows on the dozing town. Brownie trundled down the main street where stone and tin cottages flanked fields, the only lighting outside the hotel, where three cut-down Fords were parked and horses were tethered to the post.

'There's a garage,' Ernie said, as they passed a tin shed next to the hotel. 'Folks aren't doing it too badly here.' Lily nodded. If the farm subsidies had come through this year, they might have got a motor car. It was 1932 after all.

They crossed the bridge, her nerves jangling. The sheoaks clutching at the river's edge rippled, whispering to the cormorants and darters that flitted and swooped on the bank. The road turned down towards the beach, through fields and scrub, and she counted three cottages before the sea came into view, purple and choppy.

It was as Ernie had described: stone and chamferboard houses clustered the beachfront where the jetty's pylons marched into the sea. Beside a cottage stood a wooden shop boasting signs for a tearoom, Kodak film, and ice-cream, lit up by gas light. A wisp of a woman stepped out of the doorway, her thinning grey hair pulled back to reveal she was half-bald, turning her head like a sparrow as Ernie called, 'Good evening, Mrs McGinty.'

Mrs McGinty nodded, lifting her chin in a slow circle to encompass Lily and Ernie and Girlie, the horse and dray, the remaining contents of their home, and their fragile plans to rebuild their life. She held up a hand, smiled at Lily. 'Welcome, Mrs Hass.'

This woman would already know something of Lily from Ernie. Though Lily would have preferred making her entrée into the town's society with those ladies who mattered, she felt at a disadvantage. She patted Ernie's arm for him to stay the horse and stepped down. 'Hello, Mrs McGinty. My husband tells me we're to be neighbours.' She cast her gaze further up the chalky road. Beyond a stone warehouse was a row of cottages, and on the crest of a sand hill bathed in the pink glow of the sunset another, larger cottage, with a pointed roof and lattice work all round. It would have good views of both sides of the bay, she thought. The perfect place for a guesthouse – if the tourists would pay. Lily tipped her head back to Mrs McGinty. 'We should be getting on and settle into the cottage before it's too dark.'

'Cottage?' said Mrs McGinty, looking between Lily and Ernie.

Ernie cleared his throat. 'Ah . . . Lil, those 'uns are our premises.' He pointed at the old warehouse eighty yards from Mrs McGinty's tearoom. Even in the falling darkness rusting holes were evident in the roof and there were no outbuildings she could see. She'd been prepared for reduced circumstances, but this? It wasn't even a home, little better than when they would camp in the sand hills a hundred miles south from here after the harvest season. And this was where Ernie had brought his family to live.

'Mummy, are we there yet?' Girlie roused from the bench on the dray, stifling a yawn.

Ernie pulled his cap down on his head and avoided Lily's eyes. She pressed a smile at Mrs McGinty, hoping it would stop up the tears she felt forming. 'It seems so.' She climbed up beside Girlie.

Mrs McGinty patted the side of the dray. 'Be sure to come by in the morning. I can fix you up with a few things you might need.'

'Thank you. Though it shan't be too long before we're settled in,' Lily said, then turned her face to the wind coming off the sea.

~

Cold braced her limbs in the morning, dragging her from sleep. Still, she clung to Girlie's rounded back, searching for warmth and a reason to not have to face the day. She twined her legs in the sacking and blankets they'd laid on the floor and covered her eyes with her free arm, the other pinned beneath her daughter's body. But the daylight streamed in with the chill.

Ernie cleared his throat. 'You up?'

She squinted at his hazy silhouette in the open doorway. 'What time is it?'

'Morning. I've been across to the McGintys'.' He pulled out a warm-bread smell from his sack. Hunger roiled in Lily's belly and she wriggled her arm out from under Girlie, turning her gently onto her back.

'There's fresh butter, too,' he said, slathering it on a piece of torn-off crust. He pushed the lot into his mouth.

She took the loaf of bread from him as he headed outside, and gazed about the room for a place to prepare breakfast. The splintered-pine kitchen table was crowded with wooden boxes and sacks of all manner, hauled off the dray and dumped there last night by Ernie while she made up their makeshift beds. Their new home appeared bare and grubby; two wide rooms divided by a single wall. She brushed the residue of the night from the table to the floor, thick with crushed sea shells and sand that had blown in through the channel of open doorways.

Hardly a kitchen. No range, nor fireplace, nor trough. The piano looking out of place. She pulled a ball of bread from the centre of the loaf, stuck it into her mouth with her finger, just as she used to do as a child when Pa took her to the track to watch the gees.

Smoke wafted in, and she followed it outside. Ernie was crouched by an open fire, tipping the billy into an enamel cup. He looked up, held out the tea for her. His fair hair fell over his eyes. Lily's fingers hovered, instinct pulsing to neaten his appearance. A split-second, conscious thought to leave it be, and she grasped the cup, bringing it to her lips.

Ernie pushed himself up. 'I know it's not what you were expecting. But we're in a good place here. Now they've got a motor coach that brings tourists down from Geraldton in the summer. And motor cars coming here in the winter, too. McGinty says the shacks are always booked out.'

Lily cast a glance across the sand hills, counting two, three chimneys rising up between the gullies.

'The beach settlement needs a guesthouse,' Ernie said.

She arched her back. 'I still don't understand how you came upon the idea of it.'

He squinted, poured himself a cup of tea from the billy. Lily became aware of a chorus, gulls and other small birds she'd forgotten, ocean-going birds.

'Something Fred said. A guesthouse would be good business, single men about, or a pair of ladies, they don't want to take on a whole shack. And camping's a lark, but sometimes a man just wants to come home from fishing to a cooked meal.'

She considered her brother-in-law Fred's opinion, taking in the drifts of sand against the stone walls and the weathered window frames. 'Who on earth would pay to stay here?'

Ernie put down his cup and sprang to his feet. 'I'll show you.'

Lily followed him to the side of the building, stepping gingerly across shells and sticks in her bare feet, wearing only her long shift and a shawl. Ernie was rubbing his hand along the stone wall, crumbling it into dust. 'This side'll be our home, and on the other side will be the guestrooms. They'll have their own corridor running along this back wall.' Lily watched him turn towards the McGintys', taking long strides until he reached the corner of the building. 'I can divide it up into four, five rooms.' He scratched his head, scanning the ground between him and where she stood under the deep roof of the verandah, and she could see him calculating how he might fit more people in, make more money.

'But what about our rooms?'

'I was thinking on it last night after you went to sleep.' Ernie beckoned her round to the road in front of the building. She hesitated, tightening her shawl.

He motioned impatiently, tipping to his toes, eager to show her the plans he'd dreamed up the night before.

'I'm not fit to be seen, Ern.'

'Oh, right.' He turned to face the direction of the Obelisk on the headland. Lily came up behind him, grasped at the loose tail of his shirt hanging out of his trousers and tucked it in.

'Go on. Tell me.'

He pulled her to him and she breathed in the sour warmth of perspiration and tobacco.

'I'll put in a shop at the front here, groceries, things like that,' he said, gesturing at their side of the building.

'But there's a grocer's in town.' She'd seen a sign for groceries on the building by the bridge.

He jutted out his chin and she immediately regretted her words. He always made her feel bad for questioning his ideas. 'The holidaymakers will want somewhere closer,' he said, measuring his words, 'and there's retired farmers living down here.

'I could get the shop going in a month or two. And the guesthouse by New Year's, I reckon. McGinty gave me the name of the carrier. Fella called Fairclough. I'll see if he can pick up the summer holidaymakers and bring them down to the beach.'

As she moved towards the front door, her shoulders sagged at the thought of the washing and cooking, and the work of the shop and guesthouse that stretched out in front of her. It had been a long time since she'd not had any help with the household chores. Lily had fought hard to keep their domestic against all of Ernie's protests that they couldn't afford her. *But things'll change now, Ern,* she'd said. *The guesthouse will be a sure thing, like you told me. And with your talent for business,* laying it on like cocky's joy, *we're bound to come by a better life. Things are turning.*

Ernie came back to her, lifted the hair from her neck in that way that made her clench her shoulder blades together.

'Don't worry, things'll be rough for a bit, but you'll get used to it. I'll put in a kitchen stove and walls for a bedroom first.'

Her shoulders heaved and he dropped his hand from her neck. 'We'll have a proper bathroom, too. With a brick copper.' She started to smile, and he continued, 'Guests will pay extra for the chance of a nice, hot bath.'

'Where's the water for all these baths going to come from?'

'Ah,' he said, kicking at a drift of sand inside the doorway, 'that's the beauty of it. There's a concrete underground tank attached to the other side of the building.'

He had an answer to all her objections, so that she could find no more without feeling petty.

CHAPTER FOUR

LILY

'I miss Jenny.' Girlie pressed her face against the cracked window pane.

Lily wiped her brow with her sleeve and sat back on her heels. In the two hours since Ernie had left for town to look for labour and timber, she had swept the back room, found the underground tank Ernie had spoken of and hauled two buckets of water with the winch. Then she'd set Girlie to the task of washing the windows while she scrubbed the floors.

'Not half as much as I do,' she muttered. Then more loudly, 'Let's break from cleaning a while. Shall we explore the beach?'

Girlie brightened. 'Can I go for a paddle?'

Though the sky was almost cloudless, the wind that whirled through the open doorway carried a veil of sea spray that numbed Lily's hands and nose and ears. 'No. You'll catch a chill.' She shooed at a small bird that flew in. 'We can't be gone long. I'd like to see what supplies we can get from town.'

With her shawl wrapped over her hat, preventing it from flying away, she took Girlie's hand and crossed the road to the beach. To the left were two large bough shelters. Dark patches in the white sand proved as she came closer to be the remnants of fires. Lily kicked sand over the embers, just to be sure and settled beneath the canopy of a shelter, holding the flapping brim of her hat away from her face. The sea was rough, waves crowned by white foam breaking about sixty yards off shore. Closer in, three small sailboats rocked, held fast by their moorings. The jetty stretched out towards the horizon, then turned towards the north.

Girlie played on the hard, wet sand, picking up shells, cupping them in her hand to study them before slipping them into her pocket, bringing to mind Lily's own childhood obsession with pressed flowers. Her favourite place in all of Perth was King's Park, where Pa would take her for walks, never impatient when she stopped to pick a yellow everlasting, or blue Leschenaultia flowers with their paper-star-like petals. She would gently spread each petal into place between the pages of his racing form guide, then, at home, arrange them on card and stitch around the edges with her mother's embroidery silks. Those stitches the first inkling of her later passion for sewing.

Girlie kicked out, yelping. Lily rushed to her, catching her hand. 'What's the matter?' she cried, casting a worried glance at the sand etched with scallops of bubbling foam.

'It touched me. When the sea water came up. It felt so slimy.'

'Seaweed?'

A blush spread across Girlie's cheeks. 'Maybe.'

Lily straightened, starting at the sight of an old man standing by the pile of Girlie's shoes and socks and Lily's shawl beneath the bough shelter. He was hatless, and a shock of white hair waved around his head as though a seagull were settling there. He pulled a pipe from his mouth and raised it in greeting.

'Hello,' he said, wiping spittle from his lips with his handkerchief before stuffing it into his pocket. 'I saw you come down here.

Thought I'd see how you're getting on. Reginald McGinty. Call me Reg. Everybody does.' He winked at Girlie, who'd slunk behind Lily's skirt, bunching it in the back with her hand.

'Lily Hass. Please thank Mrs McGinty for the bread and butter we had this morning.'

He shoved the pipe between his lips, sucking hard to rekindle the tobacco but it had gone out, muttered something that Lily couldn't quite make out. She leaned towards him. He looked up suddenly, searching for something over her shoulder, making her turn, but there was only the jetty and the three boats on the water.

Lily couldn't step around him to the shoes and shawl without appearing rude. 'Do you own one of those boats?'

'Which boats?' He glanced at Girlie and up the beach towards the other bough shelter.

She gestured out at the sailboats moored in the calmer water.

He shook his head. 'My son's boat's still out. Two of those belong to the fishing families round here. If you want fish, George Hopkins'll sell you some – his cottage's over the hill behind your place. And that boat further out is the Chinaman's. Kang Pei. Lives on his boat. Been there more than ten years.'

Lily gazed at the masts bobbing from side to side. Foam broke around the boat furthest away. 'It looks a dangerous place to live.'

Reg smiled, his face creasing up like rumpled linen. 'Not for the Chinaman.' He tilted his head, chuckling. 'Only dangerous when he comes home from the hotel in town. Been known to miss his step down to his dinghy on occasion. Landed in the water.

'But, aye, the sea gets rough. Plenty of boats been wrecked out there.' He shook his head. 'Safest place for them is the hole.'

'The hole?'

He pointed out the stretch of calm water, darker than the shifting greens and blues around it.

'You'll see other boats coming round on occasion. Italian fella, Moretta, lives in a shack over yonder the nuns' cottage, Back Beach. He'll pull his boat into the hole for safe harbour.'

Girlie piped up. 'Italian?' Lily glanced at her sharply.

'That's right. What's your name, then?' Reg grunted as he bent forward to meet Girlie's eye level, stumbling a little.

'Girlie.'

'Well, that's a pretty name. I might have called you that anyway. Suits you.'

Lily held a smile. 'Do you have grandchildren, Reg?'

He put his hand to the small of his back to straighten. 'Grandsons. Grown up now. Never had a little girl about the house.'

She put out a hand to Mr McGinty to take her leave. 'I must see to supplies from town. I'm sure we shall see much of each other, Reg.'

When he grasped it, his hands felt like pumice stone. 'Come to our place and see what you need now. Martha'll spare you something from our vegetable garden.'

Before she could argue, Reg dropped her hand and walked up the beach towards the tearoom.

Lily squinted as she entered its gloomy interior. 'How long have you had your tearoom here?' she asked.

'Four years. Had the grocery store up in town before. Now me son Robert runs that.'

'Is he the one out on the sailboat?'

Reg spat out some tobacco. 'Only son I've got left.' He shuffled off behind the counter, and out the back.

Lily knew better than to pry; every family had its secrets that bound them together. Though, while he was gone she nosed about the tearoom. It was a shop, too. The dusty shelves held bathers and towels, swimming caps, boxes of camera film, and dozens of four-gallon kerosene cans. On the counter under glass were brightly coloured lollies, and a bucket churn stood beneath a sign proclaiming ice-cream.

Reg returned with a basket of cabbages and silverbeet.

'We've just had chicks hatch,' he said to Girlie, who'd been looking longingly at the lolly display. 'You can choose some to take with you.'

Girlie gave her a pleading look. Lily was about to say no, but the idea of fresh eggs overrode her need to pull Girlie into line. 'All right, then. But no naming them. They're not pets.'

On their way through the back room, Reg caught her looking at the stacks of furniture covered with canvas. 'Have a gander, see if there's anything you need.'

She thought of the bare walls of the port store, the kapok mattresses she'd pulled out to sleep on tonight and the easy chair she'd placed in the corner of their future sitting room. 'If you're sure Mrs McGinty can spare some chairs. I would be so grateful.'

'You're welcome to them, they never belonged to us. Just collecting dust.'

In one corner she spied a wooden cradle with a fine lace canopy, and Lily wondered just whom the furniture had once belonged to.

CHAPTER FIVE

ERNIE

Ernie wiped the shaving soap from his throat, lifted his chin and checked both sides of his face in the mirror. Satisfied, he reached for his shirt hanging on the back of the door and buttoned it up. It felt good to be a businessman again; Ernie Hass, guesthouse owner and shop proprietor.

Things could have been very different.

But he'd landed on his feet. The less he thought about the fertiliser account in Perenjori, the better. It wasn't worth sweating over. Most of the creditors had been paid out from the sale of the machinery and animals.

He whistled now, bumping the door open with his hip and letting it swing closed on the back of his leg.

'Daddy?'

His daughter stood by her bedroom door, clutching a bundle of bed sheets. He'd enclosed the verandah with lattice for a room of her own. Over the past month, blokes from town had helped build the inside dividing walls. His and Lily's bedroom was off the kitchen. The front room was now a small sitting room and the new shop.

He waited for Girlie to say something more, but she cast her eyes down, easing herself back into her room. It annoyed him when she was like this, drawing in on herself, expecting him to know the magic words to open her up.

'First day of school,' he said, finally. At church this past Sunday, Lily had been questioned about Girlie's school attendance. She'd been reluctant to let her go while there was still so much work to be done to set up the house, but Ernie knew she feared local gossip more than dirtying her elbows.

The smell of hot porridge greeted him in the kitchen. They were doing all right. He sat down at the table, leaned back in his chair and grinned. A full belly and a kiss from his wife would see him through the day.

'After you're done—' Lily said, drying her hands on a dishcloth. She pushed away the arm he slung around her waist, glared at him, shaking the dishcloth in the direction of Girlie's bedroom. 'I've got to get her ready for school.'

He stood up, pulling her in firmly. 'Lily.'

She held up a cheek, but he turned her chin to kiss her mouth. Her lips pressed together and she wriggled out of his hold.

The warmth of her flesh lingered in his hands.

The back door opened, scraping an arc already forming on the linoleum floor, and they both turned. He glanced at Girlie's leather shoes, bought almost new.

Lily bustled towards the child, holding a hair pin between her lips, elbows flapping as she coerced Girlie's wiry hair into plaits. 'Can you take her with you?'

Girlie winced, as Lily shoved the pin into her hair, trembling slightly as she held her head up straight.

He sometimes felt Lily was too hard on the girl, but it wasn't his place to step in. 'If you're quick about it.'

~

'Have you met your new teacher?' Ernie asked Girlie as they set off in the dray.

'Yes. Mr Peters.'

He nodded. That was that. They'd now sit together silently all the way to town.

But a few minutes later: 'I don't think he's as nice as Miss Glaston in Perenjori.'

He held her gaze. She had that look that could set him off-balance.

'Things could be much worse,' he murmured, glancing across to the jetty, where a fisherman carried his gear towards a sailboat.

A few days ago, children had found driftwood from the *Sea Prince*, which had been lost at sea. Ernie tilted his hat to shade his eyes from the glare. He was as fearless as those fishermen, not ocean-going, but he took risks. *Risks*: that was Lily's word. He preferred to think of them as opportunities to be grasped. Everything he saw along the Beach Road into town this morning – the tearoom, new shacks, a fish shop – served to prove his instincts right. Dongarra had grown since the days he'd come camping as a boy.

A new settlement was springing up along the beach and he was determined to be a part of it. McGinty had a jump on him, supplying the tourists who came in the summer with their ice-creams and teas. It rankled that McGinty had a post office and the only telephone line, too. After Ernie's meeting at the bank this morning, he would see about getting a line extended to the guesthouse. He would offer first-rate facilities: a copper in the bathroom to pour hot water directly into the tub, and a lounging room. The tourists would come – people who had time and money to go places, who threw off the hardships of the past few years to embrace the modern world where proving your worth meant catching a few snapper or western sand whiting and swimming past the breakers, rather than going to war. That's what had drawn him here – a fresh start where the past was wiped clean.

Ernie slowed as he turned onto the main street.

'Morning.' A fellow hailed him from beneath the awning of the paper shop. He was lanky, with tufted salt-and-pepper eyebrows.

Ernie reined Brownie in. 'Hello. I'm Ernie Hass.' He extended his hand to the man. 'We've not met.'

The man swung a bundle of newspapers from the back of his brown cut-down Ford, landing them by the door of the paper shop with a thump. He took Ernie's hand. 'Been out of town for a few weeks on a government road job. Matthew Fry. Newspaper and mail carrier.' He gestured up at the dray. 'That your daughter?'

Ernie tipped his chin at Girlie, and glanced down the street towards the corner opposite the church where the schoolhouse stood, at the children walking horses to the field. 'Yes, first day at school.' He flicked the reins gently at Girlie. 'Go on.' She hesitated, before slipping down to the road on the other side of the dray.

'You must be about the same age as my Susan. She's eleven,' Matthew said, smiling at her.

'I'm ten.'

'Well, then. You look out for her. She'll be a friend to you, I'm sure.'

Ernie jerked his chin at her to leave, before turning his attention back to Matthew. The morning sun cast a long shadow across the man, and Ernie stepped down from the dray to better see him. Matthew leaned across the back of his truck, reaching for a loose newspaper.

'Hey ho, there's something in today's paper that mentions you.' Matthew brandished the *Western Mail* at Ernie.

Ernie clenched Brownie's harness. 'What does it say?'

Matthew flicked the paper open, licking his inky thumb to turn the pages. 'Ah, yes, here it is. *Dongarra, a pleasant seaside resort.*'

Ernie's shoulders relaxed. He wiped his free hand on the back of his trousers. 'Go on. Where does it mention me?'

Matthew mumbled to himself as he scanned the lines of the article. '*A pleasant motor run of forty miles* . . . Hm, this is it. *As an indication that the possibilities of Dongarra are being somewhat recognised, it is worth mentioning that Mr Ernest Hass, recently moved on from wheat farming at Perenjori, is opening a guesthouse at the beach settlement.*'

Matthew looked up and grinned. 'Not bad. Not bad at all, considering you've not been in town for long.'

Ernie grinned broadly. The article was a surprise, sure – he couldn't guess at how the journalist knew his business – but it was just as well; that kind of thing saved him on advertising. 'It's only the beginning. I've plans for more than the guesthouse.'

'All well and good, Mr Hass. But I fear the tourist season'll be a bit disappointing this year. Sounds like the weather's done in a lot of farmers' crops. I doubt we'll be seeing much of them here after the harvest.'

'I know all about that,' Ernie said. He leaned forward, an elbow resting on the dray. 'Just gotta cut your losses and start again.'

Matthew seemed to study him, turning the brim of his hat in his hands. He nodded slowly. 'Aye. You might be right.'

Ernie looped the reins back over the horse, cutting off further conversation. 'I'll be seeing you around. I've got a meeting at the bank.' He patted the satchel holding his ledger book.

Matthew gestured at Ernie with his hat. 'You won't be coming by the hotel this evening, will you?'

'You know, I think I might.' He watched as Matthew started up his truck, then moved Brownie on towards the field further down the street.

~

Ernie paused at the door of the Dongarra Hotel, slapping the dust from his hat. The batwing doors opened, spilling out two men who'd quarried limestone for the inner walls of his house. He nodded at each one, let them get on their way lest they ask for more work. Mr Booth at the bank had warned him about his finances and he had no more money for labour.

He sauntered inside, nodding at those who checked an eye at him. It was a decent sort of drinking establishment, with a beer tap at the front bar.

'Mr Hass.'

He glanced across the bar to see Matthew Fry standing at a table in the corner with two glasses of beer in front of him. 'Come and join me, will you?' Matthew said, moving one of the glasses towards Ernie.

'Much obliged to you for buying me a beer.' Ernie swallowed a few inches off the top. The beer was cold and he'd have a drink with anyone. A man was a mate in the public bar.

Matthew chuckled. 'Weren't for you. I'd ordered two for myself just in case I couldn't get a look in later.'

Ernie grinned and glanced at the clock on the wall. Still half an hour before closing. The barman thumping down glasses, spilling beer.

'I'll get the next round now, then,' Ernie said. He swallowed another couple of inches, and as he made to go to the bar, two men came towards the table, one younger, one older than him, maybe forty. The older one was bald, his scalp pink and shiny.

'Thought we'd come and have a drink with the new bloke,' said the younger man, thin-faced and with a wandering eye.

'Can I get you gentlemen a beer?' Ernie felt the lightness of coin in his pocket.

'That'd be decent of you,' the bald man said. 'Bill Fairclough's the name.'

'Ernie Hass. I've been meaning to speak to you.' He shook Bill's hand. 'Been busy setting up our home, but I'm opening a guesthouse and shop down at the beach. I'll be looking for a regular service to bring holidaymakers from town.'

'Sure, I can do a bit of business with you. Here, have you met Gerry Paxton,' Bill thumbed the bloke next to him, 'our police constable.'

'Off duty,' said Gerry.

Ernie was unsettled by not knowing which eye to look at, so made his excuses to go to the bar. When he returned, an old fella, with the stink of fish about him, slammed his glass down on their table, stabbing one of his gnarled fingers towards Bill. 'What's goin' on with them prohibiting netting, Bill? Can't earn a living if I can't fish from the beach.'

Bill pulled his shoulders back, shaking his head. 'I don't like it any more than you do, George.'

George grunted and swiped his glass off the table, shuffling back to the bar.

'What's all that about?' Ernie asked, glancing at the fisherman.

Bill necked his beer, wiping the foam from his moustache. 'George Hopkins. Disgruntled 'cause the Fisheries Department's put a ban on netting fish from the foreshore. They didn't consult with the Beach Improvement Committee of the Road Board before making the order.'

The mention of a committee alerted Ernie. 'Anything to do with improving the beach I'm up for. How's a bloke to join that committee?'

Bill cleared his throat. 'I'm the chairman, so I suppose I can say you can throw your hat in at the next meeting.'

The constable nudged Ernie's arm so that he nearly tipped his beer. 'That's who you are,' Gerry said, snatching at the thought as though it had been dangling in front of him.

'Who's that?' Ernie gripped his glass tightly.

'Champion rifleman at the Geraldton Rifle Club. I saw your name on the board when I was a lad. So, your people are from Geraldton, then?'

Ernie's throat went dry. 'I was. My father sold his business in Geraldton and operated a wheat agency in Perenjori till he died a few years back.' It had been foolish to think there wouldn't be anyone who remembered him around these parts.

'Where've you been?'

Gerry's questions unnerved him and it wasn't just the eye or the badge. 'Me and my brother Fred signed up in '15. I came back, met a pretty girl in Perth and married her.'

'Which unit?' asked Matthew.

'32nd Battalion. South Australian unit. Assigned to the 8th Brigade when we reached Egypt.'

All three men nodded in recognition.

'The Somme,' murmured Matthew, shaking his head. 'We lost many of our local men.'

'Guess I was lucky.'

'No luck about it,' said Gerry, slapping Ernie on the back. 'Champion rifleman. Bet you knocked off a fair few of them Huns.'

'Last drinks, gents,' called the barman. Men started to shout over each other to get his attention behind the bar.

Matthew drained his beer and gestured a question at the men with his empty glass. Ernie waved his hand over his glass and was glad to see the other two men do the same. 'Got to pick up the passengers from the Geraldton train soon,' Bill said. Matthew shrugged, said he'd look in on Ernie at the beach in the morning, and left.

Bill leaned in and said what he'd clearly been waiting for. 'I read about you in the paper this morn. Says you had a wheat farm at Perenjori.'

Ernie steadied his gaze on him. 'I did.'

'So, what made you give it up to open a guesthouse here? Beach attractions?'

Gerry snorted.

Ernie was always quick to size up a man. It was how he did business. He could tell if someone wanted more from him than he was willing to give. And for him to make good on a deal, he'd have to know where the other fellow's fingers were. Bill Fairclough was out to cause trouble, knew more than he was letting on.

'Could be,' Ernie said, smirking. 'No, it was the wheat prices. And the damned rabbits and emus destroying the crop. Just like every other farmer round here, I guess. I was just smart and got out when I could.'

'Is that so?' Bill set his glass down on the table and brushed the back of his hand on his stubbly chin. 'I was down at a Road Board meeting the other week when the government agriculture men came. From what I was hearing, it takes brains to be a successful farmer.'

'Fair go, Bill,' warned Gerry.

Yes, Ernie had got Bill right. He decided then and there that he'd need to be three steps ahead; not lose sight of Bill for a moment. With what was coming soon for Ernie, Bill wouldn't need much to bring him down.

CHAPTER SIX

LILY

Unlike the Country Women's Association in Perenjori, which had its own rooms in the hall, the Dongarra branch met at the homestead residence of Mrs Liddle, its President. It was a large white house situated at the bend in the road just past the police station. Its beautifully terraced gardens sloped down to the river, where small boats bobbed gently on the glints of the late afternoon sun.

That Friday evening, Lily walked through the Liddles' rose garden, greeted by the sight of a woman, wearing a lace-trimmed shawl that trailed to the ground, stooped to inhale the scent of a rose. The embroidery on the shawl was exquisite and Lily stopped to stare at the paradisiacal design. Was this Mrs Liddle? She regretted not wearing her crepe wedding dress, though she had curled her hair in rags that day for the occasion and wore her best hat. She scuffed at the fine gravel with her heel.

The woman straightened, a faint blush on her cheeks. 'Hello! You've caught me admiring Mrs Liddle's roses. Are you joining as a new member?'

'I hope so,' Lily said, giving her hand. This woman wasn't even the hostess, and yet Lily's outfit couldn't compare. 'Lily Hass. I was Vice-President of our branch in Perenjori.' A half-truth. She'd lost the position two years ago, but those were secrets she'd left behind.

'Mrs Betsy Booth, a pleasure. I'm our Treasurer. My husband's with the WA Bank, you see.'

Lily repressed a smile, nodding at this irrefutable correlation.

'I saw you straightaway at church on Sunday. I told Darla McGinty you must be the new family down at the beach. She'd thought you would have been a different sort, you know . . .' Mrs Booth lowered her voice. 'Taking up the old port store in its condition. But we're glad to see you're one of us. So glad. Mrs McGinty is one of the ladies you really must meet tonight.'

Lily smiled at her welcome. They had been noticed. *These* were the women who mattered. Mrs Liddle and Mrs Booth, and now a Mrs Darla McGinty. McGinty – related to her neighbours? she wondered. She made a mental note that she ought to impress herself upon the old McGintys, and Darla McGinty, to quickly gain respect. Not the CWA President – in her experience, these women jealously guarded their roles at the top.

A servant brought them through to a large sitting room hung with floor-to-ceiling brocade curtains and crammed with highly polished mahogany furniture. At least twenty faces turned in her direction. The women filled every available space. Two upholstered couches were pushed against opposite walls, while three rows of hard-backed chairs formed the central flank.

'Mrs Booth, we were just about to commence.' A tiny woman stood up from one of the couches, her greying hair pulled back under a lace cap. 'Have you brought a new member?'

Mrs Booth exchanged glances with her. 'Mrs Liddle, this is Mrs Lily Hass. She's the new family at the beach.'

'Please join us, Mrs Hass.' Mrs Liddle raised her hand towards the opposite couch. 'I'm sure there is room at the back for one more.'

Lily swallowed her own introduction as she squeezed beside a young woman. How would she be noticed at the back?

'We have a lot to cover this evening, not to mention Mrs Fairclough's birthday to recognise,' Mrs Liddle glanced at a blonde-haired woman in the front row wearing a frightfully loud shade of red, 'so I shall commence forthwith. After business, we shall induct our Younger Set, and Mrs Booth will demonstrate making a hook rug.'

Lily slipped off her cotton lace glove and ran her fingers over the cloth of the armrest, tracing the silky threads of the woven pattern. The threads were worn. Now that she looked about the room, she noticed the insects lining the bowl of the oil-lamp fitting, and the wallpaper behind the office-bearers' couch, where the sunshine would fall, faded in graduating lines to a dusty pink.

'So as to ensure a more satisfactory arrangement for afternoon tea, let us agree to each not bring more than is sufficient for two,' Mrs Liddle was saying.

'What about the tea?' one of the women in the second row said, raising her hand.

'Tea and sugar may be arranged for separately.'

'Moving on to our second item on the agenda, Mrs Booth, if you please.'

Lily arched her back, casting glances across the heads in front of her, coming to rest on the faces of the four office-bearers. Besides Mrs Liddle, and Mrs Booth, whom she thought quite plain-looking if it weren't for her pretty shawl, the other two were of similar age to herself, one chinless, the other with eyes set too close together above a pinched nose but dressed in a pale blue coatdress that Lily instantly coveted. She could tell the quality hand finish from this distance.

'For the benefit of our younger and newer members,' Mrs Booth said, beaming at Lily – she snapped her attention back to her – 'I shall repeat that at the count last month, we had raised £7 over the course of three bridge evenings. Owing to inclement weather, one bridge evening less was held this past month, and we took just under £4.'

Mrs Liddle's shoulders sagged.

'As the main object of our series of bridge evenings is to raise funds for the renovation of the hearse, its wheels having been white-anted, we must devise further fundraising activities,' concluded Mrs Booth, tapping the sheaf of papers on her lap.

Mrs Liddle rose to her feet, nodding at the lady office-bearers. 'And to that end, Mrs Booth, Mrs Smith, Mrs McGinty,' – ah, thought Lily, Darla was the woman in the blue dress with the unfortunate facial features – 'and I have come up with an idea for a novelty cricket match.'

From among the older women, she heard a faint groan. But now her attention was riveted and she tilted forward. A novelty signalled something other than the same pattern of organising luncheons, sitting in the shade to swipe at blowflies and driving home a slightly worse-for-wear husband.

'Come, come,' said Mrs Liddle. 'I'm sure the Younger Set will be thrilled to hear what we have in store.' The office-bearers nodded, each evidently in their leader's thrall. 'The cricket match will be played between a ladies' team and a gents' team.'

'Where's the sport in that?' asked the blonde-haired woman in the front row. Lily's eyes skimmed across the woman's red dress. It wouldn't have been out of place in a nightclub – but here?

'Don't fret, Mrs Fairclough, the gents shall be playing left-handed.'

The Younger Set tittered beside Lily; their excitement she put down to the chance at winning the local boys' admiration. Every lad longed to be a Donald Bradman. Mrs Liddle narrowed her stare scanning the room while she answered questions about the cricket match. She would have been no more than five foot, but her presence loomed over them.

'When will it be?' asked another woman. 'My Archie's got to be working the siding come the wheat harvest.'

Mrs Liddle looked to Mrs Booth, and raised an eyebrow in question. 'It will have to be December, then.'

Mrs Pearson, who was married to the minister and played the organ at church, exclaimed, 'Don't forget the fair!'

Mrs Booth checked a calendar laid out on the bench beside her. 'We could make it the week before the church fair. The ninth, Mrs Liddle?'

Mrs Liddle nodded. 'Very well. The novelty cricket match shall be held on the ninth of December.'

There was an interval as Darla McGinty left the room, allowing Lily to shift her backside. But she kept one eye trained on Darla's movement, partly in admiration of the coatdress, partly in curiosity as to how the other women regarded her. Darla returned with a nod and Mrs Liddle cleared her throat. 'Ladies, in honour of Mrs Fairclough's birthday this past Tuesday, Mrs McGinty has a presentation to make.'

Mrs Fairclough stood up.

'On behalf of all ladies who contributed to the gift, we would like to wish Mrs Fairclough many happy returns.' Mrs McGinty handed the woman a small paper-wrapped parcel.

Mrs Fairclough slipped off the wrapping, holding her packet of handkerchiefs, edged in pink, as though she had won the booby prize in a raffle. 'Thank you. It's most unexpected.'

Lily overheard a whisper from the young woman beside her. 'What's she need them for?' Her neighbour collapsed in giggles as her friend's reply concerned stuffing Mrs Fairclough's brassiere.

She dropped a glance to Mrs Fairclough's chest and silently agreed there was no need for supplementing. The woman was the obvious sort. Lily had already decided which of the women would be a worthy alliance, and Mrs Fairclough was not one of them.

They rose for supper served in Mrs Liddle's dining room. Lily gazed at the gilt-edged dinner plates behind glass, the dust on the glass chandelier hanging over the long refectory table down the centre. Once the Younger Set dispersed away from the buffet table, she took her plate and, showing restraint, served herself a single plain scone. Mrs Fairclough had piled her plate with egg sandwiches and cold chicken and stood in the centre of the room, laughing loudly in a small circle of women. Lily took her plate to the corner, where she chewed slowly, looking at the dozen or more women in groups sitting and standing, discerning whom she might approach. These women had an air of solidity. The farmers' wives of Perenjori – most of whom had followed their new husbands from England after the war – were marked physically and emotionally by the crash in wheat prices. With these Dongarra women, their church pews would be engraved with the family name, the streets named after an ancestor and two generations buried in the cemetery. Their fortunes might have fallen in recent times, but they had foundation, and would not sink too low. Lily was starting life over again with few resources and a carefully constructed image to maintain. Everyone would know everything about each other and they would have nothing to hide. She could not compete, but she could win favour and, with it, protection from gossip.

'Hello.' Mrs Liddle appeared on her left. Up close, she looked younger than Lily had credited, her complexion clear and unlined. 'Mrs Booth tells me you were Vice-President of the Perenjori branch. I'm Daphne Liddle.' It wasn't so much an introduction as an establishment of position.

'Our Vice-President is Darla McGinty.' Mrs Liddle waved her hand in the direction of Darla seated on a couch. Lily could hear Darla holding forth in a discussion on the perils of women's cycling with three other women who nodded at everything she declaimed. As contrary as Darla McGinty's views were to Lily's, they seemed to be respected here, and the woman would be an ally. Lily's elderly neighbours, the McGintys, might prove a useful connection. But proximity was a double-edged sword. The right neighbours gave the best protection, but the wrong could make life miserable. She resolved that neither she nor Girlie were to be seen on a bicycle.

'My husband and I are opening a guesthouse and shop down at the beach,' Lily said.

Mrs Liddle continued as though Lily hadn't spoken aloud. 'I know some of the Perenjori ladies. Do you know Mrs Fulton?'

Her chest tightened. Mrs Fulton was a font of gossip and one who'd been dead-set against Lily's appointment as an office-bearer in the first instance – and the leading dissenting voice to remove her. She had found herself trapped in a game of one-upmanship with the woman who thought marrying a railway engineer was the pinnacle achievement. But hearing that particular name was not what had knocked the breath from her, it was the knowledge that there was an association between the women here and those she'd left behind in Perenjori, and gossip could easily flow along its lines, undermining her new start. She had not moved far enough away.

Brightly, and forced, she said, 'Oh, yes, I do. I hope she's feeling much better. So poorly in the autumn. Of course, having a husband out of work must have made matters much worse.'

Mrs Liddle gave an almost imperceptible nod. 'I have only pity for such men in these hard times.'

Lily gave the appearance of listening, her mind flicking through the possibilities to ensure success in this town. Her priority was to present herself as an unimpeachable mother and wife, before the women formed a picture of their own if her past caught up with her.

She turned her attention back to Mrs Liddle, who was saying, 'Even here we have been feeling strictures on our way of life.'

Lily caught sight of the Liddles' servant clearing platters at the buffet table. 'I understand. We had to send our domestic back to the mission. I think I might have been rather hasty. You don't happen to know of a woman I might get in to do?'

Mrs Liddle pressed the point of her finger to her chin. 'Not off hand, though there are plenty of ladies about who could help for an hour or two a week. Now, I should move on.' With that, Mrs Liddle escorted a pair of the Younger Set away from the buffet, where they had been making a second attack on the table heaving with jellies and sandwiches.

~

Drawing her thin cotton shawl tightly about her against the cool night, Lily walked to the corner of the bridge where Ernie would collect her. The river bank teemed with sounds that grew fantastical in the darkness. The splashing and swishing through reeds, the hissing and clicking of insects coming at her from all directions, and other, less definable, scuttling movements.

The light from Ernie's hurricane lamp swung like a beacon as the dray approached. Back in Perenjori few farmers had motor cars or trucks and she had not felt such a lack as she felt here, where every second person got about in a motor car. But the possibility was out of reach to them. Even though she'd mentioned looking for a domestic to Mrs Liddle, she knew what Ernie's reaction would be; they had little money to spare for the luxury of help. As it was, he wouldn't say how he'd found the money for the port store. She suspected he held a line of credit that stretched as far as the road to Perenjori. It would reach Perth by the time Ernie made a success of a venture.

Once he slowed in front of her, she reached for Ernie's arm to help her up.

'How was your evening?' he asked, a cigarette clenched in his teeth.

She shivered. 'All CWAs are the same, really.'

They passed a utility truck on the way down the Beach Road and Lily looked across at her husband's profile in the glare of the headlamps. He had plans for their life in this town. If only she could believe in him.

CHAPTER SEVEN

TOMMY

The Dongarra police constable trained his eyes on him; one was shifty, going over Tommy like he was assessing his stink, the other fixed on his face like a lie detector. Both unsettled him, made him feel not quite there.

'Ernie Hass, you say?' The roaming eye came home. The constable chewed his cheek before settling his evaluation with a click of his tongue.

Staying the tremble in his hands, Tommy shoved the rations into his knapsack. They were his due, so he was going to take them. He'd proved to the constable that it had been a week since he'd picked up his last rations at the police station in Perenjori, when he'd enquired into Ernie's whereabouts only to be told the family had upped and gone to Dongarra. One more week on the track hadn't mattered, no longer circling around himself. But he wouldn't believe that they were here until he saw them with his own eyes.

Tommy worked the buckles on his knapsack, but his fingers started at it again, and Christ, the constable was watching with one eye at least. He sweated and fumbled, fought to keep the tremble away. Finally, the leather strap fed through and he swung the knapsack over his shoulder and picked up his bedroll.

The constable tipped his hat back, scratching his head as Tommy backed away from the counter. He dropped his gaze; pushed the door open to the outside. To breathe air into his lungs. To cool his blazing face and neck. But the constable caught the door on the heavy back swing, holding it open.

'You might need to know where you're going.'

'Eh?' said Tommy, gripping the baggy seams of his trousers.

'Ernie Hass's place. That's where you said you were travelling to. Wasn't it?'

Tommy nodded, wavering from one foot to the other. 'Right you are, constable. Just point me in the direction and I'll be off.'

The constable came up close, hands on hips. 'You'll be wanting to keep to the road. So as you don't get lost.' It wasn't good-natured the way he said it. The police never were. Other blokes on the track had similar stories of their encounters with the law, but he always forgot this when face-to-face with a copper, couldn't hold his nerve. 'This here is Waldeck Street.' The constable stretched one arm out and pointed over Tommy's shoulder. 'Follow it round past the Liddles' house, that big white place there, down Hunts Road until you come to the Beach Road. Cross the bridge. About half an hour's walk down the road till you reach the Front Beach. You'll see a cottage with a tearoom, and a goods shed near the jetty. Just past there is a stone building. That's the Hasses'.'

Tommy stepped backwards, away from the constable's reach.

'You about for long? It's my job to keep tabs on the likes of you.'

'I can't say, it depends,' Tommy said. 'I'll be sure to let you know of my intentions, constable.' His intentions were the same ones he'd had for the past six years, three spent locked up, three on the track. But he'd never shared them with anyone.

Both eyes locked into place. 'I'm sure to know from Mr Hass sooner or later.'

~

Tommy was finally free from the tyranny of the police, out on the white-painted bridge feeling the wind come up the river from the sea, lifting his coat flaps like sails and pushing him onwards.

Ahead, where the bank of the river rolled down to the water's edge, were two tin-walled shacks side-by-side. Outside one of them, a child sat on a tricycle, his finger stuck up his nose. He stared at Tommy as from somewhere inside the shacks came raised voices, clanging and thudding. He darted a look at the child's face – as dull-mouthed as before – and scanned the scrub. The track down to the houses gave out beneath a thick stand of sheoaks and banksias concealing the way to the river mouth. Though he was weary of roads, and wondered how it would feel for the sand to give way under his feet and wash them clean in the sea, he pressed on. He'd already wandered down too many side tracks.

Chalky limestone marle from the road covered his boots, got into his boots; his feet slippery with paste, forming blisters. New blisters on old. But they didn't bother him.

Nor when the gravel cut sharp, through the worn leather soles, finding the split and lacerating him over and over again, giving focus to the sensation of each step. He stumbled, lurching and buffeted by the wind. It tore around his ears, funnelling sounds from far away, exploded close to his ear drums.

He skidded on loose gravel, flinging out a hand to catch himself. Out on the track, he often became sucked up into his surroundings. He'd forget where he was for minutes at a time, then surprise himself when he came to at a farm gate or a road crossing. Surprised he hadn't dissolved into the expansive sky. The further north he'd travelled the denser the light, and he filled his body with it.

As he reached the crest of a scrubby sand hill, the horizon line of the dark green sea sliced the sky. He began to whistle 'The Sleeper Cutters' Camp', the tune he turned to whenever he found himself kipping in his own damp funkhole of a night. In the trenches in the Dardanelles; a shanty hut with a leaking roof; a dried-up river bed.

Just as the constable had instructed, a cluster of buildings by the jetty came into view. He passed a round water trough, licking his blistered lips, tongue scraping like sandpaper. He hadn't been too ashamed to drink horses' water before. But now – now he was going to be a new man, able to taste again, fill his stomach with food, be quenched.

There was a long, stone house facing the beach. Rubble piled up against the side wall and the roof caved in at one end, but as he strode closer he saw a new latticework extension behind the house and a wash house and tin dunny at the back fence. Beyond that, dense scrub. He shifted his knapsack and bedroll on his shoulder and swallowed.

A woman came out of the wash house carrying a basket on her hip. He stood still; she was thin and pale, as insubstantial as himself, but memory was not a certain thing. Another rabbit hole down which he lost time. Then she came into focus, the clearest, most trusted memory he had.

She shook sheets from the basket, flipping them over the line and pegging them. He could have watched her all day, but the gurgle in his stomach drove him forward. He spat on his hand and rubbed down the sides of his hair.

She glimpsed him then, and clutched one of the hanging sheets to her body as though she'd been caught bathing. Her face was cast in shade. And it wasn't until he entered the yard proper that he could make out her expression.

'What's your business?' she said. Shook her head. 'I haven't got any work for you, if that's it. But you can have a crust and some water and be on your way.' She let slip the sheet and turned to the house.

Tommy called her name and she stopped cold. She didn't turn around immediately, not until he said her name again. 'Lily, it's me.'

Her eyes went wide, sucking in his appearance. Was she staring at the changes in his body – his crooked nose broken by a farmer in Merredin, his trousers held up by boot laces – or at the very fact of seeing him on her doorstep?

'Lord, it *is* you, Tommy,' she said, breaking the spell. He walked right up to her, but a shift in her eyes held him back.

She was beautiful like their mother, but Lily's red hair, faded, was pushed back into a tight knot, and she wore a dun-coloured dress. Like her light had gone out. Bleeding the colour from the picture of Lily he'd kept in the pocket of his memory. She used to turn both men's and women's heads in those frocks she ran up. A way of looking showy without showing off. She always used to say, *You never know who's going to stop by.*

'Can I come in?' he asked.

'Where've you been?'

'Stony broke and walking.'

She tied the loose strings on her apron, gesturing for him to follow, led him into the kitchen, where he dropped his knapsack and bedroll against the wall. A kettle boiled on the hob. She rested against the stone wall staring at him, waiting. His neck prickled all over. He didn't like being watched. Had to remind himself this was Lily.

She brought the teapot to the table. Without thinking, he reached for it, seared his thumb on escaping steam. He sucked on the burn while she twiddled with her empty cup, glancing up at him from time to time, then away towards the window.

'When did you leave Perth?'

He shook his head. 'Must have been three years ago.'

'How have you been living? I mean – have you been working? Are you eating?'

He shrugged. 'Bits and bobs. The susso. Chopping wood for a staley.'

She got up to check the pantry cupboard. 'It's all I've got till tea,' she said, holding out a handful of biscuits.

'That'll do.' He smiled, he'd been right about her; but she busied her hands, filling their cups. On the back of one hand a scar – he couldn't remember how she'd come by it. He cleared his throat. 'I hear you've just moved here.'

'Have you now?' A sharpness in her tone. Still guarded. 'How'd you come by that information?'

'The local copper. Thinks a lot of your husband.' Tried to make himself appear solid, like the man he'd been before. Not what she must see now.

She didn't say anything. Just wiped the crumbs he'd spilled on the table into her hand.

'Any chance Ernie can see me with a bit of work while I'm here?'

'Oh, Tommy,' she said, frowning. 'I haven't seen you for six years. You've been God knows where. So much has happened and you just show up here. Me and Ern, there's lots you don't know about behind closed doors.'

He heard those doors: a rapid volley slamming shut. *Bang. Bang. Bang.*

Bang.

The door slammed against the wall. A child, a girl, had run into the kitchen. 'You'll never guess—'

His hand flew across the table, knocking his cup to the floor where it smashed, splattering tea.

The girl stared at him. 'I didn't know . . . I really didn't,' she said, fear in her voice.

The girl dropped to her knees, picking up the shards of china. Lily said, 'I'll see to it. Go outside and play until Daddy comes home.'

Daddy? The word crackled in Tommy's brain and he opened his mouth to say something, but Lily glared at him. And his memories telescoped, so that instead of Lily it was Ma standing in front of him and he saw himself at seven years old when he'd broken her garden urn. Here and there at the same time. *No.* He squeezed his eyes shut then opened them.

His sister's face formed again, deep lines cutting her brow. The girl glanced at her, then him, her expression a mirror of Lily's, before she slunk out the back door. Lily crouched to clear away the mess he had made.

'You have a daughter.' He said it as a statement, but it was meant as a question, for the pieces didn't add up. Any daughter of Lily's could only be . . . what? Five, six at most. He didn't know much about children, but she seemed far older. Nothing added up for him anymore, and he wanted more than anything for Lily to straighten out his brain and tell him there was nothing wrong with him. 'You didn't have her . . . back then.' He fumbled for words. After he'd left Perth, he'd gone out east as far as Norseman on the edge of the wheatbelt, until the towns, the farms, the reasons had started to slip. Had Lily's daughter slipped from his memory? They'd told him he couldn't trust his memory anymore; that ghosts appeared as flesh-and-blood, and the flesh-and-blood as ghosts. The boundaries between them had blurred in the war, all that living with the dying.

Lily got up from the floor slowly. 'I don't want to talk about it, Tommy,' she said, dropping her voice. 'But there are other ways of welcoming a child into one's life.'

'Adopted, you mean?' Of course. There was no doubting Lily. She could explain what he could not.

She stood there, with that wary look again like she regretted letting him in. 'Uh-huh.' Her lips pressed to a thin line.

Before she could push him out, he said, 'See if you can ask Ernie about some work, then, eh?'

She hesitated, her eyes looking vacant for a moment, before fixing themselves back onto him. 'I'll ask. We're doing up the other side of the house in guestrooms, he'll want help with that. There's no money, but you can kip outside and I'll feed you. You'll have to be gone by the tourist season, mind you.'

He opened his mouth to thank her, but she held up the flat of her palm to stop him.

'I can't keep helping you my whole life,' his sister said, looking at him sadly.

That was what he most desired. To be someone who didn't need help. To be someone. To be himself again.

CHAPTER EIGHT

GIRLIE

Mr Peters banged the duster on the board. The hubbub of chatter instantly died away as four rows of heads snapped towards the front of the classroom. Girlie gave up trying to catch Susan Fry's eye. Since her first day of school a fortnight ago, she'd clung to her new friend's side, thrilled at Susan's interest in learning every intimate detail of her life. A close friend made it easier to cope with changes. She couldn't wait to share the news of the arrival of her mysterious uncle.

'Leave your pencils and make two orderly lines at the front of the classroom,' their teacher said. The children rose from their seats in a cacophony of clanging metal and chatter, until he silenced them again. 'There'll be my carpet slipper for the next child who disrupts the class.' They filed into lines, boys against the wall, tapping each other and grinning, the girls in a neater formation. Girlie slipped in next to Susan.

Mr Peters beckoned them to follow him outside, and with side-long enquiring glances at each other, they complied. He handed two four-gallon tins to the head of each line. 'Children, attention. Keep close behind me.'

They followed him up Waldeck Street towards the river. A cutting in the scrub fell away to the river bank, and one of the bigger boys held back the branches of a wattle as they made their way after the teacher. They assembled on a sandy stretch littered with spiky nuts and tree roots.

There was something on the ground in front of Mr Peters. Girlie ducked under a low branch to see what it was. A campfire.

'Are you gunna make us a cuppa, sir?' asked Nigel, one of the bigger boys behind her, to a round of sniggers.

The teacher gave him a wry smile. 'Ha. Not quite. It's a science demonstration. Girls go this way, boys that way,' he said gesturing up and down the river bank. 'Among the sedges is best. But don't go too close to the water's edge, I won't thank you if I have to get wet.'

Girlie watched the other children to see if they knew what was happening. Two boys, Bobby and Joe, ran ahead and poked sticks into the clumps of sedges. Mean boys. Bobby was the ringleader. With his shorn hair and scarred, lice-bitten scalp, his lip always curled into a sneer, he looked tough. Joe was smaller, his hair combed neatly and he was one of the only boys who wore socks with his shoes. But he would do whatever Bobby did. They'd thrown wads of paper soaked in spit at Mary Ellen and Brigid coming out of the girls' bathroom, and had run off, whooping. And when Susan strayed close to the boys' side of the yard to fetch a ball, the boys and their gang had called her names. But she'd stood her ground, hands on her hips, calling back, 'Those are fine words, Joe Smith, dontcha think your ma'll be pleased to learn of them?'

Susan was different to Katie. Girlie's mind roamed back to her first true friend, in Perenjori, who'd been afraid of spiders, loud noises and the dark. Susan was more like Jenny, she supposed. And just as Girlie had tried to show Jenny she wasn't afraid, she wouldn't let on to Susan how frightening she found the new schoolyard – learning whom she should be friends with, whom she wasn't to talk to, who liked whom.

'Come with me,' hissed Susan, pulling at her sleeve. The spiny leaves of the gnarled trees scratched Girlie's arms. 'We're supposed to hunt for frogs. We did this last term and Mr Peters chopped their legs off. They didn't half still wriggle about, though.'

Girlie's stomach flip-flopped.

She jerked her head at a shout from up the bank, and Susan grabbed her hand. 'Sounds like they've already caught them. Come on.'

Back at the clearing, Mr Peters had hung a tin of river water over the fire from a bough. 'Master Pringle, bring it here,' he said. Girlie looked up in alarm as Bobby moved towards the fire, cupping something close to his chest, grinning like a prince at the other children.

'Class, come closer. Not *that* close, Miss Delaney; we don't want your dress catching alight.' The boys chuckled among themselves while Brigid glared. Girlie pressed herself into a gap so she could see better.

Water began to bubble up in the tin. Her upper lip and forehead dampened. She felt sick but couldn't look away as Mr Peters cupped his hands around Bobby's to take the slimy frog from him. Too quickly, there was a splash of water and a flash of murky green as the frog jumped out of the tin.

Susan squealed. But Girlie studied Mr Peters. He didn't look worried by this turn of events, instead he gazed at them as though a magician completing a trick. What had he been trying to do? Several of the boys dropped to their knees to look for the frog.

'Quiet. Quiet,' said Mr Peters as more of the girls squealed and hopped from foot to foot. But it was only Bobby and Joe snatching at their shoes, pretending to catch the frog. 'What did you just see happen?'

Girlie found her hand creeping up her side and pointing to the sky.

'Yes, Miss Hass.'

'The frog got scared of being boiled to death and jumped out.'

'That's right. A frog's not a stupid creature,' Mr Peters paused, lifting up the second tin. 'Or is it?' He beckoned to Eddie, one of the older boys who'd been standing at the back throughout the fray, gripping another frog in his hands. Girlie couldn't bear to look. She stepped back, onto the toes of Mary Ellen behind her. Mary Ellen elbowed her in the stomach, and Girlie peeled away from the group.

Mr Peters put the frog in the tin and hung it over the fire, half-covering it with a lid. Girlie's stomach felt strange where she'd been elbowed, like great big bubbles of sickness were spreading out from her middle to the edges of her skin. The air beneath the trees was steamy and swirled around her.

The next thing she knew she was lying on the ground in the shade. A sharp nut stuck into the small of her back. Mr Peters' face hovered over her. 'Feeling better now? You fainted.'

She nodded as he lifted her up, though she felt so heavy-headed it took all her effort to do so. Though it was the middle of spring, the sun was hot even in the shade. Above her she heard a willie wagtail singing the song of a squeaky wheel, darting in and out of its nest.

~

After school, Girlie hooked her arm in Susan's as they walked towards the bridge, telling her all about the surprise arrival of Uncle Tommy.

'I didn't even know I had an uncle. He didn't know about me neither.'

Susan screwed up her freckled nose. 'That's funny. Where's he been your whole life?'

Girlie told her what she'd found out from listening to her parents through the kitchen door. 'He's been working on farms. The only things he owns fit into his knapsack.'

Susan lived near Dr Marsh's house on the other side of the bridge, and though they'd walked home together every day, Susan hadn't yet invited her inside. Girlie saw it from the road, a tin and sack-walled shack, and always two or three of Susan's brothers or sisters playing in the yard. Susan was eleven months older than her but short and thin – *petite*, Girlie's mother said – and looked much younger than Girlie, who was growing 'too fast for her knickers'. Susan usually lagged after school, not wanting to go home to take care of her brothers and sisters. Today this irked Girlie, wanting to race home to see her uncle, but she wouldn't show it. The friendship was still new and fragile. Instead of taking the bridge, Susan skipped down to the bank, hopping between it and rocks just below the water, like a dancer or circus performer. Somebody had laid planks across to an island and onto the bank on the other side. Girlie cautiously followed Susan a few feet along the plank, her heart lurching each time it wobbled under Susan's twirls.

'My uncle told me how he follows the rivers all over,' Girlie said. 'He walks everywhere, singing songs.' Last night he'd laid out his bedroll against the wash house and her mother had given him some canvas to stretch over him like a tent.

Susan leaped onto the island and skidded, bending forward for balance and then stood up, waggling her splayed hands. 'Ta-dah.'

Girlie smiled.

'How long's he staying?'

She shook her head. 'I don't know. I heard Mummy telling Daddy it would only be until he got back on his feet again. It didn't sound like Daddy wants Uncle Tommy around.'

'Why's that?' asked Susan.

Girlie shrugged. Her father said that Susan's father knew everyone in town's business, but before she could form a reply, a whoop came from above them. She and Susan cricked their necks to see Bobby and Joe thundering across the boards of the bridge. They hadn't spotted the girls yet, but they soon would. As he passed each bridge post Bobby gave it a big whack with his stick. Girlie gritted her teeth.

'I don't want them to see me. Bobby teased me for fainting in class today.'

Susan flicked her gaze at the boys and back. 'Come on,' she said. 'We can get to the other side before they do.' She stepped onto the plank, stretching out her toes in front of her.

Girlie looked at the planks leading across. They submerged just before reaching the bank. 'All right.' Her knees locked up in fear.

She had forced herself to the first rock when Bobby yelled, 'Chicken!' Susan surged, leaping across to the rock at the surface. Five yards ahead of her. Ten. Girlie didn't look up but the boys' feet hammered, and Bobby's stick-whacking grew louder, almost above her. The planks jangled beneath her feet, smacking the water, until she was skidding and spraying water. This was madness. She stopped and glanced up to see Susan bounding onto the bank. Susan cupped her mouth, shouting at her. Too late. Bobby was banging the stick, yelling, 'Chicken! Girlie's chicken!' She lifted each foot clear out of the water to avoid the pull of the current, gaining a few yards to the rock, but as she did, something hard and sharp hit her shoulder, knocking her down. Flailing, she latched her fingers onto the edge of the plank, and clung to it, sobbing. Her satchel streamed water down her wet, heavy dress as she straddled the plank and pushed herself to her feet. The boys had run ahead, probably waiting for her at the other side, but she edged her way forward to Susan, who reached out to grasp Girlie's hand and pull her to safety.

The whole right side of her body smarted. She lifted her elbow and saw a graze about two inches long on her forearm. Bobby and Joe stood on the slope above them, laughing and holding their sides.

Girlie hated them. She squeezed her lips together so she wouldn't cry.

'Stop that!' Susan shouted, running at them. They laughed, running out of sight. She shook her small fist at their backs, and then turned back towards Girlie, sunlight making a halo of her blonde hair. 'They're horrible boys.'

Girlie didn't answer, trying to control the shuddering in her body.

Susan noticed her arm and grimaced. 'Ooh, I bet that hurts.'

Girlie looked again at her graze. Fear churned with her anger. 'I can't go home to my mother like this. What am I going to do?'

Susan lifted a shoulder. 'I gotta get home – feed my new kitten, Ruffles.'

'Oh,' said Girlie, her mixed-up feelings easing with a new thought. 'Can I come with you?'

'Maybe another time.' Susan looked her up and down. 'My older brothers are home today.'

Girlie let this sink in. Katie was an only child as well, and they'd sworn each other as 'sisters'; but here in Dongarra Susan had two sisters and four brothers of her own – she didn't need another 'sister' in Girlie. 'You're lucky,' she said.

'I guess. Ruffles is the only thing I've got that I don't have to share.'

Sharing was what Girlie looked forward to the most – stories Jenny had told her, walking the fields with her father, her mother's goodnight lullabies. That was when she felt closest to her mother, didn't feel like she was being judged. She tried to look at her life through Susan's eyes. Was she really lucky and just didn't know it?

'See you,' Susan said, with a flick of her hair as she turned, and picked her way through the thicket of flood gums and sheoaks.

Girlie's teeth started to chatter as she watched Susan leave. Now that she'd calmed, her wet clothing chilled her and she didn't feel much like walking home with the wind blowing. She hadn't seen where the boys had run off to, either. They'd called her 'chicken' and now Susan must think her weak, too. Why else would she not want Girlie to come and see her new kitten?

She wrapped her arms about her knees, and rested her head on them. From where she was crouched she saw straight under the bridge to a sunny clearing surrounded by tall trees. If she wasn't seen, she could remove her wet dress to lay it out in the sun to dry.

The clearing was larger than she'd thought and she noticed an old campfire where the sandy ground sloped up sharply. It reminded her of the scene with the frog earlier that day and she felt sick again, took in deep breaths. The air was slightly smoky. She stopped mid-stride when she realised it had been a recent fire. With a stick, she poked at the charcoals in the pit, turning over a glowing orange ember. It sent out fizzing sparks and she dropped the stick, hastily kicking sandy soil over the fire in case she started a bushfire.

She knew that fire was dangerous, it hurt people. After her grandpa's house had burned down nearly three years ago, just before Christmas, their tenant Mr Sutcliffe had lost his eyebrows and his cat. He glared at Girlie and her mother every time they visited the shops in the months following, like he blamed them. And then she started to hear whispered rumours about her mother. From listening to her parents' hushed conversations, it seemed that the fire had caused her father money worries.

'Oi, that's my fire.'

Girlie stubbed her toe in the dirt. A girl had appeared on the edge of the clearing. She was holding a sack, dripping water onto her bare feet.

Girlie shrank back, embarrassed at the state of herself – dirty, wet and bleeding, even though this girl's dress was stained and too small for her, the sleeves tight under her arms. 'I thought it had been left behind. Is it really yours?' she asked, her eyes wide as she watched the girl kneel down to blow on the embers, pulling dry grass to build the flames.

'Uh-huh. Gunna boil up a crab.'

Girlie looked on with fascination as the girl pulled out the crab from her sack, holding its greenish-grey pincers apart between her fingers. She grinned.

'I'd better get going. I didn't mean to intrude.' Girlie gathered up her sludge-coated satchel.

'You can stay and have some of my crab, if you like. My name's Ruby, what's yours?'

'Girlie Hass.' Ruby shoved the crab into a tin that Girlie hadn't noticed sitting by the campfire, and Girlie was struck by a thought. 'Do you live down here?' She glanced through the dark shadows of the trees further along the bank.

'Nah. Up behind the Methodist manse. My dad's a porter on the railway. I just like to come down here after lessons.'

'I haven't seen you there. At school, I mean,' said Girlie. Susan hadn't said anything about this girl.

'Well, they don't let us mix with you lot, do they? Me and my sisters, we get our lessons at the back of the manse in the old shed. Mrs Pearson, the Reverend's wife, she teaches us.'

It was on the tip of her tongue to ask Ruby what was so bad about them that they couldn't come to school, but she remembered the way her mother used to judge families in Perenjori. Some people were acceptable and some weren't. She didn't have to understand why. It was possible she might get in more trouble than just for her dirty clothes if she stayed to talk to Ruby.

'I have to go home,' she said.

'No worries.' Ruby shrugged a single shoulder. 'You gunna be all right?' She pointed at the graze on Girlie's arm.

Distracted by Ruby, Girlie had forgotten the pain but now it did smart badly. She cradled it with her other arm, nodding.

'Here, wait a minute.' Ruby scraped some bark off a tree, then chewed it up and spat it out on her palms. She came up to Girlie, who watched unsure of what Ruby was doing, and held the spat-up bark to the graze. 'The stinging will go away now.'

She recoiled, but it was true – within minutes, the graze did seem to sting a little less. 'How do you know to do that?'

Ruby grinned. 'Something my mum taught me.'

Girlie's mother had only ever taught her the piano. But what good was that when she got hurt? 'I really must go now,' she said, her chest tightening at the thought of her mother.

'See you, Girlie.' Ruby waved at her, then settled on her haunches by the fire.

As she climbed the bank towards the bridge, squinting at the harsh sunlight, she thought about how Susan hadn't mentioned Ruby. Pleased, because now Girlie had a secret, one big enough that even Susan would want to share. Secrets had a special kind of power. When Jenny had shared the secret of her husband, Girlie had felt stronger, knowing something that had been kept from her mother.

CHAPTER NINE

LILY

Lily walked Girlie and Susan round to the McGintys' tearoom. The girls giggled, sharing glances, and she yearned for the intimacy of a girl's best friendship. For Lily, it had been Maisie Winthrop, when she was eight years old. She and Maisie had done everything together: sat next to each other in the front row of Miss Trotter's class at the Thomas Street Primary School in Subiaco, held their hands out in unison to be caned for whispering secrets about Neville Ford with his cheeky grin. He could spin a hoop thirty times before they had to go back into class again. Lily found out – second-hand – just how fast his hands were when Maisie kissed him in Samson's market garden at age twelve.

Maisie's betrayal still unsettled her, but she'd never let on how much she'd been hurt. Forming the right kind of friendships became essential to protect against future betrayals, which was largely the reason for today's visit to the McGintys'. She was unlikely to run into Darla McGinty herself, but Lily thought to impress her presence on old Mrs McGinty so that she might be mentioned to Darla. And in the right way – a mother treating her daughter and her daughter's friend.

The bell tinkled as Lily pushed in the door. Susan looked at the boiled lollies and musk sticks and chocolate freckles and liquorice allsorts under glass, her mouth forming an O. 'Gosh,' she half-whispered, her eyes shining. 'Thanks for bringing me, Mrs Hass.'

Lily smiled at her, but tightened her mouth at the sight of Girlie slouching against the door, her hair fluffed up, when Lily had combed it just before they left. Compared to Susan, whose hair was cut short at her ears, Girlie looked uncouth. Unbecomingly large, Lily admitted to herself. She hadn't started to 'develop' until she was nearly twelve.

Susan's father was well thought of around town. He brought the newspapers and mail down to the McGintys' post office each week, and if Lily was outside, he came across to admire the small geraniums she was coaxing from the dirt in front of the house. She hadn't met Mrs Fry yet, but this was a friendship Lily wished Girlie to cultivate. Maybe her daughter would learn to be more quiet and mannered like Susan.

Inside the cramped tearoom were four tables, one already occupied by a woman with her back to them, seeming entirely incongruous with her gloomy surroundings. All gleam and colour. She wore a bright red dress, and her blonde hair was fashionably shingled. Lily flushed when the woman turned and caught her staring. She flicked her attention to the girls, prodding Girlie in the back towards a chair.

It was the woman whose birthday they had celebrated at the CWA meeting.

Mrs McGinty was busy on the other side of the counter putting through a telephone call for Mr Shenton, one of the old farmers who lived in the sand hills behind the Hasses' place. He usually kept to himself. Lily assumed him a lonely old bachelor. As he waited for the connection, he gestured agitatedly, speaking in a low tone to Mrs McGinty who appeared to ignore him, pressing her hand against one ear, with the earpiece against the other.

Girlie stood, her gaze pulled towards the lolly counter. 'Sit down,' Lily admonished, seating herself with her back to the woman to dissuade conversation. She heard the woman's chair scrape the floor and forced herself to look around, arranging a pleasing expression on her face.

'Hello, Mrs Hass,' said the woman, walking the few steps to Lily's table. And then when Lily was a beat slow in responding, 'Lorna Fairclough. I saw you at Mrs Liddle's.'

Lily stood to take her hand, but the woman had already pulled out a chair at their table. 'Would you care to join us?' she asked, knowing this was how it was to be – Lorna Fairclough was the sort of woman who pressed herself into your life, and nothing short of rudeness could evict her.

Just like that busybody Mrs Fulton of the Perenjori CWA. Lily thought bitterly of how *she* hadn't lost her Treasurer's position when the unemployed Mr Fulton had been found sodden drunk in the town bar every night. All because Gussie Fulton had once been bridesmaid to the Mayor of Perth's daughter.

'I am sorry I didn't introduce myself at the meeting,' Lily said. 'It's all too overwhelming, meeting everyone for the first time, and so much to learn about the community.' She'd instinctively dismissed Lorna, with her lack of refinement, as a potential ally, but she would be civil until she formed a clearer picture of how Lorna fitted in.

'Never mind. Dongarra is just as sleepy as the people who live here. Hello, Susan.' Lorna smiled at the girl, then turned to Girlie. 'I haven't met this young lady. Your daughter? She's the spit of you,' she said, looking from Girlie to Lily.

Lily tightened her stomach. 'Yes. My daughter, Girlie.'

Girlie bit her lip and smiled, shyly.

'Your only one?'

'Just Girlie.' Lily breathed shallowly, feeling defensive.

Lorna leaned across the table towards Girlie. 'I bet you'd like a little kitten to play with, just like Susan's.'

Girlie dropped her jaw. 'Oh, please.'

Lily bristled, taking a deep breath as Mrs McGinty approached, remembering why she had come. Lily ordered a pot of tea, and, fingering the lining of her purse, asked, 'How much for ice-creams, Mrs McGinty?'

'I can give you girls a wee bit for nought today. There's some already churned up this morning,' Mrs McGinty said, lowering her voice after a quick glance over her shoulder to the back room. 'Our little secret.' She smiled. 'I always like to have children about the place.'

The girls dissolved into giggles as they watched Mrs McGinty scoop out the creamy confection into glasses for them. Lily relaxed, glad she had thought of this outing and resolved that she would bring Girlie to visit Mrs McGinty more often.

Lorna pressed her handkerchief to her lips. 'Martha, can you bring out some bread and jam?' Lorna seemed well fed, not suffering a lack of any kind, except perhaps manners. Lily shifted herself slightly away, an imperceptible distance but enough to imply she didn't approve of Lorna's poor form.

Mrs McGinty wiped her hands on some hessian and threw it over the ice-cream contraption. 'Unless old Reg has eaten the last of it,' she said, chuckling. Lily relaxed into her seat as Mrs McGinty disappeared into the back room.

Girlie clasped her hands in front of her. 'Please, Mummy, please can I have a kitten?'

'My Tabby's had a whole litter, I've more than one to give to a good home,' said Lorna.

'Mine is the sweetest ginger kitten.' Susan pleaded Girlie's case. 'With one white paw. I adore it.'

Lily pressed her fingers to her temple in small circles. 'No, Girlie.'

Girlie slumped her shoulders, and immediately Lily flashed her a look to straighten up.

'I apologise for mentioning it. I wouldn't have, if I'd known she couldn't have one,' Lorna said. She mugged a look of contriteness.

Lily couldn't tell if Lorna was genuine in her apology, but would take the higher path. 'It's kind of you, but Girlie knows how I feel about pet animals. Besides, it's hard enough to have her practise the piano at home as it is without any further distractions.'

Girlie cast a furtive smile at Susan, who didn't reciprocate. Quite sensible, Lily thought.

'Oh, you have a piano?' said Lorna, and Lily cringed at the hint of surprise. Why should she not?

'I do hope your daughter will play in the recital at the church fair this year,' Lorna continued, as though she had not meant her words the way Lily had understood. 'Susan, you went in for it last year, didn't you?'

Susan nodded, swallowing her mouthful quickly. 'Yes, Mrs Fairclough, vocals. My ma says it's the only way I can make myself heard.'

'With an accompanist?' Girlie asked.

Susan nodded. 'Mrs Pearson from the church.'

'I can accompany you, if you like. I don't think I'd much like to go in for the recital on my own,' Girlie said, licking the last skerrick of ice-cream from her spoon. 'If that's all right with you, Mummy?'

'When is the fair?' Lily asked, recalling a mention at the CWA meeting. A piano recital would be a perfect demonstration of her commitment – the years she had instructed Girlie in the piano. But she frowned at the thought of Girlie's practice this morning. Sloppy scales.

'A week or so before Christmas,' said Lorna.

Lily felt the painful throb return to her temples. Before Christmas? That gave Girlie two months to polish her repertoire.

'Here, I'll tell you what,' said Lorna, patting Lily's hand like she had known her for more than a few minutes. Though Lily was wearing gloves, she flinched at the close contact with the burn scar on her hand. 'The girls can go out and play while you enjoy a nice cup of tea and we can chat.'

Girlie sat up straight now, bright-eyed, a drift of cream on her top lip.

'Of course,' Lily murmured, and the girls sprang from their seats, holding hands as they left the tearoom.

Mrs McGinty shuffled back with the teapot and bread and jam, and Lorna exchanged words with her about her cataracts and Reg's back. Mrs McGinty answered briefly while pouring the tea, her attention given to Mr Shenton who had finished his telephone call and now waited by the counter. Lily watched these movements, taking them in, coming to the conclusion that Mrs McGinty was not put out by Lorna's manner.

She took deep sips of the milky sweetness.

'I used to care for Robert and Darla McGinty's children when they were young lads,' said Lorna, leaning close to Lily as though they were friends sharing confidences. 'Now Samuel's fourteen and George is sixteen. Imagine that. They grow so fast.'

Lily's opinion of Lorna turned. She was someone who had been intimate with Darla McGinty's household, and therefore might be useful.

'I haven't met Robert McGinty yet, though I've seen him in church with Darla,' Lily ventured. 'They seem quite devout.' The McGinty pew at church was one of the nearest to the pulpit. On the occasions that she had found herself observing the ladies of the congregation rather than focusing on the minister's sermon, she'd seen Robert and Darla, sitting attentively, their own eyes never breaking focus from the minister, and they were always one of the first to speak with him following the service. Robert McGinty appeared dour-looking, nothing like his father, Reg.

Lorna uttered a short laugh, which partly came through her nose. 'Darla would have made a good nun at the convent. She's very good at self-denial.'

'Oh?' It seemed to Lily that she and Darla might be cut from the same cloth. She'd spent years living for others, rather than for herself – yet she sensed there was more to this off-the-cuff comment than Lorna was letting on. She held her tongue. Being silent was the best way to force someone to say what they were really thinking.

Lorna took another slice of bread from the rack and spread jam on it with an air of childlike self-indulgence. 'The McGintys were one of the first families in Dongarra. Reg's grandfather was lighthouse keeper here until the port was moved up to Geraldton.'

This told Lily why Darla McGinty was held in respect by the other ladies, but something in Lorna's words had been a little cryptic. She would have to try a different tack.

'How many children do you have, Mrs Fairclough?'

Lorna took some time swallowing. 'Goodness me, none, thankfully.'

Whenever Ernie spoke of Bill Fairclough, who had the carrying business and a garage up in town, Lily had noted the edge in his tone; it usually meant he envied a man. She wondered if she'd tell him that Bill's wife didn't want children, didn't put herself about as the maternal sort of woman, quite the opposite kind. But the little voice inside her that criticised, which almost sounded like Ma's, put an end to the thought.

'It's good that Girlie's making friends already.' Lorna gestured for Lily to help herself to a slice of bread, but she refused, gaining pleasure from the self-denial and hoping that Lorna would notice.

'Yes, but I think she hasn't quite reconciled herself to the move,' Lily said. The move hadn't been what she had envisaged either – a chance for her and Ernie to start again, just as they had when they'd moved to Perenjori in 1926. But each move took them further away from each other. 'The night before last she woke me in the early hours. She'd had a bad dream and said she wanted to go home. It took me some time to convince her this is home now.'

'Aw, the little duckie. I wouldn't worry, Mrs Hass. She'll feel like one of us soon.' Lorna steadied her gaze. 'And so will you. You'll find something to do – dances at the hall, euchre parties and sporting fixtures. We Dongarra ladies are quite well known in the district for the suppers we put on. I'd say it's a little livelier than the wheat districts,' she laughed, 'though only just. Always an excuse to pull on a good frock. Do you have a dressmaker?'

Lily glanced down at herself. She was wearing the belted primrose-yellow dress, so faded that only she knew it had a white floral pattern running through the grain. The puffed sleeves had sagged and she now tied them above her elbows. But it was finished well, without the usual stamp of being homemade.

'Me. But I haven't made anything in so long.'

Lorna set the teapot down with such a thump that Lily looked over towards Mrs McGinty, who was sorting through the mail for Mr Shenton.

'Oh, what a shame,' Lorna said. 'I get my dresses made in Geraldton, with the same woman as Daphne Liddle and Darla McGinty. There isn't a proper dressmaker in Dongarra, and many of the other ladies make do with their wedding gowns. I dare say you'll have them wanting you to run something up for them. But I'd want to ask you first.' Lorna shifted in her seat, tugging at her skirt, which was riding up.

'No. Sorry, I can't,' said Lily. 'I don't have my machine anymore.'

Lorna sighed, echoing the ebb in Lily's spirit. The way to a woman's heart was through her wardrobe. To think of the friends she could have made. 'But I can alter one you already have. For instance,' Lily said, waving her hand across Lorna's chest, 'with this dress – as lovely as it is – the darts have been stitched straight across.' She gestured at the ugly, blunt points poking out. 'They don't give a smooth finish. I could take up some of this fabric and round-stitch the darts. That would help shorten the waist, as well.'

Lorna grasped Lily's wrist lightly, and beamed a smile. 'Oh, Mrs Hass—'

'Lily, please.'

'Lily, I can see we're going to get along just fine together. When can you start? I have a wardrobe of dresses that need renovation.' She giggled as Lily's mouth gaped in the realisation of what she'd got herself in for. This was what always happened – she formed an idea to fix a situation and plunged in too quickly and too far, like getting married, without a thought to the consequences, which required more drastic actions to remedy them in turn. But this was only dresses, she reminded herself, nothing more.

'I'm teasing,' Lorna said. She called across to Mrs McGinty to bring more tea, and by the time Lily had drunk enough to seep through her pores, Lorna had told her all about the unfortunate incident at last year's Methodist Church fair involving Mrs Lovett's weak bladder. Lorna peered over her shoulder to the back room, before lowering her voice. 'And the Frys' eldest boy, Larry, was in trouble with the law five years ago. The Red Cross collection can went missing just after he'd come into the butcher's. He denied it, of course.'

Lily raised both eyebrows. Susan Fry had seemed such a nice girl. She would have to keep closer watch on that family, she decided. 'I'm glad you told me, I wouldn't have known.'

Lorna pressed a handkerchief to the corners of her mouth. 'There's not much I don't know about people in this town. Take the good Reverend, for example. He went astray about ten years back, took up with a woman from his congregation.'

'Not Mrs Pearson?' Lily wouldn't be able to look at the minister's wife in the eye after church again.

'No, Gladys came later, after he repented and saw the light.'

'Well, how do the town ladies feel about that?'

Lorna tapped her lip with her finger in thought, then tilted her head. 'There are some who mutter, of course. But I am of the opinion that what's done is done. A person should be judged on how they treat people today, not on something they did yesterday. And he's a true-blue man of faith now.'

It felt almost obscene, knowing such private details of someone erstwhile respectable, especially if, as Lorna said, he had redeemed himself. Lily shook her head. 'It's always the ones you don't suspect . . .'

Lorna hooked a thumb towards the back room. 'Oh for certain, duckie. Martha McGinty'll have likely read Mr Shenton's mail already. He's waiting on news of his daughter who's eloped with her fella to Melbourne.'

Lily glanced outside to where Mr Shenton stood, his elbow resting on his buggy, reading his mail and scratching his head.

Before she could respond to Lorna's latest revelation, she was disturbed by a loud shriek and shot up from her chair. 'I'm sorry, please excuse me, Lorna.'

Susan was standing knee-deep in the round horse trough. The shock at seeing that it wasn't Girlie in trouble failed to wipe Lily's stern expression. She shouted, 'What do you think you're doing?' managing to soften the harshness in her voice by the end of it.

Girlie helped pull Susan out.

'Are you hurt?' Lily fussed excessively so the girl would not think she was a shrew. She turned on Girlie. 'What did you do to Susan?'

Girlie's face paled, she stammered, spitting out crumbs. 'N-nothing.' Girlie stared at Susan, as though expecting the poor girl to offer her an excuse.

'It was my fault, Mrs Hass. I was walking around the edge and fell in,' said Susan, slipping off her wringing socks. 'Accidentally,' she added, her glance to Girlie lingering a little too long.

Lily seized on a broken oat biscuit in Girlie's hand. 'And where did you get this?'

'Kang Pei gave it to me,' Girlie mumbled.

'The Chinaman, Mrs Hass, who lives out on the boat,' offered Susan.

Lily swung her gaze across to the sailboats in the harbour. A fisherman was tying his dinghy up to the jetty. She turned to Girlie and flicked a look towards their house. Girlie understood, walking home without a backwards glance.

'It's time for Girlie's practice now.' When Susan didn't budge, Lily pressed her, 'Your mother will be needing you, I'm sure.'

Lily watched her skip away thinking of what she'd learned this morning. There was so much work to be done. And, seeing the rubble and tin lying behind their house as a stranger might, not just in building the guesthouse and shop.

~

Lily worried a track on the kitchen linoleum. The scar on the back of her hand itched.

That afternoon she'd persevered with Girlie, repeating herself each time Girlie missed a key in a shifting harmonic progression, until Girlie had begged, *Can I go now, Mummy? My fingers hurt.*

No. She'd forced her palm down on Girlie's fingers and ground them against the piano keys. *That's what pain feels like*, she'd said, fighting against Girlie's struggles to free herself. *Do you want to play in the church fair recital or not? Years and years of piano practice and you can't even apply yourself for one afternoon.*

Girlie had whimpered, *Please, Mummy*, trying to rescue her small fingers.

Just like Lily with her own mother. The vision had jolted her, and she'd lifted her daughter's fingers to her mouth, kissing them all over. *I'm sorry. I'm sorry.*

Lily scratched at the scar. She *was* sorry, truly. Sorry that she was becoming like her mother; that something unconscious compelled her to act this way. Squashing Girlie's fingers! Her mother had burned the back of her hand with the iron when Lily had played Mozart's 'Fantasia in C Minor' poorly – after that she'd memorised it, studying its harmonic structure: finding patterns, matching bars and phrases.

She spent an awful lot of time feeling remorseful about her treatment of Girlie. She vowed to be more patient, more understanding, less critical. But then it would happen again: the reality of Girlie disappointing her. Lily pressed her nails into her palms. She was a disappointment to herself.

Sometimes it was easier to fall into her old role of mothering Tommy than to be a mother to Girlie. She picked up Tommy's enamel plate of roast potatoes and a bit of fish fried in mutton fat, and took it out to the yard. A new iron roof had gone on but the guestrooms weren't in order yet and Tommy still camped against the back wall of the wash house.

The sky was purple and golden behind the cloud bank, and she could see fishermen packing up their gear along the shore.

She peered inside the flaps of the canvas tent. 'Tommy?' She crouched, her eyes adjusting. She rested his plate on a wooden crate, and straightened the blanket twisted in a heap on his bedroll. Paper spilled, fluttering, from the open mouth of his knapsack. A tug in her stomach made her pause, let her eyes drift across the paper. Sketches. Just sketches. A broken-down windmill in a field. She exhaled. Not everyone was like her, with something to hide. Now she felt chastened for suspecting Tommy of ulterior motives. He just wanted to be close to family after so many hard years on the road. The rub of it was, when they'd moved away from Perth six years ago, she hadn't expected him to find her again. She didn't want to be found.

Lily straightened Tommy's belongings into the knapsack. Her house had to be kept in order.

~

That night, Lily buttoned Ernie's shirt as they dressed for the Saturday night dance up in town.

'Fred's wanting me to help out at his farm, Sunday week,' Ernie said, running his hand along the inside of his waistband. Casually, as though it were a favour that didn't carry the weight of its measure.

'What about church?' she said, turning away. She slipped her good crepe over her head, catching a whiff of the vinegar she used to sponge it clean. Despite her care, the pale fabric showed signs of yellowing along the underarm seams and collar.

'He's getting some blokes together for an emu cull. I said I'd do everything I could to help, of course.'

She nodded. 'Yes, of course, you must.' When they'd failed to find labour for last year's wheat harvest, Ernie's brother Fred had carted the wheat to the siding for them.

'I thought I'd ask a few of the blokes from round here along too,' he said, running his hand up her back. She shrank when his fingers lingered at the nape of her neck.

She turned to face him. 'What about Bill Fairclough? You might ask him.'

He withdrew his hand from her, tensing his jaw. 'Why?'

'No reason. I met his wife earlier today, that's all.'

He watched her, there was more to come.

'And Tommy. It would be good for him to go along, he spends too much time alone.' He laboured long hours, building the corridor at the back. When they crossed each other, he didn't speak much, but he watched her sometimes, made her think that she must have greatly changed. She understood. She wouldn't have recognised herself from the person she was six years ago.

Ernie creased his forehead. 'What are you thinking?'

'I just think it might be a nice idea for you to know each other, away from me. And from Girlie. He's different now, not like before. All that's in the past.'

So much was in the past.

CHAPTER TEN

TOMMY

Tommy sat in the tent, working his way through each fingernail, tearing it off with his teeth to reach the slick of lime underneath. If there was anything to make him feel the weariness in his body, it was hauling limestone rocks from the quarry up by the river. But he didn't get any recognition for his effort. Ernie would nod at the heap of rocks but somehow couldn't stretch to having a chat or a smoke with him. How Lily must have worked on her husband to let him stay. He spat out a sliver of fingernail. He already relied on her too much.

It felt good to be industrious. Useful. Made him remember how he'd helped her around the house when they'd lived together in Perth, the three of them, Ernie, Lily and himself. Before . . . before he began to lose pieces of himself.

Over the past three weeks, in addition to dividing off a corridor from the back of the house, he'd built the wall of one of the guestrooms. But he was still sleeping outside. This morning at dawn, before going down to the quarry, he'd sprayed the weeds with sodium chlorate. A few more days and Lily could start digging up the ground.

She had sketched how the garden was going to be. Together, they had looked out over the yard towards the scrubby bush, and he listened while she described the carnations and roses she'd have if there was water enough. Spring was slipping towards summer but she would plant them anyway; she always imprinted herself on her surroundings.

He picked up the bottle beside his bedroll and swished it about, skolling the last inch of hop beer. Shadows blurred on the inside of the canvas tent. He blinked. Lily had snuck the beer to him from the crate Ernie had bought to sell in the shop. It was strong beer; he shouldn't drink too much or he'd see things he'd rather not.

The wind picked up in gusts and slapped at the canvas. With his hat pushed down firmly past his ears, he ducked out, looking up to the sky, where a spectre of a full moon hung in the sky. Down towards the holiday shacks, three people loitered in the street, so he set off in the opposite direction of the jetty. Two sailboats rocked in the choppy waves of the harbour. One he knew was the Chinaman's but he'd seen him go up towards town half an hour earlier. The other boat was dark, tied up at the end of the jetty. Last week Tommy had walked to the turn in the middle of the jetty, not knowing whether he would keep going or not until he stopped.

In the lee of the goods shed on the foreshore, he sank to the sand, bowing his head between his knees. He was feeling untethered again, his head ringing like it might lift clear off. Sand and dried seaweed swept past, catching on his trouser leg. He slipped off his boots, plunging his feet into the sand – felt it seep between his toes – before pushing himself upright. Long strides along the harder sand until he reached the jetty. Part of it was made of new, stronger timber, but the further he walked, the more gaps appeared between the planks and the more brittle the rail. An eerie purple light reflected the sun behind the clouds.

He came abreast of the Chinaman's dinghy at the turn and peered over the rail, heard nothing but the waves battering the hull. He straightened now, his shirt sleeves billowing. If he tricked himself into thinking he was walking to the sailboat at the end of the jetty, to see if there was anybody out there, he'd be able to make it almost all the way.

The sailboat had been tied up that afternoon. Before, it had been moored in the hole with the other boats, but whoever it belonged to had come in. Dangerous leaving the boat like that. He scanned the shoreline nervously; the sun was a molten line on the horizon, but apart from a dim glow of a fire on the beach around the bay, there were no other lights.

About ten yards before the boat was a ladder. The ache in his head sharpened to a knife edge. He sat, legs hanging over the edge of the top ladder rung, shoulders hunched while he flicked the flame of his lighter until the flint sparked, lit his smoke and, cupping it, drew hard. Too hard. Smoke burned his lungs. He coughed, dropped his cigarette into the water churning below, with the hiss of a wingless firefly.

He hooked his wrists around the ladder, leaned forward, yelling his lungs inside out into the water below. Gaping faces twisted and turned in the current, disembodied arms groped for his feet, and he yelled again until they disappeared beneath the foam. The water swirled, bloody, and he feared it would pull him in. His hands jittered clinging to the ladder, splinters in his palms. The sharp sensation brought him back, made the jetty solid under him once more. He sucked in deep breaths of sea air until his blood, muscle, skin and bone reformed into the shape of his body.

The red parted.

Breathing hard, he fished in his pocket with his trembling hand for his lighter, and set about levering a protruding nail from the wooden ladder. He cursed as the lighter slipped and his fingers shook, rattling the lighter against the nail. When he'd worked the nail from the wood, he held the nail to the flame. He sat back and contemplated the planking between his legs, then scratched a feathery horizontal line with the hot nail tip. Working quickly, he burned the outline of a spray of wattle, reheating the nail tip with his lighter every few strokes.

The doctors had said it would help with the tremors, give him focus to reassemble when he felt himself shatter. Poker work had helped him keep living, keep walking to find Lily. Whenever he was down on his luck over the years, he'd managed to sell a few pieces of his poker work. Coasters, doily lids, wooden spoons.

A tapping on the jetty planks seeped into his consciousness. He looked up, startled at what seemed a woman hurrying towards him.

'Oh,' she said, the expression of shock on her face smoothening out. 'Hello.' She looked up the jetty to the end and back to him.

Tommy gazed at her. She looked just like that pictures star Marion Davies he saw on all the posters. But if she was real, what was she doing out here?

She stretched the tips of her gloves one by one. He waited for her to pinch her little fingertip, but she played with the clasp of her handbag instead, then pulled out a cigarette tin.

'Do you have a light?' She held her handbag to her cheek to shelter the flame.

Nodding, he got to his feet to hold out the lighter.

The end of her cigarette glowed hot as she sucked on it. Tommy didn't know whether to sit or stand or talk to this woman. He knew by the look on her face that he wasn't the person she'd been expecting to see out here this evening. If only he could reach out and touch her, and let her know he wasn't who he thought he was either.

She blew out a stream of smoke, bending down in front of him, so that her coat gaped open. 'What are you doing?'

Tommy's reply caught in his throat until he realised she was tapping her fingernails on the plank he'd been etching.

'Oh, that. Just some poker work.'

The woman sat, folding one leg under her and dangling the other over the edge. 'It's lovely. I have a few pieces – doily covers and so on.' She drew on her cigarette, looking him squarely in the eyes, unflinching, and lifted her chin towards the horizon. 'Are you out here alone?'

He glanced at the waves, but she wasn't talking about the ghosts, the ones who'd disappeared beneath the foam. The lighter slipped from his sweating fingers. 'Goddamn.' He flicked his hand. 'Begging your pardon.' He bent down on one knee to pick it up.

Sparks dazzled him, and he fell onto his backside, stunned to see small flames licking at his trouser leg.

'Oh my Lord!' Her hand pressed against her mouth. She sprang to her feet. 'Quick. Take them off.'

Tommy stared at the flames, dazed, unable to feel pain.

'Your trousers, take them off,' she said, the whites of her eyes bright.

He moved, afraid she would do the deed for him if he didn't, tearing buttons off to rid himself of his trousers. Balling them up and stomping on them until the flames died out. He pushed the charred remnants between the ladder and the planks of the jetty.

Her laugh was long and throaty. And Tommy became conscious he was standing beside her surrounded by inky ocean, wearing his stained shorts. 'What happened?' she asked.

What had happened? She was a fantasy, conjured to stir him up. If he were still wearing trousers, they'd combust all over again. But it had to be the sodium chlorate he'd spilled on himself that morning when killing the weeds in Lily's garden. 'My own stupid fault.'

'Come on, I'll get you to the beach.'

The glimmer of the horizon had turned dull.

'Thank you . . .' He waited to hear her name, but she didn't offer it. He suspected that not only had she thought him another man, she didn't want anyone to know she'd planned to meet him. He was grateful to her for saving him; he wouldn't ask her to reveal herself further. She was married. He'd seen her ring when she removed her gloves.

When they reached the sand, he said, 'I didn't mean to trouble you. Sorry.'

She waved, brushing his arm with the back of her hand. Up close, in the moonlight he saw her. A figure as he'd imagined it.

She crossed to the dark side of the goods shed where her horse and buggy waited and set off back to town, Tommy watching until he could no longer see the spot of light from her buggy lamp. The burn on his leg stung, but curiously another sensation rose to the surface. He could feel his arm where she'd brushed it; warmth lingering on his skin. Too long since he'd felt the limits of his body like this. And underneath something was stirring, coming back to life.

But he was afraid of what he felt for her. They had been lonely years since he returned from war, unable to feel something for a woman without hurting her. He couldn't trust himself yet – he needed more time with Lily, learning to relate to real people again, to exorcise his ghosts. But this woman helped anchor himself in his body in a way that Lily couldn't.

And a memory surfaced.

Lily fussed about their father, pins between her lips, straightening the lapel on the blue serge suit she had made for the occasion, and attached a Union Jack flag to its pocket.

Tommy looked up at her from the kitchen table from time to time, to check the angle of her chin or the curve of her ear. Her hair hung loose over her shoulder, slipped away from her ear as she glanced across to him. He rubbed out the charcoal lines he'd just sketched. She didn't have their mother's large lobes; Lily's joined at the point of her jaw.

'Tommy, you're not dressed. You'll make us late and we'll be too far back to see the parade.' Lily brushed off Pa's shoulders and kissed his cheek.

'I don't think I'll be coming,' Tommy said.

'Pa's coming.' Her tone accusatory.

Pa leaned against the table to stand up, coughing into his handkerchief. He was getting worse, his skin yellow and his eyes rheumy. 'Don't bother the lad, Lilith my girl.'

He hobbled out the back door to the privy in the garden.

Lily put away her pins and cleared away their breakfast plates, dropping them into the sink with a clatter. 'Maybe you can see to boiling the water while we're gone, then.'

He shrugged his shoulder. The morning light rimmed her silhouette through the grimy kitchen window, and he wanted to capture the effect on paper. The magic was broken by the sound from the garden of their father retching.

Lily sighed. 'He wasn't this bad a couple of weeks ago. It's the extra work covering the Flemington Races last week that's done it. It'll be the death of him.'

'He won't leave,' Tommy said. 'The paper loves him. The bookies love him.'

She went to her room and returned with her handbag, pressing two bob into his hand. 'You don't have to come with us. But you should do something, go out to a bar and celebrate. The war's over.'

Tommy looked at the coins in his hand. Lily worked hard at the dress shop. Harder now that Pa was reporting less for the *Western Mail*'s racing pages and drinking more. And Tommy hadn't been able to find work since he lost his job at the AFL fruit canning factory three months ago.

'Is that me?'

He moved his arm away from the portrait of Lily, closing his eyes while she picked up the paper. It rustled. When he opened his eyes, she was staring at her portrait with a glazed look.

'Is this how you see me?' she said, finally, holding it out to him.

She was beautiful, and he'd drawn her just as she appeared before him in their dingy back kitchen, wearing a dress with a lace collar, tiny stitches covering the sleeves.

Lily sat across from him at the table and held his hand. 'The whole world is putting the war behind them. It's time you did too, Tommy,' she said. 'We've got to look forward now, to the future. You've got real talent. Look at this picture you've done of me. I'll tell you what – one of the seamstresses in the shop has a brother who's an artist, goes to the technical school; maybe I can see to get you in.'

'No,' he said, quietly, pushing the paper away, where it fell to the floor.

'Why not?' She retrieved the paper and stood by his shoulder. 'Look at me.'

The throb started in his head. Even if he turned to look at her, he wouldn't be able to see her anyway. His eyes had gone inwards, backwards to the war. Black streaked sky. Pounding in the distance, flames bursting from the shadows, everywhere around him the smell of freshly cut grass.

'Tommy. Look at me.'

He blinked. Lily's face came into his vision, her eyes searching his face for wherever he'd disappeared to.

'I'm here.'

'You shouldn't be wasting your time on labouring jobs and factory work. You're better than that. Even with . . .' Her voice trailed off, and she stroked his cheek.

~

Lily did it. She persisted in having the head art teacher see him, and the morning of his interview at the Perth Technical School, she watched while he prepared himself. He combed out the dandruff along his hair parting, looking in the tarnished mirror hanging above the kitchen stove. In the reflection he saw her open up his portfolio on the table.

He walked over to take the folder from her. 'I'm not sure yet which ones I'll show.'

She pursed her lips. 'What do you mean? You can't make any mistakes with this. There won't be any more chances.'

'I know that.' She'd mentioned it every day for the past two weeks, when he'd sooner forget about it altogether. Displaying the contents of his portfolio to strangers was like laying his nightmares open to daylight.

'There are three I was thinking of. Can I show you?'

She nodded.

He passed her the picture from the top of the sheaf. 'You've seen this one.' It was her portrait. She smiled, running her finger across the page. 'You haven't seen this.' He handed her the second.

'But I know it. This is the parade ground in front of the barracks, isn't it?'

He had sketched it the morning she'd come to collect him. All through 1916 while he waited for his discharge, that one tree in the otherwise empty landscape had been his anchor while everything else in his environment slid about.

Tommy fumbled with the third picture he intended to show the art teacher: the portrait of their mother he'd drawn from memory.

'Oh.' She flicked her gaze at him. 'Why would you draw her?'

He held the paper away from Lily, afraid she might snatch and burn it. 'Why not?'

'She's dead.' Lily folded her arms, before flinging out a hand to riffle through his drawings.

He darted forward but it was too late. She drew her hand to her mouth, didn't speak. He wanted her to speak. She always spoke. But she had seen. Which one was it? He looked down at the drawing. Distorted faces, ripped body parts strewn on rocks.

The black swirls of his nightmares.

~

The flames spread across the ground in front of him, lashing their heads, but Tommy cowered, an arm over his head, the soil beneath him growing warmer.

Shouts.

He woke, drenched in sweat, lying on his stomach across his bedroll. He sat up, his heart still pounding. Commotion outside. He peered through the tent flap to see Lily flash past, followed by Ernie in his white singlet and trousers, carrying the kitchen bucket. He shrank back into the shadow of the canvas and listened.

'Ernie, you can't go!' Lily shouted. She pulled on Ernie's arm but he shook her off.

'Go and wake Reg, get him to call Gerry Paxton and tell him to send more men down. If I don't get to the jetty the whole thing'll go up.'

Tommy watched Lily waver. But several minutes later he heard raised voices down at the McGintys'. He leaned out of the tent to listen, looking up at the night sky – a hazy net of dull stars – thought of his charred trousers by the ladder. A breeze off the ocean brought the smell of smoke.

CHAPTER ELEVEN

ERNIE

Sweat trickled down Ernie's forehead as he dragged the sacks of flour, oats and sugar across the floor into position in front of the counter. He stopped to wipe his brow with his handkerchief, and gazed at the dust settling in the sun's rays through the front window, like plumes of yellow smoke.

He'd been stood rounds of beer at the pub yesterday and cheered as a hero for putting out the jetty fire on Saturday night, almost single-handedly. The fire had affected the old section of the jetty, just past the bend, and Mr Liddle's sailboat had taken some damage. He'd hauled buckets of seawater and had the fire under control by the time Constable Paxton and the others arrived.

Today everything began again.

He fiddled with the packets and cans on the shelves, lined up the bottles of cordial, and cleared a space on the floor by the front door for the morning papers. He looked at the clock on the wall opposite: twenty to eight. Matthew would be along shortly with the delivery of newspapers, and then he would open.

He flipped open the ledger book on the counter. Robert McGinty was bringing a crate of fresh vegetables, tomatoes mainly, off the train from Geraldton. Ernie crouched to open the drawer under the register to slip in the ledger, then jolted upright when the bell jangled above the door.

A bent-up old fellow peered into the shop.

'Good morning,' Ernie said. 'What can I do for you?'

'You're not open yet, then?'

'Just opening up now.' He wiped his hand along the counter as he emerged from behind it, holding open the door for the man, who leaned on a cane with one hand and held a box under his other arm. 'I'm Ernie Hass, the proprietor.'

'Clement Rawlins, sub-branch President of the Returned Soldiers' League. Selling poppies for Armistice Day.' Mr Rawlins looked about the shop. Ernie followed his gaze until Mr Rawlins turned to face him. 'I stopped at Reg's and sold him a couple. Will you have one, a shilling for the large, threepence for the kiddies'?'

'Glad to do my duty, sir.' Ernie helped the box out from under Mr Rawlins' arm and opened it. Inside were nestled large and small cloth poppies. He felt in his trouser pocket for a shilling and inserted it into the slot in the box, and pinned a poppy to his lapel.

'Who were you with?' Mr Rawlins hobbled towards the counter, where he rested his elbow. One lens of his glasses was blackened.

Ernie rounded the counter. '32nd Battalion.'

Mr Rawlins nodded as he picked at his teeth with a pin. 'Aye, that's what the boys told me up in town. C or D company?'

'C.' Ernie pressed his palms against the sharp corners of the register.

Mr Rawlins put the pin down on the counter. 'It seems to me, you should be the one to head off the Armistice march, my boy. Not many from the 8th Brigade made it through the Western Front.'

Ernie considered what was being handed to him, and for a fraction of a second hesitated. 'Are you sure?'

'And now a local hero too. George Hopkins told me how you put out the fire on that there jetty Saturday night.'

George Hopkins the fisherman had arrived at the scene of the fire not long after Ernie.

'Kind of you to say, sir. But I just happened to be the first man there. Surely there are local men who would be better suited to lead the march.'

Mr Rawlins picked up his pin and held his box aloft, ready to leave the store. 'I know of a lot of heroes in the Great War who were simply that – the right man in the right place at the right time. After the service is over, we'll march – there's a dozen of us – from the church down the track to the memorial stone at the cemetery.' He watched Ernie. Waited.

Ernie weighed up what was at stake. 'Very well, then. It would be an honour.'

~

Lily pinned Ernie's Victory Medal to his chest. 'That looks nice.' She pressed her hand against it. He covered her hand with his own, but she slipped it out from under him. 'I've got to help with Tommy's.' She left him to go to her brother, who'd now moved his things inside to the finished guestroom.

Ernie lit a cigarette. Today he would lead the district's returned soldiers and she would see him for the person he tried to be: Ernie Hass, local hero. So Mr Rawlins had filled his head with it. But his head was also filled with other things. He was a fraud and he knew it. At least he hadn't been discharged, not like Tommy had. But even though Ernie had told him the manner in which Tommy had been discharged, Mr Rawlins had insisted that Tommy walk too.

Aye, there's too many boys that came back that way. He's an 11th Battalion man, so he's all right, Mr Rawlins had said. *He's your brother-in-law and all. He can walk up front with you.*

The service began at half-past ten that Friday morning. Shops either put up a sign to say they were closed, or kept a junior on to take care of business while the older members of town attended church. Children were kept in school, but even so, the pews overflowed, with many having to stand to the sides and at the back. Gerry Paxton had reserved seats for Lily and Ernie in the middle of the congregation.

Lily craned her neck. 'Why are we all the way back here?' she whispered. 'You're leading the march, you should be up the front.' She flicked her fan towards the pulpit. '*I* need to sit with Daphne Liddle and Darla McGinty. If only we'd come sooner.'

Ernie watched the men filing into the front pew – Mr Rawlins, Reg McGinty, Robert McGinty, and beside Robert, his wife, on whom Lily had fixed her attention. Robert tried to speak to Darla, but she turned her face away. Ernie remembered him vaguely from his youth as a bully, and hoped Lily didn't have plans to befriend his wife; but, glancing at Lily earnestly studying the congregation, and knowing her, she liked to be seen with the 'right sort'.

Two members of the Road Board sat beside the McGintys up front, followed by Bill Fairclough, not in uniform. There'd be a story in that, Ernie thought. He'd find out tomorrow at the committee's annual general meeting; a few of these blokes were sure to be there.

Reverend Pearson approached the pulpit. Ernie got to his feet with the crowd to sing 'Lest We Forget'.

After leading them in prayer, the minister said, 'In accordance with the wishes expressed by the King, we'll hold a two minutes' silence.'

Ernie closed his eyes, and holding his slouch hat to his chest, he thought of the men he'd enlisted with – Martin, Bennett, Goodes, Slater, Thornton and Byrne. Leaving Fremantle port on the HMS *Indarra*, to join the battalion in South Australia. They left on the same ship on 18 November 1915 for Egypt, a little apprehensive of what lay ahead. Of them, only Ernie had been further than his home town before. Though he wouldn't be eighteen for another three months, those men – boys – looked to him for answers to their questions of foreign places. *Will there be girls with* – Slater made rounded shapes with his hands – *who'll not say no?*

Ernie had blushed. The only reason he'd come down to Blackboy Hill in July of 1915 was because he couldn't join up in Geraldton, where they all knew he wasn't of age. But his brother Fred had gone to war already, enlisted in the 10th Light Horse Regiment and had been sent off in February to Alexandria and then to the Dardanelles. Ernie couldn't wait until the following February when he'd turn eighteen.

Ernie's eyes opened as the minister cleared his throat to end the two minutes' silence. They resumed their seats and the minister began the Roll of Honour. Each name he read was followed by a soft cry or moan. Reg blew his nose loudly into his handkerchief when the name Samuel McGinty was read out. Sam had been Dongarra's champion rifleman back in the day, besting Ernie in competition on more than one occasion. He listened closely to the minister, recognising other names from the inter-club sporting fixtures of his youth. Lily fanned herself beside him.

'And so we seek to emulate the heroic example set before us,' the minister intoned, gazing out at the crowd. Those men not in uniform were grey and balding, eyes full of sorrow for lost sons and nephews, and young men, eyes full of admiration and envy.

Ernie turned to seek out Gerry, and the constable lifted his chin. Gerry was a young bloke, unmarried, eager to lend a hand. He was coming out with Ernie to Fred's farm to help with the emu cull. Matthew Fry was driving them, though he'd had a blue with his missus for missing church.

Ernie caught sight of Tommy skulking up the back, and half scowled that he'd given in to Lily's request to take her brother out with them on Sunday. He pressed his leg gently to Lily's, but she shifted, crossing her ankles. A trickle of perspiration dampened her calf, and he had the sudden desire to touch it.

'Can the heroic be harnessed and put to use other than violence?' asked the minister. Ernie inhaled deeply. 'Heroism is embedded in man's nature. And since war is a beastly thing, we need a substitute that will evoke the same heroism, courage and sacrifice. Such a substitute is the program of Christianity in its militant attack on vice, crime and injustice, therefore let us remember the glorious achievements of the Great War.'

There was silence as the minister recited Laurence Binyon's ode.

Ernie murmured the final line after him. Martin, Bennett, Goodes, Slater, Thornton and Byrne – all dead, and he'd not been with them when they'd fallen on the fields of France.

~

Ernie tipped his hat at the gents as they filed into the hall for the Beach Improvement Committee's annual general meeting the next day.

'You're putting yourself up for membership, I'm hoping,' said Matthew Fry.

Ernie smiled. 'I will, Matthew.' He steadied his gaze on Bill Fairclough flicking through papers with Mr Liddle. *No brains*, he thought, smarting once more.

He caught Mr Hopkins staring at him and gave him a nod. It had been the fisherman who'd put in a good word for him with Mr Rawlins after the jetty fire.

'What's Bill's story?' Ernie jutted his chin towards the chairman. 'Why wasn't he in uniform yesterday?'

'I think he tried to enlist, but had a dicky heart,' said Matthew.

'Mr Hass!'

Ernie waved at Gerry wending his way around the hall to sit near him. 'Still on for tomorrow then, constable?'

'Yes, sir, we'll be like those army men – gunna take on the birds with machine guns.'

This past week, Ernie had hung off every line in the newspaper articles relaying the military's deployment to Campion, south of here, to cull the emu plague menacing the wheat farms. The government's response was too late for him, but he'd be damned if Fred's crops would be affected. Ernie's living depended on his brother's generosity. 'I'll need a spare rifle for Tommy,' he said. 'Only got the one.'

Gerry nodded just as Bill opened the meeting.

The banker, Mr Booth, stood up, setting out the finances: the takings from the shelters and the water tanks. More tourists had come to the beach this year than last, but Ernie thought the committee wasn't ambitious enough. Tourists bathed, played sports, fished and drank beer on the foreshore, but had to make the journey into town for more than the basic supplies, including petrol. The idea he had was of a rival village, boasting the same amenities or more. Let the fogeys live and shop in old Dongarra; soon those with brains would be shifting stumps to the new. And Ernie would have beaten them to it. He had his eye on the land behind his, virgin land he could hold onto and sell at a premium in years to come.

He stiffened at the word 'fire'.

Bill nodded in the direction of the question. 'Yes, yes. The fire is top of the agenda for the meeting. And we'll discuss the ongoing netting ban, don't you worry, George. But let's keep to point. Next we have the election of members of the Beach Improvement Committee for 1933. Mr Booth, Mr Liddle, lead us through the process, please.'

~

Ernie was elected to the committee easily, but was put out that he didn't hold an office. The same men filled their positions for another year. After a smoke and a light supper, the committee opened discussion of the fire.

Ernie raised his hand. 'Why is it the older sections of the jetty don't have warning signs?'

Some grumbled. 'We've been saying it for years,' said George Hopkins.

'Quite, quite. We'll make a note of it, in light of the fire on the jetty.'

'My sailboat was scorched,' said Mr Liddle, indignantly. 'We shall have to do more than make a note.'

'Do we know yet what caused it?' asked Mr Booth.

Bill shook his head. 'Could be anything, a fisherman's cigarette,' – a snort of disgust from George – 'but the main thing is that the fire damage wasn't extensive.'

Ernie's cue. 'Could have been, if I hadn't got there in time.'

Bill hesitated, about to say something to Ernie, but looked down at his notes instead. 'As you know, I represented the committee to the Irwin Road Board meeting Saturday last. Naturally there was concern about the condition of the jetty among other matters relating to safety for the tourists on the beach during the season. The Road Board suggests a caretaker for the beach be nominated.'

Oh, yes. Ernie had had a feeling about the meeting today, knew it was the key to overcoming the setbacks of the past few years, the disappointments and secret shame. Caretaker of the beach. That would be someone who'd have influence in growing a new settlement. He'd be able to stand tall and feel proud of himself for good reason.

Bill was still telling them about the Road Board's suggestion. 'But of course, we will all be involved in drawing up the by-laws pertaining to the beach caretaking arrangements, and I'll put them to the Road Board for endorsement. I nominate Mr Hopkins for the caretaker position, if you'll take it on, George.'

George raised his hand in assent.

'Any other nominations?' Bill looked past Ernie quickly, it seemed.

'I say, shouldn't Mr Hass be given the responsibility?' said Mr Liddle. 'It was him, after all, who put out the fire.' Ernie felt Bill looking at him, taking his measure. 'And he'll be on hand should anything else arise over the summer.'

Ernie tilted his head.

'All right, both Mr Hass and Mr Hopkins have been nominated. Show of hands for Mr Hopkins.'

Ernie restrained the leap inside him as only George and Bill raised their hands.

'Mr Hass,' said Bill, lacklustre.

Booth, Liddle, and Frank Smith from the Progress Association lifted their hands. Ernie added his as an afterthought. He settled back, knowing he was a step closer to ousting Bill from his roost. Next year, he might even make Chairman.

George shrugged, gave a wry smile. 'Main thing is, has the Road Board heard anything about when the netting ban will be lifted?'

'Not till next year, at least,' replied Bill.

George grumbled some more, mainly about his hands being torn to shreds from line burn. Bill told him to wear gloves.

CHAPTER TWELVE

GIRLIE

'Rain is imminent and the washing might not dry,' her mother called out from the wash house, enunciating each syllable. 'The water will not lather, it is too hard.'

Girlie pressed the nib of her pencil to the paper on the kitchen table. *I-m-m – was there an 'a' next?*

'Read it back to me.'

She furrowed her brow; now she couldn't remember what came after 'imminent'. 'Rain is imminent . . .' She muffled the next words in case she'd heard it wrong. 'And . . . um . . .'

'*And* the washing might not dry,' her mother called, more shrilly. 'Concentrate, Girlie.' She heard water splash on the floor. Soft curses. Her father had put an old copper in the wash house, but still hadn't built the brick copper he'd promised in the bathroom.

Girlie would rather be out in the wash house than confined to her dictation on such a sunny day. She drained the last of the Sunshine milk from the tin, dribbling a bit down her chin. The shop bell jingled, sending her to her feet, wiping her chin with her hand as she went through. A woman and a man looked about the shelves and talked between themselves.

Her mother came in, smelling fresh from the laundry blue. The ends of her sleeves were wringing wet and she untied her apron, handing it to Girlie. She frowned. 'Clean yourself up, look at the state of you.'

Her mother ironed out her frown lines as she turned to the customers. 'Good day, how can I assist?' she said. Girlie trailed behind.

'Me and Mrs Godfrey wondered if you might have a room available. It's our honeymoon,' said the young man, smiling at his new wife. She'd blushed when he called her 'Mrs Godfrey'. 'We saw an article in the paper. But there was no telephone number, so we just motored up from Perth on the gamble you can take us in.'

'Yes, of course,' said her mother. 'I'm originally from Perth myself. Nedlands. You needn't fear, we can provide the essentials you might be used to. I dare say, even in the city nowadays, you must be feeling the pinch.'

'Nedlands?' the wife said. 'There are shanty camps along the foreshore now.'

'Oh.' A frown. 'That's where I used to walk with Molly.'

'Who's Molly?' Girlie asked, but her mother motioned with her hand, which she interpreted as meaning to go out back. She lingered in the corridor, pressing her ear to the wall.

'I'll need to ready the room for you, if you don't mind waiting. Perhaps you might like to go over to the tearoom.' Girlie knew that edge in her mother's voice, it meant she was controlling herself, biting back words.

Girlie peeled away from the wall as her mother came down the corridor sighing loudly as she passed. She wanted to help, following her mother into the guests' corridor. Sand ground underfoot, and only one guestroom was finished. Uncle Tommy and her mother had dragged an iron bedstead across from the McGintys' last week to furnish it. Half-walls divided the rest of the space.

Her mother pushed the door open. The curtains were drawn and through the gloom Girlie could see the shape of Uncle Tommy lying on his side, smoking a cigarette.

'Tommy. I need this room for guests,' her mother said, marching over to the window and opening the sash. A gust of wind swept up the ashes from Uncle Tommy's tin ashtray; they drifted in the sunlight before settling gently onto the wooden floor. Uncle Tommy pushed himself up.

'Now?'

'Now.' Her mother planted her hands on her hips and shook her head. 'Look at the state of this room. Kip down the other side while the guests are here. I've got to smarten this up before they come back.'

'Do you want me to help?' Girlie flattened herself as Tommy passed with his bedroll and knapsack.

Her mother was on her hands and knees, plumping the kapok in the mattress. She pushed the hair back from her eyes. 'No, go on back to your dictation.'

Girlie settled down at the kitchen table, sharpening her pencil until her mother called out, again in that clipped, clear voice, 'Rain is imminent and the washing might not dry.' Then, bustling through from the wash house with the good sheets, 'The water will not lather—'

The bell rang out once more. 'I'll go,' Girlie called, running out to the corridor, but her mother handed her the sheets. She carried them to the guestroom, but hearing Mr Moretta's voice in the shop, she tossed the bundle onto the mattress and skipped towards the shop.

'Mr Moretta, what brings you here?' her mother said. Girlie peeped into the shop. According to Susan, he'd been a sailor and had jumped ship when the port was still here. Girlie imagined him as a kind of exotic pirate. Who knew what an Italian was like? She didn't know if he would speak English properly or what colour skin he would have. He batched in the sand hills on the other side of the nuns' cottage, down near the Back Beach.

Italian. He didn't look foreign, though. Almost the same as her teacher, Mr Peters, except he had a moustache. A thick, dark moustache that twitched when he saw her hiding in the shadow of the doorway. Mr Moretta groped around in his pocket and held something out to her. She edged forward, flicking a glance at her mother to see how she should act.

Her mother tipped her head, as she weighed the flour. 'Say thank you to Mr Moretta.' Her normal voice, not the high-pitched, careful voice she used around strangers.

'Thank you,' Girlie mumbled, grasping the pear drop he held out for her.

He paid for half a pound of flour and left, waving goodbye to Girlie. 'Thank you for the lolly,' she said once more, then turned to her mother when the door clanged shut. 'I didn't know if I should take it.'

'Don't be ungrateful for what you're offered.'

'But,' sucking on the pear drop, 'I thought you might be cross. Like when Kang Pei gave me a biscuit.' She flexed her fingers. The biscuit had not been mentioned again but Girlie couldn't think of any other reason why her mother would have hurt her hand on the piano, the same day.

With a click of her tongue, her mother prodded Girlie back to the kitchen, throwing a scant glance over the sentences she'd written. 'You can see Mr Moretta is just like us.'

Girlie nodded.

'Of course, one can never forget he is still a foreigner.' Her mother took up the broom, marshalling the sand on the linoleum into drifts.

'I see.' Girlie committed her mother's words to mind, like dictation. It would account for why she'd hardly seen Mr Moretta. Perhaps he wasn't allowed to mix with town people, because he couldn't be trusted, appearing similar but different underneath. Just like Ruby. If Girlie hoped to share her confidences with Susan, she needed to know more about Ruby, what made her different. Did she dare ask her mother?

'The other day I met a girl playing near the river. I think she's Italian as well.'

Her mother stopped sweeping. 'What girl?' she said sharply.

'Ruby. She said she wasn't allowed to mix with us kids at the school.' Her arm tingled at the memory of the graze, which had mostly healed. That poultice wasn't something she had seen someone do before, but Ruby didn't seem different to Girlie in any other way.

'Doesn't sound right. Italians and Spaniards and all sorts are still allowed to go to school.' Her mother grabbed Girlie's wrist, pulling her towards the window to look at her in the sunlight. 'Did the girl look sick to you? Golden staph?'

Girlie gritted her teeth as her mother yanked her ears and pulled her eyes wide to examine her. 'I don't think so,' she said, the words coming from the back of her throat as her mother pulled her chin up, forcing her mouth open.

Ruby hadn't looked sick. Just scrawny like most of the children at school.

'You didn't go to her house, did you?'

She shook her head.

'Good. I can't think who her family might be.' Her mother patted her on the backside. 'Help me make up the bed before the Godfreys come back.'

~

After helping her mother, Girlie was allowed to leave her dictation. When she arrived at Susan's house, all she found was Susan's brother Larry out the front chopping wood.

'She's gone up to the convent school with Mum. She helps out serving in the dining room on Saturdays,' he said. He was fourteen and had a shocking rash of pimples on his chin that made her feel queasy looking at him.

There was only a wisp of wind in the air that afternoon and the sun was still high, signalling plenty of time until she'd have to find her father and go home. She didn't intend to return to more dictation, or any of the other horrors her mother subjected her to in the aim of 'improvement'.

There was no one else to play with. She remembered the elbow Mary Ellen had given her in the stomach. Being new was the same as being different or foreign. But Ruby hadn't struck Girlie as being from elsewhere, and her dad worked on the railway, she'd said. Why *wasn't* she allowed to go to school? Girlie ran her mother's reaction around her mind. It was a secret she wanted to get to the bottom of. Ruby didn't seem to care about being different, and that puzzled her more.

Instead of turning onto the road to cross the bridge to town, she took the chance and ducked under the bridge, following the bank to the clearing. The remnants of the fire were cold. Disappointed, she kicked at the ground before sitting, her skirt tucked around her legs, and watching a dragonfly dance above the sedges. Sunlight glinted on the brown river, and eventually her heartbeat, which had raced at her daring, slowed. She lay down, closing her eyes just enough that she could see the branches above her through the gauzy frame of her eyelashes.

'You're back.'

Girlie sat up, looking into the darkness under the bridge. 'Hello?'

Ruby stepped out into the light. She carried a satchel, though it was Saturday and she definitely did not go to school.

'What are you doing here?' Ruby asked, peering past her through the trees, searching for others who might be there.

'Looking for you. I thought you might want to play together.' Girlie gestured at the satchel. 'Or do you have classes on Saturdays?'

Ruby cocked her head, just for a second and then relaxed her shoulders. 'Nah, but I like to read. It's nice and quiet here. Back home my sisters are always pestering me to play hoops or pat-a-cake.' She grinned. 'Plus my mum makes me help in the kitchen if I hang about.'

'Me too.' Girlie shifted a little to the side, hoping Ruby would sit with her. 'What books are you reading?' What she really wanted to ask was what made her so different to the other children that she couldn't go to their school.

Ruby seemed to sense the question anyway, staring at the space Girlie had made beside her, before settling down about two feet away. '*Anne of Green Gables*. How's your arm?'

'Much better, see.' Girlie held it up. 'My mother didn't even notice the graze.'

Fear pulsed across Ruby's face. 'You didn't tell your mother what I did, did you?'

'No, why?'

Ruby stared at her and shrugged. 'You can't tell her. I'm not supposed to know traditional ways. My mum taught me but Dad would kill me if he found out.'

'What traditional ways?' It didn't make sense, but the shape of the secret was becoming clear.

'Yamatji, but we're not meant to be anymore, we're exempt Aboriginals, my dad says.' Ruby rolled onto her knees, bridging the space between them. 'You can't tell no one.'

'I don't understand. How can you be Aboriginal? You're white like me. Our domestic, Jenny, was Aboriginal and she had black skin.'

Ruby balled her fists. 'I am, I just am. But I gotta act like I'm not, otherwise Dad says the police will make us go live on a reserve. That's why you can't tell about the bark I put on you. Promise!'

'I promise.' Girlie held up her hands, palms facing Ruby. 'But if you're acting like white people, how come you can't come to school?' Ruby's hair was blonder then Girlie's father's. Even Girlie's own hair was dark brown. But people's lives didn't match up with how they looked.

'They might say we're not Yamatji, but they still treat us like it.' Ruby picked up a rock and flung it into the river. 'Here I'm white,' pinching the skin on her forearm, 'but not out there.' She made a wide sweep of her hand towards the town. 'They still see me as black, and so will you.'

Girlie shook her head vigorously. 'That's not true. My old Sunday School teacher said that when you close your eyes everybody looks the same.' She almost told Ruby that she would sometimes close her eyes when Jenny was washing her and pretend Jenny was her mother. She widened her eyes, looking at Ruby. Then she closed them. 'See?'

A shrill *peek-oo* answered her.

Girlie opened her eyes. 'Ruby?'

All about the clearing, shadows lengthened, criss-crossing so the tangle of floodgums and sheoaks appeared denser, more jungle-like. Sudden rustling in the high branches made her brain fizz. A startled movement lower to the ground. She narrowed her gaze through the trees towards the bridge, and ran towards it. The path became more densely littered with small nuts, which she felt sharply through her leather soles.

She focused on the space about twenty yards ahead of her, never actually seeing Ruby, just where she'd been. The path narrowed, forcing her to draw up beside the sedges to avoid plunging into the river. She'd long passed the island and plank bridge across the shallows. The water here was dark and still. She looked around for the path forward or away. Ruby had to be somewhere up further where the trees stopped and the low bushes hugged the river to the sea.

A little way ahead the sunlight revealed trampled bushes, and Girlie surged forward, pulling aside the soft fronds of sheoak until she came to a blindingly bright set of stone terraces. She squinted, looking at a large house at the top. Dr Marsh's. Could Ruby have found shelter there? She didn't know why Ruby had run off in the first place. Skirting the lower terrace, she picked up a narrow, foot-wide depression through the bushes, which sprang taller and taller around her, past her knees, almost to her waist until she felt the thick, crunchy leaves scratch her arms. She lifted her feet higher, crashing through the bushes, feeling like a giant in a sea of purplish-grey vegetation, the glinting river just there beyond her fingertips. The spit of sand across the river mouth fringed the horizon in front of her. She froze. Swallowed up by the bushes as high as her armpits about her, she couldn't even see the way she'd come. The sky was cloudless, the blue her mother smiled at on washing days. Pelicans swooped and muddled about in the rockpools at the mouth, and she thought if only she could just get there, follow the sand across the spit, she might be able to walk around the bay home. So close. It struck her that she might never be found. Imagining creatures slithering about her ankles; she panicked, heart barrelling in her chest, and lifted her feet higher, stomping down the purples and greys and silvered greens. She opened her mouth to call out but shut it. There was no one there.

A shadow flitted across the edge of her vision. She blinked. Everything fell silent: the scrub, the lulling brown water of the river, the pelicans far away on the shoreline. The pounding in her ears.

'Hey!'

Girlie whirled around, scratching her legs on the prickly stems of a bush. 'Ruby?' she cried. Surrounded by a mass of high scrub, even the way behind her seemed to have closed up.

The girl stood, revealing herself, a broad grin on her face.

'How *dare* you run off like that! I got lost, I didn't . . .' Ruby was no more than a couple of yards away, but as much as Girlie flailed about looking for a way to get to her, she remained utterly trapped. Her shoulders sagged. 'Can you help me?' she begged.

But Ruby turned and disappeared. How could she leave her stuck in this place? She'd thought Ruby was her friend. Girlie stifled a sob. She hated Dongarra, where she didn't understand the other children, where none of them were friendly to her except Susan. And even that friendship challenged her, having to practise more than usual at the hateful piano. How she longed to be back home in Perenjori with her best friend Katie – and with Jenny. Ruby was right. Girlie had seen Jenny as different in colour, but she hadn't understood what her life was like. She'd only thought she'd known Jenny because Jenny had known all there was to know about her.

She startled as Ruby appeared beside her, grabbing her hand. 'Come on. This way back to the road.'

Girlie bit back tears as she followed Ruby between scrub as tall as her shoulders, flinching at the scratches they would inflict. But the grey-green leaves and stems brushed her with unexpected softness. She would never have tried to come this way; it had seemed impenetrable.

Ruby instinctively swivelled and ducked under tree boughs to sandier ground at the top of the ridge, where the track opened out to a large market garden. Girlie collapsed to the ground, knees bent up as she slowed her breathing.

'Why did you run away?'

Ruby pulled at a long leaf, sucking the end of it. 'I didn't. I was right in front of you all the time, you had your eyes open but you still couldn't see me. Like all the rest of them – you only see what you want to see.'

She squinted. 'And you didn't have to follow.'

'I guess I don't like not knowing something. My mummy always says that I ask too many questions and I'll get myself into trouble one day.'

Ruby kicked at the ground. 'What do you want to know?'

Girlie wanted to know Ruby, know what made her so different to other children, learn what she hadn't been able to see. Of all these questions she had on her mind, Girlie could think of just one to ask. 'Will you be my friend?'

CHAPTER THIRTEEN

ERNIE

The men walked the red dusty track towards the lower wheat field on his brother Fred's property. Mid-morning, yet the skin of Ernie's nose, the back of his neck, his forearms already smarted from sunburn.

'Uncle Ernie, can I hold your gun?' his younger nephew Johnny asked, running alongside him.

He ruffled Johnny's hair, and handed him his rifle, bearing the weight of it. Johnny was six months younger than Girlie, who he'd never let near his gun, but this was the difference between sons and daughters. The boy grinned, and checked the sights.

'Pow, pow,' he said, cocking his fingers.

Ernie's older nephew Ted ran over. 'Can I have a go?' He made to grab for the gun, but he hefted it out of his reach. He favoured the younger boy. Johnny reminded him of himself, always missing out when his brother Fred got everything worth having. A kiss from Bonnie Forster at the Bluff Point plain-and-fancy-dress ball, the under-twelves footy medal, their father's wheat agency in Perenjori, a wheat harvest. Two sons, and his wife Rosie had given birth to a baby, Ruthie, only last month.

Ernie hoisted the rifle to his shoulder. 'We should have Lewis Automatics. That's what the army used against the mob of emus down in Campion the other week.'

He looked across to the men he'd brought with him: Gerry Paxton, with his .22 calibre rifle, Matthew Fry, bearing an old thirty-thirty, and Tommy, using Gerry's Remington .44 calibre rifle. One of Fred's neighbours, Wilf Wendt from the western boundary, had also joined them.

Fred playfully kicked his sons' backsides and they ran back to the homestead. He shook his head. 'I heard those machine guns were no good.'

Gerry loped up to the brothers. 'They were just going about it the wrong way. Look, I know they're Australian Army, but they don't know the land. Not like you and your brother.' Gerry seemed to realise, at the same time as Ernie, that Tommy was trailing behind him. 'Mr Adamson,' he said, 'you marched on Friday. Where did you see service?'

Tommy mumbled, 'Dardanelles.'

Ernie cleared his throat and spoke before he was asked. 'Emus are a different breed of enemy altogether. Back at Cowanup Downs, I never saw more than a dozen or so in a paddock, but they would scatter, spreading the damage.'

'Aye,' said Wilf, 'it's damn near relentless, their attacks. I seen maybe twenty, thirty a time, trampling down my grain. Fences are no obstacle to them feathered bastards. What's the use o' repairing them, when they tear through the next day, and plagues of rabbits follow?'

Fred touched Ernie's arm to slow his pace, separate them from the others.

'What?'

'Wilf's been driven barmy, his missus told Rosie,' Fred said quietly. 'He's been twitchy and playing with his rifle in bed.' Shook his head. 'I haven't seen anything like it up around here.'

'At least you still have a standing crop.' Ernie held back the strain of envy in his voice. Under the blue sky, the fields of his brother's farm shimmered.

Fred grimaced. 'Wait till you see.' He called to the men to huddle round, told them to split up in pairs: Fred and Ernie, Tommy and Matthew, and Gerry and Wilf.

'We'll fight the birds at their own game. Cover greater ground. What we don't want is to herd them together, they'll likely stampede.'

The men entered the field and within twenty yards, Ernie could see that what he had thought of as a golden crop had been decimated. 'Jesus Christ.' Large swathes of wheat plants lay flattened, and those that stood had had their heads bitten off. 'Are you gunna be able to strip a bag of wheat this year, Fred?'

Fred took off his hat and wiped his brow with his handkerchief. 'I'll try. Them subsidies would help but.'

Ernie stared at his brother, noticing that the lines around his eyes and mouth were deeper, darkened with the red dust. It was because of the lack of subsidies that Ernie had lost Cowanup Downs. The government men had promised them in exchange for increasing the wheat production. *Prices are falling, grow more*, they'd said. He had re-mortgaged the farm, buying the Sunshine Auto Header and building the new thresher shed. But those subsidies never came; the creditors had instead. He clenched his teeth – it had all started with the bloody fire . . .

Cries from the men caught his attention.

'There, north-west corner!' Wilf and Gerry came running.

Ernie shielded his eyes and saw three, no, four necks bob above the heads of the wheat.

'Tommy, Matthew, you take the south-west,' Fred said, pointing towards Wilf's property, 'and me and Ern will head towards the north-east.'

Ernie slung his rifle across his back, running his hand over the wheat plants as they walked together in silence. Far from the others the only sound was the rustle of the stalks in the dry wind. 'Fred,' he said. He'd been working up to this, and his voice cracked.

Fred lifted his chin. 'Mm.' He cast a look up the slope towards both corners, and fell in beside Ernie.

'You know I was saying my day in court's coming up?'

Fred ran the dirty edge of his thumbnail along the line of his cheekbone. 'Soon?'

'Yeah, this Friday. In Geraldton.'

'Are they going through everything?'

Ernie nodded. 'I think so. If there's anything left, they'll take it for the creditors.'

'Christ, Ern. Who else is there to pay?'

He glanced up at the sky. 'Fred, the farm was mortgaged to the hilt.'

Fred gave an exasperated sigh and shook his head, slowly.

'Well, what else was I supposed to do?' Ernie countered. 'I thought those subsidies would cover the outlay for the new machinery. I couldn't have a year like last year's harvest – the crashing wheat prices. Goddamnit, you said it yourself, you were expecting the government subsidies.'

'But I didn't stake my whole livelihood on it.'

Ernie had to wear Fred's words like a hair shirt and grit his teeth. Bite back his first response, remember the stakes. All he could do was increase his stride, putting distance between him and his brother, making Fred walk on Ernie's terms. It was childish, but Fred always brought out his jealous streak.

'You had a good thing in that farm. Just didn't know how to manage it better. Letting out Dad's house, Christ . . . You should have sold it to invest in the machinery rather than ringing up credit.'

Ernie flared, turning on Fred. 'So, I had no insurance policy on the house. That tenant Sutcliffe started the fire, I just couldn't prove it. It's just luck, just fucking bad luck.'

Fred shook off his glare. 'Just keep Dad's name out of the papers, and mine. And once all your creditors are off your back – all of them – get insurance on the guesthouse.'

Ernie slumped. Fred had him by the balls. Without Fred's help, he wouldn't have the slim prospects he did. It wasn't the financial debt that crippled him, but knowing that Fred owned him for the rest of his days.

'You're right. I'm a shitting failure. But I won't do it again. The guesthouse will come good. The shop's up and running and I've got ideas for increasing business.' Ernie lowered his eyes. 'But I won't ask for any more. Just . . . Just, I need to keep the arrangement a little longer. I'm skint.'

His brother thumped his arm. 'Ernie, I told you: I'll give you half the income from the wheat agency as long as it takes you to get back on your feet.'

Ernie smiled. 'I'd best shoot a few of them bastard birds for you, then, eh?'

He laughed with Fred, but under his skin he prickled like an echidna turned inside out. Hiding his fucking spines. His spine, more like. But he owed Fred now. He'd always owed Fred. And Fred had been Dad's favourite, the eldest, did everything right, jumped when Dad said jump. Everything Fred touched was golden, whereas Ernie's lot was shit. That's why Fred had inherited the wheat agency, which brought in £1100 a year, and Ernie had got an uninsured two-bedroom cottage.

He had arrived in Fremantle in March 1919 to an official homecoming of afternoon teas put on by the Red Cross Society at the Soldiers' Institute but not a welcome from his father, who made the long journey down to Fremantle six weeks later, the day Fred arrived home.

So, where was it, this army barracks, Ernie? London? Dad had said, buying Ernie and Fred a pint at the Sail and Anchor.

Perham Downs. Salisbury, Dad, he said. *All training requisitions for the AIF in France came through me.*

I'm a damn lucky fellow to have both my sons in that bloody war come home to me alive. Dad's eyes misted up. But looking around them in the pub, Ernie saw men expressing their feelings. Laughter, tears, haunted eyes. It had been a long war, and only a man who'd been there could know what it was truly like.

Fred firmly grasped Dad's shoulders, telling him he would join him in the hardware business in Geraldton as soon as the army let him go.

No, you won't, lad, Dad told him. Ernie's brother and father stood close, their shoulders touching. *I sold it and the house. With your mother gone, it was too big.* Dad shed a quiet tear. *Too many memories in that town.*

Ernie had already decided to stay in Perth to try his luck. He'd become fond of motor cycling while in England, joining an organisation that rode on weekends. By his calculation, hundreds of returned soldiers in Perth would have had a taste for the same, and he'd started working in motor cycle sales.

Are you coming down here to live? Ernie couldn't imagine his father in the city. He couldn't abide strangers.

Dad shook his head. *I bought a house in Perenjori. One of the new towns. And an agency for buying wheat.*

A month later Fred had selected 5115 acres of land for a wheat farm further north.

There's talk of new town sites. And there's still land about that can be used for wheat. How about it? Fred had said when Ernie came up a month after that for Fred's wedding to his sweetheart, Rosie.

Ernie had shaken his head. He'd met a girl, taken a shine to her, a pretty redhead. There she had been at the Town Hall dance, dressed damn fine in a shimmering dress cut low at her back so that he sweated, couldn't help his eyes drifting down the ladder of her backbone. He never thought he'd have a chance, but his mate Les Beveridge, whom he'd taken up with on the *Lancashire* home from England, had his eye on her friend. By the end of the night Ernie had convinced Lily Adamson of a dance and a walk to the taxi cab, lending her his jacket against the chill even though it meant he'd had to ride home in his shirtsleeves. Since then he'd seen her five times. He thought she was his girl, but she held off, saying she wanted a steady and dependable man. He said he would treat her like a princess, but she laughed in his face, told him of the shoe salesman from Dalkeith. So, when Fred asked him whether he wanted to take up land for wheat, Ernie said no. He knew what he wanted: to not be second to any man – not to his brother, not to a shoe salesman. He'd wanted the best, and that was Lily.

It was different when they were married. Every year when they met up at the coast for their holidays, Fred would crow about the bags of wheat – bags of gold – he was harvesting from his land. Rosie was always in new hats and gloves, causing Lily fits of envy, spending long nights at her sewing machine for her holiday frocks.

Nothing rattled Lily more though than the two boys, Ted and Johnny, one after another, in those early years.

Why can't we have what they've got? she had complained to him one night after they'd made love. At first, all Lily could think about was getting pregnant. She consulted older women from the women's organisation she attended, magazines, even checking out plain-covered books from the library. But as the months of barrenness turned to years, these moments of intimacy were meted out.

He'd handed in his notice at Mortlock Bros. in February 1925. Lily hadn't spoken outright against him riding motor cycles, but it was there in the literature she read to him. And the truth was, he'd seen past the craze for motor cycling – fellows were now getting into motor cars. Instead, he'd made a show of it, settling down to appease Lily when she sobbed and cursed at the luck of his brother's wife in falling pregnant so easily. Anything to make up for what he could never give her.

He became a wheat distributor. Another cog in the family business. When Lily's father died, they moved into her father's house, to be with her brother Tommy. Ernie watched as the bags of wheat from Walkaway were unloaded in Perth and as wheat prices went up and up without him taking a cut.

He discussed Fred's suggestion with Lily. There was land to be had around Perenjori, close to his dad. Smaller lots, less productive than there'd been three years ago.

No, Lily had said. *You know I can't leave Tommy, Ern. Don't ask me to make that decision.*

Now he owed his brother for their new life in Dongarra and he still couldn't make Lily happy.

~

Fred pulled up short at the fence, grasped the twisted pieces of wire.

'A great big flamin' hole. I'll have to come back for that.' He squinted out from under his hat. 'Time for some tucker first.' He scanned the field and whistled long and clear across to Gerry and Wilf near the single gum tree throwing shade in the field.

The metal of Ernie's rifle burned through his cotton shirt. Dusty heat wafted from the wheat plants. 'Throat's as dry as a vulture's crutch,' he rasped, taking the water bag Fred offered him when they reached the gum. The taste of warm rusty water filled his mouth; the wetness didn't touch the sides.

'Any left?' Tommy asked.

Ernie wiped the trickle of water from his top lip. 'Yeah.' He grunted, capping the bag. Tight. Then chucking it into the dirt by Tommy's feet. No one could doubt how he felt about Lily. He loved her. Why else would he agree to bring her brother along today? Tommy niggled more than one of Ernie's sore spots.

Tommy dropped to his knees, taking a sip from the water bag, and handed it over to Wilf.

The farmer nodded his thanks. 'So, Mr Adamson, Dardanelles, eh? Fair dinkum cock-up.'

Ernie felt Fred turn behind him to hear the answer – he'd been through the Nek and worse, out on that campaign six more months than Tommy had been, and then deployed to the Front. Fred wasn't a malingerer. But no one said anything until Tommy replied, quietly. 'Yeah, I guess it was.'

'Jesus, you blokes didn't stand a flamin' chance,' said Gerry. He looked at Ernie. 'I wouldn't have wanted to have been anywhere near the Front, neither. An uncle of mine was in the 8th Brigade.'

Ernie's chest tightened.

'Rosie's made us some grub.' Fred thrust a wax-paper packet in Tommy's hand. 'Eat up.' He handed them each a pie from the tucker bag Rosie had left for the men. Gerry and Wilf took their lunch and walked off into the field.

Ernie braced his back against the trunk of the gum, flicking blowflies away from his pie. Fred upturned the basket next to him and sat on it. 'What's this idea you're talkin' about for the store? Do you need me to give you a hand?'

He owed Fred too much. 'No, I think it's already a done deal. Just got to take care of some of that other business I was talking about, and then I'll be right. I'm getting a petrol bowser for the front of the shop. A lot of motorists come down from Geraldton to the beach, and up the midland route from Perth.'

Matthew wandered over. 'A petrol bowser? What does Bill Fairclough think about that?'

'What do you mean?'

'He's the only fella selling petrol in Dongarra,' said Matthew. 'At the garage. Forty-four-gallon drums of Atlantic petrol.'

Before Ernie could think of a way to tell Matthew he didn't care a twopenny damn about Bill and his drums, Gerry and Wilf ran hollering towards them. 'Emus! Bloody heaps of them. Grab your rifles.'

The mob of emus was about fifty yards away and running directly at them. He jumped to his feet, tossing his pie over his shoulder, and grabbed his gun. The other men did the same.

'Christ Almighty. Must be at least twenty,' Fred muttered. He whistled to ready the men, before raising his rifle.

CHAPTER FOURTEEN

TOMMY

The whistle cracked through Tommy like an electric shock. 'Get your rifles!' he heard Fred shout. The hairs on his arms stood on end, and he felt that familiar clench in his bowels. *Hold on*, he prayed, not to God but to the skin, the flesh, muscle and blood that kept him together. Feared what little left of his spirit might spew out with his shit.

Bullets shattered the air into thousands of hot knives nicking his skin. Jolted, as the men snapped their rifle butts to reload. He staggered, bent double, gasped for air, pulling it through his nostrils, gagged as the dust hit the back of his throat. The bullets ripped up the dirt, and through the clouds he saw the emus, scattering. Screaming. There was screaming.

He hunkered down, drawing his arms over his head. The crackle of musketry became a roar: of rifle, shrapnel and machine-gun fire. He squeezed his eyes shut, pressed his body up against something. Sand bags. Back in the trench, the men going over the top, throwing themselves at death, their stomachs and chests and heads spraying blood. The smell of cut grass. He'd been thinking of the strangeness of those smells, standing on the banquette, waiting for his turn to go over the top. Grass and shit and piss.

His rifle unloaded and fixed with a bayonet, he'd never felt so impotent. He prayed again, but found his prayers directed to Ma.

Two seconds to live, cried the CO, and then his whistle. Tommy could no longer remember if he heard it, or if there'd only been the pound of his blood and the mutter of his prayers. But on the movement from his mate beside him, he sprang up the ladder to hop the bags, shouting at the Turks.

A figure rushed through the smoke at him. Tommy closed his eyes. *Come get me, you bastard.* A gun shot to his left.

When he opened his eyes, he saw one of the emus keeled over, blood spurting. Like his mate, Richie Walters, beside him in the trench with blood pulsing from the hole in his neck.

He hadn't gone over, he was being pulled back. *Pull back, pull back*, someone shouted.

He struggled free, lunging for the ladder. He had to go over.

Pull back. The hands rougher.

He fell into the trench, crying.

He wiped his eyes with the back of his arm, tears burning his face.

'What do you want done with him?' he heard the bloke who'd pulled him back say.

The haze cleared. To the yawn of blue sky above.

Ernie looked down on him like Tommy was the shit he'd evacuated from his bowels. The man behind Tommy grasped his arms to lift him up. It was the copper, Paxton. He let out a whimper. 'My face. It's on fire.'

'There's nothing there.' Ernie had stepped in close to him, eyeball to eyeball, and Tommy dropped his gaze.

Back then, the medicos had covered his face with cotton gauze.

'What's wrong with him?' A woman was before him now. Thin-faced and weathered, she scrunched up her nose. 'He ain't going to stay here, is he?'

Rosie. That's right. He remembered. Ernie's sister-in law. He was out on Fred's farm, with Ernie and the men, but they were talking about him like he wasn't there.

Tommy pushed himself out of the squatter's chair where he'd been sitting, no recollection of how he'd made it from the field to the verandah of Fred's homestead.

Ernie was beside her, wiping his hands on a rag. 'No, Rosie. He's not staying here.'

'Well, what happened out there? Fred?' Her voice rose shrilly towards Ernie's brother, who stood with the other men in the circle of shade beneath the tree in front of the house, smoking.

Fred flicked away his cigarette and strode towards them. Tommy glanced away.

'It's over for today, Ernie. Go on. I'll keep going with Wilf.'

'I don't know what to say,' Ernie was saying, shaking his head.

Fred went back to the other blokes, said something that made them turn their faces towards Tommy on the verandah.

'Sorry, Ern,' he mumbled. Ernie didn't flinch. Just walked away. Tommy followed him slowly, glancing through the screen door into the darkened house, where the two boys' faces were pushed against the mesh. They sprang back as he passed.

Tommy kept going until he reached Matthew Fry's truck, hauling himself up onto the tabletop tray. Ernie and the constable ignored him, piling onto the seat under the canopy, the constable up front on the window side and Ernie in the middle, while Matthew drove them back to Dongarra.

Tommy had lost his hat out in Fred's field. The late afternoon sun beat down on his head and the wind blew through his hair, bringing him voices: *Run, Tommy, run. You're going to die. Are you a coward, Tommy? Why did you pull back?*

He'd never gone over the top. He'd stayed in that trench lined with the fallen bodies of his mates. The smell of grass and shit and piss.

Back in Dongarra the truck bumped along the wooden bridge and the setting sun burned a hole in the sky. Too late for him, he thought, leaning the weight of his face in his hand.

Suddenly the truck careened off the road.

Doors slammed. Shouting. In his face. Throwing him to the ground.

'The fucking idiot shot at me! Could have killed me!' Ernie shouted nearby.

The rifle was prised from his grip, his finger twisted around the trigger. 'Mr Adamson, remain still.' The constable's voice. 'I'm removing the gun from your hand. Do not move.'

Tommy wasn't moving. Maybe he was, his nerves jittered, blood gorged and roared in his head.

Minutes, time passed.

Then Ernie and Matthew were staring down at him from the truck, the doors open. The constable was up on the tabletop looking at the canopy. Putting his finger through a hole.

'What's going on?' Tommy rasped, his shoulder ringing with pain.

'What's going on?' Ernie said, dropping down from the truck and coming up close to him, crouching down, in his face. 'You came this close to shooting me.' He held his fingers a bullet's length apart.

'Would have been a foot in it,' said the constable, hopping down from the tabletop. 'Looks like you must have fallen onto the canopy, Mr Adamson, setting off the trigger. The bullet went through, right into the middle of the dashboard.

'Matthew, drive them home,' the constable continued. 'It's dark and we all need some rest.' He picked up his rifle, and the one Tommy had used, and walked back over the bridge towards the police station.

Ernie signalled to Matthew to start the truck as he clambered in.

Tommy watched them drive away, leaving him sitting in the dirt, his elbows on his knees.

~

All the way back down the Beach Road towards Ernie's house, Tommy gathered his thoughts. Prised them apart, untangled them, tried to pin them down. Out in that field, Ernie had been dismissive, but there was something not quite right in what he'd said. Talk of war service. Somewhere in Tommy's brain was the connection he needed to make.

Light shone out of the kitchen window at the back of the house, and he caught Ernie's raised voice. Though Tommy was desperate for Lily to see him now, he didn't want her to be scared by what he'd done. He ducked into the shadow of the back wall, listening.

'Where else can he go?' she asked urgently, quietly. 'He hasn't got anyone else.'

Ernie blustered at her, followed by Lily frantically shushing him.

Ernie ignored her. 'We're trying to make something of ourselves here, and he'll destroy it all.'

Tommy ground his fist against the limestone wall, feeling warm blood trickle down his knuckles. Lily would be on his side. She'd protect him.

'I'm not questioning you, Ernie. Of course not. I understand.'

All this time on the track, single-minded, just knowing she would be the answer to his endless questioning about what was real. He'd never asked himself whether he would get better, or how; he'd just known that she was the last person in his memory who wasn't a ghost, who cared about the man he'd been. If he couldn't prove to her that he was capable of coming back, if he was turned away now, that man might be lost completely. But if he stayed, he didn't know what he might do, maybe something worse than letting the gun go off, and then Ernie wouldn't let him near Lily again. Tommy would never hurt her. The shadow of himself might though, and that's why he had to free himself of it.

They didn't notice as he slunk across the corridor, past the room he'd been turfed out of, down to his canvas sacking. He packed his belongings into his knapsack and, throwing it over his shoulder with his bedroll, headed out into the night.

CHAPTER FIFTEEN

LILY

Lorna stood on a box in the middle of the kitchen, her arms held out palms up, as if she were giving benediction.

Lily tugged at the seams of the dress under Lorna's arms. 'I should probably take these out.' She pulled out the pencil stuck in her bun to mark it in her notepad then unlooped the tape measure from her neck and reached around Lorna's chest. Lorna breathed in. Lily added half an inch anyway.

Lorna exhaled the moment Lily finished measuring, toying with the buttons sewn onto the cuffs. 'To think I had this gown made in Perth. And you're going to make a better job of it.'

Lily smiled thinly, counting under her breath as she marked the fabric with charcoal. Reminded herself that she'd agreed to this, after seeing Lorna sitting with Darla McGinty at the Armistice Day ceremony, both of them wearing smart dresses and new hats. Lorna was more than just a former nanny to Darla's boys, she was in Darla's inner circle, was approved of by the founding families, it seemed. This was approval that Lily craved if it could lend respectability to the wanton obviousness of Lorna's attributes and deportment.

Besides, altering the dress for Lorna was a welcome distraction from her worries about Tommy's disappearance. Sewing once more, a giddiness swept through her. But she kept it in check. Remembered where such feelings might lead her – to the photograph buried in the Arnott's tin.

'You're lucky, going down to Perth.'

Lorna shrugged. 'I suppose so. I don't ask for my allowance, though. It's compensation.'

'What for?' Lily looked up from her notepad. She hoped it didn't appear too impertinent a question. But the more others spoke of themselves, the less she would have to share of herself.

Lorna stepped down from the box and took a cigarette from her tin on the kitchen table. Lighting it, she settled into the ladder-back chair and blew out a flume of smoke. 'For being stuck with him. It's Bill's way of making up for what I've missed out on by marrying him.'

Lily immediately thought of Lorna's childlessness. Lorna presented herself so boldly she had assumed there were no hidden layers to her character. 'Is it Bill who doesn't want children?'

Lorna drew on her cigarette. 'I don't know. I never asked. I just told him I'd had a gutful of looking after Darla McGinty's, so he shouldn't expect me to have any.'

In a way, she understood what Lorna meant. All she had ever wanted was to be a mother. It was a fantasy, burst by the reality of the child's dependency, the whining, the refusal to behave the way Lily had dreamed a child of hers would. Jenny had been a blessing in that regard. 'I imagine Darla has firm expectations of her boys,' she said, hoping to lead Lorna into revealing something of the McGintys' family arrangements as a way for Lily to approach Darla.

But Lorna appeared oblivious to her machinations. 'And I didn't want to ruin my figure, did I?'

Lily ducked so Lorna wouldn't see her smile. Bearing a child would have made little difference to Lorna's figure, her girdle strained to contain her.

'Marriage is always better when you want the same thing,' Lily said.

Lorna stubbed out the cigarette on the tin ashtray Tommy had made. 'What about you and Mr Hass?'

Lily bent down to pick up a pin from the floor and paused. She ran the tip of the pin across the linoleum, pricking a dotted seam. 'Yes, we both wanted children.'

But she had wanted to be a different kind of mother. Not an imposter.

Lorna stood up to unbutton her dress and Lily helped her step out of it, folding it neatly and hanging it over the arm of the chair.

'I'll have this done for you by next week.'

Lorna did up the dress she'd arrived in, and waved her hand. 'No rush. I know you're doing it by hand. Work like that takes time. Even for a proper dressmaker.'

'Some more tea?' Lily asked, laying the back of her hand – the unscarred one – against the enamel teapot. She didn't even have her mother's teapot anymore, she'd had to sell it off. Real bone china, Royal Albert Regency Blue.

Lorna crossed her legs. 'Lovely.'

She had been weighing up what to tell Lorna of her past. There were parts she felt proud of, but they'd been buried along with the many parts of which she was not. Whatever she told Lorna would probably become known by the community. 'I was almost a proper dressmaker, you know,' she allowed.

Lorna lit another cigarette. 'Before you married?'

Lily took care not to let her distaste show on her face. She sat down, pressing her knees together. 'Yes. I worked at Pritchard's in Nedlands.'

Lorna wrinkled her forehead. 'I don't know it.'

'It was back during the war. I was only sixteen when I started cutting patterns. It might not be there anymore. We had some well-to-do clientele, though. I learned to be a seamstress there.'

'And you left to be a farmer's wife.'

Lily bristled. 'Well, no. I didn't straightaway. I was a fashion mannequin for a while.' She kept her tone steady, remembered to pull up the corners of her mouth, the appearance of friendliness, though her blood pulsed loudly in her ears.

'How'd you manage that?'

Lily resented the implication. 'One day in town I was stopped by a photographer on St George's Terrace wanting to take my picture.'

'Whatever for?'

'Oh, you know, the society pages,' Lily said, tucking a strand of hair behind her ear. She sipped her tea. Small anchors to hold herself together.

'Your picture was in the paper?'

She had been on the mark with Lorna. Hungry for gossip from the world of fashion and society. Though Lorna had been nanny to Darla's sons, she appeared to be treated by Darla as a social equal, and might be Lily's way into the tight-knit coterie of CWA women, to be seen as the perfect wife and mother. She'd noticed the way the local women watched Darla hungrily, keen to mention a child's achievement or a new recipe she really must try. But Lorna comported herself distinctly from them, and didn't care about these things. A friendship could pose a threat to all Lily hoped to achieve, yet she'd made riskier decisions before, and the sacrifices she continued to make were the price she paid to keep those she loved safe. She just had to be vigilant.

'Yes, "The Racing Reporter's Daughter" was the headline. Pa wrote for the *Western Mail*'s racing pages.' Lily didn't say how proud Pa had been of her, how he'd clipped the picture out and pinned it up at work so all his colleagues could see.

'It caused a little stir, I suppose. There were certainly plenty of invitations to dances with returned soldiers after it appeared. I was photographed wearing one of my own patterns. And some of the clientele came into Pritchard's asking for me.'

Lorna shook her head. 'I would've had no idea. You look the picture of a farmer's wife.' She didn't have to say any more. It was as though the flash from the photographer's bulb had captured Lily's brightest, most colourful self, burned to the negative.

'But now I know better. Lily Hass, you've got your first customer.'

Lily frowned. 'I'm a wife and mother now, Lorna. And I've got so much work to do with the shop and we've just seen off our first guests . . .'

The Godfreys. What God-awful timing. Yesterday morning before they'd left, Mr Godfrey had said, *Thank your brother for allowing us the use of his room at short notice. I . . . ah . . . went to thank him myself but couldn't find hide nor hair of him.* And they would have heard her arguing with Ernie on Sunday night.

Lorna swiped the air with her cigarette. 'Pish. Get a woman in to help. I know of someone. I can send her along.' She flashed her hands in the air as she conducted the new aria of Lily's life. 'You could open a dress shop.'

Lily dropped her tea cup to the table and shook her head firmly.

'Maybe sell some ready-made frocks out front?'

Lily leaned her elbow on the arm of the chair. 'Even if I could, I couldn't. No machine.'

Lorna moved her hand with a flourish. 'Ernie's got his fingers in a few pies, Bill says.'

'Yes, he's the caretaker of the beach now.' She had to be careful when talking about Ernie; it was when her disguise was at its thinnest. 'I am so proud of him. He didn't put out the fire on the jetty for the recognition, of course.' The words always sounded false, that she didn't know if she'd gone overboard. 'I suppose . . . Bill's probably told you about Ernie's new role.'

'Bill doesn't say too much.' Lorna cast a sidelong look and hesitated. 'Does he know how the fire started?'

Lily knocked over her tea cup. 'Oh, blast it.' A brown puddle trickled from the table edge onto the primrose fabric of her lap. She wiped at it, but the stain set in, and she looked up at Lorna with an apologetic shrug.

Despite the distraction of Lorna coming for a fitting, Lily had been on edge all day. That morning Ernie had rubbed her shoulder and she didn't even turn away, her stomach churning with upset at Tommy's disappearance. She hadn't been happy when he turned up in her life again, to pluck at the threads she'd thought tied up; but breaking her promise to her father was worse. She'd already risked their new start in Dongarra – what else could she have possibly done to take care of Tommy as Pa had wanted?

Ernie had told her, *If we don't hear anything by Friday I'll see what Gerry can do. But I don't know what that is. Fellas like Tommy blow in off the track and shoot through again.*

She'd conceded he was right so that he wouldn't see just how shaken she was. Her body was in a constant quiver, her nails bitten to the quick, so she'd had to resort to running her knuckles against her teeth. It was hearing from the Godfreys about the newspaper article giving their names, business and whereabouts. An advertisement in the mid-west paper's classifieds was necessary for customers, but she didn't want the general public in Perth learning the same. Tommy's arrival in town had reminded her of something: she could be found.

Lily sighed. Tommy would have left before the tourist season anyway, and with them already taking guests, it was probably for the best that he'd gone. The Godfreys had only stayed a couple of days and had been exposed to Tommy's problems. One question could start the unravelling of lies. But she was well-practised at keeping up a pretence in her own home to the people who thought they knew her best, hiding who she really was, even from herself. Her thoughts rested on the photograph in the tin. Managing strangers would be simple in comparison.

'Hello? Mrs Hass?' Mrs McGinty called out in her reedy voice, from the shop at the front.

'Excuse me a minute,' Lily said, handing Lorna her hat. She closed the door to the kitchen behind her at the sound of Lorna lighting another cigarette.

Mrs McGinty stood in the shop, the mail in one hand and in the other, a packet of jelly crystals held close to her face as she squinted to read the instructions.

'Can I help you with anything, Mrs McGinty?' Lily tied on her apron to cover the tea stain. Mrs McGinty usually only came to deliver the mail; her son Robert brought down their groceries for the shop. He was a man of few words and though he was civil with her, she sensed something unsettling beneath his thin veneer of respectability. She couldn't shake the glimpse she'd had last week of him staring at Girlie playing across the road at the roundabout. A flash in his eye as her skirt flipped up. And then it was gone as he continued conducting business.

Mrs McGinty startled, as though caught out in a secret indulgence. She fumbled, putting the packet of jelly crystals back on the shelf. 'No, no. Just brought over your letters.' She tapped the postmark on the top envelope. 'Looks like you've got more responses to your advertisement.'

Lily took the mail from Mrs McGinty, sizing her up. The old woman appeared frail, bird-like, but Martha McGinty must have been a formidable force once, if the stories of her youth, scaring off the tribal blacks with her shotgun, were anything to go by. Lily couldn't forget she was also Darla McGinty's mother-in-law, a position of great influence. She forgave this intrusion on their privacy.

'I hope we haven't become a burden,' she said, her lips pressed in a smile. 'I don't mind coming to collect our mail myself.'

Holding up her hand, Mrs McGinty shook her head. 'No bother. None at all. But tell me . . .' she gestured at the packet of jelly crystals on the shelf, 'does anybody use this stuff? I've been making my seaweed jelly for decades just from the bounty that nature gives us. If you're keen, I'll give you my recipe for it.'

'Thank you. That's very thoughtful of you. I'm sorry, but I must return to the visitor I've left in the kitchen.'

Mrs McGinty clasped Lily's arm on her way out. 'Don't forget the recipe. I don't give it out to just anyone.'

There was a bounce in Lily's step as she opened the kitchen door. Lorna had pinned her hat to her hair and now flexed the brim with a finger. 'I hope you might reconsider my idea?' Lily gave her a quizzical look. 'Dressmaking?'

To busy Lorna out the door, she agreed she would ask Ernie for a sewing machine, though it would be futile. She remembered how in Perenjori he'd been determined to punish her, and the Singer had been a hard loss. Harder still because the loss of her secret income threatened her plans, the security of their position and reputation.

So much for plans. When the house they'd inherited from Ernie's father had burned down just before Christmas in 1929, not only did they lose the rental income, there had been no insurance on it either. Something she had not known. And wheat prices continued to tumble. They lost the other labourer in 1930 and Ernie hired men off the track for harvest. He said this was the year life would come good for them, investing in the harvester and new shed. *They'll pay off,* he'd said. *Just wait until the subsidies come.* She'd waited.

The sea breeze had come in early, bringing a rotten stench that made Lily want to retch. Lorna blanched, holding her nose. 'Oh, my Lord. That's bad enough to singe my eyebrows.'

Lily was about to say that one had to put up with these things living close to the ocean, but the sudden change in wind direction brought a fouler stream of air. Not from across the sea but the other side of the house. Where the underground water tank was.

Her heart lurched.

'Tommy!' she cried, realising too late what she'd said. But Lorna was here and she could be of help. 'I think there's something in the tank.'

She ran to the back of the house, pulled off her apron and wrapped it around her hands. The heavy, round lid to the tank was still in place.

'Gah, yes, you're right,' Lorna said. 'The smell is stronger near the tank. What on earth is inside – a dead possum?'

Lily's heart pounded.

'What's your brother to do with it?'

'What?' Lily snapped her head towards Lorna, grasping the handle on the lid.

'You said, "Tommy", back there.'

'Oh, something . . . a long time ago.' Lily felt her frown lines stitch together as she heaved the lid to.

~

Four months. Definitely four months since her last blood. Lily didn't dare hope, but let the knowledge well up inside her as she tipped sawdust into the dunny. Four months. That meant she had been well with child when Pa had died at the end of April, not knowing he was going to be a grandfather. But at last she was going to be a mother. The turmoil of the last seven years was over. She could finally move forward, unafraid and without guilt, as life returned to its true course.

No, she couldn't dare hope. As she pulled up her drawers there was something else. Self-preservation. If not for herself, for what might be growing inside her womb, and that meant she wouldn't strain herself, or walk to the shops, or even sew the pieces she sold at the Women's Service Guild. Thank God they'd moved back into the Nedlands house after Pa died, with Tommy whose hands were willing and helping, especially with Ernie's frequent trips away for work. Tommy chopped the wood for her and lifted the heavy bundles of wet sheets from the copper and pushed them through the mangle. Rosie had worked the thresher alongside Fred until the day before she gave birth to Ted, but Lily wasn't made the same. She was fragile.

Four months. As much as she wanted to tell Ernie, she couldn't. Not just for the fact he wouldn't be back until next week from his visit to the wheat belt, but for wanting to keep it secret just a moment longer, in the knowledge that, after nearly seven years of marriage, she had finally done it. She wanted to allow herself to dream about the mother she was going to be: caring, concerned, devoted. The things they would do together: play piano, press flowers, teach her to sew. The child her small companion.

There would be plenty of time for Ernie to puff his chest at fathering a child later.

She hummed a tune. She was going to make this child stick. She'd already unknowingly brought it through the grief of Pa dying. Grief, embroidered with relief. None of the doctors had expected him to live as long as he had. Even when an old colleague from the paper or the race track would drop in, they'd made their jokes together.

I'm going for the Grand Annual, Pa would say, referring to the steeplechase run in Warrnambool, the longest distance race. *No need to shoot me yet.* Laughing made him double up in agony. But she hadn't realised just how bad it had been for him until right at the end. When he couldn't shield her from his liver cancer anymore.

Two months ago, she and Ernie had just returned home from the Anzac Day service on The Esplanade, crushed by the heat and crowds. Tommy was waiting in the darkened corner of their front porch.

Lily, Pa needs you.

She shot a look at Ernie, he dropped his keys and turned to go to her, but she nodded for him to go inside.

Is it bad? She patted her handkerchief at the perspiration on her forehead.

I don't think he's got long. Tommy's hands shook as he rolled a cigarette.

She had put a chicken in the oven to roast while they'd been out. By the time she'd come back from Pa's house, the lamps had been lit, and the remains of Ernie's dinner were wrapped on the kitchen table. She found Ernie in the back shed, drinking a beer while he greased his tools.

And?

Tommy's right. There was blood in his pot.

What did he say?

Nothing much. Do you want another beer?

Lily let out her breath in the kitchen, picking at the chicken carcass. Pa had asked for one thing, and when she'd promised it to him, he'd been spent, closing his eyes sunken in their gaunt sockets.

Less than a week later he'd died, and she made good on her word. All Pa had wanted was for her to look after Tommy.

~

Lily closed the dunny door, still humming her tune. A rustle in the rose bushes caught her attention. 'Molly!' she called, pursing her lips to whistle for the dog.

Molly was Tommy's Jack Russell cross. But it was Lily who fed her tidbits from the kitchen table. Treating her like a baby, Ernie had said.

She smiled inwardly and broke from her hum into song. Molly yelped and dashed over to her. 'Come on in, Molly.' She held the back door open and the dog bounded up the steps and into the kitchen, sitting up begging, her tail wagging.

'All right, what have I got for you today?' She bent over to scrounge an arrowroot biscuit from the tin at the back of the dresser when she felt a bubble pop. She sprang up, clutching at her lower belly and opened her eyes wide. 'I felt her.'

Molly looked at Lily and whined, rolling over onto her back on the floral-patterned linoleum.

Lily grinned at her. 'I'll still be fond of you when the baby comes.' She ruffled the dog's ear, folding it inside out, which Molly usually loved. But she continued to whine.

'You're missing Tommy, aren't you?' She checked the clock on the wall, and frowned. Half-past four. 'He'll be home soon. Hopefully he's got that new watchman's job, that's why he's late.'

If it weren't for the help that Tommy provided her while Ernie was away on his work trips, or the joy that Molly brought in having something to nurture, Ernie would not have stood for living with him. 'I've got no choice,' she'd reminded him. 'Pa said I have to look after him, and I will.'

When it was just the two of them, Ernie would express how useless he found her brother. *Who loses three jobs in a year?* he'd sneered.

She would upbraid him. *Not everyone wants to be a successful businessman like you.* But they were hollow words, because Ernie's ambition pleased her. It was one of his few character traits she admired. He had been looking for a modern house of their own in Bassendean, as West Guildford was now called. With the change of name came a surge in progress and prosperity in the suburb. For Ernie, it would mean business opportunities, for Lily, space to hopefully raise children. Tommy would be all right; he'd have this house, Pa's house.

Tommy had been laid off again last week from digging trenches for the government. She hadn't been able to get much sense from him, only that he'd started shouting at the men to down tools, stay in the trench. The headman had hauled him out.

She looked at the clock on the kitchen wall again. Four minutes had passed. The tick echoed around the blue-tiled room. She stroked Molly's belly, shaking her head. Tommy had had episodes like that off-and-on in the ten years since he'd returned from the war. Nothing serious. Short-tempered and restless. There were plenty of men like that around. Every member of the Women's Service Guild had someone in the family – a son, husband, brother, nephew – who hadn't come back the same. A little angrier, a little more nervous, a little less likely to accept the same old routine. But who could blame them? Tommy couldn't stick at a job, or art school.

Molly pulled away, her ears pricked up, pawing at the back door. Lily pushed herself up, one hand on the small of her back. Molly barked.

'Do you want to go outside, Moll?'

The moment Lily unlatched the door and propped it open, Molly shot out, barking, and leaped from the top step to the ground.

'Wait!' Lily pulled her cardigan around her, peering out to the darkened corner of the garden where the dog scratched at the wash house door. She hadn't brought a lamp out with her, and thought to turn back in for one, when Molly's bark stopped, strangled. Lily tripped down the steps in time to see a brown snake slither into the rose bushes.

She rushed to pick up Molly, but the dog wriggled from her, dragging her hind legs to the wash house door, feebly scratching at it. Lily opened it, breath stilled.

In the thin light coming through the pebbled-glass window she saw a figure bent over the edge of the copper as though reaching inside to scrape the bottom, if it were not still full of water.

She didn't scream. She grasped her brother by the waist and pulled him back. He jerked and struggled, holding the rim of the copper to keep his head submerged. When his arms flopped by his sides she fell back, dragging the sodden weight of him with her onto the floor.

Dirty water spewed from his mouth. She cradled his head, sobbing, realising just how much Pa had shielded her from what Tommy had become.

~

Lily lifted the rusty tank lid, growing more anxious as she peered inside.

'Can you see anything?' asked Lorna.

Her heart almost hurtled into the water. She reached inside, pulling out the bloated body of an animal, ginger with one white paw.

Lorna gasped. 'It's Susan Fry's kitten! One of my Tabby's litter.'

Lily gagged, pressed her face into her arm. All the fear and worry of what could have been brought bile to her throat. It would have been her fault when she'd only been trying to protect him, all of them, by burying the past.

'Let go of the kitten. I'll take care of it.' Lorna gently took hold of her arm and lowered it, forcing her to lay the corpse on the ground. She rubbed Lily's back. 'How about we go inside and I make you a nice, strong cup of tea.'

Lily followed her mutely into the kitchen, still clouded with shock. Lorna gave her a whiff of ammonia, stinging her eyes with the smell.

The water was still boiled and Lorna had a cup of tea on the table in minutes, reviving her. 'Now, duckie, tell me,' said Lorna, setting her cup down, 'what is the matter with your brother?' She lowered her voice. 'Was it the war?'

'Yes, and no,' said Lily, cautiously. 'I thought he'd be better by now. It's been sixteen years since he left the barracks hospital.'

Lorna circled an extra teaspoon of sugar into her cup and Lily allowed her the expense. 'I lost my first husband in the war. We'd only been married a day before he went down to Blackboy Hill.'

Lily put her hand to her mouth at this unexpected revelation. 'I'm so sorry.'

Lorna pulled out a cigarette and lit it. 'That wasn't the worst of it. A week after he shipped, I found out I was pregnant.'

Lily made sympathetic noises, guessing at what had happened next. It was an awfully personal thing, and yet it didn't appear to bother Lorna to reveal it. She half resented Lorna her ease in coping with life.

'Nature has a funny way of working everything out.' Lorna stifled a sob with a hollow laugh. 'I lost the baby soon after. Must have known its daddy wasn't coming home.'

Lily looked on her curiously. Perhaps she had been wrong about the person she'd thought Lorna was. She could see a heart filled with regrets beating under all that bosom. 'Did you love him dearly?'

Lorna studied the end of her cigarette, then put it between her lips drawing deeply. With a cough, she expelled the smoke over her shoulder. 'I got on with things.'

Lily nodded. 'Bill.'

'That was a while later. I cared for the McGinty children for a few years.' Lorna picked some tobacco off her lip. 'Which reminds me. I'll send Mrs Feehely down to help out. She used to be Darla's domestic.'

'If you can vouch for her. I don't want the type that comes in and spreads gossip.' Lily hoped she could trust Lorna's word, she'd been wrong to think that Lorna hadn't harboured secrets. But a woman like Darla, pious and married into an established family, not to mention plain in looks, wouldn't have many secrets to hide in her household.

CHAPTER SIXTEEN

GIRLIE

Susan's mother had been waiting to collect her at the school gate yesterday. A signal that something was wrong. Susan took one look at her mother and ran to her without saying goodbye to Girlie.

During this morning's spelling test, when Girlie would have ordinarily glanced across at Susan's answers, quietly checking them against her own, she thought about how upset Susan must have been at losing her cat.

But *why* did Ruffles have to die in their tank?

Even though she hadn't been home when her mother found Ruffles, Girlie still felt to blame, and now she worried Susan might feel the same. Without Susan's friendship, there would be no one to play games with in the school yard or to stand up for her when she was bullied. The children were bent over their test papers. Mary Ellen, her head turned down, tongue sticking out, as she wrote; Brigid and Jane and Alice and other girls from the east end of town who never played with Girlie, all of them with cropped hair and in pressed smocks. The boys sat on the left side of the classroom. She lifted her chin to glance at them, locking eyes with Bobby across the aisle from her. He sneered before stomping his foot on the ground and looking up at Mr Peters. Several others noticed and looked up, too, as their teacher approached Bobby's desk, whacking his carpet slipper against his palm. Girlie turned her face down, but the back of her neck burned fiercely.

'Is there a problem, Master Pringle?'

'No, sir. I mean, yes, sir. That Girlie was looking at me, thought she might be cheating.'

'Is that right, Miss Hass?'

'I-I just thought I heard Bob-by say something,' she stammered.

'I'll speak with you later.'

Girlie didn't dare look at anybody else after that. She kept away from the other children at lunchtime, sitting in the classroom, pretending to study one of the class readers when really she read the same few sentences over and over until the school bell rang. Children straggled in, grumbling. She barely paid attention to the afternoon's mathematics lesson, measuring triangles, watching the clock on the wall above the blackboard.

The moment they were let out, she stuffed her exercise books inside her satchel, hoping that Mr Peters had forgotten he wanted to see her. His back was turned and he rubbed his forehead to puzzle something out.

'Hey, Girlie girl, where're you going?'

Tears sprang to her eyes, but she refused to look at the boys behind her and tugged at the straps on her satchel.

'She's got no one to walk home with,' taunted Bobby.

'We'll walk with you,' said Joe. Both boys sniggered.

'No, thank you.' Her face blazing and palms sweaty. She walked quickly to the front of the classroom to get away, planning to run as soon as she was out of sight.

Mr Peters, still turned to the board, ordered, 'Miss Hass, stay behind.'

Her heart thudded. Bobby and Joe were whispering, then Joe looked up and smirked.

'Yes, Mr Peters.' Girlie knitted her fingers together.

The classroom had emptied now, and through the window she heard the shouts of children playing The Germans Versus Us in the school yard. Mr Peters held up a finger while he leafed through test papers on his desk.

The school yard sounds drifted away. Her left leg started to cramp.

'Frankly, I'm not sure what to make of this. Your spelling-test results are dreadful. Three out of twenty-five.' He thrust the test paper in front of her, covered with so many pencilled crosses.

'I'm sorry, sir.' She cast her eyes down, staring at the knothole in the wooden floor.

'A round of banging dusters shall help you do better next time.'

Girlie crumpled. 'Can I do it tomorrow? It's just, I wanted to see Susan. She's upset about her cat dying yesterday.'

Mr Peters hooked his finger inside his collar and ran it around to loosen it. 'Very well, tomorrow, then.'

She ran down Waldeck Street, sliding in the gravel at the corner past the police station, scraping her knee. One of the milkman's boys almost hit her with his bicycle but swerved at the last moment. He shouted, but she ignored him and ran on. She didn't dare look down at her leather-strapped shoes because she knew they would be filthy and ruined, and her mother would give her trouble – The State of Girlie's Shoes. But she couldn't slow down. All morning, without Susan to defend her, the boys had made strangled mewling noises behind her back. One or two of the girls – she didn't dare look up to see who – joined in with tiny squeaks behind their hands.

She was too late.

Joe and Bobby were leaning on their elbows on the white railing; Joe throwing pebbles into the water below. Girlie scanned the slope down to the river. If she crossed the ford slowly, the boys might tire of waiting and she could slip past without them seeing her.

She skidded, putting out her hand to slow her descent, and tiptoed down the bank shaded by the bridge. A motor car rattled the wooden boards above, showering her with dust.

The water was higher than the last time she'd walked across the planks. A few of the boulders they rested on were just below the surface of the river now, and as she stepped out to the nearest rock she felt water seep into the soles of her shoes.

'Girlie.'

She slipped, turning her ankle, but sprang back to the bank. Her heartbeat rumbled in her ears like the motor car crossing overhead.

'Girlie.' A little louder.

There was someone near her on the bank under the bridge.

Even though the ground on the far side was brightly lit by the sun, under the bridge it was dark, and she paused, fearful. Then out from the dark she saw a pair of boots and then the legs and person they belonged to as he slid down to her.

'Uncle Tommy!' she cried. 'What are you doing here?' He'd left without saying goodbye. One more person who'd come into her life, only to leave abruptly.

The skin under his eyes was puffy and dark and his cheeks were stubbled, but she kissed him anyway.

'I just needed to be alone, that's all.'

'I hate being alone. I was alone today because Susan didn't come to school. Her cat died yesterday.' Girlie realised she was prattling. But it was all right. Uncle Tommy wasn't like her mother. He didn't mind it when she chattered to him about whatever was on her mind.

'Sometimes other adults are hard to be around.'

She gazed into the darkness under the bridge, finding the shape of his knapsack and bedroll. 'Is that where you've been sleeping?'

He shrugged. 'I've slept in worse places.'

'What about food?'

'Bandicooting the market garden at the convent school.'

Her mouth fell open. There were different rules for adults to children. When her mother had caught Girlie at six years old stealing a melon from Ah Lee's garden in Perenjori, she had given her a hiding. In her defence, she'd said, *But I just wanted to give it to Katie, she was going to give me a penny for it.*

'Are you coming home now, Uncle Tommy?' She slipped her hand into his. His palm felt rough and dry.

He nodded. 'If your mother still wants me around. It was all that shooting of those senseless birds that done it. Gave me nightmares. Got a shock when the gun went off.'

Girlie had nightmares of her own. Ever since Miss Glaston had read them the fairy tale of Hansel and Gretel, her nightmares usually involved being taken into a dark wood and left sleeping under a tree. It wasn't being abandoned that terrified her, it was not being wanted if she found her way home again. She leaned her head against his arm and walked with him out into the sunshine. Only when they approached the bridge did she remember Joe and Bobby.

'Thank goodness.' The boys had moved on from the bridge. 'Some boys at school are so mean to me. I don't even know why.'

He squeezed her arm. 'Girlie, in this life sometimes people will hurt you and you'll never know the reason for it. But they've got their own reasons enough. And they might not have anything to do with you.'

She didn't know how she would ever cope being an adult. It wasn't just the rules that were different. She would need tougher skin.

~

Her mother cried when she saw Uncle Tommy come home. Then she shouted at him. But in the end she smiled and didn't even say anything about The State of Girlie's Shoes. No wonder her father found it hard to be happy at the same time as her mother when she was so changeable.

Her father was especially not happy that night.

Girlie was in the kitchen, chopping onions for the soup, when he came home. She heard him swear at Brownie. Her mother met Girlie's eyes, gave her a flick of a nod. Girlie slipped away to her bedroom, sinking to the floor, back pressed against the cool of the door.

Her mother whispered, but her father's voice grew louder and louder. He said Uncle Tommy's name a lot. Her mother kept shushing him when he did because Uncle Tommy was asleep across the corridor.

At one point, her mother raised her voice, too, saying, 'I know I said that. But that was before. What am I supposed to do? I broke my promise to him, Ernie.' Her mother lowered her voice, and Girlie leaned into the door wanting to know what had been promised to Uncle Tommy. She made out the words, 'If he was to put two and two together, he would have done so by now. He doesn't look at her funny.'

Look at who? An uncomfortable feeling rippled below Girlie's belly button.

It was over quickly, though, just like the arguments before. Her father slammed the back door against the wall as he stormed out to harness Brownie back onto the dray.

~

Mr Peters lit the fire, the water all around Girlie starting to warm up, bubbling, and she lay back, swirling round and round in gentle, then faster and faster circles. Inside, she felt something swell up, like a tide surging up the beach. But the water didn't cool her down like it did in summer, she felt hotter. Burning up.

She flicked her eyes open.

Her legs were tangled in sodden bed sheets. Heaving with silent sobs, she bundled them up and pushed them in the corner behind the chest of drawers.

~

Her mother had spoken of a promise to Uncle Tommy, and Girlie knew those weren't to be broken. Had it been a promise when her mother told her she would still be the same person in Dongarra? She didn't know what was true anymore. There'd been a shift in her life, and not just in place. Her mother had changed; she would never have hurt Girlie before like she had at the piano, squashing her hand. It couldn't have just been because Kang Pei had given her a biscuit.

The next morning, she was happy to see Susan at school and slipped beside her at the desk. 'Hello, you're back,' she said brightly. 'You missed the spelling test yesterday.'

'So?' Susan didn't even look up.

'So . . . I guess that's a good thing, you know, despite . . . Ruffles.'

Susan hunched her shoulders, shutting Girlie out. A wedge had formed between them just as she had feared. She swallowed what she needed to say, to ask Susan to her house for recital practice this afternoon. She'd have to practise on her own, the duet seeming the only glue of their friendship. Willing herself not to cry, even though she felt tears brim her eyes, she focused on her reader, setting it just so on the desk, placing her pencils in the groove at the top.

She hadn't said the right words. Trying to make friends in Dongarra was like learning a whole new language, and she was a foreigner who'd jumped ship to live with the locals. Except whatever marked her out as different was invisible to her. The proof was that the actual foreigners, like Mr Moretta and Kang Pei, gave her their time, gave her lollies and broken biscuits. She was like Ruby and Uncle Tommy, an outsider. Her father didn't want Uncle Tommy around, she'd guessed from the late-night arguments, and she wasn't so sure her mother did either. Girlie had to trust her mother still loved *her*, though there was something about the words she'd overheard her mother say that hadn't been quite right. Something *was* different, and it had to do with whatever she had done to make people look at her 'funny'. What *else* could it be? There was nobody she could ask for advice. All she could do was watch and listen, try to be more like her mother.

~

After breakfast on Saturday, her mother brought a woman into the kitchen. 'Girlie, this is Mrs Feehely. She's going to help me with the chores from time to time.'

Girlie wiped a drop of Sunshine milk from her lip. 'Hello.'

Mrs Feehely had dark skin like Jenny, and pressed her lips together in a half-smile and nodded her greeting.

With her new resolution in mind, Girlie didn't dare say any more, but watched and listened as her mother gave Mrs Feehely instructions.

Her mother poured a cup of tea for Mrs Feehely, who sat across from Girlie at the table. She took small sips, her straw hat bobbing up and down like a bird. Really, she wasn't like Jenny at all, she realised. Even her mother behaved like Mrs Feehely was a woman at church rather than a servant.

'If you don't mind, the linoleum will need cleaning weekly. And dusting the shop. Oh, and the guestrooms; the sand just blows through the cracks. But that'll be when the guests come after Christmas. There's the washing and ironing, of course.'

'Hm.' Mrs Feehely cast a glance across the kitchen and through the doorway to the shop.

Her mother darted towards the door. 'If you can make it every Saturday morning, I would be most grateful.' She closed the door slowly, and sat at the table next to Girlie.

'Saturdays?' said Mrs Feehely.

Her mother nodded. 'Yes, if you have time. My husband is up at town Saturday mornings, so he wouldn't get under your feet.'

'I milk the cows at the convent on Saturdays before eight, but I can come after that.'

'Lovely.' Her mother drummed her fingers on the kitchen table, hesitated before sitting down. 'As for payment. I don't quite know what it should be.' At this, her mother's throat coloured purple. 'You see, I paid our last domestic's wages to the Aborigines Department. I don't suppose . . .' Her mother twisted her hand in the air.

Mrs Feehely set her hands on the clasp of her handbag, her back ramrod straight. 'You may pay my wages to me directly.'

'I see, of course. Well, the problem is, until the tourist season begins I don't quite have the means to pay much.' Her mother seemed at pains with the words. 'But you have daughters, I can make dresses for you. I was a dressmaker once.' Girlie shifted in her seat. She remembered clearly when her father sold the sewing machine. It had been when Girlie caused all that trouble in Perenjori; the beginning of the end, her mother had said, after the fire.

Her mother flashed her a look. 'Girlie, go outside and help Uncle Tommy.'

Girlie gave Mrs Feehely a lopsided smile on her way out.

Uncle Tommy was banging wooden stakes into the ground and tying string between them. She might ask him about her mother, how she'd behaved at Girlie's age. She hadn't even known that her mother had a brother until Uncle Tommy arrived and it struck her that there might be other things she didn't know, and that she would need to if she were to be more like her.

'Can I help?' She looked about the garden for a spade or a bucket, saw Mrs McGinty standing in the road outside the tearoom, and lifted her hand to wave. But Mrs McGinty was too far away and didn't see her.

Uncle Tommy squinted as he looked up, making his eyes almost disappear, and she couldn't see what he was thinking. He looked over to the McGintys', wiping a streak of dirt across his forehead. 'I'm just about done with this and then I'll be digging. But you can keep me company. That old woman's been giving me the willies, staring at me ever since your mother went inside with the dark woman.'

She twisted her skirt in her fingers. She was worried about talking to Uncle Tommy about her fears. Instead, she told him about Ruffles and the teasing in class and the way Susan was ignoring her, barely saying more to her than *Please* and *Do you mind?* Her throat was dry, and she wasn't the one doing the hard work. 'Can I get you some water, Uncle Tommy?'

'Thanks, Girlie. Though it's this sandy soil that needs water. I don't know how Lil's going to grow much in it.'

She filled Uncle Tommy's enamel mug from the tank, keeping a wary eye out.

He took a gulp, handing back the mug, and she poured the rest into the chicks' water dish in the coop.

'Uncle Tommy?'

'Uh-huh.'

'You know what you said about adults being the same as children, having their own reasons for things? Is it the same with promises – why do adults make promises they don't keep?'

'Now, why ever would you ask a question like that, Girlie?'

'It's just . . . um . . . I heard Mummy and Daddy arguing the other night. After you came home. She said she'd broken a promise to you, and something about sums.' She scrunched her forehead to remember. 'Two plus two. She reckons you didn't know what it makes. But that's silly. Even I know it makes four.'

His sunburned face whitened, making him look quite peculiar as he stared straight through her.

CHAPTER SEVENTEEN

ERNIE

The last of the sun's rays filtered across the sky. Ernie tossed his cigarette into the scrubby back yard where the dark shapes of the wood stack and new vegetable plots leered at him. A light shone dimly through a window on the guesthouse side. He grimaced; he was supposed to be the bloody man about the place. They hadn't been here three months and he'd lost his position in his own home; Lily trying to please her brother. He picked up the bottle and shook it. No bloody beer left either.

He could get another out of the charcoal cooler, but he needed a clear head for tomorrow. A tightness eased as he rubbed at his temples. He would prepare himself now; that way he could get away early before he could be questioned. He went inside, checking on his hat and coat on the stand in the bedroom.

'Ernie?' Lily called out from the sitting room.

'Coming.' He unbuckled his briefcase and rifled through the papers: the primary evidence against him. He'd burn them as soon as it was done. No sense leaving them around where Lily might see them.

'What are you doing?'

He clenched his jaw. 'I said I was coming, just got to put together some papers for a business meeting tomorrow.'

'In town?'

No sense in lying outright. 'Geraldton. I'll be catching the train early.' He buckled it up and pushed his briefcase behind the stand ready for the morning, and went through to the sitting room. Lily sat in the easy chair, darning her stockings. 'Rummy or poker?' he asked.

She moved from the easy chair to the stool for him to sit, keeping her eyes on him. 'Whatever you want.'

He settled on rummy. The way his luck was going, he should lay off gambling for a while.

After a few rounds, speaking only as the game demanded, Lily said, 'You should have told me sooner. I need to go up to town for an hour or two and there's no one to look after the shop. We're expecting a coach full of picnickers from the hospital in Geraldton. I would ask Mrs McGinty, but she'll be busy, too.'

'I've promised Matthew one of his boys some work every now and then,' he said. 'I'll stop by and tell him to come down.'

'Which one?' she said, sharply.

He threw out a three of spades. 'The eldest one, I don't know.'

'I suppose Tommy could look after the shop.'

Lily hadn't thrown down her card. He pointed at the pot between them. 'Your go.'

She continued holding them to her chest.

'Matthew's keen to have his boy work for me.' It was one thing allowing Tommy back in their home, for now, but he didn't want the shop run by someone not the full quid.

'I see. You've given Matthew your word,' she said, backing down. He just had to be firm with her. She threw down her card, and covered his hand with hers. 'I'm tired, Ernie. Call it a night and go to bed?'

He didn't know how to read these signals. Once inside the bedroom she leaned into him, kissing the base of his throat. He hesitated. Would she be taking him to the brink again, just to leave him there? An ache rippled in his groin.

She turned sideways. 'Can you undo me?'

His fingers fumbled with the tiny hooks running up the side of her dress. The harder he got, the clumsier he became.

'Ernie, I wanted to ask you something.'

'Ye-es.' He peeled the dress over her head.

'I'd like to have a sewing machine again.'

He brushed his lips on the nape of her neck. 'I'll buy you a new dress. Not tomorrow, but soon.'

She pulled away, turned, putting a hand to his chest. 'No, I don't want a ready-made dress. I'd like to make myself a new dress. Like I used to. And not just for me.'

He stepped back. 'Is this for the CWA?'

'I found a woman, Mrs Feehely, who can help out with a few chores, which I'll need when we're full over summer. And she doesn't want payment until then.'

He caught her wrist. 'What does she want?'

'She has three daughters. I said I would sew them some dresses.'

'Shouldn't be too hard by hand.' He dropped her wrist, to tug the buttons undone on his fly.

'It would be easier with a machine. And . . . I thought I might sell some dresses in the shop.'

'No, Lil. Don't forget what happened in Perenjori; I was made a laughing stock.' Firm. He thought she would back down again, and he grasped her by the back of the neck to pull her towards him.

She twisted from his hold. 'Not everything's about you. I just wanted something for myself.'

'But you've got a child. What more do you want?'

'Girlie's not going to be a child much longer, if you hadn't noticed.'

'Well, let's try for a baby.' He pulled his shirt over his head, tossing it to the floor. There wouldn't be a baby; it was a cheap shot but he pushed aside his shame. He needed to feel close to her.

She started to cry, silently. Damnit. The worst kind for undoing a bloke, but he was too close to the edge now. He took her around the waist with both hands and pushed his body against hers, running his tongue along her ear lobe.

'What's the point, Ernie?' Her sense of defeat rippled between them.

He breathed into her ear. 'This is what husbands and wives do, just because. There doesn't have to be a point.'

She didn't move against him, holding still as though she were a wax mannequin. He groaned and let go of her. 'Fine, then.' He took his cigarettes to the back yard to cool off.

~

He didn't disturb her sleep the next morning, creeping across the kitchen linoleum and cracking the back door open slowly.

'Where are you going, Daddy?'

Give a bloke a heart attack. 'Go back to bed, Girlie,' he whispered.

'Not sleepy.' She came inside and filled a glass with water, her brown curls plastered to her forehead.

A sigh escaped from some place within him. At first, it hadn't come naturally, caring for a child that wasn't his. Ernie only had to look at his brother with his boys to see how fatherhood should be. Ted and Johnny resembled Fred, sure enough. But Ernie understood fatherhood in the way the boys assumed the roles of leader and follower, would run chicken at a bull in a field but wash behind their ears for their mother, and eventually own up to the rascally thing they'd done when backed into corner – just like Fred, Ernie, their father, uncles and distant cousins. Fatherhood meant seeing in the child the whole family, and knowing you'd done your job in continuing it. There was pattern to life. And he'd fucked it up.

'Don't wake your mother,' he said to Girlie, closing the door gently.

It wasn't the child's fault, she was supposed to have made everything better. Fill the gaping hole in Lily's life after Tommy's suicide attempt, stop her from feeling like *she'd* failed him, give her someone else to care for. Seeing Lily's drawn face, the light in her eyes a reflection of the glare of the gas lamp beside her brother's bed at the hospital, he would have done anything to redeem his failings, to fix the life they were meant to have together: a husband, wife . . . and child.

Then Girlie appeared, four years old, and he'd encouraged the adoption.

But, *What about Tommy?* had been Lily's first question.

We'll find somewhere that can look after him. Not an institution, Lil, but a home for men with his problems. He'll understand. I know you feel he's your responsibility, but you're mine. I need you to be strong for our child.

The corners of her mouth had quivered at 'our'.

He believed he was doing the right thing by Lily, by Tommy, and himself, and by Girlie – for wasn't she in need of a home? The harder he clung to his belief of how life was supposed to be, and the more he strived towards it, the more messed up it became, and the further he got from where he was trying to go.

He yawned as he walked, stretching out his arms. The walk to the station would do him good. He couldn't go to Geraldton knotted up with his issues with Lily and Girlie and Tommy. They weren't anything he could fix this morning.

~

Ernie Hass, a bankrupt.

No matter which way he turned it, he wasn't able to reconcile it. He'd opted to go to court, as though he'd had any other choice. Leaving the Geraldton courthouse, he walked down Marine Terrace, letting the sea wind clear his head. It was a day for it.

The litany of price squeeze, over-ambition, false loyalty, retracted agreement, and poor judgement crashed over him. He hadn't gone into today's bankruptcy hearing blind, but it had been a shock, nonetheless, just how much he owed. To four unsecured creditors: £312; to the WA Bank: £880 over farmlands and buildings valued at £1100; to the WA Bank: £127 over the dwelling at Perenjori valued at £65. When examined, he'd answered he was now living in retirement in Dongarra and offered as his defence the fire that had destroyed his father's house in Perenjori, his by inheritance, mortgaged and over which he hadn't had an insurance policy. A risk he could not have calculated.

The case was adjourned for one week. His counsel had led him to expect the court to award in his favour, and he would be free of his debts.

At least one more week of being Ernie Hass, champion rifleman, serviceman, beach hero, and guesthouse and shop proprietor to the people in Dongarra. Bankrupts were reported in the papers. He just needed to keep the news from Lily long enough to see some profit from the petrol bowser. It was coming at the end of November, the man from the Shell Company had said, just two weeks away.

But Lil had the ear of women in town. There'd been three CWA meetings, where obviously somebody had been putting ideas into her head about dressmaking. Even if his name was struck from every club and credit denied from every lender, he would never see her support their family. There was something that meant more to Ernie than his name.

He had promised her that marrying him would not be a compromise.

Ernie sat down at a table outside the Geraldton Coffee Palace, as the church bells began to peal. His parents had been married at Christ Church. Otto and Anna. She'd brought to their marriage the wealth of a Victorian squatter family and he the social assurance that a generation in the boneyard could provide in a country town. If Ernie hadn't been third generation, his German last name would have seen him behind the fence of an internment camp during the war.

Instead, there'd been other fences.

He lit his cigarette, as the waitress brought his cup of tea.

'Lovely afternoon to sit outside,' said a woman's voice, and he looked up in irritation. But she was a smart-looking woman with a racy, short hairstyle, wearing a low-cut dress, and holding out a cigarette of her own. He'd seen her around, but couldn't place her. 'Can you spare a light?'

Ernie drew his lighter from his inside pocket and lit her cigarette as she bent over. He steadied his gaze on her face, but God help him, no man would have looked away from the swell of her breasts.

'Thank you.' She straightened up, and turned her head to blow smoke over her shoulder. He swallowed. 'Can I sit at your table?

I need to get off my feet.' She gestured at the bags and boxes in strings that she'd set down. 'There are no spare tables.'

Ernie cleared his throat and shifted his chair a fraction aside.

She pointed at the passing waitress for another cup. He shot a look at the clock face: still another three hours until the train. He'd hoped to spend it on his own determining his plan for keeping the news of the impending bankruptcy from Lily.

She caught his movement. 'Got to be somewhere, duckie?'

'What? No, I'm waiting on my train.'

'Coming or going?'

He let his gaze linger on her face. Better than being caught looking elsewhere. 'Going. Dongarra.'

'Well, so am I.' She moved forward in a quick motion that startled him, still training his gaze at the proper height, so it took him a moment to realise she was offering her hand. 'Lorna Fairclough.'

Her hand was already within his, but he let it drop. That's where he'd seen her – in church. 'Bill's wife?'

A smile played about her lips. 'Uh-huh. And you are?'

'Ernie Hass.' For the first time that day his head wasn't dizzy with thought, he was feeling the blood pumping in his body and the sunshine on his face. Competition did that to a man.

Lorna tipped her head to the side. 'Nice to meet you finally, Ernie Hass.'

He raised an eyebrow. Any whiff of Ernie's failure and she'd be tattling to Bill. Sure as anything, his name would be tarred, if Tommy hadn't done that already.

'What's Bill doing letting you out on your own?'

'Buying fabrics and notions and whatnots. I'm a fool trying to stay attractive for my husband.'

'I think your husband's the fool if he doesn't think you're more than half-decent looking.'

Lorna laughed, sending wisps of smoke out her nose. 'What are you doing in Geraldton today, Mr Hass?'

Ernie reached his arm out to the briefcase on the seat beside him. 'I'm on business matters.'

'They look serious.' The tip of her tongue pressed her top lip.

'Not at all. Putting things to right, as a matter of fact.'

'Best to take what's put in front of you,' she said, rolling her shoulders back, 'good or bad.'

He glanced at the boxes and bags, noted the names of dress shops and the milliner, Goody's haberdasher. 'Looks to me like Bill's been given a lot of good.'

Up and down the country, people were desperate, and farmers were Bill's bread and butter fixing up their machines in his garage. They wouldn't have the money to pay him from the yields they were expecting, unless they borrowed heavily. Ernie's stomach twisted at the thought of Bill doing well off their backs.

Ernie had had to take the bad with the very bad, there had been no other way he could have played what had happened after the fire razed his father's house. That's why he grabbed any bit of good that came along, pinned it down so it couldn't wriggle away.

Lorna laughed. 'Ha! Bill thinks throwing money at his problems makes them disappear. But you know what, Ernie Hass?'

'Ernie, just Ernie.'

'I can tell you're not a coward, you're a fighter. A real man.'

He locked his gaze with hers. The glare of the sun dazzled him and he looked away, reaching for the handle on his briefcase. He gave her a nod. 'I'm going to stretch my legs, walk around town.'

Lorna clasped her lace-gloved hands in front of her. 'Could you possibly help me with my packages? I guess you can say I am a fool, after all.' She shrugged at the helplessness of her spending.

He bent over to pick up her boxes, brushing his sleeve against her arm.

CHAPTER EIGHTEEN

TOMMY

Girlie's laughter drew him out of his room. Lily was out in the wash house, clanging the buckets about; wherever Ernie was he didn't care. He'd been thinking, turning Girlie's words over; but they were like the letters the lads kept in their breast pockets in the war. Folded and unfolded, cried on, smudged, and whole stories of disbelief read between every line, so that he couldn't remember what the words had originally been. He wanted her to repeat what she'd overheard Lily say.

Tinny splashing sounds in the kitchen made him pause at the door. He should announce himself, clear his throat, give some indication he was there in case she needed to protect her modesty.

The laughter had stopped now, like she was listening. He held his breath, inched forward, pressed his ear to the door.

Softly, another voice. 'And then he came to the river and said, "Mr Frog, will you take me across?" And the frog replied, "If I take you on my back, you'll sting me." Head forward, Girlie.' The sound of water sloshing.

Mrs Feehely, the woman helping Lily with the household chores, was giving Girlie a bath, telling her stories. He'd remembered this one from when he was young, his mother telling it to him. What was the moral of the fable? His leg cramped, and he eased his foot off the ground to relieve the tension, but it sent him off balance, and he shouldered the door with a thud.

'Who's that?' Girlie called out.

He could stand there and wait for Mrs Feehely to come to the door and catch him, think him spying on Girlie in the bath. He didn't wait to think of other options; he turned the handle, walked in.

'Oh, sorry. I didn't see you there.' He held up his arm to shield his face. The towelling cloth was hanging over the back of the kitchen chair, and he passed it to the woman, keeping his eyes focused on hers. 'Just after a bite to eat before I start work,' he said, lightly.

She said nothing, took the cloth and set to drying Girlie. Tommy whistled as he sliced off the end of the day's bread, still warm from the oven, slathered butter over it.

'So, what did Mr Frog do?' asked Girlie.

Tommy checked to see if Girlie was decent before sliding into the chair, waiting for the end of the tale. He chewed slowly. Mrs Feehely stood still, her arms wrapped around her body while he held his gaze on her.

'Go on. Tell the end of the story,' he urged her.

She flicked her eyes up at him, then to Girlie. 'You dressed? Better go and see your mother,' her voice becoming strained.

Did the woman not hear him? She knew he was looking at her all right, shivering as she reached for Girlie's shoulders. He pushed his chair back, where it fell against the wall making both Mrs Feehely and Girlie flinch. 'Sit down,' he pointed at the chairs opposite him, 'finish the story.'

'I've got to help Mummy with the washing, Uncle Tommy.'

He turned to Girlie, loosened his brow, his hands trembling. 'I need to know how it ends. I can't remember.'

Mrs Feehely's dark skin paled; her hair was done up in a bun and wearing that pink dress with a high collar like she was off to a ladies' meeting, rather than a servant. They sat down at the table, Mrs Feehely placing her hand on Girlie's as he picked up his chair.

'So . . . er . . . Mr Scorpion promised that he wouldn't.' She darted a glance at Tommy. He nodded for her to continue. 'Then when they were halfway across the river, Mr Scorpion stung Mr Frog and they both started to drown.'

'Oh no!' cried Girlie. 'It was a promise. He broke his promise.'

'Because it was in his nature.' The woman twisted her hands. 'I need to get back to my work now, Mr Adamson.' Pleading.

He rubbed his eyes. The mention of the broken promise; Girlie had told him the same thing. But now with the story finished, she had wriggled away, followed by Mrs Feehely picking up a cloth from the floor.

'Please,' she said, plucking at her forearm with the fingers of her other hand. 'I need to wash the linoleum in here. Mrs Hass requires me to.'

She was afraid of him. What had he done? He'd only wanted to hear the end of a child's story.

~

Daylight, the outdoors, and hard yakka banished unwanted thoughts. He jangled at the idea of Lily saying he couldn't put two and two together. That's what the doctors had told him. He hadn't been able to see how they could be right, thought he knew what was real and what wasn't, but all that talking therapy had made him question everything about himself, even what he could see in front of him. Seeing Lily after all this time, and her life with Ernie and their daughter – it worried him that they'd been right, that he *had* been confused, seeing ghosts. But the promise Lily had broken – *that* he could remember.

Before he went to war, he'd told her he was scared.

Don't be, she'd said. *You'll come back to us, I promise.*

Part of him had come back, but not all. Had it really mattered so much to her that she'd made a promise she was powerless to keep?

Lily was right, he hadn't found his missing part, let his soul rest inside him again. But he was safe here. He was returning slowly, and he would watch and listen, stay close and get things straight in his head again.

By the time Lily had stoked the copper for the morning's laundry, Tommy had shovelled a layer of blood-and-bone over the sandy topsoil of her garden beds. Letting Lily see he could be of consequence. Yesterday, there had been a swarm of daytrippers and instead of asking him to work in the shop for a bit when she had gone out, Lily had got a pimply lad in. He tried not to think it was her who found him untrustworthy. It had to be Ernie.

'You'll be ready to start putting in your seedlings this week, Lil,' he said, scraping the sand from his boots on the back step.

She stood in the doorway, her hand shielding her eyes, biting her lip. 'If I can get anything to grow here. Besides saltbush.'

Tommy sought out Girlie ducking under her mother's arm. 'Are you going to help me in the garden today?'

Girlie nodded, checking with her mother first.

Lily caught Girlie on the shoulder. 'I thought we'd visit the Frys together. I'm collecting the cauliflower pickles Mrs Fry made for the golf luncheon.'

Girlie screwed up her face. 'No worries,' said Tommy. 'But I was thinking of getting some seaweed in from the beach to put on the garden. I'll need some help.'

'Do you think it'll improve the fertility?' Lily asked.

He shrugged. 'Dunno about that, but plants take quicker, I've seen.'

'I suppose I could use some seaweed to make a jelly,' said Lily. 'Mrs McGinty's got a recipe she said she'll give me. Be back before I go out to the golf tournament. And don't forget that Susan is coming for practice this afternoon.'

Girlie nodded, strangely quiet. He remembered that Susan was the friend with the drowned kitten.

~

Tommy brought a bread crust and a waterbag, and they walked the chalky goat track through the dunes south to the Back Beach, past the nuns' cottage, past the Obelisk and the shacks dotted among the scrubby hills. Early tourists had already claimed them. Fishing rods leaned on the porch rail of one, and a line of washing fluttered behind another. Dinghies lay upturned on the shore.

He noticed Girlie had started to sing, something she hadn't done when he'd first met her. Just strings of babble, sounds she put together in a tuneful way as she sprang across rocks, kicked up sand and darted into the gullies. She had her own way down to the beach, picking up broken shells or smoothed glass.

'You look like you're searching for treasure,' he said, catching sight of her running her hands through the sand.

'Susan told me about some lost Spanish coins. Will you help me look for them?'

He couldn't say how many minutes passed then, using his hands as shovels as they pounced on anything that shone in the scrub.

He collapsed on his back, his whole chest shaking as he laughed. 'Look at us!' A fine crust of sand stuck to the sweat on their bodies.

Girlie laughed too, cupping her hands in the sand and throwing it at him.

He spluttered, spitting out sand. And jumped to his feet.

'I'm so sorry, Uncle Tommy.' Girlie pulled her top lip over her bottom lip, the same way Lily used to when she was small. It would always work on Pa. Strange the resemblance. What was it Lily had said? That Girlie had been her gift from God.

He pulled his brows together. 'I'll make sure you are,' he said in a gruff voice, then flung a dried hunk of seaweed at her. She squealed, ducking away.

He arrived at the Back Beach a little breathless, his cheeks stretched and aching from laughter. Tidal lines of seaweed stretched up the dazzling white curve of the beach.

'Oh! I thought we might see some of the nuns down here swimming,' Girlie said, coming up behind him.

'They keep to themselves, Moretta says.'

'Mr Moretta, the Italian?' She turned her face up to his. 'Do you speak to him?'

He grunted, sitting down to remove his boots and roll up the cuffs of his trousers. 'Not much. But he always gives me the time, and I've got plenty of respect for a man like that.' He guzzled from the water bag, wiping his mouth with the back of his sleeve before passing the water to Girlie. She took tiny sips.

After quenching their thirst, they gathered piles of seaweed like leaves on bonfire night. He grimaced, looking at the three gingham sacks he'd brought. 'I don't know how we'll get this lot back to the house.'

The smile on her face dropped.

'We don't have to go back just yet.' He formed a shovel of his hands, making the beginnings of a castle in the sand. She saw what he was doing and joined in, scooping seawater to harden the walls, decorating the turrets with seashells.

Then she sprang to her feet, landing squarely in the centre of the sandcastle. 'Whoop!' she cried, dancing around in a circle, hollering at the gulls that swooped and cawed. He could see why the nuns preferred to swim at this part of the beach, empty apart from the sand crabs disappearing into the hard, wet sand of the shoreline. It was like being on the track, feeling as wide as the sky. But he scanned the beach – the idea of people appearing here unnerved him.

He picked up a clump of seaweed, wet and brown and drooping with clusters of pods, and draped it over his bare head. 'What do you think, does it suit?'

She shrieked with laughter. 'Take it off – Mummy will have a fit if someone sees you.'

'She would love it.'

'She wouldn't.' Girlie crossed her arms.

'Lil loves dressing up.'

Girlie shook her head. 'No, she does *not*! We went to plain-and-fancy-dress dances in Perenjori and Mummy always went plain.'

Tommy pulled the seaweed off his head. He would stink something rotten now. 'Well, I suppose she was different back then.'

'Was she like me?' Girlie asked, kneeling in the sand with her feet sticking outwards, her face turned up to his, still and solemn.

He thought about it. 'Not much. She wasn't awfully fond of dirty and squirmy things, like you are. I remember one time when she was having a doll's picnic in our back garden in Nedlands,' he laughed at the memory, 'and I put worms in the teapot. Ha, did she scream.'

Girlie rocked back on her haunches, giggling.

'But then, you wouldn't really be like her, would you?' he said. 'You'd be like your real mother.'

The laughter faded from her lips, turned ashen. 'What do you mean?'

She didn't know. Since that first conversation, when he'd been overcome with disbelief, and relief, at seeing Lily again, the adoption hadn't been mentioned. Could he have imagined it? But since he'd found Lily, he'd hung on her every word, where there was safety. He couldn't have imagined it.

'You didn't know, did you?' He watched her face, her expression blurred as though something broke inside her. An echo of his own constant shattering. 'Lil and Ernie adopted you.' Lily *had* said Girlie was adopted. So, it was true. But surely Girlie should know, she was ten years old, for Christ's sake. Lily didn't keep secrets. She wouldn't lie. She wouldn't.

Girlie moved now. Streaked away up the beach, kicking up the sand behind her. He staggered to his feet and started to follow, but his knee gave him gyp. He watched her get smaller. He understood. Sometimes you needed to run away.

He glanced up the beach looking for some shade, saw a bough shelter a hundred yards up.

He blinked. There she was. The woman from the jetty the night of the fire, on her own, reading a book. Tommy ploughed through the sand until he reached her.

She looked up in surprise and flushed, deepening her sunburn. She'd caught it on her arms; Tommy let his gaze drift downwards. 'Hello,' he said. 'I thought I had the beach all to myself.'

She closed her book and picked up her bag to leave.

'Please stay. At least, don't leave on my account. I just wanted to thank you.'

She peered at him. 'Whatever for?'

The maw of Tommy's mind opened. It hadn't been real, just another one of his fantasies and now he seemed a fool. But his trousers scratched the partly healed scar on his thigh.

'I wanted to thank you for not telling anyone it was me.' He had thought about telling Lily, to come clean even though it had been an accident. But after what happened on the ride home from Fred's farm, he'd kept it to himself. One accident might raise eyebrows among townsfolk, two and they'd be saying he shot at Ernie on purpose. He didn't want the notice of the police. Locking him up again wouldn't help ground him. The opposite. He dissociated – that's what the doctors said – lost his body, found it difficult to find his way back again.

She stood up, looping her bag over her shoulder, and smiled. 'I haven't told anyone anything because I don't know anything, do I?' But she wasn't overly confident, he thought as he sat down in the sand, watching her step out of the shelter, casting anxious glances up and down the beach.

She cupped her hand over her eyes, and he followed the direction of her gaze further towards where Girlie was walking at the tideline.

'Oh, you're Lily's brother,' she said, coming back to the shelter.

He wiped his sweaty palms down the sides of his trousers. 'Tommy Adamson. Are you a friend of Lil's?'

'I am. Lorna Fairclough. Lily did me such a favour with a dress of mine. I'll be wearing it this afternoon at the golf, actually.'

She sat down on the bench close to him, the heat from her lifted the hairs on his arms. He only caught her final words. 'Golf? Oh, I don't play.'

She tilted her head, puzzled.

He smiled, clamping his lips lest he spewed out any more rubbish.

'I was talking about you with Lily the other day,' she said. 'You poor man. She told me how you suffered.'

His initial elation deflated. She pitied him.

'That's all in the past. I'm sorting myself out now, and then I guess I'll move on.'

She stood. 'Good for you.' She laid a hand on his arm before she walked away.

She disappeared up the track through the sand hills. His gaze lingered on the line where the crest of the sand hill met the sky, at the space where she'd stepped out of his sight as though she might walk back through an invisible doorway into another world where she would stay and talk to him.

He lay back and thought of Lorna. He'd found false comfort before with women who pitied him. There was the nurse who sponged him down each day at the Lemnos Hospital, and let him do things to her under her skirt that he thought only he was doing. Only, later he found out she'd treated all the other lads to the same. There was the widowed farmer's wife in Katanning who'd taken him to her bed at night but who became testy with him in the morning when he wanted a hot breakfast as well. None of them had treated him like he was somebody.

Lorna was different. She had only put her hand on him, but she could be up there in the dunes thinking about coming back to see him. She was married, it could never be real. But the fantasy warmed him. He slipped into this other world, imagining the comfort of the soft flesh of her body.

~

The line for the susso at the Barrack Street Depot stretched along the front of the building to the corner. Mostly old men, and young men crippled by the war. Tommy, blowing on his hands to keep them warm, turned to the bloke behind him, wondering what was wrong with him until he saw the twitchy grip he kept on his pipe. Wound up and ready to stab him with it, so Tommy looked away.

He'd told Lily he was going for a watchman's job, but he'd been feeling restless, no patience to stand for hours, day in and day out. It had been nine years since he'd left the barracks hospital, and like some of these men, he'd never be the same again. Foot by bloody foot he gained on the door to the depot. All the time, praying he wouldn't be sent off, like when he'd lost his government job digging trenches the week before.

He stepped forward again as a woman peeled off at the front. She was hunched over tying her belt around her thick waist as she came towards him.

His head felt hot, and red clouds settled over his eyes.

Not here. He clenched his toes inside his boots desperately clinging to the present. Ghosts from the past came unbidden now, usually at night, but a passing face might make him go off-kilter; he'd got used to it, had learned to take off or hunker down. But never this sort of ghost.

The woman fumbled at the knot on her waist, passing by him with a smell of cologne over stale sweat. His body jolted, nerves zapping, the roar of blood in his ears. The dead couldn't walk the street and collect their susso.

He stepped out of the line, quickened his pace to follow her.

'Ma,' he called. When she stopped, his body could have disintegrated into a pile of ash.

She looked square at him, hunching her shoulders.

Tommy fought, still clenching his toes, reforming his body to stay in the present. 'Is that really you? I thought you were dead.'

She jutted out her jaw. 'Is that what your father said?' Her lip curling up in disgust. This face – skin pulled taut across her cheeks, creased with grime – wasn't the one he sketched from memory.

He shook his head slowly, afraid his body would betray him, do something he couldn't control, like beating his fist on a wall, himself, or her. 'I came home, Ma,' he said, trembling, 'and you weren't there.'

He folded onto a doorstep set up high. 'Lily said that . . . Lily said that . . .' Tommy pulled his knees up.

'I suppose she wanted to believe that rather than the truth.'

He looked at her. She had come near enough to speak softly, but not to touch. She was ravaged by something other than the drink, which had finally done Pa in. A yellowing bruise bloomed across her cheekbone and capillaries had burst in her left eye, giving her the look of a ghoul.

'You weren't there. Where did you go?'

Ma turned her head away, and he saw her gaze circling the ground by her feet. 'Alfie – Alfie Bright, he was our boarder while you were away. A bit of help and extra money about the house. I fell in love.'

'The boarder?' Tommy felt sick, steaming though it was June, sweat pooling in his boots.

She opened her mouth to say something, but shut it and nodded. 'I thought Alfie'd be different. Care about me, not horses. But he hasn't a caring bone in his body.' Ma rubbed her jaw. 'I suppose I deserve everything I get now.'

He grabbed at her coat sleeve, but she slipped through his grasp. 'What is it you get?'

Her face tightened so she was no more than the skulls he'd seen baked dry and scoured by vultures lying on hilltops. She pulled away from him, muttering to herself, clearing her throat. 'At least you were safe. Your pa never laid a finger on me, any of us. You were better off with him than me.'

A shadow peeled across her face, and he saw a deep shame, torn between fear and a longing to fold him in her arms.

But it must have been a trick of the light. As she walked away, Tommy bowed his head between his knees, his chest heaving with his ragged breaths. He was broken. Lily had kept their mother's death from him for ten months at the hospital. She'd said she'd wanted to protect him while he was recovering. But what had she been protecting him from?

~

'Mr Adamson, what do you think you are doing?'

Lorna *had* come back. But she sounded hard, her arms at angles to her hips, a towel slung over her shoulder.

His penis shrivelled in his hand. He tucked himself into his trousers quickly, discomfited that warm thoughts of Lorna had led to the memory of Ma's ghost. More evidence of the disturbance in his mind.

She shot a look towards the ocean, and he followed it. Girlie, in nothing more than her knickers, wading in the waves just down from the bough shelter. Lorna trained her stare on him. Not with her warm eyes, but like he was a rotten stench. She snatched up the straw hat she'd left behind and turned on her heel, striding back to where she had come from.

'N-no,' Tommy stammered. 'Wait. I can explain.' He scrambled to his feet, holding up his trousers around his offending region, while he scorched his feet on the sand after her.

She climbed the wooden path through the dunes without slowing or a backward glance, disappearing into that other world, the real one.

CHAPTER NINETEEN

GIRLIE

When Girlie returned from the beach, her father had already left for the golf tournament. She found her mother at the kitchen table, massaging her temples with her fists.

Brimming with questions, Girlie held up the sack of seaweed.

Her mother glanced at it. 'What am I supposed to do with that now?'

'You said you were going to make seaweed jelly.' The question of who Girlie really was stuck in her throat like a lump she could not swallow.

Her mother pushed back the hair stuck to her forehead and relieved Girlie of the sack. 'Run next door to see if Mrs McGinty's there, and get the jelly recipe if she is.'

Girlie gladly set off on the errand to avoid the sight of her mother drawing out each mass of slimy tentacles and pummelling them in the sink, taking out her headache on the seaweed. And to avoid the endless questions she had about why she was adopted, which would only fuel her mother's anger. And in the state Girlie was in, she would only cry, annoying her mother more.

There wasn't anyone in the tearoom, so she ducked round the counter and down the passage Mr McGinty had shown her. She didn't realise she was holding her breath until the door slammed against the wall, letting in the voices of Mrs McGinty and a man who didn't seem to be getting a word in edgewise, and her breath rushed out in a gasp.

'Don't do anything, it'll only cause trouble, but this is the second time I've seen her over there,' Mrs McGinty was saying. She stopped talking to the man, called out, 'Anyone there?'

Girlie trembled, staying her tread on the boards, but Mrs McGinty was walking towards her.

'I heard something I reckon, Robert.'

Girlie revealed herself. She goggled at the sight of Mrs McGinty wielding a rifle, which was quickly dropped, pointing to the floor.

'That's the girl. From next door.'

A man appeared behind Mrs McGinty, towering above her by two feet. The skin on his nose and cheeks was blistered red, but he had the same thin hair as Mrs McGinty.

Girlie's eyes flitted to the gun and back to him. 'I'm Girlie Hass,' she said, pointing to her chest, hollowed out by the sound of her name.

He grunted, coiling a length of rope around his shoulder. She had heard of Robert McGinty; he brought the groceries to their shop but she hadn't seen him before. He kept a steady eye on her.

'You worry too much, Mum. People are best keeping to themselves.' He left the tearoom, without acknowledging Girlie in any other way. But she was sure she'd overheard them talking about her. Tears rimmed her eyes, guessing at why. She blinked, focusing on the brightly coloured lollies under the glass.

'What do you want?' Mrs McGinty tucked the rifle under the post office counter.

Whatever it was about Girlie that Mrs McGinty had been talking about with her son, it had made her angry; she was different to the kind old lady who had given Girlie and Susan free ice-cream. It seemed that anything Girlie did, even just being herself, made people cross. But her mother had sent her with one question.

'My mother wanted a seaweed jelly recipe she said you were to give her.'

Mrs McGinty stretched across the counter as much as her fragile frame would allow, breathing a stale stream of air into Girlie's face. 'I've got nothing to give her now. I think she's got enough of ours already.'

All the talk of jelly and now her insides felt slimy, would slide into a puddle if she didn't leave immediately. She nodded, and ran.

Her legs took her straight out of the tearoom and down to the foreshore. She hardly registered the sand flicking up about her, or the spray getting into her face. Spray from the sea, or tears, she couldn't tell which. She let out a shudder, wiping her arm across her face so she could focus on what was in front of her. Whelks and muttonfish shells, little ears in the sand, but she didn't stoop to pick them up as she usually did.

She sifted through her memories instead, piecing together the mystery of where she came from. But in the background of every memory was Perenjori. Her iron bed with its painted nursery-rhyme tiles. Digging in the vegetable plot with Ah Lee, helping him prepare greens for dinner, or sitting in the iron tub while Jenny scrubbed at her back. Jenny, in the frame of every picture. She listened when Girlie told her about falling over in the school yard and scraping her knee, when she told her the stories about the frog families who croaked in the garden beneath her bedroom window. Girlie wrinkled her brow, thinking hard. Her father? Where was he in her scrapbook of memories? Walking together in the fields when the wheat was as tall as her. He killed a snake once that had crossed their path. Her father had always been distant but there.

Now she saw shadows in these images where she'd not seen them before. Her mother *had* acted differently to the other mothers at school. Not different in a bad way, just different.

The plain-and-fancy-dress balls. Her mother made the best outfits for Girlie – at least until she sold her sewing machine. One year, when Girlie was in the infants' class, she'd been a sugar-plum fairy. That was the year she'd become friends with Katie.

Katie's mother had dressed as Little Bo Peep and Girlie had wished so hard that her mother could have been more like Mrs Lowndes. But instead, her mother dressed as always, wearing her cream dress for dances. Girlie had been ashamed of her mother going 'plain' as she did, especially when she could make such beautiful costumes. When Girlie was seven, she'd been the princess from the story 'Princess and the Frog', and her mother had made a golden ball from yellow satin stuffed with cotton.

It was the first time a photographer had ever come to Perenjori. Only Katie had seen a camera before, in Perth. All the children and most of the mothers had lined up to be photographed. But not Girlie. And certainly not her mother. Girlie had been excited – and a little apprehensive – to be photographed as the princess, but her mother had refused to allow her to take part in the photograph. It hadn't made sense. Her mother had been eager, firm even, about Girlie walking in the parade, to show off the beautiful gown she'd made from an old georgette evening dress. When Girlie had complained, begged to be included in the girls' photograph, her mother had left the dance early, before the prizes for best costume were awarded, and it was her father who took Girlie up to the photographer afterwards to have a photograph taken just of herself.

She plunged her hands into her pocket, flicking back her flyaway hair. The sun warmed her closed eyelids. There was always some way she failed her mother. Her memories jumbled. She might try to be like her mother, yet she could never be.

A shrill whistle came across the air.

She opened her eyes. Kang Pei raised his hand, loping along the jetty to the sand.

'Hello,' he called.

The ends of her mouth turned down in the struggle to speak.

He came near, his face shiny like leather from living out on the boat in the sun. 'Why are you looking very sad?'

She sniffed, turning to face the street and the McGintys', where a motor car was parked out front. She looked further towards the guesthouse but couldn't see Uncle Tommy.

'I don't think . . .' she started. She stared into his eyes, almost like toffee. It wouldn't matter telling him. Who would he tell?

'I found out I'm adopted,' she said, walking towards the goods shed. In the shade, they sat down against the stone wall, and she shared what Uncle Tommy had told her. She shrugged. 'So, you see, I don't know where I'm from.'

Kang Pei shook his head, his black hair falling across his forehead like the silk tassels on her princess costume. It was a movement that made her memories double back over themselves. Ah Lee had looked the same.

'I knew a Chinaman before, in Perenjori, but he wasn't a real Chinaman like you are. He was also an Aboriginal, they said. Half-caste.' She swallowed, forming words that might provide answers she wasn't ready for. 'What does it feel like to be a Chinaman?' She'd cringed before she finished her question, holding her breath as she waited for him to speak.

He broke into a laugh.

She let out her breath. 'Why is that funny?'

He crinkled up his eyes. 'People call me a Chinaman. But China – of China I have no memory. I was born in Kalgoorlie.'

Just like an Australian. But what was in his head? She was brave enough to ask him now.

'What is in yours?' he replied.

She shook her head. 'This morning I would have told you I was from Perenjori, and Perth before that, where Mummy met Daddy. Daddy's from Geraldton originally.' She sketched a chalk line in the ground with the point of her shoe. 'Now, I don't know. I'm like you. I don't have memories of where I really come from. So, what does that make me?'

'You are still the same person.'

'I feel like their daughter, but I'm not really.'

He rummaged about in his pocket and told her to hold out her hand. She did, expecting another biscuit. But it was something flat and hard, a coin when she looked at it more closely, though with a square cut out of its centre and no King's head. 'What is it?'

'My mother gave it to me to remember that everything changes.' He jingled his other pocket. 'But I prefer the other kind of coin.'

Her mother wouldn't like it. 'Thank you. But I can't possibly keep it.' She tried to give it back to him.

'No, no. It is yours.' Kang Pei rocked onto the balls of his feet. 'You remember I am your friend, this will not change.'

She closed her hand over the coin and nodded. This was a good secret. She'd given him her deepest secret in exchange.

~

Her mother clucked her tongue when Girlie came into the shop. 'What happened to you? Did you get the recipe?'

Girlie squeezed her mouth tight and shook her head. 'She said she didn't have one.' People should keep to themselves. That's what Robert McGinty had said, and it seemed a good rule when she had more questions than answers.

'What on earth! Oh well, I expect she's just forgetful,' her mother said, brushing her hand along the shelf beside the window, stirring up a fine mist of dust. 'Pass me those cans on the counter.' She ducked below, rummaging, until she came up wielding a rag.

Her mother's mood was gone for now, but it would return if she knew how strange Mrs McGinty had seemed just because her mother and Uncle Tommy had taken some of the McGintys' furniture. That's what Mrs McGinty had said, wasn't it? They had given enough to her mother.

The dust made her cough. With her hand covering her mouth, she studied her mother. She had the same shaped face as Girlie, with its small up-turned nose and pointy chin, and she was chewing her lip just as she always did. But her eyes were grey, whereas Girlie's were bright green. Ah Lee had once told her they were like smashed jade. It was funny, but she couldn't remember the colour of her father's eyes: it was one of those details she never noticed unless she was looking for them.

'What colour are Daddy's eyes?'

Her mother paused in straightening the packets on the shelf. 'Blue. Why do you ask?'

Girlie shrugged, and her mother looked at her reflection in the front window, patting her hair rolls. She took a deep breath and turned to face her.

'I must tell you something.'

Girlie passed the cans to her mother, mindless of what she was doing. All she could feel was the pulsing of her blood. Her mother was going to tell her, and she realised she wasn't ready. Everything would change.

'It's the Frys.'

'Is Susan not coming this afternoon?' Asking questions might slow her mother down, so that she might never come to the truth of what she was going to tell Girlie.

Girlie had been practising on her own this week; she felt as though Susan might drop her, but she hung on, determined not to let her down in the recital. She felt the weight of the secret coin in her pocket – and remembered that everything changed. Even friendships.

'Yes, she is. Really, Girlie, you must start deciding which songs you'll be playing. She said you hadn't discussed it with her yet. I have some ideas, I left the sheet music and notation on the piano.'

Girlie set down the can she was holding. 'I'll go right away and practise before she comes.'

'Not yet. I must tell you what I found at their house.'

She studied her mother's face, hoping that the worst was over, and fearful of what was to come. But now nothing could surprise her. The worst had already been discovered. She shifted her weight from foot to foot.

'Mrs Fry keeps a slovenly home. They are not nice people. I found the floor dirty, and the table was grimy when I set my bag down. Flies were on the bread even, and she did not shoo them off. I don't know how they can breathe with the stench of the privy filling the house. The walls were just sacking and tin.'

'Will I still play with Susan in the recital?' Girlie asked, a little braver now that it seemed her mother wasn't disappointed in her for a change, though a little concerned; she knew enough of her mother's rules to understand that she couldn't be friends with Susan anymore.

Her mother opened her mouth to speak but the chime of the bell sounded and she pulled her mouth into a smile – what Girlie thought of as her mother's 'outside face'.

It was Susan.

'Hello, dear,' her mother said, her voice pleasant. 'I was just telling Girlie about my lovely visit to your mother. Right,' brushing herself down, 'I'd best be on my way to help with the golfers' luncheon.'

Susan slunk through the door, barely looking at Girlie. Her first visit since Ruffles drowned, and from Susan's expression Girlie was glad her mother was going out. Susan mumbled the barest hello.

They practised the songs her mother had laid out for them – 'Waltzing Matilda' and 'My Melancholy Baby', Susan singing without her usual gumption. She didn't even comment when Girlie hit the wrong keys in the last few bars of 'Waltzing Matilda'.

Girlie stopped playing to bring them each a cup of milk.

'Why didn't you come with your mother this morning?' Susan asked. It was the most Susan had said without Girlie having to ask her a question first.

Girlie forced herself to swallow. 'I had to help my uncle. I've got so much to tell you.'

'Like what?'

She instantly regretted her haste to divulge. But Susan had taken an interest in her; maybe her fears about their friendship were not true.

Thuds came from the side of the house where Uncle Tommy was shovelling the seaweed into the vegetable beds.

'Oh, nothing. I'll tell you tomorrow at Sunday School.'

'You can come to mine after,' Susan said, 'while Mum and Dad are out walking the town.'

Girlie's thoughts tic-tacked. What would her mother want her to do? All her life she'd been learning the rules as they applied to Girlie Hass, her mother's daughter; thought they would help her learn to be the girl she was meant to be. But she could never have been that girl. Susan still wanted to be her friend and now her mother had taken against her. What did 'not nice' mean, anyway?

'You don't have a piano.'

'We don't have to practise all the time,' Susan said. Then, rolling her eyes, 'We can play skipping instead.'

'I can't come over.'

'Why not? Go on, tell.' Susan grasped her wrist, giving it a twist with her other hand, so that Girlie feared her skin might tear.

'Ouch, stop that.'

Susan tightened her grip.

'All right, I'll tell, I'll tell.' Girlie yelped a little as Susan released her arm. She rubbed at it. 'My mother said that . . .' She lowered her voice. 'That . . . you're not nice people.'

'Is that right?' Susan's cheeks flushed red, hiding her freckles. 'Well, my mother says that your mother has airs and graces she's not entitled to. Asking about town for a woman to come and do, as if you was nobs. She's not even offering anywhere what the nobs do in wages.'

Before Girlie could tell her about Mrs Feehely, Susan continued, glaring, 'All the other girls say there's something wrong with you, too. Acting like a princess, fainting that day at the river.'

They were right – there *was* something different about her. But not how they thought. She could feel tears brimming behind her eyeballs, tried not to let Susan see how she had got to her. 'Not all the girls. Do you know that girl Ruby? I met her in a clearing under the bridge and she's my friend.'

Susan snatched up her cup, draining it. 'And your ma thinks *we're* not nice people. You're going around with the Abos!'

'But she's not. She told me.'

'Ruby Feehely's a dirty Abo, everyone knows it. The Feehelys ought to be sent out to the reserve past Mingenew.'

Girlie clamped her mouth shut. Feehelys? Ruby was Mrs Feehely's daughter? Ruby had been right – she'd been in front of her eyes and yet Girlie still hadn't seen her. Focused on covering up who she really was, she had spilled Ruby's secret, and now Ruby's family might get into trouble. Her mother would never forgive her if Girlie's loose mouth sent Mrs Feehely away. Secrets weren't fun to collect when they could hurt others. Not even Kang Pei's special coin could help.

CHAPTER TWENTY

LILY

There was one slice of Mrs Liddle's sponge left among the half-empty plates of cold meat, salad, jellies, and the mutton pie Lily had asked Mrs Feehely to make for the golf luncheon.

'Do you fancy the last piece?' she asked Lorna, who'd bustled over to the pavilion, tap-tapping her heels.

'Have they all eaten?'

Lily scanned the grassy surrounds for straggling golfers from either club. 'I think so.'

Lorna forked cake into her mouth, spilling crumbs down the green dress Lily had worked on. It had taken her a week while Girlie was at school and Ernie at the shop or off on business. Time slipped by as she worked, but she did not feel her fingers cramp up until late afternoon when she grew dizzy looking suddenly into the distance. Then she would shake out the dress and press each fold, each pleat with such care.

She ran her gaze across the dress now it was filled by Lorna, who looked a little like a half-boiled crayfish on account of a sunburn. But it had been worth the effort.

When Lorna had arrived at the luncheon, Mrs Booth admired her dress and congratulated Lily on her handiwork, buoying her spirits until she remembered the ghastly hook rug at the CWA meeting. The woman's taste was questionable. Her praise for the stitching of Lorna's dress meant nothing until Mrs Booth called over Darla McGinty twirling her pink parasol.

Very nice, Darla had said, when she saw Lily's work. *Though it'll get spoiled during the game. You will partner me, won't you, Mrs Fairclough?*

Darla had given Lily only a scant glance during her appraisal of the dress. Lily's hope of being taken into her inner circle, let alone noticed, was dwindling.

Lorna grasped Lily's arm and pulled her in close to her side. *I'm afraid I've promised to help with the cool drinks.*

Mrs Booth? Darla asked.

Oh, I've already partnered with Mrs Lovett. Mrs Booth lifted her shoulder apologetically.

Darla narrowed her eyes, causing Mrs Booth to flush. It was really Darla McGinty and not Daphne Liddle, nor any of the others, who the women respected. Lily had been mistaken about Robert's odd look at Girlie. This week he hadn't even come into the shop when he delivered the groceries, leaving them by the front gate.

My husband will partner you, Mrs McGinty, she'd offered.

Darla had cast her gaze at the golfers walking in pairs towards the first tee, then looked him up and down. *It would be appreciated, Mr Hass.*

As she watched them confer on their choice of club, Lily only hoped she could trust Ernie to hold up his share of the plough. It was a risk, but a calculated one.

The dress *had* been worth the effort. Lily reached for the bow on Lorna's sleeve. 'May I?' She adjusted each sleeve, unfolding the cuffs to hang over Lorna's elbows. 'I used a little extra fabric for the trim, see.' Cannibalised from strips of a peach-coloured lawn cotton dress she'd made at Pritchard's, a long time ago.

'Did you see the hem facing?'

Lorna licked cream from the corner of her mouth, glanced briefly down at her dress and nodded. Lily picked up the edge of Lorna's skirt for her. Two rows of bias scallops circled the underside of the hem in the same floral lawn.

'But that's too lovely to hide,' said Lorna, swallowing her last morsel of cake. She raised an eyebrow. 'I'll be having to lift my skirt for all and sundry.'

Lily smiled, but like Lorna's hem it formed a straight line with more complicated feelings underneath.

'Goody's had some printed crepe-de-chine. Discounted,' Lorna said. 'You said you were a mannequin once. With a new frock . . .'

The peach-coloured dress was the one Lily had worn for her first sitting with the photographer. She shook her head. Though she was always vigilant about her past catching up with her, it disturbed her to look back. 'Those days are over for me. I'm married and a mother.' After sitting for the photographer, as with all her other dreams of how her life would be, the image of marriage and motherhood had been rudely violated, turning to ashes in her mouth. Instead of having a dutiful child, she had Girlie. Sullen and asking too many questions. Despite her best efforts, she couldn't quash the ugly thought that if she couldn't be the mother she'd intended to be, she was no better off than being childless, like Lorna.

Lorna leaned against the pillar, lighting a cigarette. 'If you change your mind too late, it might be full price again, two and three a yard, I believe.'

Lily shot a glance at Lorna – she detected a subtle barb, and was debating with herself whether to defend their financial position.

'Lily, a man'll die of thirst.' She flinched at Ernie's creeping up on them, wiping his brow with his bare forearm. One or two straggling golfers wandered into sight between trees, or over the crest of rolling slopes, but she couldn't see Ernie's golf partner, Darla.

Lorna flicked her cigarette into the bushes.

Lily waved her arms to dispel the smoke and leaned across the table, half on her tiptoes. 'What do you want? Squash? Tea?'

'Any ginger beer?'

She poured Ernie a glass of Mrs Booth's ginger beer from the flagon. 'Only chips of ice left.' She handed him his drink. He drank it down in one gulp, sweat running in rivulets down his throat.

'How are things with Darla?' She kept a level tone, conscious of Lorna listening in.

Ernie grimaced, lifting his collar to wipe his throat.

Lily flared her eyes, gritting her teeth, which Ernie mistook for a sign of annoyance or boredom or something else completely at odds with her hopes for the day, because he suggested she go home and see to Girlie.

'I'd like to stay, Ern,' she said, lowering her voice, the sound of Lorna moving plates from one place to another on the table behind her.

He squinted in the sun, shook his head. 'I just don't think she should be alone with Tommy.'

For a moment she considered leaving; the fair recital was only three weeks away and the girls hadn't chosen their songs until she'd taken matters in hand. But then a thin, pastel-coloured figure topped with a large pink parasol emerged over the crest of a sandy hill. Darla.

'Susan's with her, and the McGintys are nearby,' Lily said, though Mrs McGinty seemed confused and frail. But Lily wouldn't be swayed from her intention to sit with Robert and Darla McGinty tonight at the golf award ceremony.

With a touch of his fingers to his forehead in Lorna's direction, Ernie walked back towards Darla.

Lily turned to Lorna to apologise for not properly introducing her to Ernie, but saw a strange expression on Lorna's face like she'd swallowed her cigarette.

'Are you feeling poorly?' She filled a glass with water for Lorna.

'Is Mrs Feehely working for you today?'

Lily paused, holding the glass up in front of her. 'She left before I came up to town. I must thank you for the recommendation.' Mrs Feehely presented herself well, always a favourable characteristic.

Lorna twisted her wedding ring back and forth. 'Oh. I suppose it's nothing. It's just, I wonder if it's appropriate for your daughter to be left with your brother like that.'

Lily's hand shook, spilling water on the damask cloth. 'What are you saying?'

'I saw your brother down at the Back Beach this morning.'

'He was collecting seaweed for the garden. Not as peculiar as it sounds.'

Lorna lowered her voice, compelling Lily to move towards her. 'I will tell you what I do find peculiar. I know he suffered in the war but I wouldn't be a good friend and a decent woman if I didn't tell you what I saw him doing at the beach.'

Oh God, thought Lily. It could be any number of his behaviours. Ernie's comment about Tommy and Girlie had touched a nerve with her, though she hadn't shown it. Still persistent was the urge to protect him from scrutiny, especially after his stunt at Fred's farm. Though Lorna knew of his circumstances, Lily didn't want him parading them on the beach for all to see.

'You must tell me, Lorna. I can help him, if I know soon enough.'

'It's Girlie who needs your concern,' Lorna said, lighting another cigarette.

'Why?' He'd never hurt her. Not on purpose. But Lily tucked this thought away.

The red of Lorna's face deepened. 'I saw him doing unnatural things, things that a man shouldn't be thinking of with his own kith and kin. A child, too.'

Lily felt winded. She had been so afraid of the person in the photograph hidden in the tin, she had not thought to watch for similar dangers with Girlie. But this was what she was most afraid of – that daughters turned into their mothers. With one hand resting on the table, she faced Lorna. 'What did Girlie do?'

An inch of ash fell from Lorna's cigarette, streaking the lawn cotton trim of her sleeve. 'What did Girlie do? She's the innocent.'

Lily listened while Lorna told her of what she had seen at the beach.

'In just her knickers?' She breathed deeply, pressing the small of her back against the tap on the urn.

Lorna nodded. 'And—'

'I am sorry for your having to witness such an act,' Lily said. 'It probably isn't as it appears and it wouldn't do Tommy any good if it's mentioned. Could you please not tell anyone? I know it's dreadful of me to ask. But I can't let Ernie find out. He'd be so angry with Tommy.'

Why hadn't she known it herself? Were there signs she'd missed? Girlie *had* been moody when they'd returned from the beach.

It would do no good to be visibly agitated. She had slipped; quick to blame Girlie and revealing more than she ought. There had to be a simple explanation for Tommy's behaviour. Lily gathered herself together, released tension pulling furrows across her forehead and jaw.

The voices of a young couple blew across to them on the wind. Their laughter jagged in Lily's chest as she watched the young man feed his girl the corner of a sandwich. Giggling, the girl shoved him, and he scooped her by the waist, taking her out beyond the line of trees.

Lily exchanged glances with Lorna, letting out the air in her chest. 'Hard to believe Ernie and I were young like that once,' she said with forced levity, folding up a dishcloth. 'So young and so naive.'

Lorna didn't respond. Lily looked up to see her trace a finger along the top of the table. 'There's no shame in keeping things from our husbands – we all do. How else can we keep a marriage together? If they knew all our secrets and we theirs, no one would stay married.'

'You can't surely mean that, Lorna.'

Lorna coughed. 'Oh, I do! I've had a gutful of Bill. I wish I had the gumption to leave him, but I don't think I ever would. The idea of it keeps me going, still. If Bill ever found out . . . I know I can confide in you, Lily, which is why I don't mind telling you I loathe the man. He's a brute and he's just so, so old. Look at me. I've given up my best years for a man who doesn't even appreciate me anymore. I sometimes don't see him from Friday through to Sunday night.'

Lily flinched as a group of golfers cheered loudly. She waited until they roamed past, then leaned in, whispering, 'Where does he go?'

'I don't know and don't care. All I know is I'm lonely.' Lorna shrugged. 'But I'd rather that than be alone. You know, frying pan into the fire.'

Lily reached for Lorna's arm and gave it a squeeze. Neither of them was living the life they thought they would. 'Well, you've got me as a friend.' And she believed the words as she uttered them. She still hoped to gain other, more important women's favour, but for now Lorna was the only person who'd given her something – admiration – in return for her efforts.

Lorna shook it off, waving away her feelings like smoke. 'How ever did I get so maudlin? What will you do about your brother?'

'I'll speak to him.'

'I understand,' Lorna said, nodding. 'Bill would be the same if he had a daughter, he'd kill any man who did that to her.'

The weight of Lily's secrets pressed against her lips, formed a barrier between her and any genuine friendship she could have with Lorna. If she told even an inch of where Girlie had come from, unravelling the lie she had crafted for herself, the whole façade of her marriage and family would crumble. No longer the obedient wife and natural mother. She'd taken in a four-year-old, already too old to be rocked in a cradle and sung nursery lullabies. But Lily did these anyway, compensation for Ernie's reticence with the child. He held back, didn't know how to pay Girlie attention, and she could see her wanting it. She recognised that same hunger for recognition. The stark contrast with Lily's own relationship with her father – Pa holding her hand at the track, pointing out racehorses he fancied, and letting her ride on his back when they got home: her very own gee gee. He was the sun she spun around;

his attention turned night into day. She would have promised him anything to bask in that feeling of absolute adoration.

At least Ernie gave Girlie the protection of a safe home. Lily felt hot shame and resentment when she caught him staring at Girlie when she wasn't looking. It was like he was assessing her, drawing comparisons. Though Lily behaved as a mother should, Ernie's expression made her despise herself. For didn't she have similar thoughts? She accepted her self-loathing as her penance, doubling her determination to create a 'normal' childhood for Girlie so she would not feel different to any other child. Girlie didn't have a father's devotion, but Lily wouldn't wish her an emotionally absent and sometimes cruel mother, like she'd had. Would she have felt differently if Girlie had been a boy? Ma had never punished Tommy for his naughtiness – sighing and saying, *Boys will be boys,* and still giving him extra pudding.

A hubbub of golfers' chatter drifted across to them, and, glancing at the burn scar on the back of her hand, Lily pulled on her lace cotton gloves, raising her eyebrows at Lorna to bolster them against the onslaught of drinks requests.

Lorna shot out from behind the table. 'Darla! What happened?'

Mrs Lovett and Mrs Booth stood each side of a hobbling Darla McGinty. 'Poor Mrs McGinty's injured her ankle. Is there ice we can fix to it?' asked Mrs Booth.

Lily untied her apron and hurried out to help Lorna ease Darla onto a stool. 'I'm afraid not,' she said, looking at Ernie who trailed behind his lame golf partner.

Darla winced, shaking her fist on her lap. 'Well, at least find someone to bring my car round for me.'

Lorna paced across the field to search for a driver.

Lily brought over a dishcloth she'd soaked in water, attempting to wind it around Darla's ankle; Darla sitting with her leg straight out and resting on Mrs Booth's lap. She waved her furled parasol at Lily, knocking her arm.

'I'll be fine. I'm just concerned our club's honour's at stake. We lost to Walkaway fifteen games to five last time. If one of a foursome is out, we can't play our match. I wager Walkaway is gloating already. And moreover, Mrs Worth was to give me her felt hat. Oh. Oh.'

Lily looked up in alarm as she unrolled the dishcloth from Darla's ankle.

Darla sniffed. 'What was Robert thinking, going out on the boat today when we needed our best gentlemen golfers?'

Lily frowned at Ernie. Had he done nothing during the day to impress Darla?

Darla looked her up and down, quite cross. 'You're going to have to play in my stead.'

A small hope leaped inside Lily that she could save the day for Dongarra and make Darla grateful. But she was useless at sports. What a bind! If she played, she was likely to reveal her failings and bear the blame for losing Darla her new hat. Reluctantly, she shook her head.

Lorna arrived to rescue her from Darla's withering look.

'The Reverend said he'll drive you, Darla.'

Lily stepped back as Ernie and Lorna helped Darla upright. Ernie doffed his cap at her. 'I'll find another partner, Mrs McGinty.'

Lorna held Darla's arm out for the Reverend to take from her. 'I'll play if you like. That is,' Lorna looked to Lily, 'if it is all right with you.'

Lily checked with Ernie to see how this suited. To her annoyance, he stared at Lorna, chewing his inside cheek, when this alternative arrangement would save the Dongarra side's dignity, and the Hasses' standing.

'Ernie, this is Lorna Fairclough. We met through the CWA,' she said. 'Lorna, my husband, Ernie.'

Ernie hesitated, but Lorna was more accommodating. 'How do you do, Mr Hass? Pleased to formally make your acquaintance at last.'

The day had been illuminating. Of all the people Lily had hoped to rely on to secure her family's position in town – the Frys, both Mrs McGintys, her own husband – there was only Lorna, bold in all aspects of manner and dress. This friendship was a risky proposition. But the safe and solid options of Darla McGinty and the other lady office-bearers of the CWA were out of reach. She could see that now. Besides, she thought optimistically, the contrast with Lorna might make her appear more respectable. She wouldn't let her mind travel the other direction, that a friendship with Lorna might reveal Lily's own undesirable qualities.

Qualities she could never let take root in Girlie.

CHAPTER TWENTY-ONE

ERNIE

The golfers decamped to the hall in town for the prize-giving ceremony, but Lil hadn't returned for the entertainments.

Bill Fairclough took the trophy from Gerry Paxton and cleared his throat to say a few words. 'I'd like to thank the Walkaway Golf Club under the able leadership of Denny Worth for putting up a good show today. Unfortunately for Walkaway, Dongarra was not such a pushover this time round. Sixteen to two, eh, Denny?'

The Dongarra crowd chuckled as the Walkaway team leader gestured their defeat. The Walkaway golfers sat on one side of the hall in tables of their foursomes, the Dongarra crowd the other, though with the addition of wives and husbands, the foursomes had become a little muddled.

Lorna had proved a more than adequate alternate partner. She had the shapely legs of a golfer, Ernie had glimpsed as she teed off. They'd beaten the Walkaway pair three and two.

Bill blathered on throughout the rest of the prize giving, raising laughs from both sides of the room. Ernie forced a laugh every now and then, keeping one eye on Lorna. She didn't twitch her lips for her husband. Not once. But she was necking that sherry.

'Another beer, gentlemen?' he asked. Matthew Fry and Gregory Booth, the banker, filled out their table. Neither of their wives were present. They shook their heads; they'd been nursing the one long-neck all evening. The run of the evening was his. If Lil hadn't come by now she wouldn't be coming, and he planned to make the most of it. Somehow he'd get a dance out of Bill's wife; he could just imagine the fevered state Bill would get in when he saw that. The old fool.

'All right, then.' Lorna covered her mouth as she burped slightly.

She was vulgar. Not a patch on Lily's refined ways. But look where they'd got him – always on the wrong side of her bed.

Supper was announced, bringing Bill back to the table where he took up the seat between his wife and Ernie. They shuffled their chairs apart to let him in.

'Where's the kidney pie? I thought you said you were making one,' Bill said, knifing at the leftover cold meats on his plate.

Chewing slowly, Lorna slipped her finger into her mouth to pick at her teeth. 'The butcher didn't bring any kidney.'

Bill snorted, sending a piece of gristle flying from his mouth. 'You're just too lazy to put in an order.'

'Yes, Bill.'

Ernie shot glances at Gregory and Matthew, but they were avoiding the other man's domestic strife.

Gregory edged his elbows onto the table. 'So, Matthew says you're expanding the store for the motorists.'

Ernie's first reaction was to deny it, but that would mean making a liar out of Matthew to his face. The word 'motorists' stopped Bill in his loud mastication.

Something perverse in Ernie felt like laying into him. 'True. Putting in a bowser in front of the store this week, before the summer tourists come.' And because he just couldn't help himself: 'Bill, you're the man I need to speak to about this.'

Bill pushed his plate away and leaned heavily on his forearms.

'You sell Atlantic Petrol, don't you?'

Bill grunted.

'My contacts tell me that stuff's too rough. Good enough for farming machinery, but these modern motors need petrol that's a bit more refined, like Shell's. A man's coming down from Geraldton this week to show me a few things. What else would you recommend I stock, Bill?'

Bill steepled his hands in front of him. 'You plan to put a bowser down at the beach?'

Ernie shrugged. 'That's about the gist of it.'

'Don't you think you should have consulted with me first as Chairman of the Beach Improvement Committee?'

'Well, it's rather a private business matter, Bill.'

Bill flexed his fingers. 'Not when you get queues of motor cars down there. A safety hazard and all. What with the jetty fire.'

Ernie bristled. But Lorna leaned in, placing her hand on Bill's forearm. 'Mr Hass is the caretaker of the beach, isn't he? He's not likely to put anyone at risk.'

Bill eyeballed him, glancing at Matthew and Gregory staring into the bottoms of their empty beer bottles. He shrugged off Lorna's hand and pushed his seat back. 'I'm not much in the mood for euchre tonight. I'm going home.'

Colour returned to Lorna's face, and she gave a nervous giggle. 'Oh, don't mind him. He's such an old fogey.'

'I'll get you a drink then, Lorna,' Ernie said. 'Gentlemen?'

'Mrs Booth is feeling poorly, she overtaxed herself in the fixture today. I'll be going,' said Gregory.

'Matthew?'

'I'll get them,' Matthew said. 'Baiting him was a bit much, Ernie. It won't bode well. Begging your pardon, Lorna.'

Lorna waved her hand airily. 'I'm sorry you had to see Bill like that.' She picked up their plates to take to the kitchen, leaving Ernie alone at the table, but the hall was suddenly too stuffy and he craved some outside air. He passed by Matthew at the entrance.

'Just going outside for a smoke.' Ernie pointed into the darkness.

Matthew looked from him to the empty table. 'I'd join you, but Mrs Fry's said I got to stop smoking. On account of my wheeze.'

Ernie felt put out by Matthew telling Bill his business, when he hadn't got his story straight yet. It was like being in bloody bankruptcy court all over again.

Others stood outside, hanging around the motor cars and trucks where many of the lads stored their bottles of beer. Mostly Walkaway folk, they didn't crowd him. He looked out across the street at the dark monstrous shapes of the fig trees, pondering Bill's reaction. Lorna mightn't have been offended but Ernie sure as hell was. Bill had fairly implied he wasn't cut out for the caretaker job, undermining him with that talk about the jetty fire as if he had something to do with it. The muscles in his neck tightened in ropes.

'Don't mind some company?'

He turned, saw it was Lorna and relaxed his shoulders. The way she'd stepped in to support him like that, standing up to her own husband. If Lily had done such a thing, Ernie would have done his rag with her, sent her home. A woman shouldn't argue against her man. He smiled at Lorna. 'Sure,' he said, lighting her cigarette.

'It's pretty out here at night. The stars. You know, I sometimes wonder if they're not all the souls of people we've lost, set up there to watch over us, let us know we're going to be all right.'

Ernie glanced at the sky. Flushed, at her talking of such things as though they were intimate with each other. A Walkaway couple jostled past, and he noticed the lads were peeling away from their booze to go back inside. 'You'll miss the start of the euchre party,' he said.

'So will you. Besides, you're my partner, aren't you?'

They locked gazes with each other for a second, and he felt a flicker in his groin. 'You did well today. That tee off the ninth against the wind. Should be my partner the next time. If Darla McGinty doesn't mind.' His laughter came out thin.

'Golf I don't mind, but I'm not one for euchre.' She ground out her cigarette against the post.

He swallowed. 'I'll take you home.' She lived just up the road past the Liddles' place, but he was chancing on her taking the risk. She might appear sentimental about souls and stars and the like, but he knew her type.

'All right.' Not even a moment's hesitation.

He walked across to the paddock beside the school, leading Brownie back to the dray where he harnessed him up. He stood aside for Lorna, holding her hand, trying not to stare at her legs as she stepped up. But she caught him at it and flipped the edge of her skirt over to show him a fancy pattern. 'Pretty, don't you think? Your wife sewed it for me.'

'Ah, yeah.' The dress was a rebuke, like Lily was watching everywhere his eyes roamed. Sewing. Hadn't he told her no? That story about sewing dresses for Mrs Feehely's daughters. The flicker in his groin was more of a twitch now. 'There's a blanket behind the seat there you can sit on. You don't want to get yourself dirty.'

When he swung himself up to the bench, he found she'd slid over towards the middle, her legs crossed so that when he geed up the horse his hand brushed her knee. The first time he glanced at her to apologise but she was staring up at the sky with a smile on her. Looking at the stars so she hadn't noticed the indiscretion. The second time he was sure she felt it but didn't move. Brazen, he flung his hand out so his fingertips skimmed her thigh.

Ernie was twitching in his skin like a bag of rabbits. He slowed as they turned the curve past the Liddles'. He gave her a sideways glance. She was watching him, pushing him. He geed Brownie on, and his thumb dragged on the hem of her skirt, flipping it over and he saw that pattern. The one Lily had made. Blood surged to his head, turning a sweat on his brow. It was like Lily had done this to him on purpose. Making him fidget, teasing and then turning away.

'Nice night. We can drive for a bit, if you like. Out of town you can see more stars, less light.' His heart pounded while he waited for her to reply.

'Bill will be in a state still.'

He turned to look at her. They were approaching the Faircloughs' house now. 'So . . .'

She shifted her backside, pulling out a cigarette from her case. She put it between her lips, expectant.

Ernie leaned over, one hand still on the reins and lit it for her.

He took the dray out onto the Irwin Road past the east end of town. 'There's a bottle of hop beer beneath the seat if you're thirsty.'

She twisted around, fumbling for the bottle. She pulled out the beer. 'How am I supposed to open it?'

'Hold on, I'll stop just up the road.' Only a few folk had houses roundabout and there wasn't a light on for miles. In the thin moonlight he picked out a clearing in the scrub where he reined in Brownie.

The heavy silence of the bush night brought her presence closer, brought what was happening closer. He slipped down from the dray, inhaling the wet earth smell. She passed the bottle down to him. Drinking would give him thinking time. With a sharp flint he hacked off the lid. The beer frothed up warm over his hand and he passed the bottle to his other hand shaking off his arm like a wet dog.

'Ladies first,' he said, offering her the bottle. She stepped down from the dray, holding the blanket round her body though the nights were coming warm again and Ernie was sweating like a farm horse.

She drank and handed the bottle back to him, wiping her mouth with the blanket. 'Well, you've got manners,' she said, then laughed. 'Nice place for a picnic.'

'Not a bad idea.' He pulled the end of the blanket from her grip, and she fell towards him. He caught her, squeezing her arms, running his hand down to her waist.

He made to pull her to the ground. 'Wait,' she said, groping for the blanket and spreading it out. She lay down on it. 'Now.'

CHAPTER TWENTY-TWO

GIRLIE

The clock ticked without seeming to move forwards. Girlie fought the temptation to look through the tall windows, for any movement at all. Two big blackboards on the wall between the windows instructed the class in what they ought to be doing, but she stifled a yawn instead. So, so tired.

'Only three weeks left of school term,' Mr Peters said. 'And testing begins next week. No slacking off. Do you understand, Master Smith?' He brought his cane down with a thwack on Joe's desk.

Girlie drew her hand down into her lap quickly lest Mr Peters thought her skiving. Her limbs felt heavy, like with a flu, and she hadn't joined in with the skipping games at lunchtime.

What's the matter? Susan had asked, narrowing her eyes at Girlie.

Susan had giggled and whispered with Mary Ellen, Maud and Polly, who took turns to cast glances across at her. Was Susan sharing her secret about Ruby?

She didn't know why she was so tired. It could have been because her father had come in late on Saturday night after the golf tournament. Waking her with his swearing as he tripped over something in the yard, dropping Brownie's harness.

He must have woken her mother, too, because she was grouchy all day yesterday after church. Made Girlie practise long at the piano, only saying, *Softer, pianissimo, pianissimo* and *Louder, strike the keys* and *Play it again*. Punishing her. For Susan's house being filthy. For not being able to play the piano as well as her mother, or *her* mother, had done.

Girlie scrunched shoulders to ease the pain in her neck. Everything hurt in her body, flipping from side to side last night like the bed was made of rock. But school holidays were coming. She collected her books when the bell rang, shoving them in her satchel to catch up with Susan. If Susan thought Girlie had airs and graces, she'd have to prove her wrong, let her know she didn't think on things like the state of her house as her mother did. But first she had to find her alone.

Swish. Mr Peters' cane sliced through the air.

Girlie slowed her feet at his warning. She'd already had to spend time mixing ink today, she didn't want further punishment. Not that she'd done anything wrong; just sitting in the classroom during lunchtime while the girls were skipping.

Out in the school yard, Susan was playing jacks with Maud. They gathered the jacks when Girlie came close, knees like jelly at what they might have said about her since lunchtime.

'Will you walk home with me, Susan?'

Mary Ellen called out and Maud murmured something to Susan, running off in her direction. 'Come on, then,' said Susan, pulling up her socks. Not the rejection Girlie had half expected.

Before, they would lark about on their walks home. Now Susan marched ahead and Girlie trailed after, holding the pain in her side. 'Wait up,' she cried, folding in half to get rid of her stitch. She counted to ten and stood upright, breathing heavily. Susan was too far away, she needed to bring her closer. 'Are you coming over to practise today?'

Her mother seemed to want her to continue with the duet. But for Girlie to continue, she would need to compose an 'outside face', pretending that she and Susan were still friends.

Hands on her hips, Susan shook her head. Girlie's breath hitched in her chest. 'Can't today,' Susan said. 'Got to help Mum with the preserves for the trip.'

'Oh, I forgot about that.' She hadn't. Earlier in the school term Susan had suggested Girlie could join the Frys on their annual family holiday, melon picking near Carnarvon. Susan had to ask her mother first. And then her mother had to speak to Girlie's mother. Girlie hadn't heard anything from anybody. And she didn't think she would.

'It sounds like a dream, a holiday like that with your family.'

Susan snorted. 'Nightmare!'

Girlie summoned her energy to hurry across the bridge. Seeing Joe and Bobby down on the bank by the ford, she stopped short, catching her breath.

Susan noticed. 'They won't bother you. Catching yabbies, aren't they?'

Bobby scooped the shallow pool with his tin.

Just once Girlie wished she had the guts to yell 'Chicken!' and run towards them. But she didn't even have the strength to keep up with Susan, who'd skipped the full length of the bridge. Girlie made it a few yards before folding over. Couldn't breathe.

Susan stood shouting. Girlie cast a glance over the railing towards the rocks and the boys, and back to Susan twenty yards away. Girlie waved her hand to say, *Don't shout*, but Susan took it as a goodbye wave, turned around and skidded down the bank to her place.

Girlie felt like the girls at school had pulled up a drawbridge and she had no way to cross the moat. She didn't have the password to be let into their secrets, and desperately, inwardly she knew that those secrets were about her. Susan knew everything about every child at the school: knew who was smoking behind the dunnies, who'd been skinned by their father's belt on the Saturday, who'd been eating onion soup seven nights a week.

Had Susan guessed that Girlie was adopted, and sniggered about it with Maud, Mary Ellen and Polly at lunchtime? No one wanted to be friends with the unwanted girl.

A pang-like vomit rose sharp in her throat. Uncle Tommy had known and he'd not been in town long, never met her before. Who else in town already knew? She hung her head, feeling like the last person to know. Why hadn't her mother ever told her? Her mother who scowled when Girlie jumped in puddles, who shouted when she ran, who hurt Girlie's fingers when she didn't play well at the piano. Her mother was ashamed. Because Girlie wasn't as good as a proper daughter. If her mother had loved her more, she might have told her the truth. But her mother sang away any answers.

~

'What is that?'

Girlie's fingers trembled over the ivory keys. She'd gone to the piano as soon as she got home. No time to wash and her fingers were stained indigo, like bruises.

'Answer me. Stop being a ninny. Speak up.' Her mother grabbed her right hand, squeezing it. Her mother had hovered over her like a hawk since Saturday.

'Ink,' she whispered.

'What am I going to do with you? Ten years old with the habits of an infant.'

'Ten and a third,' Girlie said through closed lips so the words barely escaped.

'When I was your age I would never have disrespected my mother the way you do. She wouldn't have condoned such sloppiness, mark my words.'

More evidence she was not her mother's real daughter. Her stomach caved like she'd been punched. *Don't cry*, she cautioned herself.

'I'm trying my hardest. I'm so sorry, Mummy.'

Her mother stiffened. 'I won't give up on you, Girlie. Not like my mother did. I'm just asking you to do your share.'

Girlie sniffed, and spread her fingers to match the melody note with the chord. Her pinky finger only just reached. She played the rest of 'My Melancholy Baby', tensing when she hit an E note instead of an E sharp. But it was better than she'd played all week, without Susan to accompany her with vocals. They would need to be in step with each other during the recital. When she was done she turned to her mother, who stared straight ahead, running her tongue over her teeth.

Was this a good or bad sign? Did she wonder why Susan hadn't come to practise today?

'Verna and Elizabeth Liddle aren't much older than you, but they've done their third-grade examinations in pianoforte. They're at St Dominic's. I'm thinking,' her mother said, turning to look at Girlie, examining her, tucking a curl behind her ear, 'I might make enquiries about sending you there.'

~

That night Girlie kneeled for prayers before bed as Mrs Pearson instructed them at Sunday school. 'Dear Father who art in Heaven,' she muttered, 'please change Mummy's mind about sending me to the convent school. Please make her see that it's not my fault Susan doesn't want to come here, that there's something wrong with me that the girls whisper about, that I can't be like Mummy, that I try hard but the piano doesn't come naturally to me. Please make her proud of me so she forgets I'm not her real daughter and she'll want to keep me.'

She was socked in the stomach again. Slipping into bed, she wound herself into a tight ball, rocking from side to side, gaining no relief, tangled up in the sheets. She sat up to straighten them, and gasped. On the sheet was a dirty mark. She checked her hands, but she'd scrubbed the ink off with carbolic and her skin was pink. The stain on her sheet didn't look like ink in any case, more like mud.

She lifted her nightdress to see if she'd trailed it in from the privy. Buckled at the sight of a stain in her knickers – soiled.

Girlie pulled them off, blood pounding in her ears, and wiped the dirty streaks from her legs. Silently, she eased the drawer open for clean knickers, fear roaring through her body.

~

Girlie slept fitfully, seized by the memory of her shame when she woke. Throwing the sheet back, she saw she'd soiled herself again, but it was tinged crimson like blood. Bleeding like she was dying. Being punished by God. It was all her fault. Not Susan's or the other girls', or her mother's. She was the wrong one, didn't deserve what she'd been given. A cuckoo in the nest.

The loud scraping of chairs and clanging of metal in the kitchen meant the door was open and Girlie might not be able to get her soiled clothing and sheets to the wash house without her mother seeing. She scrambled from the bed and stripped her mattress.

'Girlie!'

Her breath left her all at once. Turning, she faced her mother, her shame bundled in her arms. Her mother shot a look at the sheets and covered her mouth. 'Oh no.'

Girlie blinked back tears. 'I'm sorry.'

Her mother didn't move to comfort her, and she felt her judgement, swollen with the heat of her disgrace.

'But . . . but you're only ten,' her mother said, her eyes still wide, twisting her wedding ring.

Girlie dropped her head. 'And a third,' she whispered. What did it matter how old she was, if she would be dead soon?

Her mother turned on her heel, striding to the wash house where Girlie heard her tear at fabric. When she came back, she brandished a wad of linen strips. 'You're a woman now. You'll need your monthly rags.'

Girlie took hold of the rags, uncertain.

'Follow me,' said her mother, lifting a warning finger to her lips. Girlie waddled behind her to the bathroom, where her father had installed an enamelled bath for the guests; but Girlie hadn't been allowed to use it, still having her Sunday wash in the iron tub in the kitchen. Her mother filled the bath tub with hot water already boiled in the copper that morning. 'A hot bath will make your pains go away.'

Girlie stared. Confused that her mother was rewarding her. She tested the water with her toes; it burned at first but the dreadful aching, as though her flesh were being torn out from the inside, disappeared as she lowered herself in. Blood swirled in the water. 'It's not stopped, Mummy!' she cried out.

'And it's not going to. You'll bleed every month until you're older than me.' Her mother rubbed the carbolic soap hard between her hands to get a lather. 'It's the cross we women must bear.'

Heaviness dragged through Girlie's body. How much more did she have to bear? Why had her mother never warned her this would happen? She screwed up her eyes, holding back the tears. Why had her mother never told her anything? Instead, Girlie had made a patchwork of her mother's overheard words and words unsaid, of changeable moods, and the looks people had given her, that formed a secret so terrible that her mother had to keep it hidden, from even her family.

~

After her bath, Girlie went inside for breakfast, walking self-consciously with the rags stuffed between her legs. She tried not to act shocked when she saw her mother smoking a cigarette. Nice women weren't supposed to smoke.

Her mother coughed. 'So, now you know our secret.'

If her mother was also being punished by God, it had something to do with Girlie being adopted. She felt her face grow hot. 'I can keep a secret.' She stared at her mother, daring her to tell her about the adoption. The bleeding had changed her more than she thought. Older, more courageous. Growing up meant learning what her mother kept hidden, meant being trusted.

She flicked her gaze from the ashtray to her mother's hands, to the clock, anywhere but her mother's eyes.

'Tell me plainly,' her mother said, and swallowed loudly before adding the next part. 'Has a man ever laid his hands on you?'

Girlie scrunched up her forehead and nodded. She didn't understand, but this must be part of why her mother was ashamed of her. In time she would learn how the blood and her adoption fitted together.

Her mother moaned, crushing her cigarette so the paper broke apart, spilling out its tobacco and dropping embers onto the table top.

'Mr Peters did. He carried me when I fainted.'

'And no one else?' Her mother's voice was flat and peculiar, like she was being forced to speak.

Girlie shook her head, no. All these questions that had nothing to do with the secret. Her mother sighed, gazed at her deeply, the circles around her eyes darkened and Girlie held her breath.

But then her mother nodded, looked away.

Girlie's courage seeped from her like the monthly blood. She had to let her mother know that she knew what her mother was ashamed of. That her mother didn't have to pretend anymore.

'Is Girlie my real name?'

Her mother wiped the table, cleaning away the ash and tobacco she'd dropped. 'Of course not. It's Emma.'

'Emma?' Girlie's heart dropped into her ribs. This was the moment everything would change.

'My mother's name,' her mother said quietly, rubbing at the back of her hand. 'But you're called Girlie just as your father's Aunty Myrtle was always known. It's a family nickname.'

A stabbing pain rippled in her lower belly, bending her double. A family nickname. Their daughter, but not. Girlie, but Emma. A girl, but a woman. She'd thought she'd learned her mother's secret, but now she knew even less about where she belonged.

'Hurry up and get ready for school,' her mother said, banging pots and dishes together in the sink. 'I'll take you to the tearoom for ice-cream this afternoon.'

'No!' Girlie cried, thinking of the last time she went to the tearoom, for the recipe. Her mother turned sharply, her brows pulled together in a worried question. 'I don't want Mrs McGinty to know what's happened to me,' she explained as an excuse.

Her mother sighed. 'She won't. This is how life is, you'll get used to carrying on as normal.'

Girlie tore her eyes from her mother's. She *was* becoming like her, hiding away her shame.

CHAPTER TWENTY-THREE

LILY

'Mrs Hass, may I have a word?'

Constable Paxton didn't wait for Lily's answer as he stepped across the threshold of the shop. Disconcerted, she plunged the rice scoop back in the bag. She was immediately defensive, but Gerry was a friend of Ernie's. 'I'm afraid Ernie's not home at present. Perhaps you'd like to come back another time?'

Gerry removed his hat. 'It isn't your husband I'm here to see. I've come regarding some of my other duties, which concern you.'

Lorna's allegation against Tommy. It could only be. She would tell him there was no truth to it.

Lily listened for Tommy chopping wood outside, and lowered her voice. 'Please come through to the sitting room.'

She directed Gerry to Ernie's easy chair, then closed the door to the shop firmly behind her. She hadn't known how to broach such a topic with Tommy. Men had animalistic urges, she knew only too well, and the knowledge and fear of where those urges could lead sickened her.

She sat on the chair underneath the window. The police truck was parked right outside, signalling her business to all passers-by.

Worse, Mrs McGinty would see, and lately she'd been aloof, passing Lily the weekly mail with the barest of greetings. But there was nothing that Lily could think of that might have turned Mrs McGinty against her this way. Except . . . Tommy. She glanced at Gerry, trying to remember which of his eyes was the one to look at.

'Can I fetch you some tea, constable?'

He cleared his throat, clenching his notepad between his hands. 'No, thank you. It's best if I get on with it.'

The door opened, making her jump.

'Mummy?' It was Girlie, studying Gerry from beneath her fringe.

Lily recovered herself just enough to see him thoughtfully observe her reaction.

'Go and start on dinner, there's potatoes to peel and chop,' she said, dismissing Girlie, who left the door open on leaving.

She offered a grimace to show Gerry how she was endlessly tested. 'No matter how many times she's told, she never listens.' She added a nervous laugh, getting up to close the door. 'So, constable, can I ask what the purpose is of this visit?'

He tapped his pencil on his notebook. 'I've had word that you have a Mrs Feehely working for you.'

'Yes, but I haven't paid her any wages yet,' Lily said, sitting down, flooded with relief that it was a simple matter. She started drumming her fingers on her lap to dispel her nervous tension. 'Should I arrange matters with you if I were to? I know how it works. We had a domestic servant from the Aborigines Department before.'

He cleared his throat. 'The Feehelys are exempted Aboriginals, but as local protector, it's in my remit to make sure they don't, as it were, slide backwards. I'm sure you understand.'

'I see.' She stilled her fingers. A fear of sliding backwards *was* something she understood, and in this she felt a sympathetic kinship with Mrs Feehely. But she had a constant reminder to improve herself – the photograph hidden in her tin. 'I shall make sure to keep an eye on her.' She toyed with the button on her collar. 'Was it Mrs Fairclough who informed you?'

The focus of his eyes split apart. 'I'm not at liberty to say. But we've had more than one account of your family associating with the Feehelys.'

'*Mrs* Feehely,' emphasised Lily. 'I am making dresses for her daughters, but they do not come here.'

'But your daughter, Mrs Hass,' he said. Lily clenched her fist, digging her fingernails into her palms. 'How well do you know who she spends time with?'

Her initial concern for Tommy returned; she held in her stomach, squared her shoulders. 'Let me see. There's her friend from school, Susan Fry.' That was all. Girlie hadn't talked about any other little friends. Damn. Why did Girlie have to befriend that wretched girl? That business with her brother, Larry, and the Red Cross can. To think, Ernie had asked him to help in the shop.

'I'm aware of the rumours regarding her eldest brother, but I hardly think Susan's similarly inclined. She and my daughter are practising a duet for the church annual fair.'

Both of Gerry's eyes fixed on her. 'I'm not speaking of Susan Fry. It is Ruby Feehely I've heard that Girlie associates with.'

Lily frowned. 'I'm sorry, I don't follow. Mrs Feehely's daughter? I don't see how.'

'I think a great deal of your husband and don't want to see his name tarred by rumour. It's my business to look into the blacks' affairs when they create some attention.'

'Even if they are exempted.' Lily stood up, irritated at having been frightened for one matter only to be knocked about by town gossip. She'd known gossip before, and life afterwards was a constant struggle to repair the family's reputation. 'I appreciate the warning, constable. I'm sorry, I really must get back to the shop.' While she was vulnerable, her guard down, she might say the wrong thing.

'Right you are, Mrs Hass. Just so as I'm doing my duty,' he said, pocketing his notebook and pulling on his hat. 'If you do find any cause for complaint,' he cast a look at the closed door, 'I can have them moved on.'

She nodded, though she didn't care for a discussion on the Aboriginal Problem when she had to recompose herself for the evening's CWA meeting.

She watched the police truck until it disappeared round the curve of the Beach Road. On the shore, facing the sea, was Reg McGinty, his hat in his hands and wind mussing up his hair. It looked as though he was waiting for a boat to come in, but a glance at the boats moored in the hole indicated that his son Robert wasn't out fishing today.

Reg turned back up to the road, catching sight of her staring at him. He appeared to hesitate before raising his hat and she lifted her hand in response to his greeting. But he didn't come her way, and returned to the McGintys' cottage.

Lily closed the shop door, flicking back the front blind, and wondered if the change in Martha McGinty's attitude towards her was because of some personal slight. Had she gone about making friendships the wrong way?

'Was that the constable?' asked Tommy.

Lily's stomach lurched. 'Tommy! Don't sneak up on me like that.' She smoothed down the sides of her dress. 'Yes, it was. Nothing to do with Ernie and me. He had other concerns.'

He ran his hand over his face. 'The jetty fire.'

'No,' she said, faltering. 'No. That's not what he came for.' She stared at him. What was going on in his head? The rifle accident on the truck and him running away signalled something was not right with his mind. If his troubles worsened, he could ruin everything she and Ernie had been trying to build for themselves. Oh, was *this* the cause of Mrs McGinty's strangeness towards her?

He clasped his hands behind his head bringing his elbows forward. The look of a vulnerable man. He shook his head slowly between his hands. 'It's not what you think.' He slammed his palm against his temple. 'I'm better now, I really am. You believe me, don't you?'

He grabbed at her arms.

'Tommy,' she said calmly, controlled, lifting his hands off her arms one at a time. 'Tommy, I'm here. You must tell me everything.'

~

Lily sat beside Lorna in Mrs Liddle's fading front room, presenting a façade of calm when, underneath, fracture lines had formed. Tommy's revelation posed her with one foot either side of a widening chasm. Which side was she to choose? Ernie was her husband and she had made vows of obedience, but there had been vows she'd made to her father for Tommy. When she'd had to choose before, Ernie had convinced her that leaving Tommy at the Lemnos Hospital had been for the best. Until Tommy had turned up again in Dongarra, forcing her to come face-to-face with the consequences of that decision.

Was it really so important who'd set the jetty alight? According to Ernie, the only people in town put out were the fishermen who hadn't ceased their grumbling about the netting ban. And if it hadn't been for the fire, Ernie wouldn't have been given the caretaker role.

Lily was torn from her thoughts by the Younger Set who, having been welcomed and ensconced, now enthusiastically asked questions and nominated themselves for duties. If any of them asked for Mrs Booth to demonstrate making a hook rug, she thought, she would pointedly turn around and glare at them. Mrs Booth didn't know anything about good taste but Lily had overheard her at church last week discussing decorations for the hall.

Mrs Booth and the other lady office-bearers seemed further away from Lily than ever. Their premier position among the town ladies wasn't related to matters of taste or friendship or seating arrangements, but because theirs was always the right side.

'It is decided that all members under forty years shall participate in the ladies' team,' said Mrs Liddle, to excited murmurs and low cheers from the back of the room. Lily inwardly groaned. She'd hoped to get out of having to play in the novelty cricket match next weekend.

After supper, Lily returned her plate to the table.

'Some tea, Mrs Hass? Or if you prefer, there is chicory in the urn.'

Lily shook her head. 'No, thank you, Mrs Booth. I was wondering though, who decorates the hall for the church fair recital, because, I . . . well, I think I would be happy to help. I have had some ideas.'

Mrs Booth frowned. 'The decorating committee. But you'll have to speak to Gladys Pearson about that.'

About to ask if Mrs Booth could put in a good word for her, she clamped the thought as Darla approached with her cup and saucer.

Lily bided her time waiting for it to be filled. After the golf tournament, she'd half given up trying for Darla's friendship. But this was a laxness that could lead to disaster. If there was any truth to the constable's claim, on top of what might be construed of Tommy's behaviour, there would be no redemption for the family in the town's eyes. Before Darla could turn from her, Lily cleared her throat.

Darla cocked an eyebrow.

'I wonder if I may be so bold as to ask you where you sent your children to school?' Lily asked, hesitantly.

Darla ruminated as though entertaining the idea to ignore her question, curdling Lily's stomach with anxiety. 'The boys went down to the city for boarding. At Hale School,' said Darla eventually.

Lily swallowed. 'I am thinking of enrolling Girlie at the convent school. She needs more . . . discipline.' She regretted her choice of words immediately as Darla replaced her cup in the saucer and handed it to Mrs Booth.

'Quite.' And with that, Darla left her to speak to somebody she'd gestured to over Lily's shoulder, which now slumped.

'Some tea, I think, after all, Mrs Booth.'

Mrs Booth finished pouring a cup of tea for Miss Flanagan of the Younger Set and passed a cup to Lily, saying, 'The fees are fifty pounds a year for St Dominic's, my dear. Though I hear there's the Trinity examiner coming up on the ninth to assess the girls for music scholarships. You should ask Daphne Liddle, she would know.'

Stepping aside for Miss Flanagan to pass, Lily sidled back to Mrs Booth, unwilling to show her dismay at the cost of the fees. These women hardly knew the state of economic depression felt by their counterparts elsewhere, cushioned as they were by tradition and claims to the town. 'I'm sure a scholarship won't be necessary.' She beat a polite retreat to the corner of the room by the faded tapestry wall hanging.

The ninth of December was next Friday, only a week away. Fifty pounds! It would be too much of a sacrifice. The savings in her tin buffered her from more than mere economic hardship; they meant being able to set down roots, build up her standing within a community rather than be forced from town to town. She could not take the risk.

'Cheer up, Lily,' Lorna said, swooping in from the other side of the room. 'Look on the cricket match as competition against your husband. A bit of rivalry's always good for getting your own back for any grievances.' Her eyes twinkled.

'I suppose.' Lily nodded absently. A brush at her elbow made her flinch.

'Mrs Hass,' said Mrs Liddle, appearing beside them. 'Your crab stew was delicious.'

Lily pressed her lips into their practised smile. 'Thank you, Mrs Liddle.' She'd followed Mrs Feehely's recipe, but after Gerry's visit that day she wasn't about to broadcast the news.

'I thought to tell you I find myself admiring your choice of frock tonight, Mrs Fairclough,' said Mrs Liddle. 'Lovely and well fitting.' Her tone implied the addendum of *for once*.

'Thank you. It was Mrs Hass who altered it for me.' Lorna's tone showed that she wasn't fooled by the compliment.

'My, you are clever. What a talent,' said Mrs Liddle to Lily. 'Your husband must be very proud of you.' Lily demurred. 'We all think you a welcome addition to this town.'

Not everyone, she thought, still feeling the sting of Darla's dismissal. This might be the occasion to let Mrs Liddle know of her plans to send Girlie to St Dominic's. But she had a flicker of doubt – how galling would it feel if Ernie wouldn't pay the fees?

'My husband tells me how much Mr Hass is doing for the community with regards to the beach improvements,' Mrs Liddle continued. 'I needn't mention the fire on the jetty highlights the extent of work required.'

The knots in her stomach loosened. Ernie hadn't left her to shoulder all the burden, he'd made valuable relationships in town.

'I hear Mr Liddle's sailboat is repaired as new after the fire,' Lily said. 'Mr Hass is going out with him this Sunday to see if they can find this shark that's been menacing the line fishermen.'

Mrs Liddle bobbed her head. 'Strange business, that fire. Someone must know something. It's not a very large town. I had *my* husband with me all night. I wonder, Mrs Fairclough, did you have yours?' Her left eyebrow flicked upwards. Lily followed Mrs Liddle's gaze to see Lorna's cheeks flush, a light sheen of perspiration on her brow. Had Bill not been at the dance, with his predilection to stray on the weekends?

Lorna dabbed her lips with her handkerchief slowly and deliberately, keeping her gaze locked on Mrs Liddle. If Lily's guess was correct, Mrs Liddle was being most unkind.

'It might have been a tourist,' said Lorna. 'I suppose we'll never know.'

Lily took a sip of tea to wet her tongue. 'I think Mrs Fairclough's conclusion is likely.'

'We'll see.' Mrs Liddle gave Lorna a tight smile. 'Once again, I commend your crab stew, Mrs Hass,' she said, and joined the girls of the Younger Set still gabbling about sporting strategy.

When Mrs Liddle was out of sight, Lorna harrumphed, then winked conspiratorially. 'I would recognise Mrs Feehely's crab stew anywhere. I'd say Darla McGinty knows it too. I haven't seen her eat any tonight.'

It struck Lily that perhaps Darla was acting snooty because her former domestic now worked for her, thinking Lily was acting above her station. Could it have been Darla who'd sent Gerry Paxton?

'Lorna,' Lily said in a low tone, 'why would the constable be interested in Mrs Feehely's working for me?'

'What?'

'The constable came down to the house this afternoon. Somebody in town had informed him that I've employed Mrs Feehely.'

Lorna narrowed her eyes. 'I'm fed up to dolly's wax with the double standards in this town. You can be assured it wasn't me. But I have a fair idea of who might take against Mrs Feehely.' She stood aside, flinging her hand to encompass the room of ladies sitting and standing, engrossed in their chatter. 'A small town, but they keep their secrets close. What I would give for some honesty.' Her nostrils flared, and Lily inched away from Lorna in her state. The ladies closest to them, Mrs Smith and Mrs Lovett, had turned sharply at Lorna's voice.

'Please, Lorna. I don't think Mrs Liddle was implying that Bill set the fire,' Lily said. Lorna shook her head, looking blank. 'You know,' she continued, 'what she said about being with her husband at the dance, the night of the fire.'

Lorna touched the tip of her tongue to her lip. 'Perhaps I could start by telling Mrs Liddle some truths about *her* husband's philandering. Who he was supposed to have been with the night of the jetty fire.'

Perspiration prickled Lily's upper lip. 'Who?'

Lorna put her hand on her hip, pushing out her chest. 'Who do you think? Well,' she said, tipping her chin, 'what's good for the goose, etcetera.'

Lorna and Mr Liddle?

Lily begged off the rest of the social evening with a headache, unable to pretend to Lorna's face that she hadn't found her admission shocking, and questioned her own judgement. She couldn't understand what drove women like Lorna and her mother to it – weren't the demands of a husband more than enough?

But more pressing matters vied for attention in her exhausted mind. She retired to bed early, Ernie not yet home from one of his committee meetings in town. Whatever Mrs Liddle thought, it was impossible to know where a man was at all hours of the day and night, no matter how small the community.

Lying down only made her mind race more, retrieving and examining every concern, figment and piece of information that had passed through it in the day, so she wrapped her dressing gown around herself and set about making a cup of warm milk.

Lamplight made a halo around the shelves of boxes and tins and jars, the sacks of flour lined up on the floor by the counter, and she was reminded of Ernie's diligence and care in stocking the shop, his plans for the future. What was she doing, keeping Tommy's secret from her husband? He was the caretaker of the beach, and she was withholding information he should have. Only, it condemned her brother.

She moved quickly to check for milk in the charcoal cooler to take back to the kitchen, thinking the whole time of the secrets she was piling up against Ernie. He would find out. Marriage was so much easier when the secrets could be tucked away, pushed to a dark corner so life could continue as though they didn't exist. But this was different. He'd been distant from her all week, since the golf tournament. She'd expected him to be angry at her for not partnering him on the golf course, braced to have to capitulate to his physical urges in the night. But he hadn't bothered her for so much as a goodnight this past week.

The house was silent and she found herself hovering by the guest corridor, listening, but it was only the sound of warning bells in her mind. She shook her head and strode to the stove, raking over the embers. A flume of ash spilled onto the linoleum floor. With her foot, she swept the ash towards the stove. Mrs Feehely would make the linoleum shine in the morning.

The warning bells chimed louder. She realised what else had been unsettling her this evening. Lorna had been vehement about double standards and a lack of honesty in the town. Lily had thought she'd meant Mrs Liddle's snide comments about Bill's infidelity, and so she'd never found out who might have told the constable of Mrs Feehely's employment. Piecing the conversation back together, it seemed plain that Lorna implied a town secret concerning Mrs Feehely.

Having her own knotted life was one thing, but becoming enmeshed in someone else's knots another, no matter how sympathetic she felt towards the woman. If only she didn't need Mrs Feehely's help. But Lily couldn't cook, clean, do the washing, manage Girlie, manage a husband, be concerned for her brother, participate in CWA meetings, appear polished in church, and provide piano tuition without Mrs Feehely. And the guesthouse hadn't officially opened yet! Lily needed more than she could pay for. She sucked her back teeth. So much depended on the coming tourist season.

What could she control? There was no shame in having a native domestic, but a friendship between Girlie and the Feehely girl, as Gerry had claimed, would bring the gossipmongers. The worst kind of attention.

Convent school for Girlie seemed the only solution, offering piano lessons more advanced than Lily could give her and protection against a world Girlie was not ready for. Nor Lily.

The milk simmered and she took hold of the handle with the dishcloth, pouring the hot milk into an enamel mug on the table. The skin flopped over the side of the mug like a veil, and she swiped it with her finger. The idea of Girlie on the cusp of womanhood filled her with dread. She'd only had her for six years and was not prepared for the transition so soon. Now that Girlie was 'blossoming', growing more into the picture of the woman she would become, who was to say she wasn't starting to have funny ideas? And friendship with a native girl might put them in her mind. As Gerry had said, they could slide backwards. She knew nothing about the Feehelys' background – they might have come from a mission, and everyone said that mission-trained girls were over-sexed. No wonder Girlie had been confused and acting strangely. It wouldn't do, of course, and Lily would tell Mrs Feehely so in the morning. At St Dominic's Girlie would cultivate a better sort of friend and have a happier path in life. Her chin trembled. If only her own mother had been as concerned for Lily's future.

She looked up at the clock. Twenty past eleven. She would wait up for Ernie as long as she could, determined to discuss the option of St Dominic's. The scholarship route would mark Girlie as a charity case, and she could not – would not – contend with the stigma.

CHAPTER TWENTY-FOUR

ERNIE

Flamin' heck, Ernie thought, rubbing his eyes but still not seeing straight. The pans were clanging in the kitchen, a sure sign she wanted him out of bed. Bleedin' Saturday.

Saturday! He lurched out of bed, pulling on his trousers.

'You're up. Ern—'

'Not now, gotta get going.' He splashed water on his face, running a hand over his stubbly chin. After a quick shave, and a nick on his throat for it, he opened the bathroom door to find Lily waiting.

She uncrossed her arms. 'We need to talk.'

He held up a hand, 'Later,' and made for the kitchen door, where she folded herself into the space by the latch.

'Now.'

Ernie hooked his thumbs into his waistband and stood back. 'Go on, then. I've got to be on the Geraldton train in thirty minutes.'

Lily relented, allowing him into the kitchen. 'It's about Girlie. I want her to go to school at St Dominic's.'

He furrowed his brow, staving off his banging headache. 'Why's that?'

'She's getting older. There are . . . influences.' She widened her eyes to imply he would know what she meant. He sighed. Unless she came out with it, deciphering her was going to cost him making the train.

'That's what children do, Lil. They grow older. It's not unexpected.' He picked up his briefcase, mostly to indicate he had to get on, but there would be more. He waited for it. These announcements of hers usually came after pent-up deliberation.

'The Liddle girls, Miss Marsh, Miss Gooch, Miss Brown all go. That's how it would look, Ernie. I know what you're really worried about. Paying the school fees.'

'They'd have to be at least thirty pounds a year.'

'Fifty.'

He groaned, exasperated. 'Fifty quid! What do you take me for? You know we're not flush. Close enough to skint.'

'I thought the guesthouse bookings were coming in. Why can't you pay for your daughter's education?' Hands on hips, chin pointed at him.

He waved his hands at her. 'I don't have time for this. I'm going.'

'What are you doing in Geraldton?'

Ernie twisted the latch back and forth in his fingers. It wasn't like he would be able to hide it. Only, how could he justify it now?

'Don't be reading anything into it.'

'Into what?' Her voice rose.

'It's for the business. Now I'm selling petrol and oils for motor cars, I've got to have a vehicle of my own. I'm picking up a motor car I had sent up from Perth last week.' If he could, he'd walk away now.

But he didn't. The ticking of the kitchen clock throbbed in his skull.

'A new motor car?' she said finally. 'A new motor car.' A little quieter. 'But your daughter's not good enough, or anything else that I need.'

It was never going to go well.

He looked at her. 'The sooner I go, the sooner I'll be back and we can talk about Girlie. After my committee meeting this afternoon.' He moved to kiss her on the cheek but she turned away.

For a split second before he closed the door, he hesitated. Heard her light footsteps fade down the corridor to the shop, and with a quick drum of his knuckles on the door jamb, he pulled his hat squarely on his head.

Out on the road heading to town he picked up the pace. It was a half-hour walk when his head was clear. Away from Lily and her demands, his thoughts crowded with Lorna. He'd slept with her twice now. The first time couldn't be counted, that happened without him planning to ever cheat on Lily. But late last night he'd gone to her in full knowledge of what he was doing.

He'd told her all about the shiny new blue Hillman touring car waiting for him in Geraldton, apologising for having to take her around in the dray. It didn't seem to bother her. She didn't ask too much of him and gave herself willingly. Lorna's enthusiasm had taken him by surprise and, at first, he'd thought he'd hurt her. He hadn't realised a woman made those sounds when they enjoyed it. Like a man. Even with those women before Lily, they'd treated it as a chore to be got on with – he paid and they provided. But he was afraid to disappoint Lorna with what he had to offer and last night applied himself in ways lads slyly joked about.

A man with a flash motor car couldn't be a failure. The townfolk didn't have to know it was bought against the guesthouse. Nor did Lily. But he bet she'd ask.

~

Driving back down from Geraldton, Ernie felt the same rush in his blood that he'd had when he'd ridden motor cycles, back when he first met Lily and had a glimmering future in front of him. He could almost see it again as the motor car raced forward to meet the horizon.

~

'You're off with the Racing Reporter's Daughter again?'

Ernie sat up from the floor, dodging the kickstand of the BSA motor cycle, wiped his oily hands on a rag and chucked it at his mate, Les. 'You're jealous.'

The blokes had pinned up Lily's picture from the paper on the dunny wall.

Les laughed. 'Of a girl like that? Bet she's been round the stations a few times.' He opened the petrol cap on the tank of the 3.5 horsepower machine he'd wheeled into the workshop.

Ernie clenched his fists; there was only so much he was prepared to take. He'd stomached her talk of another bloke she was seeing; but then, they'd made no commitment to each other. Not that he didn't want to. But every time he summoned the gumption to ask her to go steady, it was in the little actions – stitching a hole in his handkerchief with a flower, or asking if he had made a sale he'd mentioned the week before – that he realised walking out together was more than he deserved.

'Watch your bloody mouth, Les,' he said, backing down from saying worse to a mate. He knew, though, that if he really was the man worthy of her, he wouldn't be such a coward.

Les threw back the rag. 'Suit yourself.'

Ernie combed his hair and took a whiff under his arms. She'd said to pick her up for the picture palace at five, and according to the clock hanging upside down on the wall of the workshop, he had forty minutes.

He gave himself a quick standing bath at the back-alley water tap where they washed down the motor cycles before they went out to customers.

Les was already closing the large doors to the workshop.

'Hold up, I'm going to take a motor cycle out tonight. Which one do you think?' Ernie said. All four of the Mortlock Bros. salesmen took the motor cycles home on occasion. It was why they needed to clean them up in their own time before they were returned to the workshop. On weekends, he would put in over a hundred miles, riding out to Mundaring Weir, usually with Les or one of the other blokes in the WA Motor Cycle Club. But not so much now he was stepping out with Lily.

'Is it to impress the Racing Report—'

'Get fucked.' Ernie ducked through the doors and walked away from Les.

'She's not worth it, mate, just sayin',' Les called. 'Come down the Commonwealth with me and Charlie.'

Deciding on the 3.5 horsepower racing BSA, Ernie wheeled the machine out of the workshop and swung his leg over, kick starting it. He revved the engine several times, giving Les the middle-fingered salute with his other hand before taking off down the alley and out onto Queen Street.

Lily lived in Nedlands with her brother and father. Her mother had died while her brother Tommy was still at war, a hard thing to come back to. Ernie's mother had died when he was still a boy, and his dad had raised him and Fred, when another man wouldn't have. Tommy was short a spark plug, and though Ernie had sympathy, it made him feel uncomfortable when she discussed him. Almost like there was an unspoken question over why he had come back from the war largely unscathed.

It was convenient that Fred was up at the farm, so that Ernie could avoid any unfavourable comparisons. Fred's marriage to Rosie had been another low blow. Made Ernie look at what he had with Lily and wonder if he was wasting his time.

He opened the throttle notch by notch, letting buildings and pedestrians flash past as whirls of colour. No use keeping her waiting.

He knocked at the door of her house and heard her shout, and a man's voice – Tommy's – answer her. Then silence. He knocked more loudly, until he saw her blurry form through the rippled glass of the front door.

'Oh, Ernie, I'm not ready.' Lily was still wearing her house coat.

'Have I got the time wrong? I thought we were going to the pictures. You said five?' He shifted from foot to foot.

With a glance over her shoulder she moved towards him and the pale and pinched expression she'd come to the door with fell away. 'No, no. It's my fault, I've had to deal with something, that's all.'

He peered into the darkened hallway behind her. 'Everything all right?'

She placed a hand to her chest. 'Yes, no cause for alarm. Do you mind waiting out here while I do myself up?'

While he waited, he sat on the low brick wall in front of the house, smoking.

Lily popped out of the door in twenty minutes, completely transformed. She'd twisted one side of her hair into a roll, which gave him a view of her long, white neck. And she wore another of her fancy frocks, this one in blue and white stripes with a low neckline. Never the same dress.

Ernie ground out his second cigarette, half smoked. 'You look ravishing.' His cheeks flamed; he hadn't meant to be so forward, but she was like a goddess.

Her smile broadened and she took his arm. At the footpath, she stopped, squeezing his arm with her other hand. 'Is that your motor cycle?'

'Do you fancy a ride?' It was a mild day for early winter.

The light flashed in her eyes. 'May I?'

Ernie pulled on the leather helmet with ear flaps. 'You ever been on one before?'

'No, never,' she said, biting her bottom lip. He swung the motor cycle around and beckoned to her before she could change her mind. 'Is it safe?'

She sat side-saddle, reaching her arms around his waist. 'I wouldn't take you out if it wasn't,' he said, moving her hands lower – not too much, but just enough so she wouldn't constrict his breathing if she tightened her grip suddenly.

He slowed when they cruised the main street to the picture palace, but she tapped his shoulder and pointed to keep going. His heart leaped. Anything to keep her close to him for a little while longer.

When they reached the foreshore, he stopped the motor cycle in the shadows beneath a peppermint tree, and waited for her to alight.

'So, what do you reckon?'

Her cheeks were flushed and shiny. 'It's not how I thought it would be. I was telling my friend about your weekend motor-cycle adventures, and he put all kinds of notions into my head about how dangerous a sport it is.'

Ernie's chest tightened at the mention of her 'friend'. He knew it would be that shoe salesman from Dalkeith. He chose his words carefully. 'You're safe riding with me.'

'Perhaps,' said Lily, slipping into her usual face, inscrutable. To get anywhere with her, he'd have to find a way to get under her skin. He couldn't bloody take her riding on the motor cycle every time they stepped out together, though he half considered it.

'We can go along the river. Do a loop and back.'

'Or we could stay here a bit and enjoy the peace. Maybe go out for a drink later.' She walked towards a bench facing the river.

He hurried up to her, sat down with his arm draped on the bench seat behind that beautiful neck. She pursed her lips, staring out at the river.

'Did something happen with your brother?'

She glanced at him, then turned back to the river. 'I got him a place at the Perth Technical School and he dropped out of his art courses. It wasn't easy, you know, getting him in, not with his medical discharge. I had to persist with the head art teacher before he relented to see the portfolio.'

'I see,' Ernie said to fill the space while his mind turned over the words he should say. There was a vulnerability underneath her bold façade, the way she'd held him close on the motor cycle, and only a strong man who'd risk everything to protect her would be worthy of her, not a steady and dependable shoe salesman. 'You did what you could. There's nothing else you could have done, Lil, so don't blame yourself.'

She set her jaw. 'I just wish he would stick at something. I can't stand flip-flopping, running from responsibility.'

That's when Ernie knew he loved her, and had to win her.

~

He pulled up in front of the Road Board office, right next to Bill Fairclough's maroon Ford A roadster. Bill would be green when he saw Ernie's vehicle beside it.

As it was, Bill hardly looked at him until General Business.

'I'd like to add something to the agenda here,' Bill said, shuffling through his papers to pull out a newspaper clipping.

Ernie tensed. For a while after the hearing, he'd been waiting for it. But the trysts with Lorna had eased the exposure of his bankruptcy from his mind momentarily, made him feel like nothing could touch him anymore. When it hadn't appeared in the papers he'd assumed it had been buried.

But it was in black and white and in Bill's hands . . . with a large heading, 'Life of a Bankrupt'.

'It's been brought to my attention,' Bill said, clearing his throat, 'that our beach caretaker, Mr Hass, has been before the bankruptcy court, a fact that was reported in the newspapers this morning.'

Bill read out every sorry detail of Ernie's financial woes. They'd even reported the fire that had razed his father's house in Perenjori. No insurance, otherwise the manner of the fire would have alerted suspicion, starting in the sitting room when the only fireplace had been in the kitchen.

Ernie stared at Bill, who didn't have the balls to look at him while tearing down his name. He felt the shift in the collective mood; the stilling of the men's breath, their eyes boring into him.

'I fail to see what that's got to do with my responsibilities,' Ernie said, looking to the men for support.

There were nods and murmurs.

'But, Mr Hass, you were appointed caretaker of the beach following the fire on the jetty, and the same article telling us of your bankruptcy links you to a house fire in Perenjori.'

'It was my bloody house, Bill,' Ernie muttered under his breath. But the damage was done.

'Is this right, Mr Hass?'

'Why weren't we told about this?' Gregory Booth asked, holding his palms up to fend off other questions shot at him from the committee members.

Ernie motioned to stand and Bill gave him a curt nod.

'It is true I have been declared bankrupt. As have many men affected by these economic times. I'm not alone,' he said directly to Frank Smith from the Progress Association. He'd closed down his furniture business two years before. 'But as you gentlemen have observed I've been industrious ever since arriving in Dongarra.' Ernie looked at Bill pointedly, and the glower he received would have made him smile if the situation were otherwise. 'I am making amends for any bad financial decisions made in the past. None of which affect my ability to discharge my responsibilities on this committee or as caretaker.'

Ernie sat down.

'But what about the allegations of the fire?' asked Mr Liddle.

Wearily, Ernie stood again. 'I had no role in either the fire that destroyed my house in Perenjori or the one on the jetty. There is nothing else I can say on this subject.'

George Hopkins supported him, but the nays had it. Bill took great satisfaction, Ernie could see in the man's smirking face, in announcing the caretaker role vacant. Cast off the committee, he carried his hat in his hand, kicking at the tyre of Bill's roadster on the way past. 'Dirty mongrel,' he muttered.

'Excuse me, Mr Hass.'

Ernie released the handle on his car door. George had followed him out and, while he appreciated the man's support for what little good it had done, Ernie was tired and headed for the pub.

'Mr Hopkins.' Ernie scratched his head. 'You didn't have to stand up to them like that, it won't have done you any good on the committee.'

The old fisherman stroked the bristles on his chin. 'I wouldn't find it right in meself if I didn't tell you why I voted for you to stay on.'

Ernie shrugged his shoulders. 'Which is?'

'I know that it weren't you what started the fire on the jetty. It was your wife's brother. And he weren't alone, neither.'

Ernie grabbed George's elbow. 'Tommy? Who was with him?'

George leaned in close, winking. Ernie reeled from the man's stench. 'It were Bill's wife.'

'Flamin' hell, you should have told me this long ago.' Ernie pulled him towards the Road Board hall. The man stood his ground. 'Don't you see that Bill will be given the shove?'

George wiped the spittle from his lips. 'They'll want to know where I was that I could see who it was, and I can't rightly say, or I'll be fined. Much more than I can afford, Mr Hass. I were out late up the beach. Netting.'

Ernie was flummoxed. For a moment, he considered letting George wear the fine – but it would be saving his committee role for the sake of the man's livelihood. At least Ernie still had his. Maybe without the extra responsibilities of being beach caretaker, he'd be able to get onto the telephone company and see why he hadn't been given a telephone line yet.. Every time he had to put a telephone call through at the McGintys, old Mrs McGinty would be standing close by, listening, while his conversations with Reg had been reduced to perfunctory exchanges about the weather. It was no way to do business, when they held control of all communications, telephone and post, in and out of the beach settlement.

He let George go, gave him his word he wouldn't tell about the illegal netting, and slumped into his seat. The new motor car had lost its lustre. And Bill had bested him once more.

CHAPTER TWENTY-FIVE

TOMMY

The hot sun glared on the glass of the guestroom window. Now that the dividing walls were in, Tommy was putting together the doors and frames. Sweat dripped into his eyes. He wiped his face with the bottom of his vest, then took it off. Lily had Girlie practising at the piano in the sitting room.

He'd told Lily about the jetty fire yesterday after the copper left, but she hadn't reacted. Like his words had little effect. Later she'd gone out to her meeting, leaving him a bit of hock under the dishcloth in the kitchen for his tea.

Besides the piano, the only other noises this late in the morning came from Mrs Feehely. Earlier, he'd gone out to the bathroom, stomping his feet to warn her. Didn't want to frighten her again, but she'd continued sweeping the corridor like he wasn't there.

Tommy used his vest to wipe the sweat off his chest, then hung it over the foot of his bedstead to dry. It bothered him, the lack of reaction from Lily. He wanted her to say she believed that it had been an accident.

He placed a plank on his sawhorse, measured off the cuts and marked them with his pencil, before sawing the lines. Shavings fluttered, sticking to his cheeks. His nose twitched. He blinked, and the plank slipped. The saw shot out from his grasp and he dropped it, groping at his hand with his other, feeling the slick between them, his eyes squeezed shut. He slowly counted to three, then opened to look at the damage.

No blood. He lifted his hand to his face, smelled it, but there was nothing. Just dirt and sweat. Thought his hand had been half severed, afraid he'd not been able to feel the pain of it.

He shook the fear from his hands. Got on with the job. The plank had split; it was no good now and he'd need something to clamp the next. He wouldn't be so lucky a second time. He'd seen something clamp-like on the shelves of the wash house the last time he'd been in there. He made sure he trod heavily as he left his room, hooked his hammer into his rope belt.

It wasn't just Lily moving away from him. He'd thought Lorna had been friendly. He knew there was no chance of a relationship – not in small towns like these. But a warmth flooded his body when he was near her. The guesthouse was almost complete and he hadn't seen Lorna in the past week. He might not get the chance to see her again, apologise for his indiscretion. Maybe it was better this way. When he'd seen her at the beach, that memory of Ma's ghost had risen unbidden and clear in his mind.

Girlie's piano playing rang in his ears as he stopped for water in the kitchen. Loud, and even though he'd never learned to play, he could hear the wrong notes. They jangled and clunked. He shook his head but the ringing in his ears didn't go away, became more discordant.

The picture of Ma. She had appeared flesh-and-blood. No. He stuck his finger in his ear, twisting it. It wasn't a real memory. The doctors said. Made him say it aloud so he'd believe it.

What was happening to him? Was he going backwards? Getting worse? Back at the Lemnos Hospital, the doctors made him question all his other memories, but never made him question Lily, why she'd disappeared.

'Listen to the melody! What note do you hear?'

Lily's shouting snapped Tommy out of his thoughts. She anchored him to the world of the living, but at times he worried that she was materialising as their mother. The way she forced Girlie at the piano reminded him of Ma's strictness with her, and she never seemed affectionate with the girl.

Why did she adopt a child if she was going to treat her like Ma had done her?

He bit his lip, tasted blood. Lily hadn't been honest with Girlie. Words and actions, lies and promises weren't adding up. Had she been honest with him?

Lily raised her voice again. Tommy stumbled out of the kitchen and outside to be clear of it. But her shouting had lit a fuse, snapping in his head. Going from the bright sunshine into the darkness of the wash house was like dunking his head in a barrel of water. He flicked back his face.

White eyes loomed at him from the dark, and he swiped at them, waving his arms in circles, lurching to make the spectre disappear.

'Don't hurt me. No. No. No. Please.' Mewling.

His arms flailed still at the darkness as a panting voice registered on his consciousness.

'No, please don't, sir.'

The black woman. Pressed up against the trough, clutching at the front of her dress. She whimpered, closed her eyes.

'Tommy! What's going on? What in damnation did you do?'

He dropped his hand to the hammer at his belt, letting Lily shove past him to reach the woman, ask her if she was hurt.

'I don't know,' he said finally. Lily looked up from her ministrations, disappointment etched in her face. 'I don't know what I was doing.' He stepped aside for them to pass, his shoulders hunched over the trough as he gazed into its bottom. When he looked up she was in the doorway, rimmed gold with the sun. Her expression hidden.

He gulped breaths until his heart beat more steadily.

'What happened?' she said.

He fumbled in his trouser pocket, finding the iron nail, pushed the tip of his finger into the point. Deeper. Until a pinch of pain. 'I . . .'

Lily sighed, exasperated. 'Mrs Feehely, would you mind telling Girlie to finish practice for now and clear out the sitting room?'

The woman swallowed, nodding.

Tommy started, increasing his pulse. 'Is Lorna coming to visit?' He squinted as he came out into the sunshine.

Lily scowled. 'No. I don't want any sordid behaviour in this house. I have a child . . .'

Sordid? He looked at her shapeless form, the lack of colour in her cheeks and clothing, her eyes averted from his. She meant sex. A red heat climbed his neck. She was talking about what had happened at the beach with Lorna. He dropped his head. Lorna thought him one of those perverted kind, had told Lily. The stink of sweat cut through his thoughts. Work. He had doors to nail together.

He shrugged a shoulder at Lily apologetically. 'I'm sorry for scaring Mrs Feehely. I didn't see her there.'

'Don't.' Lily was shaking. Her head side to side, her whole form blurring at the edges. 'Just go. I don't want to lose her, I need her. She can't see you.'

He'd petrified Mrs Feehely, and Lily too. What had he done? What was he capable of doing?

Questions. Bloody questions. It had been questioning Lily's words that had undone him; he wouldn't let that happen again. Like the early days in the hospital when the doctors had taken apart his memories and thoughts and feelings – the 'talking cure', they'd said. Made him doubt he'd even existed.

He'd only got through the past six years to find Lily, to know what was true. And now she was afraid, didn't want him seen.

'Is there somewhere you can go? For the day, get out of the way?'

Tommy gazed at the scrubby sand hills behind them, felt the wind lift sand and veil his face, saw that old bat from the tearoom staring at him again. Fuzzy, like she was trembling, but that would be him. She was no different to people he'd met elsewhere, and they had also spat on the ground as he passed. He'd learned to get out of their way. But soon the tourists would come and he would have to move on. Out there, he wouldn't be able to find himself among strangers who only saw this side of him.

'Don't tell Ernie about this morning. I've just been having nightmares, not sleeping. I'll be fine.'

She nodded. 'Go for a walk. Clear your head, then.'

He stepped towards her, to touch her, meet her eyes, have her reach out to assure him. But she turned towards the house.

~

For a late Saturday afternoon the crowd in the hotel was thin. As Tommy waited for his beer, his gaze roved over the men around him, stopped when it reached Ernie tucked up in the corner on a stool, nursing his glass. A grimace flickered on Ernie's face, and Tommy gave no notice of having seen him, turned, dropped his eyes to his beer. He'd drink this and get out, though he didn't dare go home yet.

'Up to much?'

Tommy startled. 'What's that?'

Ernie kicked out the seat beside him and sat down. 'No, I thought not. I'm going to find you a job, maybe out with the lime kilns, I heard they're always in need of labour.' Ernie finished his glass and wiped the foam from his lip.

Tommy mirrored him, wiping at the shadow of foam on his own lip, wetted it with his tongue. A job was good. One not dependent on Lily and Ernie, better. Though Ernie was acting as though he would owe him. If he owed anyone, it was Lily. This must have been her way to show him she still believed in him. Twisted Ernie's arm.

'I'm much obliged to you, Ernie.'

'What I want in return is for you to stick at the job just so long as to earn enough money to move on. That's what you do, isn't it? Blow in, cause trouble, then leave again.'

Tommy circled his jaw. 'I'm not sure I know what you're talking about.'

'Get me another beer and I'll tell you.' Ernie slammed a couple of coins on the table, one spinning off towards the edge. Prepared to duck and scramble on the floor for it, Tommy scraped the stool back. But Ernie swatted at it with his meaty fist, snatching it before it teetered and fell, slowly released the coin into Tommy's hand.

Tommy returned with their beers. A bloke had wandered over, having words with Ernie. He'd seen him before, a tall ruddy-skinned fellow who took his boat out most weekends. The set of Ernie's shoulders was guarded as he listened.

'Ernie?' Tommy put the beers on the table, waiting to be told to clear out. He'd rather the bloke went than him – wanted to know what Ernie meant by causing trouble.

'Robert McGinty,' Ernie said, pointing with his thumb at the bloke. He gestured at Tommy. 'My brother-in-law, Tommy Adamson.'

Tommy put out his hand but Robert didn't remove his hands from his pockets, just gave him a once-over and continued to speak to Ernie. 'I doubt you'd find a supplier willing to take on the risk of you now. It could cost me. I've got to take care of my business, and I suggest you keep an eye on yours.'

Ernie swore under his breath as Robert McGinty walked off.

Tommy had placed Robert now – he'd seen him over at the tearoom. He swallowed. That old woman had been watching when he'd lost control this morning. Did Ernie know?

'What was that about? There's no trouble, I hope.' Tommy braced himself, and with every mouthful of beer that Ernie took he felt the job at the kiln slipping away.

Ernie regarded him. 'No, just business. Got to find another groceries supplier.'

He would have to play at Ernie's game. 'I'm sorry if I didn't sound appreciative of you slinging me some work. I always do right by a fella that does that.'

Ernie nearly choked on his beer. 'You can't stick at anything, and never have. Lily was always risking her neck for you, only for you to take the easy way out. We've had enough. This is our new start, and we don't need you to mess it up for us.'

We. Us. Our. Lily had worked on Ernie, all right. Tommy had asked her not to tell her husband about the trouble this morning. That wasn't the sister he'd thought she was. He looked at Ernie from under his lids, didn't bite back as Ernie would have expected him to.

'Always shooting through. How long did you spend in the war before coming home?' Ernie continued. 'I was on the front line while you laid about.'

A kick in for good measure to remind Tommy of his place. Ernie making sure he knew who had Lily's loyalty. It strained Tommy to keep his face from making vicious angles, thinking of how Ernie had changed her till she was a faded tissue pattern of the real thing. Couldn't stand up for herself. But Ernie had to be the big man, the hero. A fragment of memory caught, muddled, but he remembered the name and a few sketchy details, and he knew with strange certainty that Ernie would fill in the connections.

'Does the name Rex Carlton sound familiar?'

Ernie visibly shrank, took his time in setting down his glass, eyes narrowed. Tommy had hit his mark.

'He was good to me,' Tommy continued, 'flung me a bit of work out at Three Springs. Mentioned he was C Company, 32nd Battalion.'

Ernie furrowed his forehead. 'I'm not sure I remember—'

'He says he remembered you.' It was this next part that had kept Tommy confused. 'Until you blokes got to Alex, then you disappeared, didn't get shipped to France.'

'I'm no deserter.' Sweat formed into beads on Ernie's forehead. 'I was transferred to a camp back home, but I went back. I still served.'

He scratched his cheek with his thumb slowly and deliberately. Eyeballed Ernie. There was almost a look of shame seeping from his skin.

'What's the point of stirring things up?'

Tommy grinned, licking his teeth. 'If I'd wanted to, I would have said something Armistice Day.' A bluff. He'd not remembered more than the farmer's name then.

'So, what is it you want?' Ernie said. He squared his shoulders.

Tommy dropped his head in his hands, gripping at his hair like he wanted to tear his scalp off. He whispered hoarsely, 'I just want to stop the suffering.'

'Mate, the war affected us all. We're all still suffering. Just some of us would rather leave the war behind.'

Tommy was long past the point of choice. This was a matter of survival.

CHAPTER TWENTY-SIX

LILY

Lily pinned the raw edges of fabric together allowing a wide seam, not knowing how big Mrs Feehely's Ruby was, other than she was about the same age as Girlie. Using the size query as a ruse, she'd asked Girlie about Ruby. But Girlie had said she'd only seen her the one time, by the river. Lily recalled Girlie's questions about the girl who couldn't go to school, though she hadn't realised she'd been talking about an Aboriginal girl at the time. There had been no other mention of the girl since.

'Arms up.'

Girlie obediently raised her arms over her head in a diver's pose, tilting forward for Lily to guide the dress over her head so the pins didn't snag.

'Ouch,' said Girlie, jolting.

'Stay still.' Lily secured the final pins under Girlie's arms, then held her hand. 'Up you pop.'

Girlie clambered onto the timber crate in the kitchen, while Lily marked lines in charcoal, folded and pinned the hem, then gestured for her to turn around slowly. The hem was uneven, dipping low at the front; it would need re-pinning.

'It's not a very pretty dress,' said Girlie, looking down at herself.

'Chin up.' Lily nudged her with the back of her hand. 'It's fabric from the old manse curtains Mrs Pearson gave Mrs Feehely. Beggars can't be choosers.' When Mrs Feehely had brought the curtain fabric yesterday morning, she had grimaced. Garish. Large purple flowers, symbolic of something or other in the Bible.

The Bible brimmed with flower symbolism. Only that morning, the service had been from Genesis 2:4, and Reverend Pearson intoned about the Garden of Eden. Lily caught glimpses through the kitchen window of the garden, little more than geraniums and tomato plants sagging listlessly atop sandy hillocks.

She brought her attention back to the dress fitting. A simple shift, with waist ties at the side and a square neckline, giving her satisfaction in creating something almost beautiful from its hideous beginnings.

'Who's a beggar?'

The atmosphere in the kitchen shifted. Looking up, she saw Tommy slouched in the doorway to the guests' corridor. 'No one.' She tapped Girlie's legs. 'Get down.'

Since the incident yesterday with Mrs Feehely, Lily had avoided him. She had now seen something of what had happened up at Fred's farm on the emu cull, and had come to understand Ernie's reaction. Tommy had been lost in the grip of his waking nightmares. The ghosts of all those dead young men. She couldn't imagine the horror of war and Ernie had kept his recollections from her.

Girlie climbed down from the crate, lifting the hem and removing the dress. 'Get dressed quickly and do some practice,' Lily said, bundling the dress into Girlie's arms to protect her modesty. She made a cursory search for dropped pins as Girlie hurried to her room.

Tommy shoved his hand deep into his pockets, rocking back and forth on his heels. 'I saw Ernie down the pub yesterday. Mentioned he would get me some work at the lime kilns.'

'Oh, good.' She gathered the loose pins on the table and poked them into the pin cushion. 'I hope you showed him some gratitude. What happened coming home from Fred's farm is not a thing he'll forget easily. And he doesn't even know about . . .' They hadn't spoken of the jetty fire since he'd said it was an accident.

He continued to stare at his boots. The air around him seemed denser, darker, a trick of the light.

'It was an accident, wasn't it?'

He looked up. 'The rifle going off?'

'No, the fire.' She faltered. Tommy had no cause to harm Ernie. Nor Mrs Feehely. But Mrs Feehely had thought so, kept apologising, saying it was her fault, thought he'd been about to rape her. Traumatised as much by her imaginings as Tommy seemed to be.

'Yes, it was an accident.' The shadow shifted across his face, making him appear more drawn.

'You should tell Ernie the truth.'

'Truth?' Tommy's voice came hard. 'I don't know what that is. What's the truth about Girlie?'

'What are you talking about?' She came close to him, pulling him away from the corridor where Girlie might hear, and shut the door firmly.

'When I said she was adopted, she didn't know anything of it. Was it true what you told me?' He calmly ladled a cup of water from the cooled pan on the stove.

'You didn't.' She recoiled from his words. What had he done? 'Oh, Tommy, why?' Her trembling became rage, and she hit out at him, knocking water from his cup down her apron.

He set the cup down, and strode out the door and into the yard.

She waited until his shadow had left her kitchen, breathing deeply until she regained control of herself, then picked up the pinned dress with forced focus on shortening the front skirt panel and sewing up the side seams. The task eased the pounding in her temples, allowed her to consider what she could do to repair his damage. He could not blame this on his nightmares.

Sending Girlie to St Dominic's was the most sensible idea, to put a stop to the unravelling of untruths Lily had thought were tied up until Tommy had come along and picked at them.

She cursed Ernie's profligacy with money. Now the Trinity examiner was their only chance. She paused in her sewing to listen to the sounds starting up in the sitting room. Not perfect, but there was a lightness to Girlie's playing that was wholly unlike her own. Undisciplined, but not altogether displeasing to the ear. Thank goodness Girlie had been practising for the recital and her scales were quite polished apart from her fingering of the melody notes, which was always an issue. The Fry girl had only been to the house twice this past week, and Girlie, despite her fumblings, was the superior of the pair. After her initial concern about Girlie and Ruby Feehely, Lily had warmed to Susan, knowing that Girlie's friendships could be worse. But Girlie would find a better quality of friend soon. The scholarship would mean a year's worth of fees, and anything Lily set her mind to could be done, even in five days.

Stabbing the needle into her thumb, she winced, sucking on it to staunch the blood. Would she be able to smooth things over with Girlie so easily? Girlie knew the truth – partly – and yet she'd said nothing. Perhaps she hadn't understood. If Lily spoke to her about the adoption now it would look like an admission of guilt, caught out in her lie. Any authority she had would be undermined. Girlie might want to know why she'd been adopted, and the identity of her true parents.

It wasn't that she was never going to tell Girlie; only that if enough time passed she might not need to say anything at all. She'd thought often of the words she might use – she'd saved Girlie from poverty, could raise her as a nice girl, with manners, frocks, piano lessons, a mother and a father who wanted her, protection. None of them seemed adequate.

A motor car beeped its horn out the front. Lily folded away the dress, and pinched her cheeks as she went through to the shop. Beyond the fence lined with tea tree branches to buffer the sea wind, she saw Lorna alight from Bill's maroon motor car.

Now was definitely not the right time. Lily couldn't help but think of Lorna's unashamed wantonness.

Lorna rounded the motor car, sashaying through the shop door announcing her visit with a jingle of the bell.

'Lorna. What are you doing down here?'

'I had hoped to catch you out walking in town this afternoon, I'm not stopping for long. Only I have so much to do now with the decorating.'

Lily's stomach, already unsettled, dropped. 'Decorating?' The other day when watching two tourists cross the sand hills to the beach, their newly bought fishing rods across their shoulders, she had thought of a theme for the hall decorations: 'Under the Sea'. After church this morning she hadn't managed to catch Mrs Pearson to share her idea.

'The annual fair. I've been appointed in charge of the decorations.'

Lily swallowed her disappointment. 'Have you devised a theme?'

'I was inspired,' said Lorna, 'by Reverend Pearson's sermon this morning. I thought perhaps the theme might be the Garden of Eden – what do you think? We can have flowers and boughs about the hall.'

Lily shrugged.

Lorna frowned. 'Do you think we should change it to something else?'

'No, it's perfectly satisfactory.'

'Well, then,' said Lorna, smiling. 'I wouldn't want to impose on you but I am organising the ladies for various contributions.'

'To join the committee?'

Lorna laughed, brushing her hand lightly across her chest. 'I *am* the committee. Mrs Pearson couldn't say no when I offered to pay for everything we need. I don't have children to occupy me, so I can afford to devote myself to the community.'

Lily became conscious she was carving a groove in the counter with her thumbnail. Devotion? What could Lorna know of devotion other than to her base instincts and others' husbands? Selfish and self-centred. Lily's roles as wife and mother required selfless dedication in protecting her husband and her child, maintaining an image of faith and belief in them, sacrificing her own wants and needs. Fancy dress. Her family made her a better person, without them she would be the woman in the photograph she hid in the tin. Naked.

Just the thought of the photograph and she recognised that her resentment towards Lorna was selfish in itself. Lorna had suffered a miscarriage and life with Bill offered her little fulfilment.

Lily put up her hand to shield her eyes from the glare of the sun through the shop windows. 'Lorna, do you never think of . . . the baby you lost?' She immediately regretted her question as Lorna clasped a hand over her mouth, and the moment stretched on. Nobody ever spoke about the babies that died. Like so much else, they were supposed to be buried and forgotten, not carried like ghosts within their bodies.

Lorna's fingers worried at her chin as though she were composing her face for Lily. 'Not often,' she said. 'I think about Sam more.'

'Sam – was he your first husband?'

Lorna nodded, her face lifting with a smile. 'Sam McGinty. Robert's younger brother.'

The unused cradle in the McGintys' back room; the furniture that wasn't theirs. Lily wanted to reach out to embrace Lorna, but her prudish reaction to Lorna's admission at the CWA meeting held her back.

'I still feel like I am Lorna McGinty. Marriage to Bill hasn't changed that. I suppose . . .' Lorna wiped her hands together, avoiding her eye, 'I suppose that's why I don't feel any disloyalty to Bill.

'At least you have loved and lost,' Lily said glibly. 'I've never felt such strong feelings for Ernie.'

Lorna sniffed. 'We're all acting, aren't we?'

Lily nodded. Determined to befriend Darla McGinty, to find her way into the inner circle of a founding family's protection, she'd not seen what was right in front of her. She had been friends with the right Mrs McGinty all along. And she'd nearly thrown the friendship away. 'I'll gladly help you with the decorations.'

~

When Ernie returned from his unsuccessful shark hunt with Mr Liddle, Lily had already spent two hours sitting by the piano, rehearsing the pieces with Girlie, painstakingly patient in demonstrating correct technique, enduring off-key notes, conscious that she was on edge as she questioned every one of Girlie's glances and inflections. Did she know? Did she understand what was meant by adoption? So when Ernie swayed in the kitchen doorway, fiddling with the buttons on his trousers, Lily was behind on the preparations for the evening meal.

'Aren't you going up to town?' she asked.

'Not if Bill's going to be there.'

'Bill?' She looked up in surprise. 'Has there been a falling out?'

Ernie grunted.

She flapped her dishcloth at him. 'Well, you can't very well stand there blocking my way. I'm busy. Gerry or Matthew might be at the pub.'

His shoulders slumped. She stopped mid-flap, stunned at how broken he looked.

'I can't, Lil. They booted me from the committee, I'm not caretaker anymore.'

Lily stared at him. It was like this town had decided there was something unsatisfactory about the family and was closing ranks. She couldn't understand why some families, like the McGintys with their changeability, not knowing where one could stand with them, or the Frys who lived in a dreadful manner, held standing, when for all appearances, the Hasses should be seen as paragons of family and duty.

'They can't do that without giving a reason, Ern.'

He set his mouth grimly. 'The fire on the jetty. They say I had something to do with it.'

'Oh.' Lily averted her eyes from his.

'I didn't do it, but I know who did.' He put a hand to her shoulder as though to steady her for what was to come. 'Tommy.'

She'd been wrong, chosen the wrong side, and now she might fall into the chasm anyway – but not if she tried to put things to right. 'I know. He told me.'

She felt her words ripple through his body like a shot. 'You knew and didn't tell me?'

'It was accidental, Ernie. He would never have done a thing like that on purpose. It had nothing to do with his troubles. Could have happened to anyone.' Hearing the words aloud she didn't believe them.

Neither, it seemed, did Ernie. 'If I had known in the meeting, I could have told them. But I didn't and lost my position as caretaker and it's your fault just as much as Tommy's, and now the shop could suffer for it.'

'Yes, you're right.' Placating words. Better to acquiesce and take the blame otherwise he'd take it out on Tommy. She felt false, treating Ernie as though shit wouldn't stick to him, when the reason they were in this godforsaken town was because of his incompetence. But she had made a decision against her husband, something a wife was not supposed to do. 'It's all my fault you lost the caretaker's role.'

'You could try to sound sincere about it.' He pulled towards the door, leaving her grasping at his singlet.

'No, don't. Don't!' She winced as his grip tightened around her wrist.

'Not this time, Lily. You're not telling me what to do.' She turned away from his yeasty breath on her face. 'That'd be right. Can't look at your own husband. Whose side are you on, hey?'

'You're hurting me.' Keeping her voice level. She saw hatred and fear flash across his eyes and he staggered, letting go of her. Her wrist stung and she rubbed at it.

'I'm your wife. Your wife!' she cried and beat her open palm on the wall as though to knock the fact into him. She hadn't expected the whitewash to be soft, and it crumbled in her palm.

The shock of it paralysed her. Then she laughed. Shrill, as though a lunatic in an asylum.

Through her crazed vision she saw Ernie standing stock still, pale and clammy, his weakness goading her. 'Is this the best you could provide for us, for your family?' Now she couldn't stop laughing, not even if he were to smack her across the face or walk out the door and not stop. 'What a good provider you've been for us,' she sneered.

He shook his head slowly. 'You're more loyal to your brother than to me. Why's that? You'll go to the ends of the earth for him, but not a thing for me.' He thumped two fingers on his chest. 'Not even what a wife ought to give a husband.'

He grabbed at her, pinning her against the wall with his body, thrashing about under her skirt with his other hand, ripping at her knickers. She brought up her knee to hurt him, felt the fabric of her dress rent at the seam. His hand was on his trousers now, pulling them down, still pushing against her. She brought up her knee again, felt it hit against his hardening, saw him reel away from her. His reddened eyes flashed as he stormed out, slamming the door behind him.

Her shoulder blades collapsed against the wall. Lily lifted the fabric of her dress where it had ripped. Beyond salvage.

Pressing her damp cheek against the crumbling whitewash, she listened. The house was still. Girlie must have heard everything.

Lily crept back to her bedroom, closing the door behind her and breathing out only when the handle turned up with a click. From the back of her wardrobe she pulled out the Arnott's biscuit tin. She threw the tangle of embroidery threads onto the thin chenille bedspread and tipped out the wad of money. She slid her finger along the edge of the photograph, forcing herself to look at it, though it filled her with revulsion, a helpless feeling of falling.

The self-loathing that lurked beneath her skin let loose, monstrous. This was the darkest part of her; she hated that she could not be what she wanted to be, or be seen the way she yearned, because of the person in the photograph. Only once before had she made herself look at it, and only when she'd felt her disguise – the good self that she presented to her family and community – slip. It hurt to look, but strong measures were necessary so that she didn't slide backwards. Because of *this* photograph she had chosen Ernie all those years ago, and had to make the best of it.

~

'Pa.' Lily shook her father's shoulder. She had already cleared away the bottles from the table and opened the kitchen window to air out the room. 'Pa,' she said again, desperate to wake him but not frighten him when he came to.

He opened an eye, bleary. 'Lilith, my love. Whatchoo doin' here?'

'Don't you remember what day it is? Tommy's coming home.' Lily hoisted him under his arms but he wouldn't shift. He could just stay there, no point creasing her frock. She fiddled with the jet button on her black glove.

'I'll be back at twelve. I'll tell him about how things are now, but really, Pa,' she shook her head at the state of her father, 'don't go worrying him about you as well.'

It had been a year since Ma went. Left a note saying not to look for her and Mr Bright. They were in love.

Alfie Bright, our boarder? Pa had said, surprised. As though a married woman and a single man living under the same roof weren't to have noticed one another. They weren't if one had any sense of responsibility and decency. If Ma cared one whit for her family and how it would destroy them.

Lily blamed herself. All the moments she'd seen and dismissed as something else – their heads pulling apart, Ma brushing Alfie's lapel, her hand lingering over his when serving him tea. Only afterwards did she think these moments significant, forming a pattern irregular to the one her mother should have been making. Lily should have gone to Pa, but he had his obligations to the paper and a reputation to maintain.

She would find piles of smashed glass in the night bucket, shredded letters. Any reminder of her mother thrown away. Several times Pa failed to go into the newspaper office when he started drinking heavily. Try as she might to cover for him, going to see his boss with excuses of illness, she knew he'd be found out. Then a junior reporter was sent to cover the Perth Cup at Ascot in his stead.

And Tommy had returned home from the war, taken to the barracks hospital for rehabilitation.

Lily had thought it might be mended: her mother might see the error of her ways and return to Pa, might remember her love for Tommy who she'd encouraged in his art. For ten months, Lily had visited him at the hospital, every Tuesday and Saturday between ten and twelve, telling him Ma couldn't come, her nerves frayed. Hoping she would not need to lie to him for much longer.

Two weeks before Tommy was due to be released, Lily found a job working as a pattern cutter at Pritchard's. With her first pay packet she bought a ready-made black crepe-de-chine frock with a sailor collar and the new low waist.

Tommy would ask after Ma incessantly, had idolised her, drawing pictures for her on sheet after sheet of paper and sticking them to the walls of his hospital room. But now he was coming home. How could she tell him their mother had been concerned only with her own base needs?

It was better they thought her dead.

~

Ma had cared little for whom she hurt or the vows she broke – selfish. Lily had chosen to become entangled with Ernie, with Girlie, and if she did not bind herself to them protecting what they had created together, then she had nothing.

Without her family to keep her moving ahead, looking towards a better life, she was no better than her mother. As much as Ma had hurt her with her strictness, Lily couldn't fathom the way Ma had abandoned Tommy and Pa when they were at their most vulnerable. And she'd vowed to undo the damage Ma caused them. But at what cost? She'd lost sight of the fact she might be doing the same to her own husband and child.

Lily put the photograph back in the tin, and covered it with the money and threads, weaving her fingers through the green and orange and pink. She longed for the joy of pushing fabric through her Singer once more; her fingers itched to stitch the intricate patterns on sleeves and bodices and hemlines.

Heart sinking, she carefully pressed the lid onto the biscuit tin and pushed it to the back of the cupboard.

CHAPTER TWENTY-SEVEN

GIRLIE

'Keep playing,' her mother said, getting up from her sewing in the easy chair, to collect the mail from Mrs McGinty at the shop door.

But Girlie paused to stretch her fingers then bunch them up tight. She'd been practising the same bars for half an hour.

Mrs McGinty was talking about her again, and she caught words from their conversation.

'Well, her piano playing's too loud, keep it down.'

When her mother didn't say anything in response, she assumed practice was over and gathered her sheet music. Her mother came into the sitting room, distracted by a letter she was reading. She looked up with a start when Girlie closed the piano lid. 'Keep playing. The "Ode to Joy" now.'

'But – Mrs McGinty. She was cross.'

Her mother clucked her tongue in annoyance, guiding her back to her position at the piano. She turned the page in the music book and secured it with a peg, her hands shaking, the letter crushed into a ball in her palm.

'Who is the letter from?' Girlie asked, curious.

'Nobody,' her mother said, before leaving the room.

After her parents' fight on Sunday night, which Girlie had listened to from her room, ear pressed to the door, hoping to learn something that would help make sense of what she already knew, she'd felt guilty. Guilty for knowing more than her mother thought she did. She had expected her mother to be harsh with her, but instead, for the past two days her mother had been attentive to Girlie's practice, calm in her instructions, lax in assigning housework chores. The scholarship examination this Friday was all her mother cared about. As changeable as the sea, and Girlie felt tossed about by the waves of her mother's moods.

Her mother came back in with her hat on. 'Listen a moment. I'm going out to see Mrs Fairclough about the decorations for the church fair.' Her mother sighed. 'Such bad timing, but it can't be helped. Keep on with your practice until I return. Is that understood? And don't disturb your father in the shop.'

'Yes, Mummy.'

Girlie waited for the creaking rumble of the dray outside the window, then picked out the chords on the piano, wincing as she stretched her pinky finger grasping at the melody note. It wasn't enough. She tried again. Again, the skin between her fourth and pinky finger stretched and she crashed her elbows onto her knees burying her face in her hands. She could not fail her mother. But if she did – well, she might not have to go to St Dominic's cast out from her family. The alternative wasn't much better, facing Susan and the other girls, and Bobby and Joe. She just had to do what her mother wanted, if she could work out what that was.

'Girlie.'

She wiped her eyes with her palm before turning to face her father. 'I'm sorry, Daddy. I am. I'm really sorry.' Chin quivering, she dropped her gaze to the floor waiting for the sound of the door closing, but it didn't come.

'I think you've done enough practice,' her father said quietly. He wasn't angry. Just very tired-sounding. He didn't come closer to her. 'Your mother's working you too hard. That's enough for today.'

She didn't move. Was this a trick? Would her father tell her mother that she'd disobeyed?

'Go and look behind the wash house. There's something for you there. Go on.' He stood aside for her to leave the sitting room.

She slipped off the stool. 'What is it?'

He just nodded up the corridor to the back door.

She stepped cautiously, trailing her fingers along the lattice of her bedroom wall. Not knowing what she was looking for, wondering if she'd know it and what she was supposed to do with it when she got there. She rounded the back of the wash house and gasped.

Leaning against the wall was a bicycle, painted white, like the one she had back in Perenjori, before it was sold off. But this one had a little wicker basket tied to the handlebars. She'd be able to ride to and from school, faster than Joe or Bobby could catch her.

It was taller than she was used to, but after pedalling a wobbly circle around her mother's vegetable plots, she felt confident to ride out onto the street. She rode up to the merry-go-round and back to their house again, thrilled. She leaned it against the fence and rushed into the shop. Her father looked up from marking his ledger book, worrying the frown lines on his forehead with the heel of his palm.

'Do you like it?'

Only the weary expression on his face stopped her from flinging herself at him for a hug. 'Very much. Thank you, Daddy. Daddy . . . can I ride it up to town to see Susan?'

He waved at her with his pen.

She turned on her heel, with no intention of visiting Susan, who would find some way to pour scorn on Girlie and her new bike. Amid all the extra pressure of piano practice for the scholarship examination, the only saving grace had been the idea that if she did well, her mother might let her pull out of the recital. It hadn't been mentioned for over a week, relieving Girlie of the need to provide an excuse for Susan's absence. Falling out with Susan was both good and bad. Good, because she wouldn't have to share the awful secret of her adoption with Susan. Bad, because she *needed* to share her awful secret with a friend. A true friend.

~

'I've been waiting for you.'

Ruby sat cross-legged in the clearing. Girlie laid down her bike and crept towards her cautiously, afraid to make a wrong move and send Ruby off into the bush again.

'How did you know I was coming?'

Ruby smiled. 'Him.' She pointed upwards, and for a moment, Girlie's heart caught in her chest as she looked across to the bridge through the canopy, expecting to see Joe or Bobby. She hadn't breathed a word to anyone about the constable's visit last Friday, or what she had heard as she listened through the door. Just as Ruby had said. Girlie had kept that secret watertight within her.

'Nah, him, did you see him, willie wagtail? He lets me know when something's coming.'

Girlie looked up into the branches where a small black-and-white bird skittered. The blood still rushing in her ears from the ride, she hadn't noticed the symphony of bird sounds. Now the twitters and coo-coos and piercing squawks folded over each other in harmony.

She flashed Ruby a bright smile. Ruby was wearing her new dress, longer and looser on her than it had been on Girlie. 'Mummy made your dress.'

Ruby smoothed the fabric over her knees. 'She brought it to Mrs Pearson this morning. My sister Pearl wants hers next.'

'Constable Paxton came to see my mother last week. I'm not allowed to be your friend anymore.' As soon as the words were spoken, Girlie felt herself colour up.

Ruby scowled. 'I know.' She sprang to her feet, picking up a sack that had been lying on the ground beside her.

'Oh.' Girlie swallowed the lump in her throat. She had hoped she might be able to still see Ruby in secret. Kang Pei had said she would still be the same person even if everything changed – the coin was to remind her of this – but he'd been wrong. There was the blood, and now convent school. Ruby stirred a part of her that she'd thought she'd left behind in Perenjori. She couldn't lose Ruby's friendship as well.

'You coming? Gunna catch some crabs, I'm starving.'

Girlie hesitated only briefly before following her.

Ruby took Girlie up towards the estuary where she'd not been before, on the cemetery side of the river. The wattle was thick, but Ruby didn't seem to worry about snakes, walking barefoot through the scrub that scratched Girlie's ankles above her socks.

There were other hidden perils in the saltbush as she discovered, slipping up to her knee in a small rock pool. 'Where are we going?' she asked, wringing out her sodden sock. She unbuckled her other shoe and carried them.

Ruby hadn't spoken most of the way but now she stiffened, arching her back, staring at a clump of sheoaks ahead of them. She lifted her head at it. 'We're here.' She surged ahead.

Girlie followed Ruby's footprints. In a gully in the side of the steep bank was a wide rock pool, ringed with paperbarks. A woman had her back to them, bent over with her skirts tucked up into her knickers. She brushed at a fly on her face as she straightened.

'Mrs Feehely?' She never looked this dishevelled when she came to work at their house. But Mrs Feehely had never judged her, had told her stories, made her feel at ease just as Jenny had done. Now Girlie understood why she felt so comfortable with Ruby.

Mrs Feehely frowned, locking gazes with Ruby, communicating something unspoken. Girlie was able to study them together. Shielding her eyes because the sun was lower in the sky now and shone off the top of the dune, she looked over at Ruby, framed her in her eyelashes, trying to see her blacker.

Mrs Feehely broke away to look at her. 'Does your mother know you're down here?'

Girlie shook her head. 'No, she went to help with the decorating at the hall.'

'It's all right, Mum. She ain't gunna tell anybody.'

Girlie had told Susan, and then the constable had come.

'All right, then.' Mrs Feehely nodded at Ruby.

Ruby pressed something into Girlie's hand. She looked at it – sand.

'Throw it in, tell him who you are.'

'I'm Girlie,' she said to Mrs Feehely, confused. Mrs Feehely laughed, flashing teeth white like Ruby's.

'No, do the same as me.' Ruby threw her handful of sand into the water. 'I'm Ruby Feehely from,' she shot a look at her mother, 'Moore River.'

'Who are you talking to?'

Mrs Feehely put her arm around Girlie's shoulders. 'Can you see him, in the waterhole? Big bimara rainbow serpent. He can smell you, tell you're not from this country. You've got to pay your respects or he'll make you sick.'

She threw in her sand, holding her breath to see if the snake reared his head, but it sank to the bottom. 'I'm Girlie Hass. I'm from Perenjori but I live here in Dongarra now.' She had thought her country was Australia, but Mrs Feehely seemed to be talking of someplace else, someplace more connected to her in particular. Perhaps she meant the town where you were born. Perenjori was the only other place she could remember ever being. But that didn't mean she'd been born there.

'Good. He's happy now,' said Ruby. Girlie trailed her, following the chain of rock pools that led to the wide estuary.

'Is your mother coming with us?' She looked over her shoulder at Mrs Feehely groping around the slimy rocks.

'Yeah. She's just grabbing frogs.'

'What for?'

'Gunna catch some crabs.'

Mrs Feehely whistled and they stopped. She crouched by a rock pool on the reef, dangling a string into a hole. Pulled it out, with a small frog tied on the end.

'Is he dead?' Girlie clenched her skirt with her fingers. She backed away towards the shelter of the steep bank. 'I don't like it when people hurt frogs. I fainted . . .' Ruby wouldn't laugh, think her childish. 'You know when you said the willie wagtail was talking to you? I like to think frogs talk to me, too.'

'Those frogs, they have important things to say to you, Girlie.'

'What important things?'

Ruby grinned. 'That's secret business.'

Mrs Feehely leaped across to a boulder opposite, peering under the ledge of the rock pool. Not scared of the big snake that might be living there. Like she knew different, otherworldly things about creatures and trees and rock pools. Was this why they had to hide who they really were? Did they have to wear outside faces, like her mother did, like Girlie was learning to? Girlie didn't have any choice, but Mrs Feehely and Ruby knew who their own people were. They didn't need to pretend to be one of them.

'Why don't you want to live out at the reserve with all the other Aboriginal people?' Girlie asked, turning when Mrs Feehely cried out triumphantly, a crab thrashing at the end of her string.

Ruby frowned. 'If the government puts me on the reserve, what do you think would happen to me?'

Girly shrugged.

'I'm too fair to stay with our mob. The government men would send me away to Sister Kate's to be adopted into a white family.'

Adopted. Like Girlie was. And Ruby thought it a very bad thing. Would Ruby think badly of her if she knew? Girlie thought about her real mother, wondered if she'd given Girlie up, or if Girlie had been taken away from her. It hadn't entered her mind that her real mother might have wanted to keep her. She clutched at the sharp tug in her lower belly, frightened that blood was coming from her again.

Mrs Feehely emerged from behind a floodgum with her bag full of angles.

'What are you talking about, then?' Mrs Feehely asked. 'I heard you talking about Sister Kate's.'

'Nothing, Mum,' muttered Ruby. 'Just that's what would happen if I got sent away.'

'That's not gunna happen. Not even your dad knows I tell

you our stories. And no one's gunna find out.' Mrs Feehely pressed her hand on Girlie's shoulder. It felt fleshy and warm.

'What stories?' Girlie thought of the tale of the scorpion and the frog.

Ruby kicked at the dirt. 'About emu and that.'

'My daddy doesn't like emus,' Girlie said. 'He says they ruin all the crops. Him and my Uncle Tommy went shooting emus at my other uncle's wheat farm.'

Mrs Feehely sat down cross-legged in the sand while Ruby drank from her water bag. 'Those emus are just looking for water. Come from inland towards the coast, they don't know those lands have been taken for farms.' Mrs Feehely shook her head. 'Emu's not going to like it, all this shooting. He'll get his revenge.'

'The emu war,' said Girlie, widening her eyes. Her father had told her about the Australian army at war with the emus on the wheat farms down south.

Mrs Feehely laughed.

'Tell Girlie about Nol-yang.' Ruby dropped down next to her mother in the sand.

Mrs Feehely gestured for Ruby to give her the water bag and she drank from it deeply, wiping her mouth with the back of her sleeve. 'Those are our stories, girl. You keep them to yourself.' She reached for Ruby to help her up. 'You're gunna be late for your tea, Girlie.'

The scholarship examination! It felt a world away, a different reality altogether. Girlie hesitated, searching out something in Ruby's eyes to help her stay and listen to stories. But Ruby's attention was on her mother, on the crabs, looking towards eating tea. Even here she was shut out. They kept their stories to themselves, just as she had to keep hers.

CHAPTER TWENTY-EIGHT

GIRLIE

Girlie rode her new bike to school the next morning. Felt Susan's eyes on her as the spokes whirred, watching her dismount in the school yard. Then the bell rang and Susan turned away.

After school, Susan was waiting by the bike, causing Girlie's heart to skip a beat. The less she tried to please Susan, the more interest Susan seemed to show in her.

'I know you're up to something, Girlie Hass.' Susan kicked at a tyre. Girlie flinched. 'Where were you yesterday?'

Girlie scrunched up her forehead. 'At school, of course. You saw me.'

'Not then, ninny. I mean later. We saw your mother in the main street.'

A little of the tightness in her chest eased. 'I had to stay home and practise for the scholarship examination tomorrow.'

Susan's eyes narrowed. 'What scholarship examination?'

'For St Dominic's.' Girlie slung her satchel over the bike's handlebars. Susan's grudge wouldn't be helped by Girlie's going to the convent school. But if her mother let her pull out of the recital, Susan would need to be told, she supposed. 'There's a

Trinity examiner coming up from Perth tomorrow, and I've had to do extra practice.'

'So you say.'

Girlie clenched the handlebars. 'It's true. The examination's tomorrow and I'm to do "Ode to Joy".'

'But you weren't at home when your mother told me to go down and practise with you.'

Girlie blinked. 'What?'

'When I got to your house, your father told me you'd gone up to my house on your new bike. Excited to show me, he said you were. But you know what? I went back home, and none of my brothers and sisters had seen you. And I didn't see you or your new bike anywhere in town.'

Girlie scrambled through her thoughts, trying to find a reasonable story. But no lie would cover her if her mother found out, and she had no energy left for more deception. 'Don't tell my mother, please.'

Susan cocked her head. 'Oh my goodness, you were with the Feehely girl, weren't you?'

There were too many secrets. When she'd been able to share her secrets with Katie in Perenjori, as co-conspirators, giggling, they'd been a hidden treasure. But these secrets were serious. The weight of their consequences threatened to breach the dam of her defences and half-truths. She hung her head. 'Yes, with Ruby.'

'You're gunna get in trouble if the McGintys find out.' Susan crossed her arms. 'Don't you ruin our duet.'

'Why?' Girlie asked, looking up with surprise. Since the day of the jelly recipe she knew that even though Mrs McGinty said she liked having children around, this didn't include herself. It seemed strange that Mrs McGinty would be concerned about who she was friends with. 'Why would Mrs McGinty care about Ruby?'

Susan's breath was sour, warm on Girlie's cheek. 'Because Robert McGinty is Ruby's father.'

Girlie stumbled back. 'No, he's not. You're lying.'

Susan tossed her head, letting her golden hair hang over one eye. 'Do you think so? Perhaps, you might want to ask Mrs Feehely when she comes to clean your mother's precious linoleum.'

But Ruby had said her father was a porter on the railway. Robert McGinty had the grocery store up in town and went fishing at weekends. He was married to a cranky-looking white lady.

Ruby wouldn't lie to her. She remembered the way she'd spoken at the estuary, of her fears of what might happen to her, of the way people in town felt about her family. Just like Girlie, weakened by fear. Fearful of the secret of who she really was. She had to think carefully now. The way she reacted in this state might give away her own secret to Susan.

Girlie shrugged. 'So what? It doesn't matter to me.'

'I'll tell you what,' said Susan, stepping back from the bike. 'I promise I won't tell your mother you weren't practising yesterday . . . if you give me a dink home.'

Girlie pedalled slowly across the bridge, afraid of Susan's wrath if she tipped her off the bike, concentrated on the tree at the very end. Susan slid off the back when Girlie slowed, and stared down the turn-off towards the convent school.

'You know, I'd give anything to go there.'

'But you wouldn't have a room of your own or anything,' Girlie said, if Susan thought it meant freedom from her brothers and sisters. 'Mummy says the boarders sleep upstairs on the verandah.'

'I don't care about that. It's what it means, isn't it? I could have singing lessons, and play tennis and all sorts of things. You should see how much they get to eat in the dining room.'

'I haven't really thought about it.' The lie came so easily.

Susan curled her lip. 'It's not fair. They don't give scholarships for vocals. My dad would never be able to afford for me to go.'

'I probably won't pass the examination anyway, and then I won't be going,' Girlie said, showing Susan she didn't think the Hasses were above the Frys, despite what her mother had said. It could have been wishful thinking – she was still unsure what St Dominic's would mean for her. It wasn't the same, but she couldn't forget what Ruby had said about being sent to Sister Kate's, and she was unable to shake the feeling of being sent away because she wasn't what her mother had wanted. On the other hand, her mother was desperate for her to get the scholarship and Girlie yearned for her approval. 'Mummy says we can't afford it otherwise.'

Susan cast a swift look at Girlie, then swept her hand into her hair. 'I know. Dad says your father's a bankrupt.'

'What's a bankrupt?' Girlie quivered at the idea of Susan's father knowing more about her family than she did.

'He's lost all his money and can't pay back the people he owes.' Susan skipped away, free. 'You'd better practise. Otherwise, I might have to get Mrs Pearson to accompany me at the fair after all.'

Girlie willed herself not to cry.

Susan motioned buttoning her lips, and ran off down the river path to her house.

Watching as Susan's figure became smaller, Girlie felt she would drown in secrets.

~

Her mother clutched Girlie's hand as they waited at one end of the recital hall, back straight and knees pressed together, eyes trained on Sister Mary murmuring with the Trinity examiner and two other Dominican sisters who occasionally looked over to them.

Girlie breathed shallowly so as not to disturb her mother nor the dust motes settled on the parquetry floor. There wasn't a clock whose tick might measure out the time the nuns spent deliberating, stretching on and on. Her fingers hurt now, squeezed between her mother's, the ache growing more intense the more she focused on it. She cast her gaze to the pressed-tin ceiling of the recital hall, then across to the open doorway where she could see the stairs outside that led up to the girls' classrooms enclosed in green glass.

Her mother tightened her grip. Sister Mary was coming towards them holding a piece of paper, her face serene. Suddenly Girlie yearned to come to the school, to be seated in one of the desks upstairs and sleep out on the verandah with the other girls, to be enveloped in the calm of the sisters and not have to carry the weight of everyone's secrets.

Sister Mary smiled at her, then at her mother, shaking her head ever so slightly. Dread pooled in Girlie's belly. 'I'm afraid, Mrs Hass, we cannot award your daughter a scholarship for next year.' She turned, but her mother, coiled with tension, sprang to her feet.

'Excuse me, Sister, can you please tell me why?' In her loud, posh voice.

The two sisters seated at the desk glanced up. Thankfully Girlie had been the last girl to perform and they were alone, though this did not ease her feeling of shame.

Sister Mary stopped. 'Of course, Mrs Hass. While Miss Hass played adequately' – here she gave that serene smile again, which tugged at the corners of Girlie's mouth; her mother dug her fingernails into Girlie's palm – 'her technique was a little loose and she lacked focus. Perhaps with some tutoring, she might do better at next year's examination.'

Her mother went pale. 'Very well, Sister.'

~

The moment they climbed up onto the dray, her mother let loose the words simmering inside her. 'Needs tutoring! What have I been doing all this time? Am I not good enough to teach my own child? What's wrong with you, Girlie – why can't you just pick it up the way that I did when I was your age? My mother only had to show me the chords, play a new piece through once. Never twice.' Her mother wrung her hands, rubbing the back of one with the other. 'Everything I do is for you to have opportunities for a more decent life, and you spit in my face.'

Her mother didn't really want answers to her questions, and Girlie let her get it all out, sitting still on the bench seat.

'I'm sorry, Mummy, I'll try harder. I really want to go to the school.'

Her mother inhaled with a hiss. 'That was your only chance, your father won't part with the fees.' She thrashed the reins, causing Brownie to whinny as she urged him out of the Priory grounds. Girlie clutched at the bench seat. If Brownie bolted, injuring himself or them, it would be all her fault. For not practising on Wednesday when she rode her bike to see Ruby, for not being as good as her mother was when she was her age. If she'd only had proper tutoring.

Oh. She darted a look at her mother's face, clenched so all the lines around her eyes were sharper. The way her mother had looked when Sister Mary suggested getting a tutor. Her mother didn't like people thinking she wasn't very good at something.

But it wasn't her mother's fault. It was hers. And she deserved this. Hadn't she prayed that she wouldn't get in because she was fearful of being sent away? Either way, she would feel her mother's disapproval, because it wasn't based on whether she performed well on the day, it was because of who she was, who she'd always been. Her mother had done everything to make-believe that she was her daughter, but Girlie was simply not 'decent'. No matter how she might appear on the outside, like the scorpion crossing the river, she couldn't change her nature. And now she was drowning.

What could she do? Everyone would be at the church fair recital and, even though it was the last thing she wanted, she would practise doubly hard for a whole week. Put aside the thoughts of what Susan was saying about her, think about her mother. What Susan had said about Girlie's father and bankruptcy was confusing, but she knew it was bad. Something was happening, bigger than just the secret of her adoption. There had been her mother's letter this week, and it hadn't been from 'nobody' – it had made her mother upset. The way she'd crushed it up and suddenly had to go up to town. Anything Girlie did or said might anger her mother further.

When they got home and unharnessed Brownie, her mother stormed off into the house. Girlie glanced over towards the guest-house side. Maybe she could unburden herself to Uncle Tommy; he didn't speak to anyone really, just stayed in his room drawing pictures or worked in the garden, shovelling dirt. Telling him would be like telling nobody, and she would feel lighter for it.

She knocked lightly on the door of the rear corner room and Uncle Tommy appeared like a ghost, his face coated with whitish grey dust. His blank eyes searched through the crack in the door, before they settled on her. 'Girlie?'

'Can I come and sit with you for a bit? Mummy's angry with me because I didn't get the scholarship.'

He wiped his forehead with his arm, smearing the dust into grey sludge. 'I'm beat. Just got home from burning lime all day. We'll talk another day.'

The door closed on her. Blinking back tears, Girlie slunk away to the back yard, settling down on a sleeper that edged her mother's garden beds, facing the chicken coop. Only three months ago, the chicks had been balls of feathers that fitted in her palm, but now they'd grown to half their adult size. She made kissy noises at Sally, Softy, and Silky – she had named them in secret though her mother had told her not to – to get them to come to her, but they squawked, flitting away to the far perch.

There was nobody to help her make sense of anything. She only had herself, whoever that was. Wrapping her arms around her body, Girlie started to softly sing.

CHAPTER TWENTY-NINE

LILY

Lily must have slept for two hours or more, for the light through the open curtains was fading. The turmoil she'd felt before lying down had now dissolved.

It had been a false sense of safety these past years. She had been found. His letter nestled in its grubby, paper-thin envelope, among the bills from suppliers and subscriptions Mrs McGinty had brought over this week. Bearing bad news as surely as a telegram does. But thank Christ he hadn't written his threats on a telegram – otherwise, she could only imagine how the news of it would have reached the ears of the CWA, greedy for gossip, within mere minutes, Mrs McGinty getting onto her telephone to expose what Lily had laboured to conceal. Speed was imperative in meeting her blackmailer's demands, though giving him money would merely provide respite, not free her from fear. The beach settlement wouldn't be far enough away from the main town to protect her from that.

The house was still. Either Ernie hadn't come home yet, or he'd already gone out to whatever meeting or drunken carousing was expected of him on Friday nights. It was how business was done, he'd said, she wouldn't understand. There was nothing she could say to that. And given their straitened circumstances, any business partnership was an important one.

She found Girlie in the kitchen eating bread and dripping. Girlie looked up warily, and Lily's heart sank. It was she who had failed Girlie, who'd wanted to win the scholarship just as much as she had. But all she could do was observe her outer self scold her daughter.

'Mummy, I'm sor—'

Lily cupped Girlie's head, pressing her lips against her hair. That look reminded her of her own when she was the same age, frightened of her mother's bile. 'Would you like to help me with the church fair decorations?'

She held Girlie's gaze until she nodded, then smiled. 'Good. We have to make crepe-paper flowers for the tables.'

'Wouldn't real flowers be nicer?'

'Yes they would. But it's what Mrs Fairclough has decided. She's the decorations committee – her theme, her directions.'

The job of cutting out and twisting the flowers proved more difficult than anticipated. Over the kitchen table lay mounds of torn crepe-paper strips and confetti, in red and white and yellow, dipped in wax. A smaller mound of formed flowers grew slowly in front of them. Roses were more simple to master – Girlie completed another, laying it gently on the pile – but the daisies that Lily attempted wore her nerves down, the thin petals inevitably tearing.

'Did you see your father before he left?'

'Yes. But I said you were sleeping and he went out.'

'Did he say when he was coming back?' Lily's finger tore through the paper in her hands. Damn. Another daisy petal ruined. She threw the mangled mess into the pile in disgust.

'No, Mummy.' Girlie held up another mangled flower. Lily sighed. Girlie was right, real flowers would have been better. Easier, certainly, and more beautiful. Mrs Liddle had a garden full of roses.

The best they could hope for was these few rooms attached to a shop and guesthouse, and the scrubby vegetable plots and shrivelled geraniums in the yard. And that motor car. Ernie aimed at a grander life than they had means for, spouting plans for buying the land behind and extending the guesthouse, but these would come to nothing. He hadn't turned out to be the safe bet she had thought he would be. At first, perhaps, but over the past four or five years he had acted rashly when other farmers were cautious about expenses, hadn't reined in their spending. Told Lily that after the harvest they would be able to pay off their debts at the shops in Perenjori. Except the harvest had never been bountiful enough. She couldn't square all the blame on his poor choices. Nobody could have predicted the economic depression.

If anything, it was her fault. Whenever he'd come back from carting the wheat with that empty look in his eye, and she knew the butcher, the haberdasher and the general store wouldn't be paid, another wife might have eased his worry, performed as a wife should. But the idea of going through the motions caused an attack of anxiety. She endured it as she must, for there was no other way to try for a baby. But when this had proved elusive, there hadn't seemed any point to relations for the sake of them. Rather like sewing a wedding dress for a jilted bride, as had happened once with a client at Pritchard's. Pritchard himself designed it, of course, but she'd worked on the delicate appliqued daisies.

She looked at the twisted white crepe paper between her fingers. Here she was making daisies again. Who could say whether dressmaking would have been a more rewarding path than being a wife and mother?

Girlie reached to drop another rose on the pile and recoiled, a flash of pain in her expression as Lily slapped at Girlie's arm. The blood-splattered carcass of a mosquito stuck to her palm. 'Close the back door,' she said.

For a time, Lily had tried to do both. In Perth, she'd made occasional piecework for ladies at the Women's Service Guild: children's smocks, nightgowns, aprons. It wasn't until Perenjori that she'd started to sew properly again, without telling Ernie of the money she'd needed to raise to pay off the photographer when he began to blackmail her. She couldn't take a job, of course, with Ernie's pride at stake. He hated the look of a man not being able to provide for his family. But the women of the Perenjori CWA had, like Lorna, seen in her a means to bolster their wardrobes at minor expense, keen to have something to wear that the other ladies didn't have. She made it appear she was doing *them* the favour.

Early in 1929 the prices had crashed. One of the labourers was let go before the harvest – or left to go elsewhere; she hadn't been privy to these dealings. All October leading up to harvest, Ernie had been on edge, more brutish, demanded from her what the earth of the farm would not yield.

Girlie had begun to write letters to the 'Dear Aunt Gloria' column of the *Western Mail.* They weren't anything to be worried about – usually of the kind seeking advice for her costume for the plain-and-fancy-dress ball, or asking what games a seven-year-old might play with pencil and paper. After the first few letters, Lily had stopped reading them before posting. Until the column in December. Ernie had shaken the newspaper at her, his face as red as hell.

What game are you playing at?

Lily put down her pencil. She'd been adding notations to a music score for Girlie. *Calm down*, she said.

He flung the newspaper at her, sending her sheet music fluttering to the floor. She bent down to reach for it but Ernie grabbed her wrist. *Everyone probably thinks me the biggest fool, laughing behind my back now.*

She pulled her wrist away and slid onto the piano stool. *You're not making any sense. What are you talking about?*

He jabbed at the newspaper with his finger. *Read it. Go on, read what that daughter of* ours – she ignored his emphasis – *is telling everyone. Not just in Perenjori but the whole state.*

She edged the newspaper from beneath his finger and read the print.

Dear Aunt Gloria, Daddy is always complaining he does not have enough money. I have been trying to sell fruit from cook's garden and Mummy is making dresses to sell to other ladies. Can you tell me what else a girl can do to help make money? From your little friend, Girlie Hass, Cowanup Downs, Perenjori.

She looked up at him, kept her voice level. *It's just childish nonsense, Ernie, means nothing. Nobody reads the Aunt Gloria column, just children*, she said.

I see you're not denying what she wrote. Is it true? Have you been working behind my back?

She listened for the welcome distraction of Jenny or Ah Lee, but the only sounds were a plover's warbles outside. The humid air in the sitting room closed in on her, roiling with Ernie's anger and expectation of an answer, and pressed against her lungs. He was right but he was also very wrong. The work she had been doing was fundamental to being the wife and mother he expected her to be, so that the photographer wouldn't expose the lie at the heart of their marriage.

She nodded. *But only to cover the costs of the fabric and notions, nobody thinks I am a seamstress, just that I'm helping out where I can.*

He chewed at the inside of his cheek. There was still the fact of his wounded pride. Finally he spoke. *I can think of one way you can bring in some money.*

Her sharp intake of breath.

He darted his eyes round the sitting room, coming to rest on the open piano. *You'll sell the piano.*

No! She banged her hand down on the keys and the discordant jangling made her protest sound more combative. She calmed her voice. *Please, anything else. Just not the piano.* It had been her mother's. When she'd been small, Lily had cried at the beauty of her mother's piano playing. After Ma left, the piano became a reminder of the choices she'd made, a path Lily was determined not to follow. She was nothing like her mother, and she would not abandon the piano as Ma had done.

But the piano was also a reminder of the best qualities of her mother, her attentiveness to Lily's improvement, her gift of an innate grasp of rhythm and progression that Lily had to work so hard to imitate. Consumed by her loathing of Ma, it was easy to think of her as completely bad, when Lily needed to believe that anyone could find redemption.

Ernie smiled as though expecting her to say this. *Very well, the sewing machine.*

~

Lily caught the flower Girlie threw into the basket, plucking off the tissue sepal she had somehow mangled when twisting it onto the stem.

She couldn't even control her own life let alone be an example for others. When she had married Ernie she thought she would have babies, join the ladies' auxiliary, bake biscuits and have her dresses made by proper dressmakers.

She'd never expected to have a husband who couldn't settle in a job and make a good go of it, nor to be looking after a child who wasn't her own. And after all these years, to still be sheltering her brother. Putting Tommy into the Lemnos Hospital hadn't been a simple choice between what was 'good' or 'bad', but it fulfilled her promise to Pa in a way he never could have contemplated. But she would have done anything then to protect her family. Keeping Tommy here might expose her decisions. More than ever, Ernie's business with the shop and guesthouse needed to be a success. If it wasn't, the consequences could be devastating.

Taking a deep breath, she realised that it was up to her – it had always been up to her – to have the strength to decide, no matter how difficult and heartbreaking, to keep her family and the life as she had, safe.

CHAPTER THIRTY

ERNIE

Ernie squinted against the setting sun as he pulled down the front blind on the shop window. The door opened, jingling the bell above it.

'Evening, sir,' Ernie said to the man who shut the door behind him, casting a cursory glance about the stocked shelves. Taking in the man's attire of a shirt and waistcoat, the anticipation of bad news settled on Ernie as he sidled behind the register.

The man ran his hand along the counter coming to a stop with a soft thump. 'Are you Ernie Hass, proprietor?' he asked with the manner of a man who already knew the answer.

Ernie stared hard at him then gave a measured smile. 'I am. What can I do for you, Mr . . .'

'Royce. Crispin Royce, from Customs in Geraldton. Do you sell beer, Mr Hass?'

'I do, but it's all above board here. I've got my suppliers, pay ninepence a bottle to them and retail to the public for a shilling and threepence. No more.'

Mr Royce tipped his head. 'Can you bring me one of these bottles?'

'Of course.' Ernie went over to the charcoal cooler, checked over his shoulder. Mr Royce was watching him. He pulled out a bottle of beer, felt uneasy, the ground beneath him swelling.

'Unlabelled. But the supplier assures me it's hop beer,' Ernie said, handing it to him.

Mr Royce held up the bottle. 'And that supplier would be Mr John Jackson White?'

'Yes, sir.'

'Are you aware that Mr White does not have a licence to brew beer, contrary to the Beer and Excise Act?'

Ernie shook his head, thoughts spinning fast – how to get out of this without dragging his name through the mud, or dump it on White. He swallowed. 'Mr White assured me he was legitimate. I've had no complaints from customers.'

'Fortunate for you, Mr Hass. Samples we took from Mr White's indicated the bottled beer was at seven point three six per cent proof spirit. Much higher, as you would know,' Mr Royce hefted his words, 'than is allowed.'

'Good God. I had no idea.' Ernie placed his hands squarely on the counter. 'What are you planning to do? I'd like it if this goes no further.' Following the announcement of his bankruptcy, there'd been repercussions such as the loss of both the caretaker position and his groceries supplier, though he could understand this had been a business decision for Robert. Matthew, Gerry, and a few of the others had nothing against him personally and he could count on them to stand by him. But he understood the 'appearance' of things; the suspicion of the jetty fire clung to him like a rotten stench.

'You do understand it's our duty to follow up every charge that's brought before us.'

Ernie clenched his jaw.

'But I think in this case, if you do the right thing and bring in all the bottles you have to us by Monday, I'd say we're done.' He handed Ernie a card from inside his coat pocket.

'Of course.'

Ernie opened the door for Mr Royce, the bell jangling his already frayed nerves, and when the Customs official got into his car, Ernie slammed the door with his fist. *Follow up every charge*, the man said. Ernie knew just who would be making allegations against him, wanting to ruin his business. Fucking Bill Fairclough.

~

Last Friday he had picked Lorna up from the bridge end of Hunts Road, but not tonight. He pulled up right out front of Bill's house. The bastard wouldn't be home anyway. The curtain twitched, and three minutes later Lorna appeared at the door, working her hand beneath her hair.

'What are you doing here?' she hissed, climbing into the front seat of his car. 'I thought we'd meet at the usual place later.' She moved over to him, resting her hand on his crotch. He shifted, and she ran her hand down the inside of his trouser leg.

'Wait till we stop, woman.'

Lorna pulled away to the other side of the car, pretending offence, silently demanding an apology. He dealt with that every day; she could bloody well wait.

He took the gravel track to the cemetery fast, spinning the Hillman's tyres. The gravel gave way to sand, and the steering dragged until he pulled over behind a thicket, where they could see the white foam of ocean waves through a gap in the sand hills.

Lorna pushed herself on him. 'The lights,' he murmured between her teeth and lips, flinging out his hand to switch off the headlamps. He grabbed her fleshy arms to throw her down onto the leather seat. Pinning her with one shoulder while he fumbled with his buttons.

'You're hurting me,' she said. Bit his tongue. He reared back from her.

'But you like that.' He grunted as he shoved himself inside her. She tried to push him off but he wasn't having it. She'd wanted it rough before, taking control like a man, and he was sick of playing games. He pushed down on her harder, banging his right shoulder against the door handle and his hip on the gear lever, laughing as she wrestled with him.

Once he was done, he sat up buttoning his trousers.

'You brute.'

The moonlight cast a strip across her face; she was smiling. He dropped his head, his elbows resting on the steering wheel, ran his fingers through his hair. 'What am I doing?'

She rested a leg on the dashboard, clipping her stocking. Ernie looked about the darkened dunes nervously. 'Get dressed.' Her scarf was draped over the gear lever and he threw it at her.

'We're not going already?'

He reached for the ignition, but she circled his wrist with her fingers.

'Not yet,' she said, softer.

Ernie shook his head.

'We can sit and talk a while, can't we?'

He sighed. 'What for?'

She ignored him, groping about behind the front seats. 'Got any beer?'

Beer. White's hop beer. 'No, I don't bloody well have any beer, Lorna. Your bloody husband—'

She cleared her throat.

'He's causing me all sorts of trouble, sending Customs officials to look into my business. Accusing me of shady dealings. I can't have it, Lorna.'

'I know nothing about Bill's business, you know that. It bores me. He doesn't care what I do, neither.'

'He's trying to ruin me.' He looked to her for confirmation.

Lorna twisted her neck towards the side mirror, pinching her cheeks in the glint of light. She pressed her lips together. 'You're being so serious. If this is about the petrol bowser, that was just a silly tantrum. He wouldn't try to ruin you for it. He doesn't know about us, if that's what you mean. For all you know, it could be the McGintys. They're right next door.'

Ernie had begun to weary of the 'us'. He'd only wanted to put one over on Bill. Bill deserved what he got on that score and it was more Lorna's fault than his own, flinging herself at him, putting her legs up on his dashboard. Letting him wear the blame for the jetty fire, when she knew all along it was Tommy.

'No.' He shook his head. 'This started before the night of the golf tournament. He took against me the moment he met me. Doesn't like someone else coming onto his turf, that's what it is. And it's not the bowser or the beer I'm selling in the store. Bill accused me of starting the jetty fire, did you know that? But, you see, somebody saw who did.'

Her fingers jittered across her forehead, smoothing away phantom strands of hair.

'I didn't even know Tommy then,' she whispered hoarsely. 'I was just walking down the beach that evening, thought to help him out, take him home. I was rattled, that's why I didn't say anything to Bill about it.'

Ernie straightened. 'Rattled? Lorna, many a woman would be rattled, but not you. But I get it,' his face burned, 'I get it now.

You just happened to be walking on the beach in the *evening*. There was someone else.' He gripped her thigh, pinching her flesh between his fingers and she cried out. 'Who else have you spread your legs for?' Spit flew from his lips.

'Nobody, Ernie. Nobody but you.' She put her hand to his cheek. Smothered him with her rose scent.

He shoved her hand off. 'You make me sick to my stomach.'

'I make you sick, do I?' The purr in her voice was gone now. 'Bill told me you're bankrupt.'

A chill ran through him. 'What? Have you told Lily?'

'Well, no, I didn't believe Bill, did I? Not till now,' Lorna said quietly. 'Is that why Lily can't have a sewing machine when she's just what we need around here? She would have a lot of business for her dressmaking skills . . . oh, I see. How embarrassing to have her support you.'

It had been bloody Lorna filling Lily's head with those ideas.

'That's never going to happen.' He gripped the steering wheel. 'Anyway, it was her choice to marry me, so she's got to put up with it.'

Lorna shifted, slipping her hand between his thighs. Christ, the woman was persistent. 'It doesn't matter to me, Ernie. I can see you're the sort of man who'll come good again. Lily doesn't believe in you like I do.'

He wanted to shake her now, open the door and push her out of the car. The car he had bloody well bought to impress her and all the rest of them. Goddamn fool he was.

'Don't you dare speak about Lily. I should never have let this happen.'

'I just don't get you, Ernie,' Lorna said, her eyes darting out the windows. She pressed against the door. 'Fucking me and defending her. Why?'

He wished he really had the gumption to hit her, but it wasn't in him. 'We have a family together.'

Lorna pulled a cigarette from his packet lying on the dashboard. 'You'd better see me home and get back to your wife, don't you think?' Swiping away the light he offered her.

CHAPTER THIRTY-ONE

TOMMY

From the base of a grave Tommy pocketed two half-smoked cigarettes on instinct, though now he could buy his own pouch of Champion tobacco with his week's wage from the lime kiln. He found a bench and sat, rolling a smoke. The moon hung like a giant spotlight over his shoulder. The two stubs made a fat roll-up, and he lit it with satisfaction, drawing the smoke deep into his lungs and blowing it out in rings, one inside the other.

Graves weren't quiet. Wind whistled past the statues and urns, waves crashed against the shore just over the sand hills, and the dead clamoured. The black shadow of the war-memorial stone stood over him like a commanding officer, raining down orders and abuse – discipline, they called it – on his shattered head. He cradled his head in one hand, cupping his chin with the hand holding his cigarette so he could draw from it like a baby at his mother's teat.

Comforting, his need to walk the cemetery at night. He'd come here several times this week, heavy in his weary body, missing the sound of the voices of the dead that had kept him up at night, his constant companions. He found them here. Made him keep at the job though he wanted to chuck it in already, burning like a bastard all day while he lit the fires in the lime pits. There was easier work to be had out on the farms, but there was no work that could bind his mind, make him feel solid. He couldn't leave yet.

Every day on the track he'd put one foot in front of the other; led by need and hunger, drifting in search of himself, becoming more lost, disappearing whenever the town turned against him, or used him and threw him away. A stranger to them. To himself. Now, the journey frayed, fizzling out like the tail end of a wick. Like the bits in his brain, those that didn't join up as they used to, making him remember things all wrong: his mates' names, the name of a village, the month, season, year it had been back then. He'd thought Lily would sort out the pieces, make the right pattern out of them, with her tiny stitches. But all she saw were the ghosts that crowded his memory coming back to life, tormenting him. Yet he was a man – he'd had urges for Lorna but Lily had kept her away from him. He knew Lorna was married, that he could never have her, but he needed to be around her. Those urges were the only thing that made him feel a man.

Lily was afraid. Afraid of him for the ghosts that tormented him. Afraid of him for having carnal urges for a woman. If she really knew him she would see he needed to feel more than bone weariness. But she shut him out. Pushed him away whenever he hit a nerve. What was it she'd said? Closed doors. He was going to open them. It was the only way he'd be able to force her to see him clearly.

A light – no, two lights – swung over the crest beyond the war memorial stone, headlamps from a motor car coming towards the cemetery. He dropped his cigarette, ducked behind a standing headstone, waiting until the beams of the lights passed across the graves. Peering over the top edge of the headstone, he saw moonlight glint off the chrome as the motor car parked by the thicket on the edge of the cemetery. With a jolt he straightened. What the devil was Ernie doing out here?

A blonde head popped up, turning slightly, framed by the window. Lorna.

Tommy froze, standing straight in the moonlight watching as those things he'd longed for she did with Ernie. They didn't see him, but he could see her – flashes of her waiting on the jetty, expecting somebody else. Could it have been Ernie? He trembled, impotent that he couldn't be the man Ernie was.

CHAPTER THIRTY-TWO

ERNIE

Ernie let the door shut with a light thud, and removed his coat, hat and shoes to make his way through the kitchen quietly. Moonlight flooded the room, showing up a mass of shredded paper and baskets of flowers on the kitchen table. Lily had been busy that evening. Always making something for the ladies in the community or worried about their welfare. Like her concerns for old Mrs McGinty.

Guilt caught like a lump in his throat that he couldn't swallow down. The nerve of Lorna implying the McGintys had something to do with the Customs man. Stirring up animosities would cause him more trouble than he was already in. But if it wasn't Bill who ratted on him for the beer, then who was it? He cast a weary look at the flowers on the table, picked up the water jug and drank from the lip.

If George Hopkins had seen Tommy on the jetty the night of the fire, then maybe Reg McGinty had too. And if he suspected Ernie wasn't the war hero the McGintys' eldest boy Sam had been . . . That would be enough to set the McGintys against him. He'd had difficulties getting the telephone line in, and then there was Robert cancelling his delivery of groceries because of the bankruptcy. But what if that were just a coincidence? Old Reg had seemed civil enough in the street or up in town, but a man could bite back a lifetime of resentment.

'Lily,' he whispered. Then louder. 'Lily, wake up. We need to talk.'

She rolled over in their bed, sitting up on one elbow. 'Ernie? What time is it?' Her voice groggy. 'Come to bed. We've a long day tomorrow with the cricket match.' She reached for him.

'The McGintys haven't been strange with you lately, have they?' he asked. 'Said anything about me . . . or Tommy?'

She leaned over to the lamp, lighting the wick. 'Strange? Martha McGinty's not said much to me for a while.' Flickering shadows on her face twisted her expression, making her more vulnerable. 'Why, what are they saying about Tommy? Has he done something to them?'

He pushed her gently back down to the bed and put out the lamp. 'Something like that. I'll sort it out.'

CHAPTER THIRTY-THREE

TOMMY

The next morning, Lily bustled in and out of the kitchen to the outside washing lines, and Girlie sat on the back step counting or singing, the household behaving as though all was right. Tommy sat inside his room, the air blue with smoke.

The sound of Lily's footsteps came towards him along the guests' corridor. He ground out his cigarette, tying the rope belt around his waist. She pushed open the door and, a fraction too late, smiled at him.

'Good, you're up. Are you working today?' Her voice, its brightness seemed forced as though she was playing some part in a pantomime.

He thought of how he could make her face him, tell her what he'd seen last night, Lorna and Ernie carrying on together. What that would do to her. See her face cave in with regret at the life she'd chosen with Ernie – used up and thrown away just as Tommy had been. She would become as insubstantial as he was. But she was smiling at him, trusting, thinking he was well again. Happier than she'd appeared in ages. She had taken him in like he'd known she would, stood up for him; she was the old Lily again, the one who'd visited him in the barracks hospital, who'd supported his art, who'd mended his clothes and cooked him meals and fretted where he was at all hours of the night. Tommy was wrong. Lily was real. It was he who was weak, weak, weak.

He grunted.

'There's a novelty cricket match today.' She stepped closer towards him, smiling and squinting in the gloom. 'Don't laugh,' – he couldn't – 'it's the ladies against the men.'

'I don't think that kind of thing's for me.'

'Oh no. Not that. It's just that, well . . .' She pulled a biscuit tin from behind her back, opening it. Coloured threads lay in bundles, but she was sorting beneath these. His eyes bulged at a wad of bank notes in her hand. She held the money out to him. 'Take this, please. It's all I have. You should go home to Perth, make a home for yourself, maybe even find someone to settle down with.' She avoided his eye, studied the floor.

Tommy took it from her.

She lifted her eyes to meet his briefly before leaving the room.

He stared with disbelief at the money in his hands, reckoned it had to be at least twenty quid. Enough for him to make a start on all the things she'd urged him to.

It wasn't what he wanted anymore, to move on, find a place to settle down. If he set off again, no matter how long or rough the road, the ghosts would bring him back to her, and he'd despise himself for being drawn to her – for protection, a centre of calm. And he would still find no peace, because now he knew it was his memory of Ma's ghost that tormented him, materialising in Lily. He remembered how he'd scared Lily six years ago, made her vanish.

It was a lot of money, more than she could part with, he knew. The money was a bribe to get rid of him because he'd told

Girlie about her adoption, disturbed the solid picture of domestic life Lily pretended. His accidents caused questions to be asked.

He wouldn't take the money. If neither of them existed as others saw them, then they needed to see each other clearly.

He put away the picture of her face like Ma's; he was a man with a job, and it was his excuse to stay. They were both victims of Ernie.

~

Tommy stumbled, tearing his trousers, the barbs coming at him, sticking him; around him sharp, angular shapes. He fell to his knees and pain shot through them – hard tree nuts littered the ground.

The bush.

It wasn't yet dark, but the air felt cooler than during the middle part of the day.

He lifted himself to his feet. There was a path here, trampled through the lighter bush, but it split into three. He followed the one to the left.

Had he gone a hundred yards? He didn't know, he could be turning around on himself. He caught his breath and groaned from a stitch. His heart shuddered when he heard the thrum through the trees, but his mind clicked over and realised what it was. A motor car engine. He ran now, catching a stick on his ear, didn't stop until he reached the edge of the thicket. A paved road led to the crest of the hill where the war memorial stood overlooking the Swan River and the city of Perth. King's Park, but how the devil had he got here?

He tapped the side of his head. The last he could remember was the ladies from the Returned Sailors and Soldiers' Imperial League auxiliary giving a concert at the hospital. Wednesday.

It was Wednesday afternoon. Maybe. They had started singing 'Home Sweet Home' and he wended his way to the back of the room, pressing himself into the corner. Why had he done that? The headaches. They'd started the night before. Got worse in the morning. The nursing sisters looked at him, watched him; he couldn't open the windows in the ward, wanted fresh air. They opened all right, but only six inches. Chocked. He'd stood on his bed, pushing open the window at the top of the wall, six bloody inches, gulping that morning air. The taste of hot sunshine.

Now he was here. Tommy gazed about himself. There had been other times he'd wandered off, come to in the hospital grounds, among the lawns and the flower gardens, been taken back to the wards by an orderly – Smith or Johnson, he'd been with the Light Horse that one, seen action in Tripoli. Four times? Yes, four times Tommy had wandered off since he came to the Lemnos Hospital in July. What month was it now? It was hot. Must be December. Sister Landon had put up the nativity scene in the day room. Little baby Jesus asleep in the manger. He looked over his shoulder. No one was there. Not the matron, nor Smith or Johnson. He'd got away far this time.

Far. Not going back. No one bringing him back. Not going to talk any more about his 'experience' – the doctor's word – in the Dardanelles. Dr MacGregor making him talk, calling it psychotherapy. Talk. Nobody had made him talk at the barracks hospital when he came back after the war. They'd told him to forget and move on. That's what he'd been trying to do for ten years.

Can you tell me why you tried to drown yourself in your sister's copper, Mr Adamson? Dr MacGregor had asked, pulling his glasses down his nose and staring at him.

The other patients at the Lemnos were wide-starers. Not Tommy. He shut his eyes. Like he did when the doctor asked about that day. Dizzy, inhaled, counting one, two, three until ten, then he would know he was safe. Since he'd come to the Lemnos he realised there were other blokes like him, worse and better. He had the blackouts, wandering off, headaches, nightmares, couldn't hold down a job, couldn't stay long at art school. Symptoms, Dr MacGregor labelled them. Malingering, said Ernie.

He clenched his fists. It was Ernie's idea to send him to the Lemnos Hospital after the incident with the copper. Lemnos. If his ghosts hadn't already begun to torment him, the name of the hospital might have been enough to send him crazy, remind him of his recuperation on that island in the war.

King's Park. Now that he knew where he was he could right himself. Nedlands wasn't too far away, twenty-five minutes' walk. If he could get to Lily before Ernie came home from work – even better, if he was away on one of his trips – he'd tell her he didn't mean to scare her. It had been a blackout. He didn't even know if he'd truly wanted to kill himself, there had been something that happened that day but whatever it was blurred into the edges of his memory.

There was still daylight when he got home, but without his watch he couldn't tell what time it was. They'd taken that at the hospital. For his safety. The windows of the brick house were dark, though the curtains weren't yet drawn and he supposed Lily was out at one of her women's meetings. At any rate, Ernie wasn't home, otherwise all the lights would be blazing. Ever since they got the electrical on.

Tommy tried the back door. Counted on them not fixing the dodgy latch. A jiggle and the door opened. It must have been later than he thought, for the kitchen was in total darkness. Finally home. He felt the ache of his day's exertions, the mental exhaustion of the past five months, drag on his limbs. He found his way to his room in the dark, the last in the passageway, and flipped the light switch. The change in the furnishing made him think that he'd entered the wrong room. But the top louvre in the window was still missing. His room, but they must have taken out his bed, thinking he wouldn't be back from the hospital for a while. Instead, they'd put in a table, chair and mirror. Books he'd not seen before were stacked on the table. He sank onto the chair, unlaced his shoes and eased them off his throbbing feet, then his brown jacket, torn at the left elbow. His black-and-white striped shirt was wet through, too, and he began to unbutton it.

She screamed.

And he turned, clocking something hard on the side of his head. A book. His hand went to his head, and he turned towards her but she slammed the door, clicking the key in the lock. More hysterical sounds from the hallway, the light streaming under the door.

'Lily!' he shouted, banging on the door. He pulled at the handle but it wouldn't budge. He battered it again with his open palm. 'Lily!'

She responded with loud sobbing interspersed with gasping. What had he done now? He would wait for her to calm down. He sat down, elbows on the table.

Later, there were male voices in the hallway. He made weak fists with his hands; if it was Ernie and a friend he'd be in for it.

The door opened.

Instead of the shouting or fists he expected, the two men threw him to the floor, one with his knee in Tommy's back and the other wielding handcuffs, clamping them around his wrists.

'You're under arrest for trespass, breaking and entering.'

He strained his head around. Uniformed police. He looked towards Lily for help. But she wasn't Lily; this woman was about fifty, with grey hair and a large round face.

'Who are you?' Losing his grip again, people changing shape.

The knee pressed harder into his back. 'Who are *you* is more to the point,' said the policeman.

'Tommy Adamson. This is my sister's house.'

'Mrs Lister says she ain't never seen you before.'

Tommy looked at the elderly woman, who was nodding tearfully. 'I came home, unlocked the front door and here he was – naked, the lights on.'

It must be some hoax. Each time he tried to turn, the knee was pushed deeper. He slumped to the floor, speaking to the side. 'Is this 55 Thomas Street?'

'And if it is?' said the policeman standing beside him. The other pulled him up roughly, but his legs buckled under him.

'Then I was living here . . .' he trailed off, uncertain of time, buzzing in his skull. 'Until July . . . this year. With my sister and her husband, Ernie Hass. They live here.' Tommy glanced from one blank policeman's face to the other, and then to the woman for them to anchor him, give him some understanding of the situation. 'Is it 1926?' he asked faintly, in desperation.

The lines in her face relaxed. 'The Hasses moved out in August. I live here now.'

'Righto, got to take you down to the station, find out what to do with you.' He was marched down the hall between the two policemen.

He twisted his head towards the woman. 'Do you know where they moved to?' he called.

She put her hand to her forehead. 'A wheat farm, I think.'

~

There was no address Tommy could give the police down at the station other than the Lemnos Hospital in West Subiaco, and he was put back into the police van, driven down the night-time streets, his head leaning against the window panel. Occasional words from the policemen in the front seat drifted into his consciousness – 'lunatic' – followed by throaty laughter.

He didn't pay them any mind. All he could think about was that Lily had left him. He'd gone into the hospital in July and she'd left Perth in August, couldn't get away from him fast enough.

It's not an asylum, Tommy, she'd said. *Just like a home, really. All the comforts. They'll help you get better.*

He thought that meant she would wait for him to get better, like she had last time. Sickness twisted in his stomach and he took in a deep breath.

The day of the drowning. His memory came back from the edges, forming a clear picture. That's what it had been – his mother. He had seen her in the line for the susso, found out the truth of it. Had lost her again.

The policemen's laughter roused him. He realised he was chanting under his breath, 'Bye baby bunting,' rocking his rolled-up suit jacket like a child. *Go to sleep, Tommy.*

~

At the showgrounds, the teams and their spectators had already assembled and the mood was light, laughter and shrieks heard above the hubbub of chatter. The players stood out in a motley crowd of whites and day clothes. Ernie was talking with another fellow Tommy couldn't see from his position at the refreshment table, a cup of tea in hand. He asked somebody for the time.

Play wouldn't start until ten o'clock and it was only half-nine now. He walked up to Ernie, tapped him on the shoulder. Ernie turned and Tommy momentarily faltered when he saw his companion, the police constable.

'Yes?' Ernie said, waiting.

'Might I have a word? In private.' Tommy averted his eyes from the constable.

Ernie looked him over. The constable pinned his good eye on Tommy, the other drifted toward Ernie. 'Hurry up about it, Ern. We're deciding the toss in ten.'

Tommy allowed himself to nod at the constable. 'I'll only need five.'

The constable stared at him hard with both eyes, and then turned away.

'What's this about? I got you a job, didn't I?' Ernie's eyes narrowed.

Tommy no longer feared what Ernie might do to him, in sticking his neck up. He'd spent too long saying nothing, letting himself be moved on, shut away, locked up when he discomfited other people.

Blood fizzed in his head when he realised it was Ernie who was afraid. 'I saw you last night.'

Ernie looked about, then closed the space between them. 'Where would that be?'

Tommy's balance shifted and he rolled back onto his heels. Steeling himself, he held Ernie's gaze. 'The cemetery, with Lorna in your motor. And I saw what you were doing.'

Ernie pulled him away from the ladies close by, who gave them the glad eye before turning back to their chatter. He pushed Tommy behind the pavilion, blocking Tommy's sight of anyone approaching.

'I don't know what you think you saw, but don't you be spreading rumours. It'd hurt Lily for no reason.' Ernie looked at him pointedly.

Tommy rubbed his shoulder, nodding. 'I wouldn't want to. But it's bloody hot work at the lime kiln. You know, if I found easier work around here, I might save enough to go back down to Perth, make a home for myself, maybe even settle down with someone. Just like you.' Sweat beaded across Ernie's brow, giving Tommy courage to keep going.

'Do you think you might let me stick around a bit longer, maybe into the new year? You'll need some help when the place fills up with tourists.'

Ernie sighed, relaxing his shoulders. Tommy shifted his balance forward slightly, waiting while Ernie studied his hands. Then he looked up, jaw slack. 'You'll go back to Perth?'

Tommy nodded.

'Imagine you, married and settled down.' Ernie looked over Tommy's shoulder, making a firm line of his lips. He tilted his head and turned away.

Tommy spun around, searching the crowds for the one person he believed was there. And she was. Lorna. He saw her body, encased in purest white, the skirt cut to her knees, tight at her waist. But as his gaze travelled upwards, he ran cold. She was staring straight through him to where Ernie had gone, couldn't see Tommy at all.

CHAPTER THIRTY-FOUR

LILY

'Mrs Booth's looking exhausted already.'

Out in the middle of the pitch their treasurer swung her bat at the ball, her cheeks shiny from exertion in the sun. Lily was glad of the shade of the fig trees that lined the grounds on the manse-side.

She turned to Sylvia Lanagan, one of the Younger Set, on whom the ladies were counting to guide them to a less uncomfortable defeat. 'So, as I understand it, if the ball hits those upright sticks—'

'Stumps,' said Sylvia.

'—stumps, then the batsman or woman is out?'

'Yes. The point is to defend the wicket, hit the ball away and run.'

Lily chewed her lip. She was going to appear ridiculous. Just then, a cheer went up from the men on the field and they ran into a congratulatory huddle.

'What's happened?' she asked Lorna who had come to sit beside her.

Lorna stared at her then flicked a glance at the players on the field. 'Oh, Mrs Booth's been caught out.' She said it with such an air of vagueness that Lily was able to study Lorna without her noticing.

Lorna wore an ensemble of white broderie blouse tucked into a pleated cotton skirt that only just came to her knee. Even in sporting wear she seemed provocative. But the corners of her lips dragged downwards. She'd been uncharacteristically quiet that morning, amid the animated chatter of the other ladies.

Lily took the chance, guessing at the source of Lorna's upset. She leaned towards her. 'Is Bill not playing on the team for the men? I haven't seen him this morning.'

Lorna's eyebrows snagged quickly upwards. 'I don't care what Bill does.'

Lily didn't respond, thinking how unhappy Bill and Lorna made each other. The ladies shifted their positions along the bench. Miss Lanagan walked out onto the ground, taking the bat from Betsy Booth.

'Good luck!' called Mrs Liddle. 'Give the gentlemen pause for thought!'

'I'll give her pause for thought,' muttered Lorna. Lily inclined her head in a gesture of warning.

Mrs Liddle shot a look over at them, a wrinkle appearing in her brow. Lily turned out of her line of sight. She did not want to become party to whatever had happened.

'Try to forget about any unpleasantness,' she said to Lorna, 'just for today. This is a charity match, after all. We can start our grumbling again tomorrow.'

'Do you have something to grumble about?' Lorna fixed her with a look.

Lily looked towards Ernie standing at the far side of the field. He sensed her gaze, removed his baggy flat cap to wave it at her. 'There's always something to grumble about, I suppose. But I think we'll be all right now.'

A funny expression came over Lorna, greenish, as she fidgeted with the button on her blouse.

The men on the field cheered while the ladies on the bench groaned. Lily looked out to see Mr Fry restacking the wicket and Miss Lanagan walking towards them.

'You're next, Mrs Hass,' called Mrs Liddle, pointing at her with her parasol.

Lily looked to the grassy hill in front of the railway line where the spectators had spread out their deck chairs in the shade, but she couldn't see Tommy. He had been here earlier, she'd seen him talking to Ernie in the pavilion, the damn fool. Why hadn't he left town already? She worried that he'd spoken to Ernie about the money. Ernie wouldn't understand that everything she did was to stop the family from getting hurt. But what if sacrificing the blackmail money ended up breaking them?

She strode out onto the grass, nervous as she approached the stumps. Ernie gave her a low whistle and she glared at him. He came into the centre to see her, flicking the cricket ball from hand to hand.

'Don't worry, Lily, I'll bowl slowly for you,' he called out, to the jeers of some younger fellows behind him.

She smiled for their benefit. 'Thank you,' she said under her breath. Mr Fry showed her where to stand, turning her shoulder gently with his finger so that she was side-on to Ernie. With one hand leaning on the bat, she adjusted her cabbage-tree hat and gave a curt nod. Ernie ran towards her. His arm came over quickly. She didn't have time to think before it lobbed towards her and she reacted. She struck the bat towards the ball, squeezing her eyes shut and was rather surprised by Mr Fry's voice. 'You can run, Mrs Hass. You hit the ball.'

Mrs Liddle and the ladies waved their arms, urging Mrs Lovett, holding the bat at the other end of the pitch, to run also. Lily began to run towards her, past Ernie, his back turned to her, shouting at the men to return the ball. She stopped at the end of the pitch, puffing slightly. Ernie caught the ball and loped past her to line up to bowl against Mrs Lovett.

'So glad you decided not to patronise me,' she said.

He laughed, rubbing the ball on the front of his trousers.

~

The men won, of course, even batting left-handed. One hundred and twenty-two runs to forty-three. Lily was pleased to have contributed eleven of these, considering her usual abysmal performance at sports. Reverend Pearson handed the trophy to Robert McGinty, the captain of the gents' team.

'Today's result serves to prove one thing,' Robert said in his speech to the members of both teams and the spectators gathered in the hall. The nobs sat close to the stage, Darla McGinty, Daphne Liddle and Betsy Booth among them. Lily and Ernie sat somewhere in between the front and the back, at a table with Mrs Pearson.

Tommy hadn't shown up after the match either; whatever he'd said to Ernie must have been his goodbye.

'Though they may try to play us gentlemen at our own game, women are the weaker sex.' Robert didn't smile, but evidently others thought he was jesting and laughed. Lily noticed Darla tighten her shoulders.

Mrs Fry made a loud catcall from the back, 'Gentlemen!' A chorus of men's voices rose up in mock protest. Darla twisted in her seat, narrowed her eyes as she scanned the room, her glance drifting across Lily without acknowledgement.

Mrs Pearson said something Lily didn't catch. 'I'm sorry?'

'I was just saying, you played very well.' Mrs Pearson sipped at her tea.

Lily pressed a smile keeping an eye on the ladies at the front. Lorna wasn't anywhere to be seen. Robert McGinty stepped down from the stage and uttered something at Darla that made her face pinch. He held out a finger, and she stood immediately, following her husband out of the hall.

Lily became aware of Ernie's gaze on her. 'Wonder what that's about – Robert and Darla.'

Ernie cast a vague look in the direction the McGintys had gone. 'He always was a bit of a bastard—' He cleared his throat. 'Begging your pardon, Mrs Pearson, Reverend.'

Heat rose to Lily's cheeks as she realised that they had been joined by the minister. She shifted in her seat, twisting her empty water glass in her hand. Reverend Pearson discomfited her, as though he could see into the dark spaces inside her – might he recognise a kindred soul seeking redemption?

'Will you stay on for euchre?' Mrs Pearson asked Lily.

'Yes. No,' she and Ernie replied at the same time.

'Oh dear, that is a shame. I've managed to convince the Reverend to stay for a game, when he never does.' Mrs Pearson gazed on her husband.

The minister cleared his throat. 'Sunday is my busiest morning,' he said by way of excuse.

'Girlie can't stay out too late.' Lily glanced over at the children playing on the stage. Girlie was alone, staring at the girls huddled in the corner clapping each other's hands in some rhyme. She tried to catch Girlie's eye, to indicate she should join the girls, wondering if she and Susan had fallen out. Even though Girlie had promised she'd only spoken to Mrs Feehely's daughter once, perhaps Susan had heard the same rumours as Gerry Paxton, and this had put an end to their friendship. Whatever the reason, Girlie's unhappiness was apparent. And Lily was at a loss as to how to resolve it. Were other mothers, natural ones, such as Mrs Fry, Mrs Liddle, she wondered as her eye drifted across the women in the hall, just as baffled by their daughters' moods?

Now that she had found a solution to the problem of Tommy, she needed to refocus attention on Girlie. Perhaps the pressure to play for the scholarship examination had exhausted her. There could be no success in being forced to take up something if it wasn't natural and the work involved couldn't be endured. After the recital, Lily might give up teaching Girlie to play altogether.

Ernie excused himself to go to the bar without offering to fetch her a drink.

'How is Girlie and Susan's recital piece coming along?' asked Mrs Pearson.

'They've both been practising so hard.' Lily pressed out the frown lines she felt pulling at her forehead. It was hardly likely Mrs Pearson knew the intricacies of girls' friendships. 'We are disappointed, of course, at not receiving a music scholarship for St Dominic's yesterday' – there was little shame in Mrs Pearson knowing of their financial position, she was not one to judge – 'and she is all the more resolved to do well next week.'

Mrs Pearson raised an eyebrow at the minister.

'I wonder if your daughter performs nicely at the recital the Sisters of St Dominic's might reconsider her for a scholarship,' the minister said, smoothing his beard to a point. 'I do know they are fair-minded. Perhaps I can have a word with Sister Mary to recommend Girlie to the school? A second chance, as it will. And I do believe in second chances.' Mrs Pearson smiled at him and put out a hand to his arm.

Lily caught her breath. 'Oh, I cannot thank you enough, Reverend,' she said effusively, then remembering to keep herself in check. Her sacrifice, Girlie's effort, would not be in vain after all – and for the reward to be offered again so easily after being snatched away, felt incredulous. The tension from the letter she'd received simmered below the surface, imbuing any display of emotion with a sense of desperation. Lily had to protect Girlie.

Ernie came back to the table, holding out her coat.

'I'll have a sherry, Ernie. I've decided to stay and play, after all.' She smiled at the Reverend and Mrs Pearson. Her world could be put to rights. She only had to believe in second chances.

And that meant believing in Ernie, that he could make a success of the shop and guesthouse. If they had a good summer season when the tourists came after the new year, then next year they would build a guests' lounging room off the back corridor.

Lily had been wrong. She had to appear a good wife not to the women of the CWA, but to Ernie. Because her belief in his success was their only true defence against the blackmailer's efforts. She must keep the promises she had made to Ernie in marriage.

~

The minister was more competitive than Lily would have given him credit for, taking three tricks, and ringing the bell with undignified vigour.

The Pearsons left soon after euchre but Ernie was still grumbling about the minister's play when supper was served. He slurped at his vegetable soup. 'Not much of a man of God, when you think about it. Thought card playing wasn't allowed for that lot.'

A little of the minister's former dereliction, thought Lily, but she refused to entertain the idea of being given a second chance only to slide backwards. How many chances did one have for redemption?

By the end of the meal, she was light-headed; a swoony feeling that she put down to the effects of the sherry, and the gaining of hope once more about Girlie's schooling. But there was also something about the way Ernie held her gaze, not talking much, not about work, nor what had gone on between him and Tommy earlier.

He was forging a path to the bar when Mrs Liddle tapped Lily on the shoulder.

'Mrs Hass, once you've finished, you'll need to remove yourself. The gentlemen are clearing the room for the dance.'

'Of course.' Lily got to her feet, the sudden rush to her head making her keel to the side. Mrs Liddle studied her, and moved on.

'Ernie,' she said, spying him coming towards her through the crowd carrying their drinks. Girlie was asleep in the back of their motor and she had little else to worry her for this night. 'Put those down and clear the table away. We're going to dance.' She flung her hand to indicate the side of the hall where the men were stacking chairs and spreading grain on the floor.

Ernie drank half his beer on the spot, set the glasses aside and did as she asked. Lily realised she had a power that women like Darla did not have.

~

Lily housed one and a quarter turns to her left, facing Matthew and behind him the band – a violin, drum and piano. She felt flushed, but more from the energetic dance figures than from any amount of sherry she'd drunk.

'Quite a dancer, Mrs Hass, and a cricketer, too,' complimented Matthew as they made an arch. She turned under clockwise and came out to face him.

'Hardly. I think it was luck. Either that or the bowler was taking it easy on me.' She looked sideways at Ernie dancing with Mrs Fry.

'You held your own.'

Lily housed again to the left, turning towards Ernie back in her home place in the set dance. When she had first danced with him, he'd held her in a tight vice, his perspiration reeking of beer and she had been glad to be let go for Mr Peters. Girlie's teacher had held her loosely with his papery hands, his thin-skinned cheeks reddening at every misstep. Then there had been Mr Waites, the market gardener and then Matthew. She advanced with Ernie for the second dance, and the way he held her felt different. His hand on her hip was strong but not grabbing as it had before – protective – and she leaned into the arc of his open arms.

They danced until after midnight, first in sets and then the couples' dances. Outside the hall, the air wasn't any cooler than the inside crowded with sweaty bodies. 'Building up. Has to rain soon,' someone said. Mosquitoes swarmed and Ernie wrapped his coat around Lily to take her to the motor car, where Girlie lay fast asleep.

With every oncoming beam of headlamps that crossed them Lily glanced at Ernie and he at her. They would be home soon and whatever spell she was under would then be broken.

Once inside the house, she forced open the windows to let out the steam, but quickly closed them against the mosquitoes.

Ernie sat on the edge of their bed peeling off his shirt and singlet. The ringlets of fair hair on his chest glistened dark. Her cream crepe dress had damp patches under the arms, and her slip stuck to her skin. 'I'm drawing a bath,' she said, feeling her skin tight with dried perspiration.

The water in the brick copper was still warm. She unbuttoned her dress, letting it fall into a heap on the floor followed by her soaked-through slip. Resting a foot on the rim of the tub, she rolled down a stocking, then the other leg, and released the drawstring on her knickers. The relief of the water was immediate. Every pore on her body was thirsty. Lily pushed herself under the water, her arms above her, holding her breath. The water quelled the prickling sensation all over her scalp. She herself pushed up, filling her lungs with air and looked down on her naked body. Drops of water hung from the tips of her nipples.

The air shifted.

Ernie stood in the doorway, watching her, his face in shadow. Out of instinct, she covered her breasts with the wash cloth and sat up, sloshing water to the rim of the tub. He moved from the shadows into the light, longing etched on his face, and peeled the wash cloth from her. She said nothing, watched him kick off his shorts and climb into the bath with her. She pulled up onto her knees and leaned over the top of him, kissing the salty skin on his throat, pressing her wet body against him, the water thwacking gently between their flesh.

~

Afterwards, he held her in the water, rubbing her arms. 'You're cold. Goose pimples. Come to bed.' He kissed her shoulder softly.

The water chilled her now, and she nodded gratefully, standing while he dried her down with the towelling cloth until the blood came back to her skin. She wrapped herself in the cloth and followed him through the kitchen into their bedroom. She slid under the covers with the sheet up to her chin. Ernie sat up against the bedhead, his arm stretched out along her pillow, smoking a cigarette.

It struck her that she hadn't had to go through the motions. Instead, there was a curious sense of looseness in her body. At the dance, she'd let herself be carried away, not caring that the nobs were up front, and they'd been shuffled to the back of the hall.

'I need to tell you something, Lil.'

She lifted her face towards his, hesitant. 'Is it about Tommy leaving?'

He blew out a stream of smoke, rubbing her forehead with his thumb. 'What? No. Tommy's all right. I've said he can stay on for the tourist season to help us out.'

Lily's blood chilled. She shook her head to remove the pressure of his thumb, feeling the thud of her heartbeat. 'Tommy's still here?'

'I thought that's what you wanted.'

Lily opened her mouth then closed it. All she wanted was a feeling of ease in her relationships with her husband and daughter. But she would need more than a magic spell to undo the tension from years of covering up secrets.

'Of course.' She took a breath deep in her abdomen, counting out as she exhaled. 'So, what is it you need to tell me?'

He held her gaze. A mosquito buzzed near her ear but she ignored it.

'Why we had to sell Cowanup Downs.'

'But you told me already. The wheat prices were no good and you didn't get the subsidies they promised.'

'Yes, it's true. But there were others, Hepburn, Smith, Lancaster, even Fred, who faced the same, but are still going.' Ernie plunged his forehead into his hands. 'The reason I was booted from the caretaker's role. It wasn't just the suspicion of the jetty fire. They found out.'

Lily sat bolt upright, her nerves snapping taut. Was it too late? Was there not even hope of saving their reputation? 'What? What did they find out?'

'I got into debt, big debt. I'm not going to make excuses for it. I had to declare myself bankrupt.' He almost whispered the last word.

Anger flared through her. Because of Ernie, they would be ruined. Financially, once more, but also as a family. Conflicting thoughts roiled in her mind. She felt revulsion, too, because he wasn't to know how precarious their existence was if she was exposed. And an unsettled feeling of guilt that they might not have lost the farm if it weren't for what she had impulsively done three years ago. 'I see. I'm glad you've told me.'

He let out his breath, rolling his cheek into her open hand. 'Oh, thank Christ for you, Lily.'

'What for? I'm your wife, I'm here whatever happens.' She allowed herself the sensation of intimacy, the stickiness of their bare skin against each other, the futile hope.

~

The next morning when walking out from church, they each held Girlie's hands, smiling and tipping their hats at the townfolk. But for Lily it was an act, waiting for the ugliness to break the façade.

'Looking forward to the recital on Saturday?' Mrs Pearson stooped to ask Girlie, smiling at her expectantly for a reply.

But Girlie stood mutely, her palm clammy in Lily's hand. Lily shook her head. 'Of course she is, Mrs Pearson. Girlie's ever so grateful for the Reverend passing on a good word to the Sisters. Aren't you, Girlie?'

Girlie tightened her grip, murmured something that sounded affirmative.

Lily flicked a glance at Ernie, hoping to transmit something of the awkwardness of the encounter for her. The moment he tipped his hat to Mrs Pearson, she could have kissed him.

'We'll be glad to be at the recital,' he said. 'Should be a good day for it.'

Lily exhaled as Mrs Pearson moved on to the next family.

Ernie passed her his jacket to pop the hood of the motor car and check on the engine. 'I've got to see the Shell petrol supplier in Geraldton tomorrow, there's something stuck in the mechanism.' The petrol bowser had been constructed in front of the store nearly a fortnight ago. It was twice as tall as Girlie, standing out on the road like a yellow beacon.

For once, Lily wasn't going to reprimand Girlie for her sullen behaviour. She touched her on the back, urging her to go and play on the street. Other children were playing, running circles around each other, but Girlie held back as though reluctant to join their games. 'Go on,' Lily called to her. Girlie ran, shoulders slumped and dragging her feet.

Lily slid into the passenger seat, hidden partially from the view of passers-by. She'd been able to deal with the letter hidden in her handbag, but what if another came tomorrow? She'd never be able to scrimp enough money together, now that she knew Ernie was bankrupt. When she'd spoken to Tommy this morning, forced an assurance that he was still welcome, he'd returned the twenty-seven pounds – but it wouldn't be enough. The only straw of hope was that Girlie might be safe in the protective enclosure of the convent school when she received the scholarship.

Girlie was drawing designs in the dirt with the toe of her shoe. Pale, nervy when Mrs Pearson had asked her about the recital.

There was nothing more Lily could do to prepare Girlie, it was up to her to perform nicely so that the Reverend would put in a good word. Ernie had made a mess when it came to providing for the family, and Lily had let her selfishness take them to the brink of ruin, but Girlie – Girlie was the only person in this family who could hold them fast, so they didn't all slide backwards. Such a burden for her young shoulders and she didn't even know it.

Lily wouldn't let her feel the weight of responsibility for the rest of the family. That was Lily's role. The bankruptcy didn't matter – her marriage did. For Girlie's sake.

'Do you think I might be able to join you?' she asked Ernie. 'We could spend the night in Geraldton and come back Tuesday morning. There are some notions I must buy for Girlie's recital costume.'

'What about Girlie?' Ernie glanced up at their daughter.

Lily stepped from the car and slid her arm through the crook of Ernie's arm. 'I'll ask Mrs Feehely to look in on her and Tommy.' A flicker of worry crossed her mind, but Tommy's troubles had seemed to settle down since he started working at the lime kiln. No matter what the McGintys might think of him. He was here for the summer and that was that.

~

After a night in a room on Marine Terrace, Lily smiled at Ernie at their breakfast table as he poured her tea and buttered her toast. She'd never seen him so attentive, so less likely to say a cross word.

'We really shouldn't be spending money like this, Ernie.'

He licked his thumb and finger, finished his mouthful. 'Fred's been helping me out. Half the income from the wheat agency.'

'Oh,' she said. It must have been galling for Ernie to accept his brother's charity. Ernie could never speak of Fred without bitterness, always comparing what Fred had to what he did. It was partly why she'd resented Rosie's ease in child-bearing. But Fred looked out for his brother, just as she did hers. She couldn't bear him a grudge.

As they stepped out into the street from the hotel, Ernie threaded his arm around her waist, pulling her in for a kiss on the cheek.

Lily put her hand to his chest. 'Not here, Ernie.' They stood on the footpath at the corner of Marine Terrace and Cathedral Avenue, in full view of a steady stream of motor cars and buggies, not to mention pedestrians. 'A Tuesday morning – what will people think?'

He kept his hand in place. 'That we're a newlywed couple.'

'Lily!'

Ernie stiffened. Lily turned at the sound of her name, pulling away from Ernie's grasp and bringing her hands together. Lorna stood across the road from them. She looked both ways then darted towards them, clutching her billowing skirt close to her thigh.

Lily set her features. 'Lorna, what a lovely surprise. What are you doing here?' she said, holding out her hand.

Lorna took it, glancing at Ernie, a sour expression upon her face. 'Shopping for a new hat to wear to the recital. I didn't think I would see you here.'

'Ernie had some business to attend to. I thought we should spend some time together, alone.'

Lily stepped back slightly for Ernie to greet Lorna, but he stood immobile, hands in his trouser pockets, staring across to the ocean beyond the train tracks. Lily's neck warmed at his incivility. If she could accept Lorna as she was, with her faults, then Ernie should too. Flustered, she made her goodbyes and promised to see Lorna in the morning to help with the hall decorations.

CHAPTER THIRTY-FIVE

ERNIE

Ernie lined up the empty four-gallon tins on the ground beside the bowser, unhooked the petrol nozzle and watched the fuel spurt, fanning out in the driving wind. When he'd been with the supplier in Geraldton the other day, he'd had the idea that tourists might want to pay extra for petrol they could take with them in their motor cars, rather than be stuck between here and Mingenew on the drive back to Perth.

Petrol flooded over the rim of a can, pooling in a greasy puddle on the gravel outside the store. He couldn't concentrate. He hooked the nozzle back up onto the bowser and went inside for the sand bucket.

Last night he'd received a letter, left on the counter by the register. He tossed the sand onto the petrol spill watching it darken and swell.

She was pregnant.

He wasn't any good at these things, but he'd wager it had been less than three weeks since they'd first been together. She said she knew, could tell, had been this way before.

The top of his head felt like it would lift clear off, the fumes making him groggy. His vision blurred.

Ernie staggered back, inhaling great lungfuls of the sea breeze. He lined up the tins along the front wall of the store and pulled out a cigarette, raised a hand to shield his eyes from the glare of the setting sun, glowing like a fireball. What he'd give to have the whole shithouse go up in flames – incinerate the past few weeks, years, start again.

Fucking Lorna. And fucking Tommy. They weren't to blame for all of Ernie's troubles, but they knew enough to break him.

Lorna wasn't pregnant. Not by him at any rate.

He coughed, crossing the road to the beach where he lit his cigarette, drawing deeply. No one would find out. She'd given him an ultimatum: drive up to Geraldton to see her Saturday night or she would tell Bill she'd been meeting Ernie on the jetty the night of the fire – and tell Lily that she was pregnant with his child.

The wind blew Ernie's hair over his eyes and he pushed it back. Saturday. The recital. Christ. He ran his hands through his hair, cradling his head. How could he miss the recital? Lily had so much set on Girlie's performance. And he wanted Girlie to do well. It wasn't the idea of convent school he was against as it was the fees. But if she could get that scholarship . . . It would make Lily happy, and that could only be good for him.

He cringed. Just yesterday he'd felt like he'd been pardoned – treated with respect by the supplier in Geraldton, and finding a closeness with Lily that he'd craved, his loving wife by his side. Now Lorna was going to destroy it all.

That bitch.

She was trying to lure him back to her, couldn't stand seeing him with Lily in Geraldton. Three weeks? It had to be a lie. But that was a risk he would not take. He had to start digging himself out of this mess. He tossed his cigarette and rocked to his heels, dusting the sand off his trousers.

In the corridor, Lily stood, hands on her hips. She glanced down at the floor. 'Have you been across to the beach?'

He followed her gaze, seeing the sand he'd tracked through the shop. 'I spilled some petrol out front, had to soak it up.'

She bustled him into the back yard to shake out the sand from his shoes. 'You'll scratch the linoleum,' she said, leaning on the rail of the back steps, watching him with a smile on her lips while he patted himself all over. He reached up to her for a kiss.

She even kissed him back. His chest clenched for what was to come, what he had to say.

'I got a telegram from Fred today.'

'Is everything all right? Rosie and the kids?' Lily put her hand to his arm.

'Yeah. It's the crop. He hasn't finished the harvest 'cause the emus are causing strife again. He asked me to come out Saturday to Sunday.'

Her face swung shut. 'But Girlie's performing at the fair . . . it's her chance. You said you would be there.'

The sound of piano music in the sitting room twisted his guilt like a knife in the gut. He shook his head. 'Can't be helped, I'm sorry. He has to cart the harvest to the silos by the new year.'

A wind came up off the sea, spraying sand like a whip.

CHAPTER THIRTY-SIX

LILY

Thursday, Lily woke with purpose to the fresh smell of dirt on the air. There'd been a light rain throughout the night, but it wasn't enough to revive the wilting leaves in the garden. She stood in the open doorway, perspiration already pricking her forehead. Only eight o'clock and the sky was overcast.

The sound of Tommy clearing his throat, spitting, came from the guesthouse. She might still be able to count on him, even if Ernie and Lorna had let her down. Yesterday, she'd gone up to the hall to help Lorna with the decorations. Mrs Pearson had met her at the door, worried to distraction, scratching at her elbows until they were almost raw.

She's pulled out, taken it all with her, every last ribbon, every table setting, everything! She'd paid for it, so she could take it, she said. Well, I never, in all my years. She could destroy the entire fair for this. Mrs Pearson was gasping.

Calm down, Mrs Pearson. Breathe. Words Lily said to herself each day. She handed the minister's wife a handkerchief, which she clasped to her throat. *What's happened? Where's Mrs Fairclough?*

I was to meet her here this morning. She guided Mrs Pearson into the hall, empty bar the trestles stacked up on their sides against the wall and three rows of wooden chairs. The shadowy shape of the upright piano visible on the stage.

Mrs Pearson shook the handkerchief at Lily. *But that's who I'm talking about. Mrs Fairclough simply came in last night, and took all the decorations for the fair away with her. The lovely flower baskets you made, the ribbons, the large centre pagoda shaped like a tree.* She sniffed. *I helped make that.*

Lily's mind raced. She'd seen Lorna in Geraldton on Tuesday. Lorna had been in a peculiar mood, but Lily had let it go when Ernie displayed such poor manners towards her. Just for a moment, she'd suspected that Lorna might have tried to seduce Ernie. Banished the thought quickly.

What are we going to do now? sobbed Mrs Pearson.

I'll do it.

An appearance of calm was essential, like the hole in the ocean, a safe spot, belying the turmoil surrounding them if her blackmailer made more threats. If she and Ernie and Girlie, and Tommy, stayed close, anchored themselves to each other, they could withstand any onslaught.

You will? But you've only three days. The tree took us that long to make.

We won't have a tree, then, Lily had said.

No tree? But it's the Garden of Eden.

Suppose we have a different theme? I have a few ideas. You'll see, Mrs Pearson. No one will be any the wiser.

~

'Tommy.' Lily placed her hand inside the doorway to his room. She peered in, finding him sitting on his chair, scratching at something with a nail. 'There you are. Aren't you going to work today?'

He raised his eyes a fraction, still focused on his endeavour. She moved closer and saw he was burning designs onto a roundel of wood. Flowers and gumnuts. The nail skidded, falling to the floor. He blew at the wood and rubbed his hand across it. 'I've quit the lime kiln. Ernie'll give me work round here.'

She wanted to tell him not to count on Ernie's word, that they didn't have the money Tommy expected. Instead, she held out her hand. 'Oh. That's a pretty thing you're making there. Can I see it?' She glanced at the poker work as she took it from him, and passed it back. 'Do you paint anymore?' she asked softly, guiltily.

'Depends. The only paintbrush I've had in my hands these past three years has been for whitewash. I suppose so,' he said, not looking at her directly.

'I am rather pressed for time. Lorna Fairclough has pulled out of decorating the hall, taking all the decorations with her, and yesterday I foolishly offered to take over. With a new theme, too. "Under the Sea."'

The creases in his forehead deepened.

'I've organised Mrs Hopkins for craypots and old rope cable, and Mrs Pringle has a large collection of shells that will do nicely for a simple table decoration. I didn't bother asking Mrs McGinty for help,' she said, shooting a look at him to see if he reacted to the woman's name, to confirm her suspicions that he might be the cause of this friction between the neighbours, but he was staring down at his hands. 'I thought I might paint a mural and hang a few globe lanterns, and that should cover it.'

He coughed, picking at the dirt under his fingernails. 'And you want me to paint the mural?'

Lily crouched so he'd be forced to look at her. 'Would you? It would mean so much. Ernie's skipped out on me, he's not even coming to the recital.' She felt no shame in openly stating Ernie's disloyalty.

Tommy pushed the chair back, scraping it on the floor. She bit her lip, waiting while he wiped his hands on a rag. 'What story's he given you?'

'He's helping Fred with the harvest.' The question had startled her and she answered before thinking. She tried to hold Tommy's gaze while heat rose to her cheeks. 'It's a good thing he didn't need you this time. Now you can come to the recital to support me. And Girlie.'

'He'll be away on Saturday?'

She nodded. 'And overnight to Sunday. But after the way he's been since Tuesday . . .' Things were supposed to be different now that she'd capitulated to his physical needs, yet she still couldn't depend on him to support her. She pulled back her hair, tying it into a loose knot at her nape. 'I just wish he weren't missing Girlie's performance. It's a really important night for us.'

Tommy buttoned the neck of his shirt and rolled up his shirt sleeves. 'I don't think I can come either, I'm sorry. It's just the hall . . . crowded with everyone like that. But I can help with the painting.'

Lily caught his arm as he brushed past her, forcing him to look at her. 'Headaches?' He nodded, the red-crazed whites of his eyes glistening. She put her arm around his shoulder. He didn't look well enough to be seen at the recital; better for him, and Girlie's performance, if he stayed home. Lily had given Mrs Feehely two bob to make up for her fright the day Tommy had come upon her in the wash house, but she didn't have the money to pay off the whole town.

Together they dragged the length of canvas from the wash house and pegged it out on the scrubby dirt.

'The paint might crack when it dries. I haven't done canvas like this before,' said Tommy as he sketched charcoal designs of seaweed and giant clam shells.

Lily dabbed a bit of the oil paint they'd mixed with lampblack on the corner of the canvas, and rubbed at it with her thumb. 'I wonder if I can thin it.'

She dissolved soft soap in boiling water on the stove, mixing in the oil paint, one ear listening to the strains of Girlie's piano practice. Girlie had pretended a stomach upset to stay home from school. But it hadn't stopped her from scoffing down her porridge and Lily had seen through the ruse. When Girlie offered no excuses, Lily set her to piano practice. She really needed to have Susan come down and rehearse with her.

Satisfied with the results of her mixture, she and Tommy set to work on the mural. Occasionally he directed her to make up a colour of paint, or to fill in the outlines of the shapes he'd sketched. A piece of seaweed between the rocks, or bubbles coming from a fish's mouth.

The light rain that had fallen during the night held off, but the thick air dampened her skin. She sighed, arching her back. Tommy looked up. His hair streaked with blue paint flopped over his eye. He shoved it back behind his ear. 'Lorna took all the decorations away?'

Lily nodded. 'She's not who I thought of as a likely friend before. I mean, she's a little vulgar . . . adulterous,' she flushed, lowering her voice lest Girlie overhear. It had been at least five minutes since she'd heard the sound of Girlie playing. 'But we all have our faults, and carry our burdens from the past.' She held his gaze.

Tommy pushed himself to his feet, his hands visibly shaking. 'Time for smoko.'

Lily gazed helplessly as he retreated to his room, then back to the painting. It was a small mercy the Lemnos Hospital hadn't destroyed the essence of him. He still had artistic talent – that was evident in the lifelike fish and coral – but he was no better mentally, maybe even worse, than when they'd left him there. The doctor had assured her they offered the very latest treatments. No electrotherapy. He'd told them about the tennis and cricket instead. *Your brother will think he's having a long stay at a country club.* In her weakened condition from losing the baby – the baby she had never told Ernie about – she hadn't thought to question the doctor's word. Thought them proper specialists, providing Tommy with better care than she could have given him at home. But later, later when she fretted to Ernie if they'd made the right decision to put Tommy away, he'd flared at her in anger, as he did whenever his authority was questioned.

She exhaled. Ernie needed to be admired. Always. But this abrupt change in mood, especially after the night away in Geraldton, was new. She'd thought she'd done enough to strengthen their relationship. But to revive a marriage after so long of little intimacy – a dampened wick couldn't catch with just a spark.

Girlie's piano playing interrupted her thoughts, snapping her attention back to the painting. Tommy was taking his time; it had been far longer than he needed to smoke a cigarette.

By the time Tommy came back outside bringing the warm smell of tobacco with him, Lily had got Girlie to work, washing paintbrushes.

'Are you helping us?' he asked her. 'What do you think – should I paint a mermaid with a clump of seaweed on her head?' Girlie laughed.

It was strange to see him smile as he did, painting Girlie's likeness as a mermaid. From time to time, Lily glanced at them from the far end of the mural, Girlie focused on the task in front of her, bottom lip buttoned over top, while Tommy studied Girlie's features.

Lily flung her hand out to order Girlie back inside to practise, knocking over the jar of turps. At the same time, Tommy sat back on his haunches. 'Smoko.' Abrupt this time.

His lip was beaded with sweat and he got up clumsily. Lily nodded at him as he went back inside and began to wipe up the spill. A fat drop of rain landed on her face.

'Quick. Help me get the mural inside,' she said to Girlie, grasping two corners of the canvas and dragging it to the kitchen door. Girlie stumbled, holding onto the other two corners.

Lily shoved the kitchen table aside to stretch the canvas over it, frowning as she heard the squeal on the linoleum. Girlie said something she didn't catch.

'Don't mumble. What did you say?'

Girlie blinked several times, twisting her fingers in her pinafore. 'I don't want to do the duet,' she said, running her words together.

Impossible. Lily grasped Girlie by the shoulders, ignoring the small cry she emitted. 'You can't pull out of the recital now, Girlie Hass.' Being lax with Girlie's practice this week had been for both their sakes. Doing the very opposite of what Ma would have done. Lily rued every choice and sacrifice she'd made, because none of them seemed to have mattered. All she needed from Girlie was for her to do what was asked of her; a small thing, but one that could rescue them all.

Girlie opened her mouth several times before sound came out. 'I can do the pieces I did for the examination. Just not the duet.'

Lily realised she was shaking Girlie, the child's eyes wide in panic, her hair flinging backwards and forwards. Lily caught herself, and began to stroke Girlie's hair. The burn scar was shiny on the back of her hand. How had she become this person? 'I'm sorry. You'll forgive me, my darling, won't you? But you can't say things like that. Nothing can be changed at this late stage. You'll let Susan down. And you'll let me down. Can you imagine what people will say?' Girlie gave a half-shake of her head but corrected herself, nodding slowly, then quicker when Lily smiled at her. 'Your father's trying very hard to make his business here, you don't want to anger him. Remember Perenjori?'

Two bright spots of red burst in Girlie's cheeks.

'Good girl. I've prettied up your dress with some new ribbon I bought in Geraldton. Just for your recital, so that you can get into St Dominic's. That's what you want, isn't it?'

Girlie stiffened. 'Snake.'

Lily turned slowly, darting her gaze across to the pantry cupboard, seeing the flicker of a black tail slip into a crack. With Tommy in his room down the corridor, it was just the two of them alone. 'Stay back,' she ordered, picking up the flat iron from the dresser, and slowly moved towards the corner. A rustle pricked her senses, and she crept, arms held up like a swordfighter with the iron in front of her, her left arm behind for balance. She used this hand now to gently ease open the pantry cupboard door—

'Uncle Tommy, there's a snake.'

'Goddamn!' Lily said, startled, voicing her swear aloud at Girlie's disturbance. She looked back at the pantry shelves, moving tins and jars aside, but couldn't see the black snake. 'It's gone now. Hopefully back through the hole it came in.' She picked up a pile of newspapers from the corner, handing half the stack to Girlie. 'Here. Help me stuff the gaps in the walls, there might be more.'

Tommy nodded. 'It's the rain that's brought them.'

Lily forced a wad of paper into a gap. *Goddamn rain*, she thought.

CHAPTER THIRTY-SEVEN

GIRLIE

Girlie blew a stream of air upwards at her damp fringe. Earlier, they had watched the novelty competitions in the shade of the pavilion, but now the sun slanted under the eaves, forcing her to squint.

Her mother clapped her hands together. 'Goodness, who would have thought old Mrs Green had that kind of strength.' She wiped her eyes. Girlie glanced at Mrs Green wincing and holding her finger which she had just hit with a hammer.

She tugged at her mother's sleeve. 'I'm thirsty. May I have a cool drink?'

Her mother brushed her hand aside. 'I'm not leaving now. After the ladies' nail-driving competition is finished, I want to watch the men trim hats.'

Girlie fidgeted. That morning, they had made the rounds of the fair stalls, spending too long by the fancy goods when she willed her mother to walk towards the sweets and ices. Her mother was acting strangely, laughing when Girlie couldn't understand what was so funny that the other person had said. But she'd looked at her mother sideways, seen that smile fall, like Girlie's socks to her ankles, only to be picked up again. Talked to the hundredth person that day about the weather, saying how she hoped the rain would hold off. At the shooting gallery Girlie had sighed, looking longingly at the doll on the end of the stick she could have won for a prize if Uncle Tommy had come along. But her mother didn't know how to hold a gun, and Uncle Tommy had had more of those nightmares last night. She'd come upon him at the privy, and he held the door for her, shivering and shaking like he'd seen a ghost. And it wasn't even cold.

She'd rather be home with Uncle Tommy and Mrs Feehely. Since Girlie's adventures out at the estuary, Mrs Feehely hadn't looked at her twice, pretending, she supposed for her mother's sake, that she'd not seen Girlie skiving. But that hadn't stopped Girlie from watching Mrs Feehely, wondering at what other stories she kept quiet. She couldn't quite picture Mrs Feehely with Robert McGinty. When she'd met him at the tearoom, he'd ignored her. But then, that had been the day she'd found out she was adopted. The day she'd found out she'd been lied to, and had felt lost ever since.

But Ruby didn't have to be lost. She belonged here, to the white people in town; she wouldn't be sent away, she would go to school. Resolve sharpened Girlie, made her determined to help Ruby. Not knowing who her own real parents were made Girlie question every glance, cross word, and snippet of memory, wondering if her mother's silence was because she knew the answer to who Girlie was and where she came from. She wouldn't let Ruby feel lost like this, she would tell her the answer. But with the recital this afternoon there wasn't an opportunity to slip away, especially not with the second chance she'd been given at a scholarship. The pressure closed in around her.

The moment Mrs Green unexpectedly won the competition, Girlie got to her feet. All this sitting made her feel wound up like a top.

'Up, down, up, down,' said her mother, pulling her back to her seat. 'Go and play with your school friends. I saw Susan's public schoolwork entry in the bazaar, you might find her there. I think she might win her category.'

A chance to make amends with Susan before their performance. During their practice this week Susan had found fault with Girlie's accompaniment – too fast, too slow, not lively. She could pay Susan a compliment on the essay she'd penned on the value of a girl's education.

In the bazaar area of the showgrounds she found the essay, as well as a dozen iced cakes, five needlework samplers and more quilts than could fit the beds of Dongarra – but no Susan.

'Are you looking for your playmates?' asked Reverend Pearson.

Girlie nodded, remembering her mother's instruction to be on her best behaviour for the minister today. She held the fingers of her other hand behind her back. 'Yes, Reverend. Would you happen to know where I might find Susan Fry?'

The minister tapped his finger on his nose. 'Hm. I did see some young scallywags earlier out the back near the tracks. Would your Susan be friendly with them?'

Girlie thanked him and skipped off, remembered he could still see her and slowed to a walk. Along the slope between the showgrounds and the railway tracks was a thicket of gums and wattle. There, several of the boys from school, Joe and Bobby among them, were playing leapfrog. The grass was swampy from the heavy rain the night before, and boys and girls alike poked sticks into puddles. Girlie turned away – Susan wouldn't risk dirtying herself before the recital, she had to be somewhere among the stalls and competitions – when she saw Susan with Mary Ellen whispering behind a large pepper tree.

She walked towards them, nervously flicking her glance towards Bobby as he leaped over Joe's bent back, crashing to the ground just a few yards from where she walked. But they paid her no attention. Mud sprayed her leg and she bent to wipe it down. When she straightened again, Susan was looking directly at her, pulling Mary Ellen away up the slope.

Something wet hit Girlie on the side of her head. She screamed out, whirling around to see Joe and Bobby, and three other boys, holding their sides laughing.

'What's the matter, Girlie, scared of a frog? Think it's been boiled alive?' taunted Joe.

On the ground behind her was a bloated dead frog, its innards trailing out of its mouth. Her stomach heaved and she sucked in air to calm herself, glancing for help at Susan, who stared wide-eyed before tilting her head knowingly.

Girlie gathered her courage to tell Joe off, prove she wasn't a cry baby, but the words stuck and she felt a feverous blush rush to her cheeks. It wasn't leapfrog anymore. Bobby had Joe by the waist pulling him to and fro like he was riding a horse, yelling crude obscenities. Both of them laughing.

'You're a filthy pig, Bobby!' cried Susan, marching towards them, her arm raised in the air.

Bobby let go of Joe so that he fell to his knees, rolling over onto his back, grabbing at his aching sides. 'I'm not some gin you can stick your johnny in,' Joe said, between gasps of laughter.

Bobby made to kick at Joe. 'Nah, I guess I'll have to find one of the Feehely girls instead.'

Girlie locked eyes with Susan, who cocked an eyebrow and

turned to the boys. From the square set of Susan's jaw, Girlie saw what was going to happen.

'You boys want to know where you can find Ruby Feehely?' Susan said.

She rushed at Susan. 'No!'

But it was too late. Susan had caught Bobby's attention. She shrugged her shoulder at Girlie. 'Girlie's been playing with her at the river, just down from the tennis courts. Says it's Ruby's special place.'

Girlie stared, couldn't speak.

Susan's lip curled. 'Abo lover,' she said softly, and raising her voice, 'Abo lover.'

'Yeah, Abo lover,' echoed Mary Ellen, adopting Susan's stance of hand on hips. 'She must be an Abo herself if she loves Abos.'

Girlie's heart thudded. She wanted to rush over and grab Mrs Green's hammer and smash every one of them with it. Smash those laughing faces, the sneers, the mouths that yelled such filthy words at her. Her secrets. But she wouldn't be able to wield a hammer, her arms felt weak and watery.

'She ain't no Abo,' said Joe. 'Her ma and da are white as flour.'

Girlie ran. Towards the pavilion where the hat-trimming competition was now underway, to the sanctuary of her mother's side, but her leather-soled shoes skidded across a patch of muddied ground and she fell to her knees, grazing the palm of her hand.

~

When her mother saw The State of Girlie's Dress and Shoes and Hands and Knees, she tightened her mouth until her cheeks flushed mauve.

~

Girlie settled onto the piano seat, running her damp palms under her skirt. She'd managed to avoid Susan the past two hours, stuck by her mother's side after being reprimanded. Rather than go home – which Girlie begged for, in part so that she could find some way to escape on her bike and warn Ruby – her mother had cleaned her up in the hall kitchen. Mrs Pearson applied mercurochrome to her grazed palm, told her if she played well, and won a scholarship place at St Dominic's, her mother would forgive her a soiled dress.

But Girlie wouldn't forgive herself if Bobby discovered Ruby's special place.

'And singing with Miss Hass this afternoon is Miss Susan Fry,' announced Reverend Pearson. The audience politely clapped, its numbers boosted by members of Susan's family. Girlie glanced at the faces, ladies in their best hats trimmed with ribbon and felt flowers, girls and boys from school.

Susan came in too soon on 'My Melancholy Baby'. Girlie sped up to cover the mistake, her fingers continuing on, forcing Susan to skip the pause for breath in the second line. Girlie grimaced in apology, looking up at Susan who stood, one arm rigid, gripping the corner of the piano.

It seemed the audience hadn't noticed the mishap at the beginning, and clapped with enthusiasm when the song finished.

Susan turned so only Girlie could see her face, and without moving her lips, said, 'Ribbit.'

Girlie looked down at her fingers hovering above the keys, trembling, the back of her neck flourishing with heat. She glanced to the front row of the audience where her mother sat, the minister beside her. She would find no quarter there. Her mother would tell her she'd dreamed it – why would Susan say such a thing?

Susan announced their second song. Girlie placed her fingers down clumsily for the first notes of 'Waltzing Matilda', until they slipped into the familiar pattern she had played repeatedly over the past few weeks.

By the chorus, she felt silly. She'd only imagined Susan saying such a thing to her.

She darted a glance at Susan, daring a smile. Susan met her look, singing, 'And he sang as he watched and waited till his froggie boiled.' *Sotto voce*, but there was no mistaking the word.

Girlie froze. Her hands crashed down on the keys and a horrible clanging sound echoed around the hall. She stared at the black-and-white keys until they blurred into grey. Try as she might, her fingers struck into a rigour and she couldn't prise them away. Susan didn't falter.

The audience tittered from the back rows, the faces in the front rows contorting into apologetic looks as though she, Girlie, was an awful mistake that her mother had to endure. Her mother's face was pinched into a scowl like a rubber band had gathered her skin from ear to ear. Girlie made a pleading expression to her mother, to make Susan stop singing, to make the recital stop, but Susan kept on and her mother sat rigid, the nightmare continuing until Susan finished the final refrain and curtsied as though the act had been a complete success. The applause this time was measured, strained, stopping abruptly when they left the stage. Only then did she look up. Susan giggled. But before Girlie could question her, her mother strode over and yanked on Girlie's arm.

'Mummy, it wasn't my—'

Her mother raised the palm of her other hand and slapped her across the face. Girlie's mouth hung open in shock, her ears ringing though she could hear the whispers and gasps among the women in the audience. She lifted her gaze to the minister in the front row. He raised his eyes to the heavens; Mrs Pearson touched her fingers to her lips. Behind them, the old ladies shook their heads in unison. Her mother pulled her roughly from the hall, fingers digging into Girlie's arm, as Girlie stumbled to keep up. She didn't dare look at the Fry family as she passed, or the other children waiting in the back for their turn to perform. She felt their scorn, and the relief that their performance wouldn't be the worst envelop her. Only once they reached the front entrance did her mother slow down. A couple of men stood smoking by the church across the road, but then her mother marched past them.

'Where are we going?'

Her mother whipped around, crouching low to Girlie's face. 'We can't stay now. For goodness sake, I was sitting next to the minister. How can I show my face among those people after that?' She wrenched Girlie's arm, half-dragging her towards the paddock where Brownie was munching on the grass.

Her mother pulled Brownie by the bridle over to the dray where Girlie wordlessly helped harness him. 'I don't know what else I can do for you.'

Girlie felt her chest crush.

'What – did you think we'd stay on until the end for the awards ceremony and supper after?'

Girlie shook her head slowly, climbing up to the seat. She felt dirty and sticky, and she'd ruined all her mother's plans to send her to St Dominic's. Her cheek where her mother had slapped her smarted hotly.

'Just wait until your father hears about this. You have no idea what you've done, what this means, to the family, to me. We'll lose the guesthouse, the shop, the roof over our heads. We'll have to move, pack up all our things in a swag like Uncle Tommy. Is that what you wanted? Is it? *Is it?* And all because you couldn't play two little piano pieces.'

Girlie wiped the tears that sprang to her eyes with her palm, making her cheek sting worse, not caring if she smeared mercurochrome across her face. She couldn't possibly have made a bigger mess. And it was all her fault.

CHAPTER THIRTY-EIGHT

ERNIE

A shaft of sunlight filled the corridor with an orange glow. Lorna's room was at the end. Ernie had told the publican he was Bill, as Lorna had instructed in the letter. She'd said to meet at the Geraldton Hotel; she would take a room, expecting him to stay the night, as though she thought announcing her pregnancy would make all the difference. That he'd leave Lily because Lorna was having his child.

Ernie paused mid-way down the corridor to steady himself, to steel himself.

He'd driven like a mad man, taking the second turn of the S-bend on the road too fast. The Hillman had careened, shifting weight to the left side of the chassis. No point killing himself over her, he'd thought, easing off the accelerator. He had veered off the road and lit a cigarette, smoking it down while thinking over what he had to do. He'd lit another, looking up only as a motor car slowed while passing.

There was little chance he'd stay overnight. He would say what needed to be said. Lorna would be hysterical, put the hard word on him some more. But for how long? As long as he stayed in Dongarra, Lorna would hold that over him. Enough.

He would not give her the chance to blackmail him. Not with this, a baby; it would do Lily in.

Ernie rolled back his shoulders and walked noiselessly on the thick hotel carpet. He knocked twice on her door.

A rustle inside, then the door opened a crack. Lorna peered through the gap and, seeing it was him, opened it wide. She seemed to exhale, as though she'd been holding her breath, thinking that he wouldn't come.

Ernie grimaced. He wasn't here to do her bidding.

'Ern,' she said huskily, pulling him to her. 'Did you get away all right?'

He shook off her embrace. 'This is over.' He shot a look across to the cabinet, hoping for a bottle of courage. The lamps had been turned down, and the room was bare apart from Lorna's dressing gown hanging on a hook.

She pursed her lips. 'You can't mean it. What about our baby?' She dropped a hand to her stomach and reached out with the other hand for his. He tightened his hand into a fist.

'If you really are pregnant, it's not mine.'

'How dare you.' Lorna's eyes flashed. She threw down his hand. 'Treating me like a whore.'

Ernie rubbed at the stubble on his cheek, searched the corners of the room as if answers were there instead of threadbare carpet and dust balls. 'By my reckoning, you are what you are. Because I cannot father a child.'

Lorna had looked like she was going to slap him, but now she was caught by his words. She collapsed onto the edge of the sagging bed. 'How do you know?'

Ernie pulled out the chair from the dressing table and sat astride it, resting his forearms on the ladder-back. 'I got the clap in the war.' She had the gall to recoil at his words. 'Lily's never been able to get pregnant. So, I must have been one of the unlucky ones.'

'How do you explain Girlie?'

He pressed his palms into the corners of the ladder-back. 'Adopted.'

'No! You're lying, Lily and Girlie look so alike.'

'We took her in when she was four years old. Ask Lily.'

'Oh.' Lorna drew her hand to her mouth, holding her elbow with her other hand. He watched her calmly as she stifled a sob. But then she drew herself up, her face taut, expressionless. She studied him a few moments, and he wondered what was flashing through her mind. She could use his shame against him, and Ernie knew he'd have nothing left to defend himself with.

She curled her upper lip. 'You disgust me.'

Disgust was his constant companion. That and self-loathing. What kind of war hero was secretly shipped back from Cairo to the Langwarrin Camp outside Melbourne, with several hundred other disgraced men with venereal disease, treated as pariahs, sidelined from the action of real war heroes, and made to feel broken and ashamed because of their condition.

He stood up. 'I think I've said enough. I need to get back to my family.'

Lorna flung herself to the floor, clung to his knees. 'I'm sorry, Ernie, please forgive me. Don't leave. What am I going to do?'

Fair credit to her, she'd managed to squeeze a tear out.

'Go back to your husband.' He pried her hands from his legs. 'Remember what you told me – you've got to accept both the good and the bad in life. That's what I'm doing.'

~

There had been a time early in their marriage when Lily couldn't keep her hands off him. But month after month of not getting pregnant had worn away at her, until she couldn't even look at him without him imagining it was with an expression of distaste.

How would their marriage have been different if she'd known she wasn't to blame?

Ernie would tell Lily everything. Sweat prickled his back at the thought of her reaction. Would she accept his remorse or pull further away from him? He couldn't breathe at the gamble he was taking.

He banged at the steering wheel with his palm, and drove away from the hotel, working out where he should start. The beginning. One night he'd taken her out on the motor cycle and later for a few drinks, and seized his opportunity to best his rival for her affections. The way she would sprinkle that Dalkeith shoe salesman's name into their conversation, knowing it barbed Ernie, kept him keen. Playing her game, but it only made him more determined to have her. There had never been another girl like Lily. It was how she spoke about her father and her brother, the work she did to support them. Her commitment to family. He'd seen this truth in her.

And then he'd taken the cheat's way. Taken advantage of her in her drunken state. Afterwards, she had sobbed. Worried she might have got pregnant. How it would crush her father and that she'd lose her job at Pritchard's.

Ernie had proposed to her the very next day. And he'd won her over his rival. He had buried his initial feelings of deception, at tricking her into saying yes.

Here was his second chance to be a good man and he would do it right, so they could start again and she could have the life she deserved.

CHAPTER THIRTY-NINE

TOMMY

The box lay across his knees. One-and-a-half yards long and six inches wide, solid oak. Tommy fumbled with the latches, sweat stinging his eyes.

He'd told Lily he'd take care of the shop while she took Girlie up to the fair and the recital. Then he set to looking for evidence. Without realising, he'd started making connections. And now his mind sharpened to one point.

Lily had been telling a lie about Girlie.

It had all become clear while he was drawing her. Girlie had the same upturned nose and cheekbones as Lily, darker in complexion, like a negative. Except Girlie's ear lobes, they had thrown him off, and he'd checked Lily's ears when she wasn't looking, absorbed in her painting at the end of the mural. Girlie's ear lobes were large, whereas Lily's were attached. Still, there was too much likeness in all other regards. What with Lily merging into Ma, and now Girlie, no wonder he'd reacted as he had last night, coming upon Girlie near the privy so soon after one of his nightmares. She'd been humming, and when she caught sight of him, bit her lip. It was in that gesture that the picture formed.

She had to be Lily's child.

He slipped into the darkened kitchen, everyone still out at the fair – except Ernie. Rage coursed through his body when he thought of Ernie and Lorna together tonight, but he stilled his trembling hand with his other. Lily's secret was a thread to be pulled, and when he did, all the other secrets and lies would be exposed, leaving only the truth visible.

The bedroom door creaked when he opened it, his heart ricocheting off his ribs.

He tossed aside clothing in the drawers, picked up books then slapped them back down on the bed where he collapsed, elbows on knees, thinking. Across from him, the wardrobe door stood ajar, and he keeled forward, flinging it open. He knew what he was looking for now. The biscuit tin she kept the money in; money, he was pretty certain, Ernie didn't know about.

He didn't rummage long before he saw the worn lettering of the Arnott's Biscuit Company at the back of the shelf, behind old newspapers. The tin nearly slipped from his hands as he prised it open. Out spilled a mess of threads and a flutter of money. Ignoring the money, he tossed the threads onto the bed until a shiny rectangular card on the floor caught his eye.

He picked it up, the backs of his arms and neck prickling as though peppered by shrapnel.

His sister undressed, young, topless from the waist up apart from a flimsy see-through blouse, her hair bouncing over her shoulders, her eyes closed. A professional photographic portrait.

A cold sweat broke out on his neck. Mind reeling, he stumbled, reached out for the dressing table. He gripped the edge, staring blindly as though it were dark, unable to shake the image of his sister from his head. It wasn't natural. He wanted the old picture back – Lily his sister who took care of him when he came out of the hospital, who took him in when he turned up on her doorstep, defended him even against her own husband. Lily who became more mother to him than their own. But Lily hadn't just disappeared when he'd been sent to the Lemnos Hospital – she'd betrayed and abandoned him long before.

Tommy blinked his eyes and the picture became clear. This was proof. Everything Lily had said was a lie. Girlie was her child but now that he could see for himself what Lily was like, he doubted Ernie was the father. The years weren't adding up for him, he tried to count how many years Lily and Ernie had been married, when Girlie must have been born.

Lily had infected everyone with her lies.

He beat his fist on the dressing table, pain shooting up his wrist and into his elbow, his punishment for trusting. The way he'd seen it – that Ernie had been the one to dump him in the institution – could be wrong too. It could have been all Lily's idea. Perhaps she had always tried to be rid of him: art school, enlisting – he tried to remember whose idea that had been, but that memory had gone, slipped away with the rest of them – the barracks hospital after the war. She had told him he had to stay in that place, waiting for the army to discharge him, kept visiting to appease him, when she might have been telling the authorities to hold him further.

Afraid of being found out.

He'd been wrong about what she was afraid of. But he *had* found her out. And there he had been thinking Lily the dupe while Ernie carried on with Lorna, when it was Ernie who was the dupe, not knowing he'd adopted Lily's bastard, the shameful truth hidden away from the family. Everything Tommy had held true about her had been wrong. She had betrayed him and she would betray him again.

Truth had long been sucked into the black hole of his mind, no matter how much he tried to dive in after it. He ended up swimming against the direction it swirled him in, exhausted. Easier to give up and disappear.

Would he?

He had come this far, had to see it to the end. But what would he say to Lily? What if she came home from the recital early, found him in this state? All she cared for was sending Girlie away to that school. Sending her away.

He was thinking clearly now. He stood up, took a deep breath, moved towards the door but stubbed his toe. He bent down to move whatever was blocking his way. A wooden box sticking out from under the bed, and from the length of it, he knew what it was immediately. Ernie's rifle. He undid the latches and felt the cold steel barrel inside. Solid, supporting Tommy's disbelief that Ernie was at Fred's farm, culling emus. He couldn't very well without his .22 calibre with the reflexive trigger, not like Paxton's .44 calibre that required some force to fire it.

The shock on Ernie's face when the rifle had gone off. Oh, he'd been forced to see Tommy then. Decayed and rotten, but then that was who he was now.

His blood roiled, the thoughts in his head confusing him, fleeing down the centre of that black hole. An acrid taste in his throat.

He lifted Ernie's rifle, tucking it under his arm, and made his way down the corridor to his room, dropping it on the bed just as he heard noises, rumbling, the nickering of the horse, outside. He attuned his ears to listen out if they stopped, the rain falling softly on the roof.

CHAPTER FORTY

GIRLIE

Her mother marched towards the back of the house, closing the door to the bathroom behind her as rain began to fall. Girlie rubbed Brownie's nose, feeling him nuzzle into her hand, and pressed her face against his. What would her father have to say? Would he take away her new bicycle because she didn't deserve it? Her mother didn't love her, but she deserved it. It must have been difficult for her mother to wear her 'outside face', always pretending to care for Girlie as though she were her own real child. And now she had ruined her mother's life and they would have to move again. Her throat tightened at the fear of what might happen to Ruby, and her heart quickened.

Brownie pulled away from her grasp.

Something hissed at her. Breath squeezed from her chest. She squinted her eyes, searching the shadows behind the house, and started when a figure moved out into the half-light.

Ruby. Shaking, her new purple flowery dress wet.

'What are you doing here?' Girlie whispered, glancing across to the back of the house, dark except for the pane of glass lit up in the bathroom.

Ruby gasped, swallowing, and then formed her words. 'I didn't know where else to g-go.'

Girlie beckoned Ruby to follow, and placing her finger on her lips in warning, led her into the wash house.

'I'm so frightened of my dad,' whispered Ruby, widening her eyes.

Girlie caught her breath. 'Robert McGinty?'

Ruby scowled. 'Not him, my dad.'

Girlie looked at her friend. The time had come. She shook her head. 'Didn't you know? Robert McGinty is your real father.'

Ruby spat on the wash house floor, shocking Girlie. 'He's my mother's old no-good boss. My dad's my father, he reared me up.'

Shame burned Girlie's cheeks. Ruby hadn't believed her. 'Why are you afraid of him, then?' she asked, her voice catching on a cry.

'I did something very bad.' Ruby's voice was solemn. 'The police are gunna take me away now, I know it. All day, I was being warned . . . the signs of danger were there . . . And I still did it.' She shook her head and Girlie moved to put her arm around Ruby.

'What did you do?'

'That boy, Bobby. He came down to the river. He knew I was there, came looking for me, calling my name. I tried to run, but he was bigger and faster, he caught me, started touching me—' Ruby stopped. Shaking all over, she pulled away from Girlie. 'I wasn't thinking. I just picked up a rock and hit him. On the head.'

Girlie shivered. Her blood felt cold, and not just from the rain. It was because of her that Bobby knew where to look for Ruby. 'Is he . . .'

Ruby spat on the ground again. 'No! It was just a small cut, not even much blood. But it was bad enough. Don't you see? He's gunna go straight to tell the police.'

'Oh.' Girlie's mind reeled.

‘I didn’t know where else to go. I can’t go home. My dad will kill me.’

‘He won’t!’

‘I’d get given a bad beating for it. He’ll lose his job for sure. The police won’t let us stay in Dongarra no more.’

Girlie swallowed, stilling her questions. ‘I know what you have to do.’ She ducked out the wash house door, creeping until she could see the McGintys’ house. There was a dim glow in one of the windows. The rain splashed off the side of the wash house wall, coming down harder, wetting through her hair and the shoulders of her dress. Holding her arms over her head, she dashed back to Ruby waiting inside the doorway. ‘We’re going over to the McGintys’.’ Ruby shook her head firmly. ‘The old McGintys. They’ll speak to the police and you won’t be taken away.’

Ruby’s eyes gleamed brightly against the dark. ‘No police. You don’t understand.’

Girlie wanted to hug her, hold her tightly, but instead she placed her hand on Ruby’s. ‘I do. I’m adopted. I don’t know who my real parents are. That’s why my parents can’t love me. I’m not blood related. They don’t have to love me.’ She paused to take a breath before all the words spilled out. Words she didn’t even know she’d been holding back. ‘But the McGintys, they’re your blood relatives. When they find out about you, they’ll want to help you. Besides, what other choice do you have?’

Ruby stared at her, then laced her fingers with Girlie’s. ‘I’m too scared. Won’t your dad help me?’

Girlie shook her head. ‘He won’t be back until tomorrow. And then I’m going to be in my own trouble.’ Emboldened by the risk she was taking, she tugged on Ruby’s hand. She might not be able to find out who she really was, but she wouldn’t let Ruby miss the chance, especially not when it might save her. ‘Come on.’

'It's raining hard. You'll get wet,' said Ruby, not budging.

Girlie sighed. She was still wearing her good frock, trimmed specially. Searching the shadows of the wash house for something to cover herself with, she spied her mother's old greatcoat hanging behind the copper. A thick mildewy smell escaped when she shook it out. It wasn't until they'd dashed across the muddy yard to the back fence and she held the fence down so that Ruby could clamber over, that she realised Ruby's new dress had been ruined from the mud and rain.

CHAPTER FORTY-ONE

LILY

Lily moved her hand in circles, feeling the warm eddy of water against her ribs. Her breasts were two islands. She stared at her small brown nipples and splashed them. Water dribbled down their sides. They weren't large breasts, not like Lorna's. They were as small as when she'd married Ernie. Lorna was right on that account – having children would have altered her body. But Lily hadn't borne children, and that changed her on the inside. She hated this body with its appearance of womanliness when it was a lie. Instead of feeling natural, alone, naked in the bath tub, she felt exposed.

Lily clamped her hands to her breasts.

She stifled a sob remembering how vulnerable she had been, allowing that photographer to take those filthy pictures of her. At first, he had posed her as 'September Morn'. She couldn't recall – had it been Howard, the shoe salesman, or Ernie with her that day on St George's Terrace, stepping out, when Mr Ambrose Forbes slipped his card into her hand?

My dear, I simply must take your photograph, you look exquisite, he'd said, doffing his hat.

Taken aback by his approach, Lily scanned the card, noting his credentials.

Why would you do that? her companion demanded of Mr Forbes. It must have been Ernie. Howard was never so forceful.

Mr Forbes smiled his thin-lipped smile. *My photographs have appeared as society cabinet cards from here to Sydney, sir. But this young lady would outshine most of the posers I capture.*

Her heart had beaten fast. *Would I be paid to sit for the photographs*, she glanced down at his card, *Mr Forbes?*

He showed his teeth to her. *Of course. Let's say, my studio next Wednesday around five?*

Tommy hadn't been in work for nine months since he'd lost his job at the AFL fruit-canning factory, and her father had been passed over for races he usually reported on. They relied on her wage from Pritchard's, but she wanted more than making do, she wanted them to have the lives they were meant to lead. Art courses for Tommy, and a doctor for Pa. Ever since her mother had left he had been drinking heavily and now he was always unwell, his reputation at the track and on the paper deteriorating.

She had gone then, sitting for a dozen pictures modelling her own creations and dresses from Pritchard's shop as well as the fancy dress poses, which the photographer said were popular. One of the photographs was released to the *Western Mail*, her father's newspaper: 'The Racing Reporter's Daughter' the headline.

Though she hadn't sought it, the attention from Pritchard's clientele over the following month had flattered her. It had been her smocked, peach-coloured lawn-cotton dress design featured in the newspaper that had drawn well-to-do ladies to the shop requesting copies. Mr Pritchard even asked when she would pose for the photographer again, because he had new frocks for her to model, and hinted at apprenticing her as a dressmaker.

Another sitting for Mr Forbes might be all that was needed, so that Pa could retire from the paper to recuperate. She'd gone back to Mr Forbes, asking if he had any society commissions she could pose for. His studio smelled more sour than before, of stale perspiration and cigar smoke.

He ran his fingers through his pomaded hair. *There's a client in Sydney requesting a girl with a certain style.* He cocked his head, looking at her figure. Lily turned slightly to afford him a fuller viewing. *But I have other girls on my list.* He threw up his hand, and turned to fiddle with his leatherette folding camera.

She had paused at the doorway but now pursued him into the dimly lit room. The shades were drawn and the only light came from a lamp covered in red cloth in the corner. *I'd really appreciate the opportunity,* she said. She had style, just as the Sydney commissions required. Had she been aiming too low, could she be better than an apprentice dressmaker – perhaps have her own shop, dress the young starlets of the theatre and darlings of the wealthy pastoralists in Sydney? She could already feel how proud her father would be of her, a warm glow spreading from her chest and up to her cheeks.

The next part was a blur. The session had started as the other had, fully clothed. But the combination of the musty smell in the enclosed darkened room, like in a moving pictures hall, and her ambition to be admired, led her to the perilous state. He had offered some sort of wine and she'd drunk the lot, nervous because she rarely looked on herself undressed.

The next day, in the grey winter light, her arms up to the elbows in suds as she dollied her father's work shirts, she felt revolted by what she had done. She kept her mind on the Sydney commission. If she won that, then she could put the ordeal out of her mind and behind her. No one would ever need to know about it.

After a week her enquiries remained unanswered.

She rapped on Mr Forbes's door, marching in when he opened it wearing only his trousers and vest.

Darling, he said, reaching out for her, his gaze skimming her body. She felt sickened. He shrugged his shoulder. *I'm sorry, the client took another girl. Perhaps, I can still change his mind.* He licked his lip, advancing on her until Lily was pressed against the back of his chaise longue.

I'm not that kind of girl, she cried, hitting out at him. He stumbled backwards, then lunged at her.

Oh, I think you are. I can see the headline now – 'The Racy Reporter's Daughter'.

Lily felt the hard swell in his trousers push against her hip. His breath was rancid, and she gagged. No commission in Sydney was worth what she thought he wanted from her, but was he threatening her with blackmail now? Would he send those awful photographs to her father's newspaper? She blanched at the thought of her father seeing her scantily clad. His colleagues. His reputation. The very opposite of what she had set out to do.

The room began to spin when she realised what she had to do to make amends.

After the violation, he threw the photograph at her. *For you.*

On the omnibus home, Lily palmed her eyes, calming herself with deep breaths, feeling sick with shame. Mr Forbes had taken her chastity, but before that he had taken something far more precious – her resolve to be nothing like Ma. Lily had sacrificed the family's wellbeing for her own selfish designs. Yes, at first, she had thought only of helping her father and brother have a better life – but the attention and admiration had gone to her head, making her break her vow to put her family's needs before hers.

She gasped, put her hand to her stomach, feeling it heave as she realised she'd neglected more than she'd realised. A pregnancy would be unforgiveable.

She had thought to tear the photograph to shreds, but stopped herself. How could she avoid sliding backwards into wanton selfishness, if this was who she really was, no better than Ma? Where were her strength and determination? If she kept the photograph – no matter how painful – she would be constantly reminded of the person she would not let herself be again.

The following evening when Ernie came to take her out to the pictures, she kept him waiting outside while she made herself up carefully, selecting her best frock. Steeling herself for the sacrifice she had to make.

You look ravishing, he'd said when she stepped out to the porch. He blushed, before leaning in for a kiss on the cheek. She hooked her arm inside his, and hoped very much that she did look ravishing. When her courage faltered that night, she found it in alcohol. And Ernie went where she led him.

As she left for her lunch break the next day, she saw Ernie waiting by the front of the shop. He got down on one knee, and she felt a flutter in her stomach.

~

A crack of thunder rattled the swollen window frame of the bathroom. Moments later the pane lit up. The flame in the lamp guttered. As she watched it flicker shadows on the walls above her, she thought of how she'd felt when she discovered she hadn't been pregnant after all. If she hadn't tricked Ernie into marriage, she might have chosen the other fellow, or waited for the right man to come along.

A hasty decision with a lifetime of consequences.

Lightning lit up the bathroom again with stark clarity, and a gust of wind blew under the door extinguishing the lamp.

CHAPTER FORTY-TWO

GIRLIE

Girlie hammered on the shutters of the McGintys' cottage. 'Mrs McGinty, Mr McGinty, it's Girlie from next door.' But a roll of thunder smothered her voice. She shifted the collar of her mother's coat a little higher, beckoned Ruby to follow her. Ruby shivered violently, wrapping her thin arms around her body.

At the back door, she smelled onions frying. Ruby would be safe and warm here. Girlie lifted her hand to knock but the door opened, and she stumbled forwards.

The doorway framed Mrs McGinty. 'Child, go home.'

Girlie stepped aside for Mrs McGinty to see Ruby. 'This is Ruby. She needs your help.'

Girlie stood between the old woman and Ruby, both of them frail and small, and expressionless. Mrs McGinty clenched her jaw. 'There's nothing for me to do. I don't know this girl.'

This was Girlie's chance to mend one family, connect blood with blood. She grinned in anticipation, flutters in her belly, but became solemn remembering the seriousness of the situation. 'Ruby did something wrong, but not too bad, and now her father is going to punish her and she's scared the police will take her away. Mrs

McGinty, you have to help her, because . . . because she's your granddaughter.'

Ruby shifted close, pressing her bony hip against Girlie's thigh.

Mrs McGinty also moved, turning aside to the kitchen.

Lightning cracked over their heads. Ruby clutched at her and both girls held their breath.

Mrs McGinty was now holding a rifle.

'Like I said, get away. You think we don't know about her, that she was a secret?' She pointed the rifle at Ruby. 'It's our secret to keep.'

CHAPTER FORTY-THREE

TOMMY

The crack of lightning jolted Tommy, nearly knocking the rifle box to the floor. The room lit up, drawing long shadows in the corners. He took the rifle and aimed it at those shadows, goading them to attack.

But then all went dark again. Tommy stood to attention, rifle held across his chest, listening, waiting. Nobody in the house. The room hardened. Just darkness. He fumbled for the sash on the window to let in cool air. Keep him focused. There was only one way he would be free – to take the road out of this town, with what he had left of himself, and never have to come back.

Ma. Lily. Women were all the same: you went to war to keep them safe, but they turned on you nonetheless, ungrateful, wanted to hurt you.

The sky raged with thunder, and another bolt of lightning lit up the street front, the sea with its raging white foam. And two figures, a man and a woman, running out of the McGintys' house in this direction.

If they came here, they'd find him. They'd ruin everything. He hitched the rifle under his arm, and stole down the corridor, letting himself out the back door without closing the latch. The only place to hide was inside the wash house, and along the shadow side of the wall, he snuck to the open doorway.

CHAPTER FORTY-FOUR

LILY

The lamp was extinguished. Lily lay in the bath tub in the pitch black, running her fingers down her arms to cradle her stomach. She couldn't change what she'd done. It didn't matter if the ladies in town loved her garden, thought she made beautiful dresses, or sneered at her in the street because of her behaviour at the recital, whether she kept a good house or a filthy house. It didn't matter, because she couldn't change who she was. Lily felt her body buoy, relieved of a burden she hadn't known she'd been carrying.

Thunder rattled the roof sheeting, louder.

She shot up from the bath and pulled on her robe, letting her hair stream water down her back as she hurried into the house. The back door pushed open easily, and she fell inside, groping about for the matches in the darkness. But the shelf on which they usually sat was bare. *Damn, damn, damn.*

She felt her way in the dark to the bedroom, groped for the newspaper in the wardrobe. Lightning flashed, brightening the window panes once more, and she tore off a strip for a taper to hold at the still-warm charcoals in the stove. That's when she caught sight of it lying on the dressing table.

The photograph.

It was weakness that made her keep it. Too weak to face up to herself. Too weak to stand up to Mr Forbes, anything to stop him from ruining how Pa saw her. After Pa died, the photograph gave her strength when she wavered in her dedication to the marriage.

It was at the plain-and-fancy-dress ball in Perenjori that Mr Forbes had recognised her, taken Ernie's name from the photograph of Girlie. Two weeks later a letter arrived asking for blackmail money or he'd reveal the photograph in the paper. So, she'd scrimped on household expenses, and sewn dresses for ladies around town to pay him off. Until Ernie made her sell the Singer, and desperation had driven her to act, left alone by the blocked-up fireplace in the sitting room when she'd stopped by to collect the rent from Mr Sutcliffe.

And now the photograph had been discovered. But by whom? If it was Girlie who'd found it, Lily might be able to explain it away, but she would lose all moral authority. If by Tommy, she would feel humiliated, unable to look him in the eye again. He would leave and she would hope to never see him again from the shame of it. But if it was Ernie?

The photograph had to be destroyed. She raked the charcoals in the stove.

CHAPTER FORTY-FIVE

TOMMY

Tommy twisted the metal in his hands, counting out the seconds. How many seconds to live? But he didn't need his CO to goad him this time. He wasn't a coward. He was going over the top, his rifle loaded.

He stepped out of the wash house into the driving rain, and in that instant recognised the two figures. They weren't the McGintys.

Girlie in that floral dress he'd seen Lily making for her, and Lily behind, wearing Pa's greatcoat, the one he'd always worn to the races. Lily and Ma, both of them to blame for their father's ruin, Tommy's ruin.

He lifted the rifle to his shoulder, just as lightning fractured the sky, sending a whistle into his skull. And he charged.

CHAPTER FORTY-SIX

LILY

A crack of lightning rang out. Lily soaked two lumps of charcoal in the kerosene from the lamp, waiting for the thunder to follow. Dread crept through her.

It had sounded like a gun shot.

She dropped the photograph, threw open the back door, hesitated, peering through the pelting rain, until her gaze fell on shadowy figures near the vegetable plots. Fear flooded her veins like ice water. She ran out into the yard, her thoughts confused, racing wildly.

Lily pushed the wet hair from her eyes. There was a girl, soaked through, filthy and clutching at something beneath her. 'Girlie!' the girl cried. 'Girlie's been shot.'

Lily scrambled through bushes that scratched at her arms and legs, and pushed the girl aside. The night lit up like day, exposing what seemed a bundle of wet clothing tumbled to the ground. Girlie's body lay still, soaked, blood splashed over her chest and pooling around her, diluted by the rain. Shivering and crouched beside her – Tommy, a shotgun hanging limply from his hand.

'Do you know what you've done? Who Girlie is?' she screamed.

CHAPTER FORTY-SEVEN

ERNIE

On his way through town, Ernie slowed past the hall, searched among the stragglers – a few buggies and motor cars, but no dray. Lily must have left the recital early on account of the rain, though he didn't think she'd let a storm get in the way of securing a spot for Girlie at that school. Lily *was* the storm, always getting her way. He drove on, but as he neared the bridge, a bedraggled figure lurched out into the beam of the Hillman's headlamps: Mrs Fry, waving her arms at him. Soaked through.

'Mr Hass, you've got to get yourself to Geraldton,' she gasped, as he leaped out of the motor car.

His first thought was Lorna, that she'd done something drastic in revenge for his rejection. 'What?'

'Your girl, she's in the hospital. There was an accident. Dr Marsh's away in Perth, so Reg McGinty rang through to the ambulance in Geraldton. Mrs Hass has gone with them.'

Ernie stared at her, trying to take it in, and then started up the motor car, turning it around.

~

Ernie rushed through the reception of the Victoria Hospital, past the nursing sister calling after him, running up the stairs and along the landings to each of the two large wards filled with patients in beds. A stern-looking nurse came over to him.

'Where's my daughter? My wife, Lily Hass?' He grabbed at her wrist.

'I'll kindly ask you to go back to reception, sir,' she said, shaking her arm free. 'You can't be in here.'

'He came straight past me, wouldn't stop,' said the nursing sister who'd pursued him up the stairs.

'My daughter, Girlie Hass, has been brought here. I need to find her. I need to know what happened to her,' he implored. The stern one tilted her chin at the other nursing sister.

'Take this gentleman to see Mrs Hass.'

'This way, sir.'

He followed, asking her what had happened.

'You will have to speak to Mrs Hass about that, sir,' she said, indicating for him to go through to a room beyond the stairs.

When he saw Lily sitting in that room hugging her arms around herself, he paused. She looked awful. Wet through, blood smeared on her clothing. His leather shoes squealed on the floorboards and she looked up, face white and drawn.

'Lil.' He pulled her up to him in an embrace.

A shudder went through her body. 'She was shot.'

Ernie stiffened. 'What? Girlie's been shot?'

Lily wouldn't look at him, staring over his shoulder.

He released her, running his hands through his wet hair. 'Tommy.'

Tiny lines pulled between her brows. 'It must have been an accident. Why would he . . .' She swayed and he wrapped his arms around her.

'He had no reason to.' Ernie hoped to reassure her.

She nodded, her mouth making shapes to talk but no sound came out.

He lowered Lily to the seat. 'Where is she?' She pointed towards a set of double doors.

'Don't,' she said faintly. He ignored her. A doctor and two nursing sisters stood over the bed, Girlie so small he could barely see her body beneath the sheet.

The doctor came over to him. 'You can't come in here, sir,' he said firmly. 'We'll be taking her into theatre shortly.'

'Can you tell me if she'll . . .'

The doctor nodded. 'It's a flesh wound in her upper arm. We'll do the best we can.'

A nurse laid a hand on his arm.

'Make sure she survives,' he said.

~

The operation took more than an hour. Occasionally Lily would brush his sleeve with her hand, but by the time he registered her movement and reached to grasp her hand, she had dropped it to her lap. When he got up to smoke cigarette after cigarette, pacing the hall, she did not follow. They were allowed a glimpse of Girlie, sedated, her body obscured by sheets and bandages, as she was wheeled past on the trolley to the recovery ward, and for the briefest moment, Lily turned to him, let him enclose her in his arms.

'I can't, Ernie. I just can't . . .'

He did not wait to hear what Lily was unable to do. But his attempt to follow his daughter was thwarted by the nursing sisters.

When he returned to Lily in the waiting room, she'd been joined by two men, one of whom he knew.

'Ernie—' started Gerry, clearing his throat. 'Mr Hass, can we speak with you?'

'Tell me you've caught the bastard, Gerry.' Ernie looked from Gerry to the sergeant accompanying him, older, grim-faced. He was a good six inches shorter and had to lift his chin to meet Ernie's eye.

Gerry motioned for Ernie to come with them down the corridor. Ernie glanced at Lily but she sat with her eyes closed. He nodded at the policemen and followed.

'So?'

The sergeant watched Ernie through eyes like narrow slits. 'I'm Sergeant O'Hara.'

Gerry hung back now, letting his superior take the lead, but offered, 'The sergeant came in from Walkaway. Needed a bit of help with this one, mate.'

'But it was Tommy. Tommy Adamson,' Ernie said to the sergeant. 'My brother-in-law was the one who shot my daughter. You just need to get him, though he's likely absconded by now.'

'Constable Paxton and his man couldn't find any trace of Mr Adamson near your property.'

'So, why are you here?' asked Ernie, looking to Gerry for an answer, unsettled to see him avoid his eye.

'The fire, Mr Hass,' said the sergeant.

That bitch Lorna had gone to Bill or the police, called his bluff. Ernie's blood raged. He had more important concerns right now than his affair with Lorna. 'Whatever she said, she's a liar.'

The sergeant raised an eyebrow. 'She? Are you talking about Mrs Hass?'

Ernie put his hand to his brow, clammy, worrying his fingers in small circles. 'What are you talking about?'

Gerry opened his mouth to speak but the sergeant spoke over him. 'A fire broke out at your property.'

Ernie swallowed air. Rubbed at his scalp until it was almost raw.

'You seem quite disturbed by the news.'

Ernie dropped his hand, squaring up his shoulders. 'Of course I'm upset, man, you've just told me Tommy's set fire to my business as well as tried to kill my daughter.'

He flicked his gaze to Gerry and back to the sergeant. Gerry's mouth was firm now and he'd stepped closer to Ernie, shielding him slightly from the sergeant. 'The fire didn't get to the shop on account of the rain putting it out. It might not be so bad as it sounds.'

The sergeant cleared his throat. 'Constable Paxton tells me you weren't at the church fair, nor at the house when your daughter was shot. Can you account for your whereabouts this evening?'

It was a quick movement, but one he knew had given him away the moment he looked over at Lily. Sergeant O'Hara caught it, and curled his lip. 'I see, Mr Hass.'

Ernie lowered his voice, leaning towards Gerry. 'I was driving to Geraldton but thought better of it, so I turned back. Then one of the women in town stopped me, told me that Girlie had been brought to hospital here and I came straightaway. You can check my story with her.'

The sergeant put his hat back on, reached for the notebook in his inside coat pocket. He made a few notes and looked up. 'And you didn't go back to your property?'

He was writing it down. Words that could be used against Ernie. Treated like a criminal. 'No.'

Gerry shifted from one foot to the other as though finding his sea legs on the hospital floor. Ernie felt similarly uneasy.

'If that is all, I must comfort my wife. Our daughter has been shot tonight, must I remind you, Sergeant O'Hara.' Ernie made to leave, and Gerry at least had the decency to look embarrassed for putting him in this position.

But the sergeant cleared his throat.

'Ern, we haven't finished with you.' A note of apology creeping into Gerry's tone.

The sergeant flipped back several pages of his notebook until he found what he needed. Ernie closed his eyes briefly. It seemed words would be used against him anyway.

'You've been involved in a run of unfortunate incidents over the years, haven't you, Mr Hass?'

'Yes, but so've lots of fellas. There's a depression on.'

The sergeant's lips made a grim line. 'Your name was recently noted in relation to a Customs report. You were engaged in selling unlicensed liquor.'

'I explained to that official. I had no idea Mr White wasn't on the up and up. And I stopped selling his hop beer as soon as I found out.'

'Quite,' said the sergeant, with little regard for Ernie's explanation. 'I rang through to the Perenjori station, where you were a resident, I believe, until late August.'

'That's correct.'

'Sergeant Smith had some interesting information regarding a house of yours in Perenjori that burned down December 1929. According to reports, the fire had been started in the sitting room but the only working fireplace was in the kitchen.'

Ernie had heard the findings before, but he had a solid alibi. Rabbits had got into the top paddock and he and several farmers had been shooting at them all day.

'And you have recently been declared bankrupt.'

It felt like he was being scrutinised in that courtroom all over again. It was bad enough the first time, having the litany of his mistakes and errors of judgement read out to him. 'I don't see how any of this has any bearing on what's happened tonight.'

The sergeant stepped up close to Ernie. Ernie could see the hairs protruding from his bulbous nose. The sergeant sniffed and chewed the inside of his cheek.

'There's a whiff of petrol about you. Now, why would that be?'

Ernie didn't back away or back down. 'I own a petrol bowser. I suppose petrol gets onto my clothes sometimes.'

'I notice a burn on your hand there, Mr Hass.' The sergeant shook his head. 'I tell you, this doesn't look good from where I'm standing.'

Ernie looked down to compose himself, studied the back of his hand, contemplating the ridiculousness of the sergeant's claim.

'It's a cigarette burn, sergeant. I was careless when driving. Are you charging me with arson? Because you haven't got any proof, and what's more, I won't stand for it. My daughter was shot by a lunatic and you're not doing anything about it.'

'Steady on, Frank,' Gerry said to the sergeant. 'Can't we give him a fair go? After all . . .' He motioned at Lily. 'Ernie Hass is a local Geraldton boy, served in the war. And it could have been the native I've got locked up in the cell back at the station.'

Ernie hesitated. 'What native?'

'We found an exempt native, name of Jim Feehely, loitering in the sand hills behind the house. He said he was looking for someone. Wouldn't say who. We gave him a good kicking, and he won't be out of the native cells too soon.'

The sergeant spat at the floor. 'Bloody blacks. We can charge him with arson, it'll make it a lot easier for you and us, Mr Hass.'

Ernie sagged with relief. This charade had been all about making him sweat a bit, to throw the sergeant's authority around and punish Ernie without the hassle of going through procedure.

He walked the policemen to the front doors. It was dark out and they turned up the collars of their coats in case of rain. He turned back to the waiting area, where Lily was standing, shoulders hunched and eyes glassy though she held back her tears.

'Sit down, Lil.'

She sat on the bench beside him. 'What did they want?'

He slid closer, tried to take her hand. She flinched.

Ernie sighed. She was nervy – he couldn't tell her about the fire on top of her worry for Girlie. 'There was a fire at our place. They caught a black nearby.'

He still couldn't shake the feeling Tommy was involved in the fire, but that Aboriginal still wasn't innocent – hanging about his house where Ernie's wife and child lived. Ernie felt no shame at letting him wear the blame.

Lily tilted her head towards him, watching, waiting for him to say more. Her mouth tightened and Ernie watched the lump roll in her throat as she swallowed. She was looking down at her fingers opening and closing the clasp on her handbag, then stopped and looked at him blankly, the glassiness of her eyes gone.

'Is there anything else?'

'Yes,' he said. The set of her shoulders flickered. 'I'm sorry I wasn't . . .' He had to let her know that he'd broken his vows to her. Would promise no more compromises. But he couldn't tell her about Lorna when their child had been shot. '. . . I wasn't there for her.'

The nurse came towards them, and he was grateful for the intrusion.

'Mr Hass, Mrs Hass. Girlie is awake.'

'Can I see her?' Lily reached a hand to her throat.

The nurse smiled. 'Of course. I can only allow a visit for twenty minutes. She needs to rest.'

Lily hurried along the covered walkway to the recovery ward and he followed two yards behind, watching her heels flick up and down in front of him.

He held back, standing with the nurse at the end of the bed while she approached Girlie, laid a hand on Girlie's chest, and sobbed. Ernie's gaze lingered on the swelling of padded bandage on Girlie's right shoulder. Her gown was open loose at the neck and her hair was pulled back under a hospital cap. She stirred, her eyelashes fluttered and a small smile crept across her face.

'Mummy.'

Lily sniffed, forcing her own, much larger, smile. 'My brave poppet. Does it hurt? Mummy will make sure you get better.'

Girlie nodded weakly, turning her head around until she saw him. Though dulled from the morphine, her eyes lit up. 'Daddy, you came.'

He rounded the bed the other side from Lily, taking Girlie's face between his hands. 'Of course I did. I rushed straight here as soon as I heard.'

Girlie winced, shifting her body under the sheets and stretched her left hand up to him. He didn't move as she ran her finger under his eye, smearing the wetness there. 'Don't cry, Daddy,' she said. 'It wasn't you that got shot, it was me.'

He blinked as tears blurred his vision of her. He didn't care if they all saw him crying, and instead of making him feel less of a man, he felt more of one. Girlie's love was more than he deserved, but it was his. He placed his hand gently on Lily's.

CHAPTER FORTY-EIGHT

GIRLIE

If she didn't move, she could bear the hot, throbbing pain in her arm. In fact, Girlie didn't want anyone to move. Her father had put his hand on her mother's.

'Where's Uncle Tommy?'

Her parents pulled their hands apart. 'Don't worry about him, darling,' her mother said, bringing her face close. 'He's gone—'

'For good, I hope.' Her father's eyes turned angry and dark.

'The police will find him,' said her mother, frowning at him.

Girlie moved her gaze between her parents, willing their hands back together on her chest.

'Can you tell us what happened, Girlie?' her father asked, softening his eyes again.

She closed her eyes to remember.

'It's too soon, Ernie. Don't pressure her, for goodness sake.'

Girlie rolled her head towards her father. She blinked several times to clear away the fog. 'I don't know,' she said, her voice coming out in a whisper as she struggled to form the story. 'I went outside – to the privy – and heard a noise. I think that was the gun. And then I just fell down.' She shut her eyes and remembered.

It's our secret to keep, Mrs McGinty had said, the end of the rifle waving in front of them.

A warm trickle had run down Girlie's leg.

Best you go back to those parents of yours. They've got their own nasty secrets.

Girlie wished she had put her hands over her ears as Mrs McGinty spat out horrible stories about her mother and father.

Put it down, Martha, had come Mr McGinty's voice from inside the kitchen. He'd taken the gun from his wife's hands, holding eye contact with her. *They're only children. No need to scare them.*

He'd placed his hands on his wife's shoulders, then turned to the girls, gesturing with his head for them to leave. *We know that Robert's not been a good man, he did bad things to that woman, your mother,* he'd flicked his eyes quickly to Ruby, *but he's the only son we've got left. Please understand.*

Girlie didn't need to be asked twice, prodding at Ruby to run.

Ruby was the faster runner, slipping over the fence and into the Hasses' yard ahead of Girlie. Girlie hadn't yet reached the corner of the wash house, the wind lashing her wet hair across her eyes so that she hadn't been able to see anything except for the drops of moonlight on the window louvres.

Beneath the howl of the wind she had heard Uncle Tommy. Girlie wished she hadn't heard, strained to remember it differently.

Lily? he'd said, just before the bang.

Girlie opened her eyes to look at her mother.

Mrs McGinty had told Girlie who her real father was. Mrs McGinty had opened one of her mother's letters that had come to their post office, read what Girlie's real father was demanding her mother to do if she wanted to keep Emma, as he called her.

Her mother leaned over her. 'It's time to rest now. I'll be just here. I won't leave your side, I promise.'

Her mother's promise was everything.

The corners of her father's mouth quivered as he tried to smile.

Mrs McGinty had said awful things about him, that he'd been doing those disgusting things the boys teased about in the playground, with Mrs Fairclough. That Mrs Fairclough was going to have her father's baby, so she wrote in a letter to him.

She flung out her hand as he stepped away from the bed. 'Can you make a promise to me as well?'

'Anything.'

'Promise me you'll still love me.'

His eyes looked wet. 'Always.' He cupped her chin and walked away.

It didn't matter that she was adopted. She saw that Mr and Mrs McGinty would do anything to protect Robert McGinty, even if he wasn't the son that they really wanted. Her parents had chosen her; they weren't perfect but she would keep their secrets.

She stretched her toes towards the end of the bed. Her mother was right, she might be turning into a young lady after all. Growing up meant knowing which secrets to keep and which to tell.

'Girlie . . .' her mother began. Her brow wrinkled. 'Girlie, there's never the right time—'

Girlie squeezed her hand. 'I know who I am.'

Her mother's eyes glistened, swelling with tears.

'Is it still raining, Mummy?' she murmured. She didn't want Uncle Tommy to get wet. She knew where he would be – under the bridge where he'd hidden last time.

'Maybe, darling.'

Girlie smiled but felt it droop to the side of her face. Very, very tired now. The overhead lamp was bright still, like headlamps coming towards her in the darkness. She heard humming. She was safe, her mother singing her a lullaby.

CHAPTER FORTY-NINE

ERNIE

Ernie squatted in the rubble, watching the boats approach the jetty, the wind ripping at the sails. The men clambering up the ladder from their dinghies with a speed that meant news. All morning, he'd sifted through muddied and twisted bits of iron and charred timbers, setting aside any object that had escaped the fire.

He straightened up, hand over his eyes as he watched the men run towards the McGintys'. Reg dashed out in his mackintosh, conferring with the men, line fishermen, among them George Hopkins and the Italian, Moretta, then disappear back inside the shop. Moretta appeared to be walking towards him, but stopped when George called out.

No one had come to speak to him since he'd got back from Geraldton, except Gerry Paxton and Matthew Fry. No witnesses had come forward about the fire. He kicked at the wall, showering a clump of limestone onto the scorched remnants of Lily's good linoleum. The McGintys had been home, but neither had seen or heard anything amiss at the Hasses until the shot had rung out.

It had been four days since the operation and the wound had started to heal. The doctors said Girlie might be released in a day or so. But where were they supposed to live? Lily was staying in Geraldton while Girlie recovered, but Ernie knew she would not come back to Dongarra unable to survive the mood in this town. Not that anyone would hold her responsible for the fire.

Thank Christ for insurance. The man from Geraldton had been down to see him, checked his documents were in order, the police report satisfactory. Gerry had seen to it that they had a culprit, and Ernie was free to collect the insurance money on the kitchen and bedrooms. The guestrooms were still habitable, though the insurance man had commiserated when Ernie's tourist bookings for the summer fell through, one by one. No, it did not take long for news to spread in this town.

'Excuse me.'

Ernie started at the sound of Reg's voice. He was standing in the doorway to what had been the kitchen, dripping water, his face downcast. He snuffled into his handkerchief before tucking it into his trouser pocket.

'Reg. What's all the hullaballoo out on the jetty?'

'Ah . . .' Reg began. 'The fellas have caught a big 'un. A shark,' he added. 'They've slit his belly open and there's . . .' He lowered his voice, shuffling on the spot. 'There's human remains inside.'

Ernie's stomach clenched. 'Tommy?' He'd wanted him caught, but not like this.

'Could be.'

'Is Gerry coming down?'

'I just called him on the telephone,' said Reg. 'He's on his way.'

It was some sort of justice for what Tommy had done to Ernie's life. Damaged his business, reputation, daughter. He imagined that the only reason Tommy hadn't hurt Lily was because of all she had done for him.

Christ. Lily needed to know if it was Tommy they'd found, so that they could move on, never come back to this town looking for answers.

A death certificate wouldn't be issued until later – the doctor not back from Perth until after Christmas, so they'd need to send Tommy's remains up to Geraldton. But he'd get Gerry's confirmation and head back to Lily, to his family, tonight.

That would be the answer to this whole disaster, he thought, looking around what had been the kitchen, where it had started. Only the iron range remained, its door open on its hinges. Burned out, ashes all over the floor. A straight edge emerged from the ash drifts. Like a piece of card.

He picked it up, flicking off the ash. The photograph had been singed, the woman's face obscured by heat bubbling, but he would know her body anywhere, no matter how little she had let him gaze on her.

Ernie stared at her body. All his feelings of insecurity, at being made to feel dirty and shamed during the war flooded his veins. He peered at the background of the photograph, to give him some clue as to where it was taken. The velvet curtain behind her and the pot of basil on the pedestal stirred a memory.

That photographer on St George's Terrace.

Ernie had escorted Lily to the man's studio himself, leaving her in the corridor while she smiled at Ernie, thanking him. It had made him feel special, whole again, after several years of being ashamed of who he was.

Bloody hell. They'd married less than three months later. And he had been so grateful for having been chosen over his rival. He'd won Lily and for a while, he was in clover, until she pushed him away. In time, he almost forgot that it was his fault he wouldn't ever amount to much as a man, unlikely to father a child as the doctors had said – the consequence of a few moments of illicit pleasure in the arms of dusky prostitutes – and blamed Lily's coldness instead.

This Lily was not a cold woman. He ran his thumb over her uncovered breast, sick of feeling ashamed, of feeling unworthy.

He filled the Hillman with their remaining possessions, pantry items he'd rescued from the shop, all of it stinking of mildew and smoke. Ernie slid into the driver's seat, but a long-handled pan obstructed the space for his legs making him climb back out again to rearrange the objects in the front.

'Ernie.'

He banged his head at Gerry's voice. He swung around, gripping the edge of the roof. 'Reg says you found him. Is that right?'

Gerry's queer eyes had never bothered him before, but now as one eye dropped to Ernie's waist, he felt the photograph burning in his pocket. 'I'm afraid not.' He ran water off the back of his hair with his hand. 'It seems it could be the Chinaman who lived out there. Black hair was found in the shark, and no one's seen Kang Pei since the night of the fire. I always warned him he'd fall off his boat drunk one night.'

Ernie's stomach heaved.

'I've had pleasanter tasks.' Gerry rubbed at the back of his hair again, nervous. 'Are you heading off?' He gestured at the motor car.

Ernie mumbled, 'Yes.'

'How's your girl? Is she making progress?'

'Uh-huh. Look, if you're certain it's not Tommy you found, I'd like to get away, get to Geraldton, don't want to get stuck in the mud.'

'Oh, sure. Well, so long. I'm sorry things have worked out this way.'

Ernie gave him a wave and set off, slowing down as he passed the McGintys' and gave Reg a nod. The fishermen bowed their heads, averting their eyes from him.

He gritted his teeth.

~

Lily wasn't at the hostel when he arrived. After he'd unloaded their things into the small room above the pawn shop, he headed over to the hospital, feeling as heavy as the motor car was now light of its load. He had planned to tell her everything, redeem himself for having compromised her when she'd been so trusting. But the photograph changed everything.

All he'd ever wanted from her was that kind of intimacy, the only way he knew how.

Girlie had been moved to the children's ward out the back of the hospital. Her face was turned away towards the window, and from the rise and fall of her chest he could see she was asleep. Lily sat beside the hospital bed crocheting, the tip of her tongue touching her upper lip. Birdsong outside the window now the rain had eased.

His movement into the room disturbed the stillness. Lily dropped her hands into her lap, turning her head towards him, smiling.

He raised his eyebrows. 'She's sleeping well?'

Lily nodded.

'I brought up things from the house. Dropped them off at the hostel.'

She tilted her chin in acknowledgement and picked up her needle. 'Did you speak to anyone?'

Ernie shuffled his weight to the other foot. 'Gerry.'

'And?' She didn't look up.

'They still haven't found him.'

'I see.'

Lily jerked her head up as Girlie murmured something in her sleep.

'Blokes seem to think I had something to do with the fire. Because of that Perenjori business.' He cleared his throat. 'Just so you know, I didn't.'

'I know,' she said. 'I know you didn't start the fire.'

His chest deflated. 'Um . . . Lily, can we talk? Outside?'

'What about?' she said, wrapping her crochet around the needle.

He led her by the elbow out to the courtyard where they stood beneath the dripping leaves of the large fig tree. 'Do you remember when we were still stepping out . . .'

She wrinkled her forehead.

He lowered his voice. 'I took you to a photographer's studio. You had your picture in the papers, remember – "The Racing Reporter's Daughter"?'

Lily's gaze didn't flicker but her jaw tightened, becoming defensive. 'What are you talking about?'

He fumbled in his pocket, and withdrew the photograph.

Colour spoiled her cheeks. 'What are you accusing me of?'

'So, you don't deny it?' His chest felt hollow, caved in. How could she not have been the woman he'd thought she was, all this time?

She took a deep breath. 'No, but it's not what you think. He blackmailed me. I did it to save Pa's reputation . . .' The corners of her mouth trembled.

She was telling the truth. How much had she suffered for her father's sake? Ernie had only ever wanted her to feel the same way about him – obedient, loving, fulfilling a promise no matter how the world buffeted her. She had tried. But he should have given her the attention she craved, the way her father had treated her as though she was the centre of his universe. Ernie saw all of who she really was, and this woman in the photograph wasn't her.

She had been the only true thing in his life and he'd risked losing her.

'Mr Hass. Mrs Hass,' the nurse's voice called them, shrilly.

Ernie rounded on her, annoyed at the interruption. 'Can you give us a moment?'

Lily held up her hand at him, and faced the nurse. 'Is it Girlie?'

'Yes, ma'am. You need to come immediately. She's taken fever.'

They'd been in the ward just minutes ago and Girlie had been sleeping peaceably. But Lily had already left his side, half running into the ward.

He looked on helplessly as the nurses fussed about Girlie's bedside wringing out wet cloths to cool her forehead. When the doctor was summoned, he and Lily were told to leave the room. Beneath that giant fig in the courtyard they held each other, not talking. He prayed; there was nothing more he could do. Girlie had held them together, given shape to their family. If Lily ever found out about his affair with Lorna, it would break her. It would be like gluing a dashed sandcastle back together. All those times he'd railed against Lily for not acting how she should, when she'd suffered and it was he who hadn't fulfilled his share of the bargain of marriage. He made promises to God, gambling on the bet that He even existed. Ernie would never be a man like Fred, he might never be a champion at anything ever again. But he had to be Lily and Girlie's champion, make sure he was the best husband and father he could be. If Girlie survived, he would bind them together into whatever shape Lily wanted them to be.

He was a man made new.

CHAPTER FIFTY

TOMMY

Tommy shivered, huddling, his hands pushed into his armpits. The hunger gnawed at him. It had been three days since he'd eaten raw eggs stolen from the convent chookyard. But now the river had risen higher, higher, and the plank bridge was fully submerged.

The bridge rumbled overhead as motor vehicles crossed it, their headlamps cutting beams through the pouring rain. He held his breath, waiting for them to pass over scanning the scrub for signs of him as they had done since he'd run. After he'd . . .

What had he done? Tommy clawed at the sides of his head, pressing into his skull as though the insides might spill out.

Girlie. He'd shot Girlie. And learned too late the truth of whose child she was. He gritted his teeth, moaning, the edges of his picture of Girlie disappearing, falling away into the abyss. He jerked his head, bit his tongue, and held out his hands in front of him, turning them over to stare at his knuckles, his eyes tracing the popping veins.

Lily. He'd meant to shoot Lily. She was a lying bitch.

Abandoning him to the institution, leaving him there to be terrorised by his nightmares. Put away because he'd learned the truth of her lie. Ma wasn't dead. He'd seen her. He'd *seen* her.

Lily had screamed at him in the rain, beating him with her hands. He'd cowered, dropping the rifle beside him in the mud, staring at Girlie bleeding. Why had she been wearing Lily's greatcoat?

What? he'd said, stunned, looking into Lily's drawn face.

She pushed him over so he lay sprawled prostrate in the mud. *What have you done?* Wailing over and over.

What had *he* done? Six years since Lily had disappeared. First, he'd had to get out of the institution, then find Lily, to touch her, make her real, the last person left of his blood. Let him find peace.

Tommy shook the pieces of his memories from his hands, watching them snake down the bank to the rushing river.

He'd found her. And he'd started to feel himself return to life.

All he'd wanted was family – to be reclaimed, recognised, brought to safety.

Girlie? Why? What did Lily mean? How could Girlie be his half-sister? What had he done?

Tommy stretched out one leg then the other and slid down the bank after his memories.

EPILOGUE

LILY

The bell rang in the shop and Lily plastered on a smile as the door opened, shivered at the cold gust of July air. The customer was a middle-aged woman wearing a felted coat over one of the pleated coatdresses that Gray's sold. Lily cocked her head. She could do much better for this woman.

'Hello, you're new here, aren't you?' the woman said. 'Mrs Robinson, my neighbour, said you made her a lovely frock for the Easter service.'

'Yes. We moved up from Dongarra about six months ago. Can I help you select a design or do you have something specific in mind yourself?' Lily glanced at the small blonde-haired girl beside the woman as she motioned her towards the design books on the shelves lining the wall. A Singer ran in the back room.

'I rather had something in mind for my daughter, Sophie, for the children's ball next Saturday. Velvet with lace?'

'The children's ball?' With the rush of orders following the opening of the dressmaking shop, Lily had forgotten to stock trimmings for the children's ball *and* the Tourist League Ball this month. She exhaled. In time, she'd have a handle on the business side of things, maybe employ someone to oversee stock matters.

The woman looked Lily up and down with a practised eye that she had learned to recognise. She wondered whether she should be embarrassed; she sometimes forgot she wore black and not many people here in Geraldton knew her personally.

No, she would not be ashamed of who she was anymore.

She measured Sophie, who raised her arms in compliance and turned when directed.

'Can I put my arms down now, Mummy?'

Lily gave an almost imperceptible nod that the measurements were finished.

'What do you suggest, Mrs . . .' Sophie's mother glanced at the window and the walls for a sign of Lily's proprietorship of the shop.

'Hass. Lily Hass. The velvets are there,' she gestured to the wall lined to the ceiling with shelves of fabric, 'and I'd think a smart peter-pan collar, in lace, with a smocking bodice, falling to just above the knee would be perfect.'

The woman tapped at a navy velvet fabric and Lily took her details: Mrs Simpson of Brede Street. 'Oh, you live just round the corner from me,' said Lily. 'We've taken a house on James Street.'

'That's a lovely area.'

Mrs Simpson arranged for a dress fitting on Thursday and, taking hold of her daughter, left. Lily stood at the large window watching her walk down Marine Terrace stopping to talk to a pair of grey-haired matrons. She straightened her back, standing tall, when Mrs Simpson pointed towards the shop.

Lily closed her eyes, feeling a shudder go through her. Tommy's bloated body was found when the flooded river waters had receded and they'd buried him at Karrakatta Cemetery beside Pa's grave.

She didn't blame him for what had happened. It was her fault: she'd seen all the signs and instead she'd focused on Girlie, on the community, on what people thought of her. If she had tried to help him, Girlie might never have been shot. Lily inhaled, pulled out the navy velvet from the shelf for the client, and took it through to her apprentice with the instructions.

She sank to the stool behind the large mahogany table Ernie had found, perfect for laying out paper to sketch her designs.

The consequences were never as one might think they'd be. And there were always consequences. Before they'd moved to Dongarra, she had sold off almost everything of value of Ma's and paid Mr Forbes his blackmail money in full. If she hadn't, he'd threatened to publish the photograph of her. She'd been the Vice-President of the Perenjori CWA then, women looked to her for advice on gardening, Girlie had won school awards for presentation and penmanship, and Ernie employed several men from the district. She would have done anything to save them from ruin. Though she'd later lost respect anyway when rumours spread about her starting the fire; all for nothing it seemed, when the crushing news came that there was no insurance money to claim. It had served her right to be impetuous.

She'd made sacrifices and thought she would never be blackmailed again.

Until Ernie's name and business were written about in the *Western Mail*. Those tourists, the Godfreys, had come from Perth on the strength of it, and she knew then, waited for the letter to come. When it did, it wasn't from Mr Forbes.

She could hardly believe her eyes when she'd seen his name: Alfie Bright. He wanted compensation for Lily 'stealing' his child away, as he put it. And if she didn't pay him fifty pounds, he would stake his claim on Girlie, and deliver her to a children's home.

And then she'd nearly lost Girlie anyway.

In the stretches of time during which Girlie had battled her fever, unwanted thoughts had bloomed. If Girlie died, Lily would be free – free from the blackmail, free from the grinding reality of motherhood. But Girlie had recovered and Lily knew that she really did love her.

It had been Ernie's suggestion to open a dressmaking shop in Geraldton with the insurance money from the guesthouse. He wasn't left wanting, though. *Mr Gregson, who I'm dealing with over the insurance claim, says I'm a natural negotiator, wants to take me on as a salesman.*

It was a perfect occupation, she thought, keeping him on the road for weeks on end, leaving her to make her own decisions day-to-day, while Ernie sent money home to pay for Girlie to board at St Dominic's.

It wasn't the ideal of marriage and family she'd struggled to conform to; she now realised she had no control over that. It had been a revelation, living openly without fear of being found out that she couldn't always be a good woman, selfless and dedicated to her family. And in doing so, she'd found herself again. Also, an affection for Girlie that she'd not expected, eagerly anticipating the weekends that Girlie came home. This coming weekend was extra special – Girlie's eleventh birthday celebrations and Lily would be entertaining three of her Very Best Friends from school, taking them out to the pictures and for ice-creams.

'Lily.'

Her hand careened across the paper, ruining the pencil line for Sophie Simpson's frock. She looked up at the familiar voice and smiled, patting herself down.

'Lovely to see you, Lorna.' Lily brushed her cheek to Lorna's.

'Mary,' Lily called to her apprentice, 'can you bring through Mrs Fairclough's dress.' The whir of the Singer stopped and Lily took a moment to appreciate the changes in Lorna since she'd last seen her a fortnight ago. She smiled. 'Oh dear, perhaps I'd better let out the seam allowance.'

Lorna laughed, dropping her hand to her rounded belly, obviously close to term. 'Of course. Daphne Liddle said she came by here last week – tell me you're not going to make her look prettier than me.'

The ladies of Dongarra had been a more forgiving and welcoming group than she had given them credit for. Somehow, the tragedy of her brother and the near-tragedy of her daughter had brought out their generous nature. The men, on the other hand, still bore a grudge against Ernie, their suspicion about the jetty fire having an enduring effect.

'Not possible, Lorna.' She passed her a brown paper package containing her altered dresses. 'Impending motherhood suits you.' Lorna had a permanent flush to her cheeks, and her eyes sparkled like emeralds. Lily couldn't have found a better friend than her. 'Bill's a lucky man.'

Lorna sighed contentedly, rubbing her hand in large circles over her belly. 'Bill simply can't wait for this baby to be born. He's speaking of moving to a bigger house.' A stray golden curl fell across her brow and Lily caught concern in her eye. Lorna swept her hair under her hat. 'Can you see me for another fitting next week?'

Lily checked the client register and made an appointment. Brushing her cheek against Lorna's once more, she settled onto her stool to complete the Simpson girl's dress design.

Her new home, an old homestead from when Geraldton was nothing more than a patchwork of farms, sat atop the hill the locals called Mount Misery. But it wasn't a miserable life.

She was at peace with herself. Happiness wasn't the opposite of misery, she had learned, nor even the absence of it. It was facing up to all of it: the good, the fearful, the dangerous parts that made her who she was. Pretending they didn't exist made her life miserable. Lily had thought she had to be a natural mother to be happy – to look at Lorna now it was easy to see how this could be the case.

Before Tommy had run off into the night Lily had told him the truth. That Girlie was their mother's child, their half-sister.

It had been not long after Tommy had tried to drown himself in their copper. She hadn't recognised her mother at first, decrepit, grey-haired and stout. And carrying a small child.

Her name's Emma, Emma Bright, Ma said. *I thought . . .* Her eyes searched the hallway behind Lily. *Where's your father?*

Dead.

Ma bowed her head. *I'm sorry I left you. And Tommy.*

What are you doing here? Lily held the door rigid in her hand, ready to shut out her mother and the child.

Ma put the girl down on the ground, shaking her head. *I'm no good as a mother. She's better off with you. You're her blood.*

If Lily hadn't been broken by losing the baby after Tommy's suicide attempt, she would never have considered adopting Girlie. Girlie was a living reminder of her mother's betrayal. But she had not told Ernie that she had finally, and briefly, been pregnant, to protect Tommy from Ernie's wrath. The Lemnos Hospital had been the answer to her problem, fulfilling her promise to Pa to take care of the family members she had left. Both of them.

But she could not have foreseen the further consequences of her actions. In another time, when she was a different person, she had thought she had nothing to do with the Aboriginal Problem, that she could walk away and dismiss it with a cup of tea.

But Jim Feehely had been sent to the gaol on Rottnest Island for the arson of her Dongarra house. Of Mrs Feehely and her daughters, she'd heard nothing. She'd last seen Ruby when she asked her to send word to Gerry Paxton and the doctor. That was the last anyone in town had seen of the Feehelys. Mrs Feehely had taken off into the night with her daughters. Lily had to admire her courage and determination in surrendering the only protections she had as an exempted Aboriginal, for the sake of her children.

Lily carried the burden of guilt for destroying a family. This too was part of who she was and she had to accept it.

Her fingers ached and she realised she had pencilled the same line repeatedly until the tip had broken through the paper. She leaned back on her elbows, gazing out onto the street. The sun glared off a mirror of a passing motor car, temporarily blinding her and she closed her eyes, blazing colours seared onto the inside of her eyelids.

A shadow crossed in front of the sun. As she opened her eyes, her chest contracted. A man glanced into the window and looked away, a bedroll slung over his shoulder. Just like Tommy when he'd come to her.

Lily let out her breath in a rush and rummaged inside her handbag, finding a ten-bob note. If she could just get to him before he disappeared. She cracked the door, jangling the bell, and when he heard her, turned his head towards the shop, glanced back over his shoulder.

'You!' she called. 'Come here.'

He strolled back up the footpath, uncertainty spreading across his face. He rearranged his features in defence. 'I ain't done nothin'.'

She waved this away, brandishing the ten-bob note for him. 'Take it.'

The swaggie swallowed, his gaze fixed on the note. He reached for it before answering. 'Thanks ever s'much.'

She smiled, stepping back inside the shop. Before she could close it between them, a willie wagtail flew in through the open door, darting from corner to corner inside the shop, trapped.

AUTHOR'S NOTE

The setting of this story is Dongarra, divided into a main settlement or 'town' as the Hasses refer to it, and the beach settlement. In real life, the beach settlement is known as Port Denison, but I have chosen not to use this name for simplicity's sake.

The present-day main town, approximately four hours' drive north of Perth, Western Australia, is called Dongara. The second 'r' was dropped in 1944. It was said to have been named after the local Wattandee word for 'place of sea lions': *Thungarra*. Aboriginal people with continuing connections to the Dongara and Geraldton area include the Amangu and Naaguja claim groups.

During my interviews, an elderly non-Indigenous woman, Phyllis Money, remembered an Aboriginal family living beside the Irwin River and that the children weren't allowed to go to school with her. This was about five to eight years after the time my story is set, and it stood to reason, they or others like them would have been living in Dongar[r]a in 1932. As this family's Aboriginal group identity is not on record, I have described Ruby Feehely and her mother as *Yamatji*, a word used by Aboriginal people in the Mid-West to mean 'people'. I acknowledge and am grateful for the confidentiality and generosity of the Wajarri Yamatji Traditional Owners and custodians who shared their culture and knowledge with me more than ten years ago, when I was a native title anthropologist working in the Mid-West.

I also have a slight personal connection to the town of Dongara, as well as to Perenjori and Geraldton. The character of Ernie Hass was sparked by an ancestor of mine, who was briefly a butcher and shop proprietor in Port Denison. I have adapted the newspaper article announcing Ernie Hass's business plans from an article describing the same of my ancestor. Likewise, the article announcing Ernie's bankruptcy and a suspicious fire of his house in Perenjori.

Research informs plot, and I hadn't realised how 'multicultural' Dongara and Port Denison were during the Depression until I read some of the oral histories transcribed by local historian Trish Parker. There was an Italian fisherman who had jumped ship when passing, and lived alone in a cottage near the Back Beach. There was also a Chinese man, Old Charlie, living on a sailboat, who apparently one evening the worse for wear, fell overboard. A little while later, a shark was caught and black hair found inside its stomach. They'd thought the mystery of what had happened to Old Charlie was solved until they identified the black hair as belonging to a pig used as berley by fishermen.

Fact informed fiction in other ways. In October 1932, there was a small fire that damaged part of the jetty, and a caretaker for the beach was appointed by the Beach Improvement Committee. The culprit was never found. I copied text from a newspaper article, 'Service at Dongarra', *Geraldton Guardian and Express*, 2 May 1929, p.1, found on Trove, for the minister's speech during the Armistice Day service in chapter ten.

And there really was the Great Emu War, from October to December 1932, when the Royal Australian Artillery was deployed to fight plagues of emus with Lewis machine guns. The emus won.

The rest is fiction, but there is always a greater truth to be found in a story. My daughter was born in Geraldton and we lived in the old farmhouse on top of Mount Misery. *The Secrets at Ocean's Edge* is a story of family and belonging, and I hope through this story my daughter will know a little of where she comes from.

I am privileged to be able to find and tell my story. It cannot compare with the experiences of the many Indigenous Australians undertaking journeys back to family and country as they access oral histories and archival records that demonstrate the extent of government control over Indigenous people's stolen country, stolen wages, and stolen children.

ACKNOWLEDGEMENTS

I'd like to acknowledge the Traditional Owners of the country on which this book was written – the Jagera and Turrbal peoples, and of the country on which research was conducted – the Amangu and Naaguja peoples, and pay my respects to their Elders, past, present and future.

This book has taken me on physical, emotional, and critical journeys. And I was not alone. I would like to acknowledge and give thanks to the following people.

To the Queensland Writers Centre, for your enduring support of local writers and for facilitating the Hachette Australia Manuscript Development Program in 2015, in which I participated with a previous manuscript.

To my publisher, Rebecca Saunders, for seeing something in that manuscript and deciding that you wanted me to write something else! And this is that book, and I could never have brought it this far without your belief in me, and your focus and guiding hand to shape the story; the valuable contributions of my editors, Alex Craig, Claire de Medici, Libby Turner and Karen

Ward; and all the wonderful people at Hachette Australia who made this story a book.

To those who gave me time and consideration during my research trip: Shirley Scotter and the Irwin District Historical Society; local historian Trish Parker; Don and Aileen Barrett; Phyllis Money; staff of the Priory Hotel in Dongara; staff of the Dongara library; Melody Cartwright of the Geraldton Historical Society; Thomas Cameron, Reg Brockman and the RSL Museum in Geraldton; and the anthropologists from Yamatji Marlpa Aboriginal Corporation.

To the Traditional Owners, custodians and Elders of the Wajarri Yamatji native title group, in particular, Colin Hamlett, for welcoming me onto your country and sharing your stories.

To Raina Savage and Anthea da Silva, for fabulous company and an open door.

To Gary Napier, for helping me get there (and here).

To Victoria Carless, Wendy Davies, Susi Fox, Patricia Holland, Karen Lee, Magdalena McGuire, Kate Murdoch, Imbi Neeme, Sue Pearson, Mary-Ellen Stringer and Angella Whitton, for acting as sounding boards to both my words and my life.

To the coven: Melissa Ashley, Cass Moriarty, Sally Piper and Sarah Ridout, for forging the way and being my cheer squad.

To my writing mentor, Kim Wilkins, for trusting that I can do anything I set my mind to.

Finally, to my children, Ruby and Rory, for letting me have just enough peace and quiet to write a book. And because I love you.